MADMAN

MADMAN

TRACY GROOT

MOODY PUBLISHERS
CHICAGO

All Scripture quotations, unless otherwise indicated, are taken from the *New American Standard Bible®*, Copyright © 1960, 1962, 1963, 1968, 1971, 1972, 1973, 1975, 1977, 1995 by The Lockman Foundation. Used by permission.

The quote from Homer's *The Iliad* was taken from Robert Fagle's translation, published by Penguin Books, copyright 1990.

The portion of 2 Maccabbees is taken from *The Apocrypha,* translation by Edgar J. Goodspeed, published by Vintage Books, a division of Random House, copyright 1989.

Editors: Andy McGuire and LB Norton
Cover Design: John Hamilton
Cover Image: Photonica

Library of Congress Cataloging-in-Publication Data

Groot, Tracy.
    Madman / by Tracy Groot.
        p. cm.
    ISBN-13: 978-0-8024-6362-3
    1. Bible. N.T.—History of Biblical events—Fiction. I. Title.

PS3557.R5655M33 2006
813'.54--dc22

                                                                2005032108

ISBN: 0-8024-6362-2
ISBN-13: 978-0-8024-6362-3

We hope you enjoy this book from Moody Publishers. Our goal is to provide high-quality, thought-provoking books and products that connect truth to your real needs and challenges. For more information on other books and products written and produced from a biblical perspective, go to www.moodypublishers.com or write to:

Moody Publishers
820 N. LaSalle Boulevard
Chicago, IL 60610

1 3 5 7 9 10 8 6 4 2

Printed in the United States of America

To Larry Haney, with love.

I

In the tombs of Kursi sits a man with his back to the sea. For a long time he will sit, his back bowed tight against the sea.

Some tombs of Kursi are caves in the hillside, some are rock piles, old mounds staggering like steps to a sacred altar. The altar is nothing more than a barren hilltop. In this desolate place the man dwells, and sits with his back against the sea. He cannot say why the tombs afford safety, but they do for him, the unliving among the dead.

Someone watches him. Someone he once knew. And though he hates to be watched, hates the relish of the morbidly curious, hates their freedom most of all, humans no longer hold significance for him. If they come to stare, he rages at them for a time, then forgets them. He only knows to keep his back to the sea. He learned it as a child learns about red glowing embers, learns not to touch such fiery wonders.

Across the Sea is important to him because it is important to Them. Across the Sea has dreadful consequence. He looks at the last time he gazed Across the Sea—purple bite marks up and down his arm. He takes what he has closest and smears it over the marks.

The watcher with the old familiar face sat a distance apart from the man with his back bared to the lake. Watching, idling with a weed.

"Who would have believed that one day you'd sit among the dead covered in your own filth?"

The madman never responded. Never showed a sign of who he used to be. Sometimes he sat silent with his eyes half closed, locked in impenetrable trance. More often he was not silent at all, locked, then, in careening frenzies no man could still.

This didn't stop the once-familiar man. If there was a way into madness, logic said there was a way out. Logic said.

"I don't know what to do that I have not already done," he said softly.

If he could have understood the shout of the madman, upon whom not a single word was lost, this is what he would have heard:

Do not leave me to Them!

Do not leave me!

You! I once knew you. . . .

The watcher lifted his head. Did he hear words? Or was that his wishful fancy? The madman grunted sometimes, made long garbled nonsense sounds as if he were clearing a throat full of sludge.

Once he spoke with perfect clarity—in a voice the once-familiar man had never heard before. The madman looked right at him, black eyes peering from behind filthy matted hair, and told him a thing no one could have known, a thing he had long pretended never happened, spoken in the ancient windswept tombs in a voice just as ancient and windswept: *I know what happened behind the stable when you were fourteen.*

The madman's eyes glowed then, and his face changed for a moment into a leering hideousness that made his eyes water and his skin leap; it was a wavering of flesh into a form not his own; for an instant the madman's features became the face of the voice, and then came a flickering of faces, a cacophony of images, people he had never seen, some he thought he knew from old dark memories. In that moment an odor came from the madman, an incarnate foulness, a stench with no match upon the earth; he vomited at once and crawled away, vomiting.

The watcher listened carefully, then sank into himself once more. It was no response; just another grunt.

The madman's head was tilted, his mouth hung open. Saliva ran from his gray tongue into his beard, stiff with spit and filth, with blood from the animals he ate. Sometimes when the madman was sleeping, the once-familiar man would come and cut off as much of the beard as he could. The madman used to be clean shaven and proud of his appearance.

The watcher rose. He had nothing much to record today, not about the madman anyway. He had a new thing to record about himself, something vaguely disturbing. He wondered how to word it, and tried it out in the air. "I am attracted to evil. It fascinates me. I do not know if this makes me a bad man."

He almost wanted the Other to speak again, and it troubled him. Rather, it *should* trouble him. "Yes, it should," he mused aloud. The encounter had disturbed him deeply, frightened him to his core; it also evoked a tumult of sensation. It evoked questions so enormous he could not yet frame them.

He strolled away from the man with his back to the lake, hands clasped behind him, as he used to walk in the colonnades. "I am not a bad man, but evil fascinates me. Evil intrigues me—this does not make me a bad man...."

You! Do not leave me to Them, you!

Do not leave me.

I once knew you....

The watcher stopped. He waited, motionless, hands clasped behind his back.

He heard only the cry of seabirds and the gentle rush of wind come down from the heights, rounding on the hillside tombs, coursing down the slope to the lake. He waited a moment more and then strolled away, trying out the new thing to record before he put it to parchment.

To Callimachus
At the Academy of Socrates, West Stoa
The Acropolis
Athens

From your servant Tallis
At a backwater barn of an inn
In the dreadful Roman province called
Palestine, on the Galilee

Greetings.

I would tell you the details of my journey, but you would only skip them. If this dispatch is late, it is your fault—the ship did not put out from Alexandria on the kalends of the month, as you assured me it would. I am sure you did not mean for me to stay an extra intolerable week with Aristarchus. Yes, that is what happened. Go ahead and laugh, Cal. I was not amused.

Palestine. I will describe it, though I know you will skip it. It is dry, dusty, foreign, dirty, hot; dusty doesn't do it justice, and when I say foreign, I mean barbarian. (Bathhouses? Two miles south! And never mind finding a decent launderer or fish sauce.) I am staying at a place the locals call the Inn-by-the-Lake, and that lake is called the Galilee. I've wedged a tiny writing desk under a tiny window, and I can see the lake from here. It's the only thing to soothe my longing for the Mediterranean, for Athens and all that is familiar. I am miserable for intelligent conversation.

The innkeeper has a fake smile, the locals skirt me like dung, and I miss cheese, for gods' sake, cheese. Though the innkeeper's daughter is an interesting conundrum, the inn itself is dreary, the common room dark, and—no. You are skipping this. I know you too well, dear Callimachus.

The Decaphiloi. Have I now your attention?

Tallis nibbled on the end of his pen. The moving water invited his glance, and he looked long before putting pen to parchment again.

Decaphiloi, League of Ten Friends. An amusing designation in this land called the Decapolis, League of Ten Cities. We thought so long ago, didn't we, when they chose to name themselves so?

He rubbed his brow. This wasn't the letter he was supposed to send. It should have been filled with assurances of the academy's welfare, with anecdotes of the teachers and students. This letter was never meant to be.

Cal, I don't know how to say it, so I'll say it. The League of Ten Friends is no more: the Decaphiloi have vanished, and the Academy of Socrates in Palestine is dissolved. Our little school has ceased to exist. Callimachus—it's as if it never was.

Worst of all, I am not joking. You know I wouldn't joke about this.

How well do I know you? You shook this letter and set it down in your lap. You looked long about the colonnades with those great gray brows plunged in consternation. You read over the last three or four lines, but it hasn't changed anything—Athens has lost one of its most promising satellite schools, it has simply vanished, and attend this: No one will speak with me about it.

Sometimes I laugh, Cal, the whole thing is so preposterous.

My attempts to learn more are constantly frustrated—most deny it even existed! The only place I get information is from the riffraff, at a price I can scarce afford, and now attend this: You received regular reports from the school up until a few months ago. What if I told you the portico they had rented has been empty for three years? (Go ahead and shake the letter. And get some strong drink; it doesn't get any better.)

The fellow in charge of public rental properties told me to my face he'd never heard of the Decaphiloi, or the Academy of Socrates either, and why don't I try Jerusalem. I laughed in his face, Cal, I couldn't help myself, and was summarily escorted to the door.

You did not send me to the outermost edge of the earth (that's what Palestine feels like) to be greeted with this kind of time-wasting riddle. I am not smart enough for this—you couldn't send a teacher? Or a student, for that matter? Do you know how often your name has been ill-used since I've arrived on this scorched puck of a province?

This I know, that the more I investigate, the more I—

Tallis chewed the end of his pen, made himself stop. Most of the styli in his vase back home were chewed up.

—am angry. I am unaccountably uneasy staying at this inn; there is an oddness in the air (I hope you skipped that). I am vexed at the delay in returning to

Athens, furious at the lies and the lack of information, and am now determined beyond pale to learn the truth. (Somewhere Socrates is smiling.) I know the Decaphiloi existed, you know they did, ten teachers know, and great gods and goddesses, the students know—to insist on this to a pie-faced magistrate who well knows the truth is absurd.

Did the Romans disband the school for fear of insurgence? You've spoken of the revival of Greek pride to Aristarchus, but the notion that your little school should have a hidden democratic agenda is as ridiculous as it is hilarious. Where is a parchment, I feel a play coming on. . . . (I hope you didn't skip that, it was funny.)

Well, I will write again when I have a firmer grasp on what has happened—if I'm still alive; they don't feed you much at this inn, and my purse is getting lamentably light. Of the Decaphiloi, I give this present accounting—accurate or inaccurate as it may be, it is all I have, and that from the riffraff. Six members—whereabouts unknown. One member was murdered in a most horrifying manner; I shall not put it on parchment. One is allegedly a priestess in a temple of Dionysus—you read right, Dionysus. Don't be alarmed: I've forsworn all things Dionysiac, you know that, Cal. Anyway, one member committed suicide.

And one . . . one is a madman.

Tallis sat in his chair with his lunch in his lap, eating steadily and watching the fishermen on the lake. He had been at the inn for a week now, and the innkeeper's daughter finally gave him a little variety in his meal. Showing him his whitened toga accounted for nothing in these parts. Tallis ate scorched bread for one week straight, and cheese only because he'd stolen it from the worktable in the kitchen. Today he ate boiled eggs with salt, unscorched and tasty bread, and cheese, for gods' sake, unpilfered and cumin-scented cheese.

He could have easily purchased fresh bread in the city, and did indeed on the first day, after a charred and hungry breakfast. Once he discovered the lack of a certain school of Socrates, he tightened his purse strings. His meager cache of coins would have to go for bribes, not bread; room rental, not a hammock on the next ship out of Caesarea.

One week in this backwater province, and he had no answers to the disappearance of an entire school. Eight years it should have been in operation! According to Lysias, the slave Tallis had questioned a few days ago, the school had operated for five years—three years ago, it vanished.

Tallis watched the fishermen put out their boats and row north, toward the mouth of the Wadi Samakh on the northeast side of the Galilee. The seasonal riverbed emptied into the Galilee during the rainy season, and there at the mouth of the Wadi was the best fishing on the lake. The fishermen caught thousands of the little sardines so popular around here. Not that Tallis had *tasted* any. Boiled eggs and cheese today gave him hope of smoked sardines in the future.

A rustle drew his attention from the waters. The innkeeper's daughter came up the path from the inn with what was surely an amphora of wine on her hip. She offered it to Tallis.

He brushed the crumbs from his front and accepted the amphora with a nod. He drank long and wiped his mouth and handed back the amphora as naturally as if this occurred daily—as if he did not have to water himself with a ladle from the well, no wine about it. Any wine he had, he purchased in the common room of the inn.

The girl rested the jug on her hip and looked under her hand at the fishermen. "Are you going to Hippos again?" she asked, eyes on a boat.

"I am."

"Can you deliver a package for me?"

Ah—the reason for the tasty meal. "Of course."

She hesitated. "He may not be there anymore. Leave the package on his doorstep if he's not."

She turned to go back to the inn, and Tallis caught a glimpse of her face. It was clear and hopeful, a freshened look Tallis had not yet seen from her. It was the look a young woman should have, and her returning step to the inn was light and quick. She'd also just spoken more words to him in a minute than she had in an entire week.

Are you going to Hippos again?

"Yes, I am going to Hippos again," Tallis muttered, and ended his meal by tossing the remnants to a waiting dog.

He stood and shook out his toga, which was growing more dingy by the day. He would have to find a decent launderer, and Kursi did not have a launderer who cleaned togas. Surely he would find one in Hippos; he'd have to ask one of the occasional Roman soldiers he saw. If he had known this journey was to last so long, he'd have taken his entire wardrobe—which meant his other toga.

Tallis scowled at the lake. *Yes, I'm going to Hippos again.* To find a school that has been defunct for three years, a school no one will talk about; to find out who stole the money Callimachus has been sending for the past three years, money to pay salaries and rent—money from his own pocket, and from Tallis's pocket when funds were low. Cal, of course, didn't know that.

Callimachus of Athens was the sole patron of the school in Palestine, and Tallis was his servant, the one who saw him worry and fret if he didn't send the money on time. *The teachers have families, Tallis, they risked everything; they left their jobs for our school, and they trust us. What can we do this month? Can we take on another boarder?*

Callimachus was never good at managing his money. If he had it, he gave it, and forgot monthly commitments in favor of serving immediate needs. If it weren't for the money, Tallis would be on his way back to Athens—desperately strange, the disappearance of the school, yes—but all he cared about was making someone pay for stealing from Cal.

He smiled grimly. With interest, they would pay, and interest on the outskirts of the Roman Empire was high indeed. He had already made the calculations—to debtors' prison they would go, roaringly cheered by Tallis, a thought nearly as satisfying as his Tiberius fancy: Callimachus was a great and revered Greek philosopher, in favor with the Roman emperor Tiberius. The thieves could be remanded to the emperor himself, where they would meet justice in its most unpleasant possibilities.

When Tallis thought of Cal's sacrifice, and his worry, and his depleted state of affairs, only to find someone had *stolen* from him—the fury made his eyes glow.

"Never mind—if he's not there, you can have it yourself." The girl stood before him, holding a bundle. Her freshened look faltered when she saw his face; instantly he smiled, smoothing away thoughts of dripping murder. He took the bundle, and by its fragrance knew it was one of the loaves he'd seen on the table that morning.

He held it to his nose. "I hope he's not there."

The girl smiled, the first real smile he'd seen in a week, and she skipped down the path to the inn.

❋ ❋ ❋

Tallis set out on the two-mile walk to Hippos. He was to deliver the bundle to a fellow named Demas, who lived on the other side of the city in the amphitheater housing, a building with a double tar smear on the side. The errand would take him away from his task, but no matter; despite certain misgivings at losing the loaf, he hoped to find the fellow. He was curious about whoever rated a fragrant loaf from the enigmatic young mistress of the inn. That smile was the first real conversation he'd had since Egypt.

The time he spent visiting the academy in Egypt with Cal's colleague, the insufferable Aristarchus, didn't count in the way of conversation. Aristarchus never once forgot that Tallis was a servant. It was Callimachus, Tallis's master, who had trouble remembering, and Tallis himself who had to remind him. Nothing aggravated Cal more than to hear that reminder. The great gray brows would plunge, and he would snap, "If I didn't want your opinion, I wouldn't ask for it."

It worried Tallis to think of Cal receiving the dispatch without Tallis himself at his side; Cal was getting old, and the letter would be a tremendous shock. He hoped, by then, that Aristarchus had returned to Athens. Aristarchus would take care of him. And what would *he* think of the situation in Palestine? Tallis snorted—Aristarchus certainly wouldn't trust its investigation to Tallis. A servant was better suited to run the backwater inn.

The innkeeper's establishment was tucked into a fold of landscape on the east side of the Galilee, on the Roman road running north and south. The inn was south of the little fishing village of Kursi, north of the much more cosmopolitan Hippos. It was situated on a rise that afforded a splendid view of the lake; and in a certain secluded place behind the inn, not far from the shore, Tallis had taken to eating his meals in blessed solitude. He couldn't stand the darkened common room. He spent the first day or two there, looking for affable conversation, but soon learned he was a whitened stranger, that perhaps to folks around here a toga meant only higher taxes. He was asked his business in accents that pinched his fourth or fifth vertebra, and when he saw that only suspicion prompted the questions, he learned to make his answer this: that he was a traveling scholar from Athens. Scholars were generally left alone.

He'd made the mistake, once, in an easy moment brought on by wine, of telling a local that in his spare time he was a playwright and an aspiring historian of Alexander of Macedon—called now "The Great," an appellation courtesy of Augustus Caesar. Tallis also mentioned to his drinking companion, as a casual grand finale, that he was the head servant of the great philosopher Callimachus, and was here in Palestine on business for his master.

And his companion had replied dully, "Who's he?"

"Who's he," Tallis now muttered as he approached the west side of Hippos. He sighed up at the city on the hill and began the long traversing walk to the top.

"Callimachus is one of the finest scholars of Socrates short of Socrates himself, but you wouldn't have heard of Socrates, you wine-soaked slophead. Callimachus is a greathearted old soulringer, his sum is wisdom and earnestness and passion for truth—more in his toenail than you possess in your entire being." Tallis paused to blot sweat with his sleeve, and grimaced at the sleeve. Sweat became instant grime with all the dust around here.

If everything in his life were going well, Tallis would have enjoyed discourse at the inn, even sullen and suspicious discourse. The people of Kursi who came to the inn were not exactly a cheerful lot; they had the look of people who expected to be cheated, and expected the cheater to be Tallis. Their look said a person had to work mighty hard to earn trust, and at one time Tallis would have enjoyed the challenge. He suspected beneath it all they were as good-natured as the fake-smiling innkeeper himself.

He envied the way Jarek, the innkeeper, exchanged greetings with long-known friends. It made Tallis long for Athens. Keeping to the cliff made him feel like the outsider he was, but once he realized someone had stolen from Callimachus, it put him out of countenance with the world.

He gained the top of the hill and paused, perhaps breathing harder than a thirty-seven-year-old man should. The weight of the loaf in his shoulder pack made him think of the innkeeper's daughter, and he turned into the busy city of Hippos.

So a fellow from the big city had captured the heart of the close-mouthed mistress of the inn. . . . Tallis didn't think her capable of anything but dark and sizing glances. Had he only stayed a day or two, he would not have guessed it was the girl who ran things, not her father.

Tallis watched her manage things in ways so subtle perhaps the innkeeper himself was fooled.

Every other day she fixed a basket full of food and left it at the back door. Tallis never saw who came to pick it up. (He had first, foolishly, hoped the basket was for himself.) He once caught the father giving the basket a grim, inscrutable regard. The laden glance went from the basket to the daughter, who received it with an equally inscrutable evenness. Her father had dropped his eyes and shuffled away.

One week under her roof and he still didn't know her name. Tallis only called her "Excuse me."

Jarek seemed affable enough, as innkeepers should be, but his courteous ways seemed deliberate, and his smile was quick to disappear, replaced by a somberness that seemed more usual to him. Even so, it did not appear the girl had inherited her taciturn ways from Jarek. If she had gotten them from her mother, Tallis didn't see such a woman around to compare.

The daughter was about ten years younger than Tallis, maybe more. The fact that she wasn't married did not surprise him, since this was Palestine, Palestine near the Parthian borders, and the ways here were often strange. Back home, even an ugly girl would have been married off at sixteen. If the innkeeper's daughter was not beautiful, she was not plain.

Maybe that explained why the people of Kursi seemed so morose— they lived at the eastern boundary of the Roman Empire. Tensions ran higher at the demarcation where countries met, and the Parthians were supposed to be barbarians, Persian blood crossed with wild nomad blood. Kursians would be the first to know if the Parthians had taken a fancy to win back lands lost by their ancestors to the Seleucids.

Well, the Seleucids were no more; their weakened dynasty had fizzled nearly a hundred years ago with Pompey's campaigns. The Roman general had united local cities into a federation called the Decapolis, a league of ten cities banded together to keep Greco-Roman bloodlines Greco-Roman. Hippos was one of the chief cities of the Decapolis, an impressive metropolis situated on the top of a flat diamond-shaped mountain, and entirely walled. Parthians would think twice about taking Hippos.

The innkeeper's daughter told him to stay on the main street through the forum, go past the marketplace and the public baths and the temple of Athena, until he came to the amphitheater in the southeast corner of the city. Demas lived in the neighborhood behind the theater.

"Look for the double tar smear," Tallis murmured.

He walked the main street to the forum, wove around shopkeepers who had laid their wares on blankets right in the flow of foot traffic, and stopped when he came to the portico of the temple of Athena on his right. He gazed at the columns and at the wide steps in front of them.

There should have been clusters of students on those steps, each cluster with its own teacher. Instead, the entire north side of the portico was rented out to a multiware merchant who didn't know the previous renter before him. Days earlier, the merchant had told Tallis to ask at the municipal building, and pointed to it on the north side of the forum.

What do you mean, you've never heard of the Academy of Socrates? Tallis had said to the pie-faced magistrate. You collected their rent for years.

Never heard of it.

I am in Hippos, right?

No answer.

How long have you worked here?

No answer.

What about the Decaphiloi?

(Interesting, the blink of the magistrate.)

Never heard of it.

Really. Mind if I look through your rental archives? They are public records and I, after all, am the public.

You won't find anything.

(Interesting, the smirk.)

Why don't you try Scythopolis. Better yet, Jerusalem.

The next day he had wandered the forum and its busy marketplace, questioning merchants in the vicinity of the temple, employing an instinctive caution, and his instinct was well-placed: A few were genuinely ignorant of the school that had rented the portico, but others did not appear happy at the questioning. Interestingly, the unhappy ones denied that the school and the Decaphiloi ever existed. The others simply said they didn't know.

The third day in Hippos he had merely walked the streets. There were nice wineshops and tawdry ones. There were bathhouses of the affluent and bathhouses of the not. Pleasant Greek statuary adorned certain places in the forum, and cheap miniature imitations were displayed on merchants' cloths for souvenirs. Hippos was like any other Greco-Roman city in the Decapolis . . . except this one had swallowed whole an enclave of philosophers, teachers, and artisans calling themselves the Decaphiloi.

On the fourth day in Hippos, he'd met Lysias.

Tallis had been watching a gang of public slaves repair a portion of the eastern wall by the barracks, when he had an idea. Surely the forum and the temple of Athena were kept clean and in repair by such slaves, perhaps these very ones he watched. If he couldn't get answers in high places, he would try low.

Tallis spoke to the overseer, and here his decent toga and Greek manner stood him in good stead. He told the man he needed to conscript one of the slaves for a quick service to the *agoranomos*, the market controller of Hippos. He slipped the overseer a few coins and promised to have the slave back in an hour.

By the smoldering look on the slave's face, he had a different suspicion for his conscription. It occurred to Tallis such practices must have been commonplace, for the overseer to acquiesce so easily to losing one of his workforce for an hour. Either that or he had paid the man entirely too much.

"I prefer women," Tallis had cheerfully informed the young man as they walked the main street back to the forum.

The man's stiffness eased then, and he ventured, "Then where are we going? You're not from around here."

"I need information. How long have you been in Hippos?"

"Eleven years. I came with my master from Scythopolis." His look soured. "I'd served him well and hoped for my manumission upon his death, but it turned out he owed a lot of money. The city confiscated all of his property."

They walked the streets of Hippos as Tallis questioned the man, whose name was Lysias.

"Yes, I've heard of the school. They used to meet on the corner steps of the temple."

For the first time since he walked beneath the western archway of Hippos, Tallis gave a great sigh. "Can you tell me when they met last?"

Lysias frowned, dodging a man carrying an armload of planks. "I don't know. Three, maybe four years ago."

"*Years* ago? Three or four years ago, are you certain?"

The slave shrugged. "Something like that. One of the teachers used to give me a tip if I cleaned the portico well." He thought and nodded. "Yes, it was at least three years ago."

"What was his name? The one who gave you the tip?"

"Polonus."

Polonus! At last, a name, a familiar name. Polonus ran the school. "What do you know of the other teachers?"

Here the man must have sensed profit in the questions. He hesitated, with a glance at the purse strapped to Tallis's waist. Tallis seized his arm and pulled him to the side of the street. "I paid one man today; I'm not about to pay you. I need information, and you can either spend a pleasant hour talking with me, or I'll bring you back to the gates. What's it going to be?"

Lysias chose a toil-free hour, and Tallis learned more in that one hour than he had in days.

The slave did not know the names of the teachers, only that there were nine or ten—two were women, he noted, one pretty and one plain. They met every day for hours in the northeast portico; they were a fixed part of the forum—had been for several years. Then one day the teachers didn't show up. For days the students had congregated on the steps, their bewildered state apparent as they asked questions in the forum. But the teachers never returned, and the students eventually dispersed.

When he cleaned the portico Lysias would sometimes speak with Polonus, a man he called kind and smart. He knew the name of one other teacher, Antenor. In fact, Lysias was certain he had seen Antenor since those days, only he couldn't remember where. He never saw anyone else.

Tallis and Lysias had returned to the eastern gates at the end of the promised hour, and Tallis thanked the slave.

Lysias turned to his work, then called Tallis back. "You know that wineshop we passed, the one where I said you'd find good imports?"

Tallis nodded.

"If you come again tomorrow and take me to that shop and buy me a meal and some wine, I'll have more information for you."

"I thought you told me that was the most expensive wineshop in Hippos," Tallis countered dryly.

The man grinned. "My master had excellent taste."

The fifth day Tallis was in Hippos, the slave Lysias was again conscripted for service to the *agoranomos*. While they sat over expensive wine, and a meal bought only for Lysias, the slave offered more information. This time, despite the wine, the man was not as sociable as he was the previous day.

"You've put your toe into some muddy water, my friend," Lysias commented quietly, after sizing up the occupants of the wineshop. A few servants were making purchases for their masters; a few masters were enjoying cups of wine and platters of olives and cheeses in the sitting area near a small back garden.

"How muddy?" Tallis asked. He sipped his wine, very nice indeed, glancing over the cup's rim at the people around him.

"We will not meet again," Lysias said.

Tallis studied the slave. What had changed? How far could he press him? By the stoic look on the sun-darkened face, not far. Tallis lowered his cup.

"Fair enough. Earn your meal, and we'll call it good."

Lysias told Tallis the names of a few more teachers, names Tallis already knew. He also told the fates of some of those names.

"Polonus ran the school, and Antenor was his . . ." He gestured for the word.

"Assistant." This Tallis already knew.

"Yes. One of the women ran things too, in a way my friend said was hard to define. Her name was Portia. She's supposed to be a priestess in the temple of Dionysus in Scythopolis."

Tallis kept his face smooth, while the name cleared his senses like a slap. Dionysus, god of wine . . . god of madness.

Tallis blinked. He pushed it down, he pushed it away. He took a slow sip of wine.

"There was a teacher named Bion," Lysias was saying, "who committed suicide. And one, a fellow named Theseus, was found—in large chunks—outside a disreputable bathhouse on the bad side of town."

Tallis was not aware he had slammed down his drink until he saw the surprise on Lysias's face and noticed the purple slop of wine on the table. He took his napkin and blotted the mess, cheeks growing warm. It came too quickly on the heels of Dionysus. For the first time in a very long time, memory threatened to push back, and sweat broke on his scalp. He refused to remember. Callimachus forbade him to remember.

"If they were your friends, I am sorry," Lysias murmured.

Tallis inclined his head to acknowledge the gracious comment. "They were friends of my master. He will be grieved at these tidings. Please continue." Then he said suddenly, "This—thing that happened. To Theseus. Was it before or after the Decaphiloi disbanded?"

"Before," Lysias had responded, after thinking it over. "Shortly before."

"What do you know of Portia, the one who is the priestess?"

"Nothing, except what I said. She serves in the temple of Dionysus in Scythopolis. She was the plain one."

They all came to Athens the summer before the school started in Hippos. Tallis had been much occupied with lodging details, food details, endless errands. It was eight years ago. He rubbed his temple. Portia . . .

Lysias continued over his thoughts.

"The other woman, the pretty one whose name I do not know, she simply disappeared like the rest of them. Except, of course, for the one named Kardus." Here the slave had snorted. "Everyone around here knows him. Most don't know what he used to be, only what he is now: a raving lunatic. The local legend. Crazier than a rabid dog on hard ale. Possessed, they say. And that is all I have to tell you."

Weakness entered Tallis's limbs. What he had tried for years to forget pursued him like Achilles on a rampage.

Lysias stood and wiped his mouth with the fine linen napkin, then folded it carefully and laid it on the table. He lingered for a moment, gazing first at their small table and its leftover evidence of an elegant meal; he watched a haughty servant sweep past with a silver platter on his splayed palms. He looked at the neatly trimmed ivy in the latticed arbor, beneath which genteel customers engaged in languid conversation, and he smiled a little. Then he bent to inhale the fragrance of the sprig of lavender in the bud vase on their table. He wished Tallis well, told him not to come for him again, and was gone.

Tallis sat motionless. Callimachus would tell him it was his fancy, tell him it was only old grief rolling over, it would go to sleep again.

Tallis knew it was more. Knew it by the strange uneasiness he'd felt at unexpected times at the inn, knew it by too many blows in one single conversation, too many suggestions of one certain conclusion, though Callimachus would tell him he was wrong. Callimachus would forbid him to remember.

Dionysus, god of wine, god of madness. Dionysus was here.

Tallis stood in front of a building with two tar smears on its side. He'd last spoken with Lysias two days ago. Yesterday he had sent his dispatch to Callimachus.

He thought of earnest young Kardus. He was one of the few Tallis had had occasion to speak with on that weeklong gathering in Athens. There were two servants for fifty guests, and a few of the newly recruited teachers had volunteered to help with the endless details incumbent upon a collection of fifty scholars at the estate of Callimachus. Kardus was one.

Tallis remembered him because of their mutual interest in Alexander the Great. Kardus had made a proud comment that he was descended from Macedonian colonists in Hippos, colonists who had been with Alexander himself on his great march east. He owned a small clay replica of Bucephalas, Alexander's beloved horse, which he claimed had been given to his ancestor by Alexander's own hand. Kardus had produced the trinket, and though Tallis doubted such a treasure to be genuine, he afforded the object due respect, and Kardus had been satisfied. The one named Theseus—the one now dead—rolled his eyes behind Kardus's back.

Tallis vaguely remembered Polonus, the leader of the Academy of Socrates in Hippos—a kind man, as Lysias had said; that had been Tallis's own impression. Kind and enthusiastic. A purposeful man, as suited a leader of one of the academies.

He didn't remember much of Antenor, Polonus's assistant, or of the women, or anyone else. What he did remember was excitement. He remembered a simmering enthusiasm in the crowd, a near giddiness . . . he had watched for their reaction upon meeting the great Callimachus, and he remembered it. And as Tallis watched Callimachus speak to them of the new academies, he felt privileged himself to be a part of this great undertaking. Even as a servant.

He looked at the two tar smears on the side of the whitewashed building. He barely remembered Portia. *Egyptian*, he thought. Had he known then what he knew now, of her association with the cult of Dionysus, he would have afforded her the respect due a snake pit.

He had one more idea to play out in this quest to discover the truth of the Decaphiloi, conceived just today when he passed Athena's temple with his fragrant loaf. In front of the temple, in the center of the forum, was the public message board of Hippos. For a few coppers he could post a notice.

It could prove to be a dangerous idea, but seeking the truth always meant risk. And it might take patience, a commodity Tallis had never learned to hoard. What he did have was a nice supply of calm fury. For three years someone had stolen rent and salary monies from Callimachus, the only person on earth he loved. For three years someone had sent progress reports to the academy in Athens, reports that were carefully crafted lies, all for the bilking of an honest old man out of his life savings.

Did Tallis care what had happened to the Decaphiloi? Not as much as he cared about revenge. He could hold out at that backwater inn as long as it took.

He hefted the loaf in his hand and took an envious sniff. He was already formulating the words for the message on the public boards. First, he had a loaf of bread to deliver.

In the silent tombs of Kursi sits a man with no silence within. He used to have a name. If he could remember the name, it would change things.

Remember. Poor stupid man, remember.

They won't let him remember.

Ancient babble, endless babble, a cacophonous din within keeps an endless frenzied pace where no remembrance is possible. He often screams above the din to create his own silence. If he screams, he does not hear the voices. When he stops, he hears.

Blasphemies. Abuses. Accusations. Worst of all, plain babbling nonsense.

WOULDIFICOULDIFICOULDIFIWOULDBARLEYANDPEAS
BARLEYANDPEASBARLEYANDPEASBARLEYANDPEASSOMASEMA
SOMASEMASOMASEMASOMASEMACHEESEWITHYOURBREAD
CHEESEWITHYOURBREADCHEESEWITHYOURBREADCHEESE
WITHYOURBREAD . . .

If he could remember his name, it would stop the voices. He thinks it is in the endless stream of information passing through him every second. He could dip into the stream and pluck his name from it.

He dipped into the stream long ago, and it unleashed hell.

He can't remember his name because he can't get Them to *shut UP!* Ancient babble, endless babble, and an abandoned name tumbling within.

Remember. Remember.

Poor stupid man. Remember.

STUPIDMANSTUPIDMANSTUPIDMANSTUPID MAN . . .

II

Tallis knocked until he was irritable. He blotted more sweat on his sleeve, dismayed at the smudgy look of it. This loaf did not deserve to be left on the doorstep. A dog or a beggar would have it before he turned the corner.

"Excuse me," he called to a woman across the street. "Do you know if a fellow named Demas lives here?"

She gave an airy wave. "I don't keep track of that lot. They come and go. Try the theater."

Tallis considered the loaf. He could give it to the woman to give to Demas, but if Demas was not at the theater, the loaf was rightfully his. He unwrapped the cloth and stole another sniff—ground cinnamon, grated gingerroot, and other intoxicatingly fragrant spices. He groaned and rewrapped the loaf, and reverently placed it in his shoulder pack.

The theater was not the biggest Tallis had ever seen, probably seating around five, six hundred. He'd expected Hippos to have a decent theater, but thought this city on top of a hill would have given more consideration to housing space and fortification. He knew Hippos dated back at least three hundred years, not long after Alexander's time, but this theater couldn't be more than fifty years old. It was probably added under the influence of Herod the "Great"—an appellation likely courtesy of himself.

Tallis came to the public entrance and paused before going through the archway. He noticed the stone columns on either side, twined with stone ivy. He had only to look up and see what sort of archway the columns supported. He knew he would find sculpture work in honor of the patron god of the theaters . . . Dionysus. The god's tie with the theater was the only association he had not been able to break. He had learned to live with the Dionysiac theater guilds as a mere consequence, like being a servant for the privilege of living in fashionable Athens. Or being near Callimachus.

He had learned to ignore any emblems or symbols associated with the god: Cal taught him to reduce the symbols to mere elements of composition, to see sculpture as stone, pottery as clay, carvings as wood. He had even learned to drink wine again. Why, then, this sweat when he looked at the ivy on the columns, why the cold on his heart, and why was he here—why didn't Cal send Aristarchus? If he looked up at the archway he would see what Cal had taught him to nullify. Slowly he let his gaze travel up an ivy-twined column.

The archway was only a bas-relief of Dionysus and his women, only stone, an element of composition. Tallis told himself this as he studied the ringleted, pointy-bearded god and his adoring women known as the Maenads. He ignored the unCallimachus-like tumult in his belly as he regarded Dionysus as most knew him, the merry god of wine, the cheerful companion of those gathering for entertainment. Any theater in Greece had depictions in some form of Dionysus. Any drunkard in his cups knew the good old god of comfort.

It was only stone, and he was only a myth, conjured by the minds of the needful . . . so Callimachus said. He was myth. Myth and legend.

Olympias, the mother of Alexander the Great, was a devotee of Dionysus. The mother of his hero, such a shrewd woman . . . devoted to myth. And in the form to which she was devoted, Dionysus did not remotely resemble his theater-guild or wine-god persona. There was another side to Dionysus, a side that oceans of wine could never make Tallis forget.

"The posting for performances is regrettably late," a voice called.

He broke from his study, felt the cold instantly lift, didn't know he'd been cold. He came through the archway of the amphitheater a little disoriented, relieved for the distraction, and looked down to the stage. There an elderly man with a white tumbling beard sat on a stool. Seated on the stage around him were five or six young men.

"Oh—I'm not here for the performances," Tallis began.

"I don't blame you," one of the young men quipped; and the others, including the bearded one, laughed. He shook his finger at the young man.

Tallis left the archway behind. He came down a few steps, already enjoying this, grateful for the beguilement from his troubles. He gazed about the amphitheater.

The stage components had contemporary styling. There was a fine row in the left bank of seats near the front of the stage, fitted with tiny tables for refreshment. The very front row of seats had not only tables, but footrests and seat backs.

"If I did come I would surely sit right there." Tallis pointed.

"If you can afford one of those seats, I will call *you* my master," the same young man said.

This time Tallis laughed with the others. "A pleasant company I am in," he said as he came down the steps. "I miss the theater."

"You are an actor?" said the white bearded one.

"No. I am a playwright—in my spare time. You probably haven't heard of my works yet." Then he added hopefully, *"The Day of Odysseus?"*

They looked at one another and shrugged.

"Agamemnon's Regret?"

No response, though someone offered politely, "I may have heard of that one."

Tallis sighed as he reached the bottom of the stone steps. "You're being kind. It's probably the best I'll get."

"These do not sound like the wretched raucous comedies of the day," the old man on the stool said, tapping his lips with his finger. "You are a student of Homer?"

For anyone associated with the theater, the question was a familiar challenge. Homer was out of style, as were all the classic tragedies. Tallis lifted his chin and declared, "I am. When I die he will be immensely popular again, and my plays may see stage time. I'll be postmortem rich."

Tallis had passed the test: With a deepening twinkle in his eye, the old man slowly grinned, then clapped his hands. "Wonderful! Students, attend this man—the spirit of Homer lives, and we may yet put on a book or two of the *Iliad*. Sir, my name is Patroclus, master of the theater. May I have the honor of your name? And how may I be of service to a student of Homer?"

Tallis smiled and gave a little bow. "The name is Tallis of Athens, and the service would be to point out the fellow to whom this loaf belongs —it was baked by a pretty maid just for him." He unwrapped the loaf and displayed it high, to a chorus of appreciation.

Later, when Tallis thought on it, he would say the jovial air in the elderly man faltered then—before he ever mentioned the name of Demas; and this, Tallis later decided, was very important.

"And what is the name of the man who should receive that loaf?" asked the young man who had spoken earlier. "I hope it is Claudius, a man infinitely worthy of such splendidly fragrant fare."

The others groaned.

"The name is Demas," Tallis said.

"Why, fortune favors me!" Claudius cried. "That's my second name. And if the maid is pretty, I am definitely Demas."

Tallis chuckled with the rest—it was good to laugh; he hadn't laughed since he left Athens—and glanced for advice at Patroclus.

Patroclus was not smiling. He gazed on Tallis with an unreadable look. Then he said, "He is in a traveling troupe. They just left for Caesarea."

"*I'm* Demas . . ."

"No, *I'm* Demas . . ."

Tallis held the look. Now that he was closer, the man did not seem so elderly. A white beard grown amok, wild even for native Palestinian tastes, could not conceal eyes without enough wrinkles to match the white of the beard.

"Tell the maid he left." There was polite dismissal in his tone.

"Tell her he left other women as well," someone sighed. "Remember the nut pies from Sophronia?"

"Pastries from Anna?" sighed another.

"Remember how he used to share his goods?"

"He even shared his women!"

Claudius held out his hand for the loaf. "I'm sure he wouldn't mind sharing this. He'd insist that I, his former best friend, should have it."

Tallis smiled tightly, aware of the new atmosphere. The young men didn't sense it. He rewrapped the loaf and said, "Sorry, lads. I have strict instructions to enjoy this myself if I cannot find Demas." He nodded to them and to Patroclus. "Good day, good sirs."

"Come for one of our performances," one of them called as he ascended the stone steps.

Tallis inclined his head, said he just might, and left the theater. He glanced behind only once, when he reached the archway. The man Patroclus was watching him.

He concluded his business for the day at the public message board in the forum, regretfully paying out a few coppers to the man with the ink-stained fingers, and left Hippos for the two-mile walk to the inn.

Tallis's own name had brought upon Patroclus some strange speculation. Did he know Tallis? Did Tallis know him? Was he a former teacher of the academy? Tallis couldn't place him; that wild beard concealed much.

"I didn't know you had returned," came a surprised voice.

Tallis roused from his ruminations. It was the innkeeper's daughter.

She stood to the side, arms clasped about herself, looking at the lake. "You're back early."

She didn't like to look in the eyes, Tallis had noticed. Today that fact irritated him.

"Why can't you look at my face when you talk to me?" he groused. "Is it a superstition of foreigners, or is it because I am a man?"

Ho, that brought her eyes around. They were fresh and snappy now, a vivid shade of light brown. Her hair was thick and very wavy, deeply auburn, nearly brown. The wind tossed what wasn't captured by braid or band. The loose strands blew across her smooth, freckled face, and she pushed them aside to glare at Tallis.

"Why are you always unpleasant to me?" he asked more mildly.

"I am not unpleasant," she snapped.

"You're not *pleasant*," Tallis pointed out. "Nobody around here is, except for your father and the little boy. Even your slave looks at me funny."

"Samir?" she asked, surprised enough to leave off her glare. She glanced toward the barn where the slave stayed. "What do you mean he looks at you funny?"

"I don't know. Funny. Like he thinks I'm up to something—I think *he's* up to something. This whole place feels odd. It's much more pleasant in the city."

The barn still had her thoughtful attention. Then she looked at Tallis, and the thoughtful look hardened. "Then why stay here?" She flicked her hand toward Hippos. "Go to the city and pay for pleasant."

Tallis grimaced and settled back into his brood. Pride forbade him from telling her the Inn-by-the-Lake was the cheapest place he could find.

Both of them gazed sourly on the waters, Tallis sitting in his seat and the innkeeper's daughter standing. It grew increasingly uncomfortable, her being with him in his private place. He shifted in his seat a few times, hoping she'd take the hint. Why didn't she leave; didn't he have enough to think on? Then he remembered.

He scratched the back of his head. "I tried to deliver your loaf . . ." He saw her quickened expression, saw she realized the news wasn't what she had hoped.

Her shoulders sagged just a fraction, but she shrugged stiffly. "No matter."

"They think he's in Caesarea." *And he sounds like a wharf rat, so you're better off.* "The bread was delicious, by the way," Tallis said. "Best I ever had."

When she didn't respond, he offered, "I will likely be sick because I ate the whole thing. Couldn't stop myself."

She didn't seem to hear. Her gaze on the lake had gone vacant. After a moment, she turned and started down the path, and this time her step was not lithe.

Tallis rose from his seat and followed her a few steps down the path. "Wait . . . please," he called over a sudden gust of wind off the lake.

She turned, the wind silhouetting her form in her rippling indigo tunic.

"What is your name? I've been here a week; it is ridiculous that I do not know."

He didn't like this Demas for the disappointment in her face. Tallis knew enough actors. Traveling actors and low morals were synonymous. Demas was probably handsome, athletic, and spoke with the honey tongue of a god, the scoundrel. Taking advantage of peasant women who didn't know any better.

This young woman was just pretty enough to interest a wharf rat. Her face was clear and beautifully freckled and proud. But her eyes were mistrustful. What was it with the people around here? At least hers seemed an honest mistrust.

She had not yet answered; she simply regarded him with that sullen unhappiness. Likely she was thinking on Demas; either that or he had broken a local taboo by asking for her name. Too bad they didn't hand him a list of Palestinian taboos when he docked in Caesarea.

A movement behind the maid caught his eye. The girl noticed and turned to see.

A man stood at the back doorway of the inn's kitchen. He looked just as grim as the rest of the locals, but his dress was unusual. Most of the people around Kursi wore common tunics; this man wore a gray robe frayed at the bottom, belted, layered over with a long, darker gray vest. He was notably tall, his thin frame accenting his height. His untrimmed beard spilled like gray moss to his chest, making Tallis think of Patroclus.

He seemed surprised to see Tallis notice him, and not happily. He fetched up the basket just inside the doorway and strode away.

Tallis watched him go. "Who is that man?"

"Do you know him?" the girl asked.

Did he? He had a strange force of presence. He seemed elusively familiar. Seemed he *should* be familiar.

Tallis did not know he had muttered aloud until he saw the girl looking full into his eyes.

"What is elusive?" she asked. "What does that mean?"

He considered her. "It means many things. It's the color of your eyes. I thought they were brown. I see now they are green."

He turned to watch the man walk away, but the barn concealed his path on the road. *Elusive means I cannot tell why this man seems familiar to me.*

"Do you know him?" she asked again.

Elusive is the way I feel now, Tallis thought, his gaze coming back to her, *because you have asked me twice about him, and there is worry in your voice.*

"No," Tallis finally replied, because it was more truthful than not.

He did not miss the change in her demeanor—a relief she could not hide, because she was not entirely skilled at whatever intrigue she was playing at.

"My full name is Kes`Elurah. I am called Kes." She smiled her rare smile, and Tallis was sure it was only because he did not know the stranger.

He smiled back, and she turned and walked the path down to the inn.

"Kes`Elurah." Tallis tried out the unfamiliar name, strolling back to his seat over the Galilee.

Early the next morning, one of the theater students told Patroclus to go look at the public boards. Patroclus thought it would be a reviling review on the last comedy he'd put on, and, if so, the comedy deserved it. Not the talent, the talent was fine; the comedy itself should have never seen a public stage. He was fully prepared for the backlash, and even, in a perverse sort of way as the master of the theater, looked forward to it— hoped it was blistering. Hoped someone in this city had the taste to call it a debacle. When he read what the student meant for him to read, he understood why it had been Urbanus who told him, and in such a way that the other students could not hear.

Calmly Patroclus removed the nails from the scrap of stiff leather, as if he himself had posted the message. He rubbed the leather between his fingers as he wove through the marketplace. He had checked the boards two days ago. This message wasn't there then, he was sure of it. How long had it been up? Who else had read it?

He had known someone would come—it was only a matter of time. It wasn't until the man had given his name that Patroclus realized who he was. He had last seen Tallis eight years ago, serving at the house of Callimachus in Athens.

I SEEK INFORMATION REGARDING THE FORMER ACADEMY
OF SOCRATES, WHICH USED TO MEET IN THE PORTICO OF
THE TEMPLE. I ALSO SEEK INFORMATION REGARDING AN
ASSOCIATION CALLED THE DECAPHILOI. INQUIRE AT THE
INN-BY-THE-LAKE, ON THE ROAD TO DAMASCUS, JUST
SOUTH OF KURSI. ASK FOR TALLIS.

Patroclus halted, fingering the scrap of leather, tempted by the almond roaster's fire. One toss would end it. The seller thought he had a sale, and offered a steaming pouch to Patroclus.

He could destroy this, but Tallis would learn of it and post more. He might even launch an official inquiry. It would not take long for him to learn what he wanted to know, with everything hidden in plain sight. No one had ever cared enough to learn the truth. Until now.

Julia still lived near Hippos, and there was Polonus. If Tallis found either of them, he would learn enough. Patroclus gripped the leather and walked away from the fire, followed by a mild curse from the seller.

Who else had seen the message? What if Portia got wind of it?

Was it time for truth?

He stopped short at this. He thought on it, turned it over in his mind as he turned the scrap of leather in his fingers. He resumed walking.

He told himself he had let the progress reports lapse because he didn't have time to write them.

"Fine performance last night, Master Patroclus," someone said in passing.

He smiled and nodded, looked again to see if it was any particular critic he needed the favor of, and let the man pass with no further comment.

Was it time for truth? Was he glad to have been caught? Was that why he'd let the reports lapse, because he *wanted* to be caught? Was he finished punishing Callimachus?

"I'm getting old," he muttered. He left the marketplace and walked the side alleys.

The theater was beginning to do well. He didn't need Cal's money anymore. A few new patrons had been added from the wave of new blood from Antioch; they were easily impressed fools, some of them newly come to riches, who felt that patronage of the theater was only suitable to their standing. Who cared if they loved the comedies? They and the comedies paid the bills and made it possible to put on the *real* works.

"I am glad to have been caught," he said in surprise to himself as he strolled the byways. Writing the progress reports had grown tiresome. But was this Tallis ready for the truth? Callimachus had spoken fondly of his servant, and the servant had seemed equally fond of Cal. Honest, trusting, naïve Callimachus. His blithe belief in the goodness of all mankind had murdered people. Good people. The best.

Patroclus rubbed the leather scrap in his pocket. Callimachus wanted to know what happened? Very well. Callimachus would find out. He hoped it brought hell on his soul.

"By the way, Tallis of Athens," Patroclus muttered on his way back to the marketplace, "I have indeed read your *Day of Odysseus,* and I'm glad I know who wrote it. It will see stage time, but not on mine—I'd sooner face Portia as Dionysus incarnate than put on a play from a servant of Callimachus."

The madman did not speak anymore. If he tried, the words came out wrong, as if he spoke through a mouthful of stones. It was a strange impediment laid upon his tongue.

Ironic, he would have thought, if he could have thought clearly, considering how much he used to talk, how his friends always told him to shut up. Now he could never say what he meant to.

What he was trying to say now was *water.* They were always thirsty. If he could have thought clearly, he would have laughed at the word he wanted to say. Fancy, him taunting Them. The thought to say it came from a mysterious place. Maybe from a place They had not yet found. Maybe the place where he was safe, and this poor man wasn't really him.

Poor man!

"Wuahh . . ."

He saw a face across the clearing, and rage came. He screamed and lunged—and jerked short in midair, dropping like a felled deer.

Leg iron. Prisoner, imprisoned. Nothing enraged him more.

He screamed and clawed at the chains. Then he threw himself wide, arching taut, and freed himself to Them. He did not know how he did it. They filled him and he hated it; he was wrong to let Them go there; They shouldn't go there, it was wrong.

He knew it was wrong the first time—knew with dreadfulness he couldn't take it back. They had slithered down into the last of himself while the shell called the body concealed their invasion from the world. Rape, incubated.

He snapped the leg iron as if it were brittle glass. Filled with Them, suffused with foul intoxication, he forgot the face across the clearing and began to run.

RUN, STUPID MAN—RUN! They lashed him on and so he ran, up the hills and down the hills. He tore up the southern slope of the el-Kursi Valley, where he had played as a child, tore down the slope into the floor of the Wadi Samakh, raced the half-mile across, slogging through muck in the middle, tore up the northern slope of the valley.

He ran long into the night, past exhaustion, but They weren't done. He wasn't done. He hated, and he gloried in, the venomous power.

RUN, HUMAN MAGGOT! DOG OF A SLUG OF A PIG! RUN!

Foul hot breath on his neck. Whooping malevolent glee. *RUN!*
He ran.
He saw villages light up in the course of the night, and on he ran.
Foolish people. So blinded to the Realms.

III

Tallis waited for three days for someone to show up in response to his message on the board.

He tried to keep busy. He brushed his toga with a stiff-bristled brush and managed to take some of the grime away. He started another letter to Callimachus, which sat half finished on the tiny writing table under the tiny window. It had no real news, and Cal hated trivialities—though he might appreciate the comical little fellow Tallis had made out of an ink splotch in the margin.

He tried to put time to his third play, *Alexander and Barsine*, but the Muses were off frolicking on Capri with debauched old Tiberias. He tried to analyze his dreams because he'd once overheard a philosopher back home say the gods communicated through dreams. If so, the gods were trying to scare him to death. Last night he had a nightmare such as he hadn't had since he was a boy. But he could not remember any details—only fear; his dream analysis came to no appreciable conclusion.

His own forum message held him hostage at the inn. He could not venture far for fear of missing anyone who came in response. Mostly he sat and watched the fishermen on the Galilee.

He missed the clamor and the craziness back home. Every day there was something new for Callimachus to tell him at mealtime. He'd no sooner have his master settled in and his wine poured than Cal would sound his trademark declaration: "Much has transpired since last we conversed, Tallis, old friend." And he'd tell of the latest political brewings from Rome, or the newest philosopher-king scouring Athens for support in a nostalgic bid to retake old Greek independence. *Much has transpired since last we conversed, Tallis, old friend. . . .*

Yesterday he allowed himself a quick excursion to Kursi, with strict instructions to Kes`Elurah to tie up anyone who came for him. He walked the half-mile north and toured the city in ten minutes. Not much to see, not much to do there. He learned that the trade of Kursi was fish and livestock. Shepherds tended hogs in the rocky hill country while fishermen hauled in catches at the fishing grounds by the mouth of the Wadi. Hippos afforded far more beguilement than Kursi.

On the way back, he had climbed to the top of a slope overlooking the small Kursi harbor because he could not resist. He allowed himself a few moments to gaze on the glittering Galilee and on the austere beauty all around. Some of the hills were dun-colored and barren, others forest green, mottled with rock. The mountain range far north of the Galilee had a crest of snow and an aura of cool purple. Directly below him was the valley of el-Kursi, the Wadi Samakh, which brought down the winter rains to the sea.

He found an area on the top of the slope that perplexed him at first, then surprised him—he was in a graveyard. He wondered how old the rock mounds were, if some of the buried dead were Macedonian colonists settled in this area by Alexander. He found a half-buried tablet of commemoration, but the script was old and worn, and not in a language he could read. He saw the bones of a few small animals and, curiously, a set of broken shackles, the kind slaves wore on their ankles at the slave market. An escaped slave must have stopped here until he freed himself from his bonds.

He sat now in his chair overlooking the place the locals had the temerity to call a "sea." His favorite time was not long off, late afternoon. The breezes off the lake became cool and the sun became friendly, casting a luminous golden pathway across waters made pebbly from the wind. Sea grasses in the fore spiked a dark contrast to the pearly background of the lake.

He couldn't stand much more of this uselessness. Today he'd asked Jarek if he could help hang the new barn door, but was politely put off and had to watch instead as Jarek and the slave, Samir, did the work. Sometimes the slave sent considering glances his way, glances that became unnerving. Once Tallis glared back to put him in his place, but the man received the glare with an unperturbed calm, and Tallis ambled off to watch Kes'Elurah feed the chickens.

Tallis couldn't tell Samir's age because he had very brown, very oily skin; perhaps the oils concealed wrinkles. He worked slowly but steadily, and smiled only at the little boy on the premises, the son of the servant girl in the common room. Samir always wore an ivory-colored caplike head covering; none of the other men Tallis saw wore such things. He likely called a long distant tribe his home. Tallis couldn't find out because the fellow acted as though he didn't speak the language. He had tried to engage him in the simplest of conversation, "Good morning, nice day," but if he even came near him, Samir found reason to ease away. From a distance he regarded Tallis with a silent wary interest.

Kes'Elurah wasn't pleased with Tallis watching her feed the chickens. Her glances became scowls, and he finally ambled off to watch the fishermen. He hadn't meant to be rude, he wasn't watching *her*; he was only bored, interested in new people with different ways, desperate for talk. But the people around here did not talk, and he realized it had been a relief to visit Hippos every day. Too long he had been with Cal, where life itself was a running dialogue. Here at the inn, where one supposed a livelihood in accommodation would imply at least friendliness, the mood was morose, and Tallis hated morose. The girl did not speak to her father, and the father avoided the girl. Jarek spoke more with the slave and the young child named Zagreus than he did with his own daughter.

The man had an affability easily tapped into, and when it was, it came to the surface with relief. Tallis watched well-known customers do that to Jarek, watched as they seemed to raise him to an old familiar place. Then he would exchange good-natured insults, and flick boys on their heads with his forefinger, and sometimes take a mug from a customer to test the ale himself. Those around would laugh, and the customer would holler a protest; Jarek would act surprised, offended, and then hand back the ale, chuckling, his big belly shaking.

The fishermen from the lake took special care to tap into the innkeeper's good nature. They all seemed to share some trial—perhaps the Roman government tacked unjust assessments on inns and the fishing trade. An old salt called Bek seemed especially solicitous of the innkeeper. Tallis saw it in those first few days he hung about in the common room. He saw them first share a grim, knowing look, then saw old friends settle into a routine. Kes`Elurah would greet them and bring a platter; Jarek would serve their ale and sit with them for a time.

They'd sit quiet at first. Then Bek would calmly offer comments, watching Jarek's face. Soon Jarek would talk, and by the time they left, Jarek and the fishermen would be joking. What the fishermen did not see, perhaps, was the way Jarek stood at the doorway watching them go, arms folded over his belly, the contented look on his face settling into something Tallis found oddly poignant. It was wistful, sad, and finally grim. He'd gaze at the northern Kursi landscape, and when he turned back into the inn, his look was back to the workaday moroseness.

In the early years of serving Callimachus, if Tallis ever emerged from his rooms with less than a cheerful countenance, Cal sent him back until he came out with a serene expression. It infuriated Tallis at first. Sometimes he remained in his room the entire day, just to spite the old man. His hunger usually won out when kitchen smells wafted down the corridor to his room. He'd go and display a fixedly serene look to Cal, and head for the kitchen. Soon, cheerfulness became as much a part of Tallis as it was of his master.

Cal wouldn't like this place.

Tallis shifted in his chair. Maybe Kes`Elurah thought he fancied her, when he mistakenly watched her work, and he'd like to tell her he preferred the servant girl to the frosty-eyed mistress of the inn. The servant girl, Arinna, skulked the common room flicking a rag here and there, sometimes slipping behind the doors of paying guests. Her attempt at a subtle offer to Tallis on his second night at the inn was instead quite plain; plain, as well, was her desire to conceal her activities from the inn masters.

She had a small son, surely sired by a former guest. The child's name was Zagreus. Tallis had paused when he heard the name. He pitied the boy for having a silly mother who would give him a ridiculous name.

Kes'Elurah pitied the boy too. She dignified the child by giving him work to do. While his mother nibbled on the hair she curled around her finger, wandering the common room in listless attention to whatever duty commanded her, her small son worked with a will, eager to please not his mother but the mistress of the inn. Indeed, Tallis had thought the child belonged to Kes'Elurah, until Jarek corrected him.

"I'm lonely," Tallis declared to the lake in surprise. It had been so long he'd forgotten what it felt like. "I'm so bored and lonely I'm having nightmares just to entertain myself. I'm as fascinated as an old gossip in the affairs of the people around me." Pathetic. He didn't like this feeling. It felt *needy*.

He leaned on his knees and watched for the fishermen to return. If Tallis knew the fishing trade, he'd ask if they needed help. Not to vanquish boredom, this time: One thing he had plenty of time to think about was the uncomfortable reality of his finances. The purse Cal had given him was carefully counted out to last one month; he'd been gone from Athens a month and a half.

He'd indulged himself only once on this trip, and that was for a semiworthless scroll purchased at the bookstalls in Alexandria. It was unthinkable to visit Alexandria, with its famous library, and leave without a book. It was what you did in Alexandria; no matter how poor you were, you bought a book. Even if the book was a drowsy piece of the *Iliad*—the insufferably drawn-out funeral games for Patroclus—it was still as respectable a purchase as he could afford. And a foolish one.

The scroll could have bought him two more weeks at this inn, with extra for incidentals—like reward money for people who answered his message. No one would walk two miles from Hippos for nothing; they would expect compensation. It left Tallis with a horrifying conclusion: He would have to earn his keep.

This morning he had slumped at the writing desk, idling with a silver coin. Coin was the only solid thing left of the Seleucid dynasty. Seleucus was one of Alexander's mighty companions, one of a handful left holding the reins to a gargantuan empire after Alexander's untimely death.

What if his lineage had been stable; what if his heirs had not been murdered? There would be no "King Antiochus" on a silver tetradrachm, no tattered remnants of a Ptolemaic line in Egypt. What would Alexander have thought of the decadence to tumble down after his glorious eleven-year reign? Ptolemy spawned a line of rulers with incest as its primary measure to ensure Macedonian bloodlines. Seleucus's line produced a ruler with ideas so twisted the Palestinian locals took the name he gave himself, Antiochus Epiphanes—Antiochus, God Manifest—and parodied it with Antiochus Epimanes—Antiochus, Madman. Antiochus Madman had none of Alexander's love of culture, nor respect for religion; he'd made the Jews sacrifice pigs to his own god. Alexander would have strung him up by his tongue.

Tallis grimaced: His own *stupidity* had put him in financial straits; his hero worship had. If the cheapest inn in Palestine did not need his help, if he could not find other local employment, he would be turned out. Well, and had he stayed in the more respectable establishments in Hippos he'd have been on his poverty-struck way back to Athens long ago.

He'd have to talk to Jarek and see if he could earn his keep. He'd have to *work*, like a slave. The only indignity worse than a childish nightmare was swapping his toga for a tunic.

Zagreus sat on a stool in a corner of the kitchen, sitting quiet with Mistress Kes. He was cleaning off the crusty black from the sides of the cooking pot where his mother had let the porridge boil over. His mother got the scolding and he got the cleaning. Zagreus didn't mind. He liked to sit quiet with Mistress Kes.

She was making a paste with leaves in her mortar and pestle. Sometimes she put salt into the paste, sometimes oil. She worked it smooth, and gave Zagreus a smile now and then. He wished she wouldn't. Once in the morning was enough, because it was her real smile. When she didn't give him unwanted smiles, she frowned at her paste. Something vexed her, and what vexed Mistress Kes vexed Zagreus.

"I had a bad dream last night," he offered.

"Did you?" She wasn't paying attention. "What was it about?"

"It was scary." He hesitated. "Samir said he came last night."

She worked the paste and pretended not to hear, and he pretended it didn't matter.

Zagreus knew when things bothered Mistress Kes. He knew when she was sad. He worked extra hard then, tried to be extra good.

Was it basket day? Basket days were sad days for Mistress Kes. Twice a week she took the empty basket from the tall man and filled it again. She filled it with loaves of bread, smoked fish, whatever she had on hand. Sometimes she made the paste and put it in a small jar and put it in the basket. She put other things in and made it look nice. Sometimes a posy of herbs, sometimes a piece of parchment, broken off from a scroll she kept hidden from Master Jarek.

Once she did an odd thing on basket day. She placed a bunch of fresh greens in the basket, then got very still and gave a strange cry. She clutched the bundle of greens close, pressed them on her cheek, then kissed them. She put them carefully in the basket. He saw a tear drip off her nose. He pretended not to see and was extra good that day.

A while back she had Demas days. Those days her cheeks were flushed and her eyes bright. He liked Demas days. He didn't like Demas —his mother did, and Demas liked his mother—but he was glad for Mistress Kes on Demas days. She was happy then, and things felt fine.

New days had settled on the inn. Maybe these were Master Tallis days, though he didn't make her cheeks flush and didn't brighten her eyes. Zagreus was a little scared of Master Tallis because he was so different from the other guests. He dressed different; he spoke funny. His skin was pale, and it burned in the sun. He was fussy, Mistress Kes said, and nosy. But things felt right around Master Tallis; things felt safe. Sometimes he winked at Zagreus, and there was kindness in his eyes. Demas had never noticed Zagreus.

"Finished?" said Mistress Kes.

"Almost."

"Clean your nails when you're done."

"Yes, ma'am."

Mother never asked him to clean his nails. Mother never saw if his nails were dirty. Mistress Kes took care of Zagreus, and Zagreus took care of Mistress Kes.

Troubled, he stopped scrubbing. "Is it Auntie day, Mistress Kes?"

She stopped working the pestle. "No."

"Is it basket day?"

"Tomorrow is basket day."

Ah. He applied his brush to the pot again. Then days when she was quiet-vexed must be Master Tallis days.

He raised his head at a sound in the common room. He hopped off his stool and set down the pot. He wiped off his hands and went to the doorway. He observed for a moment to see what he could see, then reported to Mistress Kes.

If the gods were trying to communicate with Tallis, why would it be through dread? It was the sum total of the dream last night, its substance, its detail, and its interpretation: dread. What would the philosopher/dream-interpreter think about that?

"There is someone here to see you."

He jumped at her voice. He rose from his chair at the lake and smoothed his toga in a huff, cheeks flaming.

"I'm sorry—I should have walked loudly," Kes`Elurah said, and he glanced at her.

He smiled wryly. "I was deep in thought," he replied, looking down the path to the inn.

Finally, an inquiry! Would they settle for the scroll in payment? He had a small bottle of his favorite scented oil, for which he had little use since visits to the baths had been reduced to a once-a-week luxury. To part with his oil, however, was unthinkable. He'd become a barbarian for certain.

She started down the path, and he followed. Was now a good time to bring up possible employment? Any time would be humiliating. He caught up to her.

"Kes`Elurah," he began.

"Kes," she replied.

"I, ah, was wondering—does your father need any help around here?"

"You can't pay?" she asked.

For the second time his cheeks flared. "I did not intend on staying in Palestine this long. I didn't bring enough money."

He stopped with Kes`Elurah outside the kitchen door, and slipped off his sandals to slap them together before crossing the threshold. "I suppose we can discuss employment opportunities another time. Where is my visitor?"

"In the common room. I gave her some wine."

He looked up from his sandals. "Her?"

Kes shrugged. "You were expecting a he?"

He knocked the rest of the dirt from the sandals and slipped them on. "I hadn't thought about it. I posted an inquiry in the forum, I suppose anyone could—" And a thought stopped his words. Nearly stopped his heart.

Kes was entering the kitchen doorway, but he seized her arm and pulled her back. He held her aside while he peered through the kitchen to the common room door. It was opened, but from here he could not see any visitor.

With an indignant look at his grip on her arm, she began to speak, but Tallis quickly pulled her around the corner to the back of the inn. He covered her mouth and spoke low.

"This woman—did you see an imprint on her forearm—a mark—a tattoo?" What did he remember of Portia? Nothing, he could not see her face. "It would be ivy or grapevines."

His mind raced with his heart. What else did Lysias say about Portia? She was plain—he said she was plain. But nothing would identify her more clearly than the tattoo that accompanied an initiate of the Bacchantes. A priestess of Dionysus would proudly bear such a mark.

He carefully removed his hand from Kes's lips. Her green eyes searched his, quick with surprise.

"I did not see any tattoo. Would you like me to look? I can be discreet."

Portia had dark hair, he suddenly remembered. "Is her hair black? Is she plain?"

The green eyes flickered. "Far from it. She's quite beautiful. That I can tell. And her hair is light brown, with sun in it."

He held her a moment longer, closed his eyes in relief, and was quite suddenly aware of himself. He pulled away, murmuring, "I'm sorry. I—"

But there was no explaining his behavior. He smoothed down his toga, avoiding her face, and started for the kitchen. This time she seized his arm.

"There is fear in your eyes," she accused quietly. "If there is one thing we know, running this inn, it's where fear belongs and where it doesn't. It doesn't belong with you." Her eyes narrowed, more with curiosity than accusation. "Why is it there?"

He snatched his arm from her. Who did she think she was, Callimachus?

"You don't know me," Tallis scoffed.

"I know what I see. My father thinks you are a good man. If this is true, why is fear now in your eyes?" She was clearly unperturbed by the fact that she detained him from the person in the common room. Unperturbed by her honest words, which perturbed Tallis greatly.

"How do you know fear so well?" he asked, and when she did not answer, he started for the doorway.

"Tallis," she called, and he stopped from surprise. He looked over his shoulder.

"I just wanted you to know . . ." She nodded in the direction of the common room. "Zagreus says there is no fear in her eyes."

After a moment he nodded and went to receive his guest.

She was standing in the doorway of the inn, her back to him. Her image, the one he would carry with him, was of folds of pearly green fabric, softly illuminated by the late afternoon sunlight in the doorway, artfully draped on her frame. An alabaster buckle held the folds of fabric at her shoulder; her undertunic was creamy, matching the tone of her skin. A mother-of-pearl clasp caught her hair, a light brown arrangement of softly curled and artfully arranged loveliness, tendrils of which lay on her neck. Sun was in her hair, as Kes had said. She was smiling at someone through the doorway, a short someone.

She clasped her hands together and laughed, then knelt in the doorway and said something Tallis could not hear, though he heard her gentle tone. Here was a lady, an elegant, patrician Greco-Roman lady, Athens come to him, whose expensive perfume finally reached his nose. The scent was fresh and lovely, foreign in this common room, quickening his heart. Alluring, in the sweetest sense of the word.

He should clear his throat to alert her to his presence, but he didn't want to. She finally noticed him herself, and turned, bringing to bear the full loveliness Tallis knew he would find. Who was Tallis, that she should come to him?

"You should have sent a servant," were his first words to her, tinged with reprimand. He would remember this later and wish he had said something else.

Even her half smile ignited the dreary common room. What would a full smile do, spray it with lightning?

"I came with a servant. He is outside with my son."

My son, she says, and that is an instant pity.

Tallis and the woman regarded one another until the woman glanced pointedly at the long table where a goblet of wine waited. He quickly gestured for her to be seated and joined her across the table.

Kes`Elurah arrived with another goblet of wine and a pitcher. She placed the goblet in front of him, filled it, and topped off the goblet of the woman. She addressed Tallis, saying, "Will there be anything else, sir?" in the only servile tone he'd ever heard from her—the only time she'd ever addressed him with an honorarium, and the only time she'd served him table wine without her palm out for payment. It made him glance at her, and the look on her face was passive dignity. She could have been an actor.

He deferred to his guest, asking if she or her child required any further refreshment, but she shook her head. To Kes`Elurah he said, "No, Thank you." She nodded, and he watched her head for the corner counter near the kitchen.

"I'd like to guess at your name," Tallis said, turning to the lady. "Are you Julia?"

"I am. Do you still work for Callimachus?"

Had he mentioned Callimachus in the posted message?

To answer his mute surprise, she said, "You told me you wanted to be an historian of Alexander. Have you written anything?"

"I'm afraid you're mistaken. We never had a conversation. I never would have forgotten it."

She laughed softly, and the sound freshened the room. "Apparently you already have. It was quite a long conversation, and I entertained hopes, back then, that it *wouldn't* be forgotten." She tilted her head. "Don't you remember? They were running you ragged, and you finally had a chance to sit down on the back porch. You thought you were alone."

Dumbstruck, Tallis sat back. "That was you?"

It was past midnight, and Tallis had been up before dawn, chasing down last-minute accommodations for the people who had arrived and were not on the list—Tallis was always the last to know when Callimachus had invited more. He had to find seven more beds, scare up seven more place settings (they had borrowed all the fine servingware they could, and now Tallis had to scour Athens for more), and inform the cook of extra arrivals. The cook had a fit because seven more people meant another bottle of fish sauce, and it couldn't be any fish sauce; no, it had to come from a place on the west side that had closed its doors by sundown. He had to find out who owned the store, find where he lived, and beg for another bottle. The fish sauce alone took two hours.

The new leaders of the satellite schools had filled Callimachus's house to overflowing, and the chatter and excitement and the wine had flowed on that first day until all were littered about the estate either asleep or in contented whispering enclaves. When Tallis thought no more was required of him, he collapsed on a chaise in what he thought was the only empty place on the grounds.

"We had quite a conversation, didn't we," Tallis said, marveling that she was the one.

"Well, *I* thought so . . . you didn't even acknowledge me the next day," she replied in a twinkling rebuke.

"I couldn't find you," Tallis protested. "It was dark—I never got a clear look at your face." Finally, an interesting woman—lost to him the very next day. Lost to him until eight years later, when he finds out she's not only the loveliest creature he's ever seen, but she's married and has a child. "Tell me you remember Aristarchus finding me."

"I remember."

"He was furious. And now I am furious at him. And don't think I didn't try to find you." He shifted in his seat. "Do you know how many conversations I eavesdropped on, listening for your voice?"

Do you know I've listened for you for years?

Fatigue and the concealing darkness and the amphora of wine Julia shared with him had loosened his tongue; they had spoken of everything from Alexander to mosaic, Julia's field of work at the new school in Hippos. They talked for at least a half an hour before Aristarchus found him and dragged him off.

"Why didn't you . . ."

"I thought the choice was yours," she said lightly.

They held the look as long as they dared, then became aware of the muted sound of children playing outside. And whatever fancy had begun on the back porch in Athens, eight years ago, was quietly laid to rest.

"You posted a message," she said, reclining in her chair with her wine.

"Callimachus sent me to visit the satellite schools; in particular, to find out why we stopped receiving reports from the school in Hippos. From your . . . Decaphiloi."

Her eyes narrowed slightly. Kes`Elurah was right, there was no fear in her eyes; if, to Kes, this made her a good person, fine. Tallis still had to find answers.

"You're a little late, aren't you?" she asked. "Three years late?"

"So I've learned—of course, we had no idea the school had disbanded."

Surprise in the light brown eyes. Confusion. Then wariness. The soft tone gained an edge. "What do you mean? What are you talking about? It's been three years since I've taught a class."

"I didn't find out the school has been defunct until I visited Hippos —*last week*."

She stared at him, and in that moment Tallis knew he could trust her. So many elements flashing in those eyes—incredulity—growing in- dignation—but guile was not there. "You are telling me Callimachus never knew what happened?" she said carefully.

Tallis leaned forward. "What did happen?"

"What about my letters?"

"What letters?"

Her eyes flashed, and she looked away. She touched her earring; she smoothed her hair. Finally, deliberately quiet, she demanded, "Why has it taken *three years* for an inquiry?"

"The reports showed us no reason to come out."

"Reports?" she exclaimed, then put her hand to her throat. "Reports of *what*? That the students taught themselves? Do you know how many gifted students I had to abandon? Do you know I have no idea what hap- pened to them? If they continued with their talents or if they went back to—" She pressed her fingers on her lips.

"What happened?"

She would not answer, simply kept her eyes on him. She was not really seeing him. Her gaze soon drifted. She drew a long breath and placed her hands in her lap. "I didn't tell my husband I was coming," she said softly. "Philip rescued me from everything—I owe him my life. He thinks it's all in the past. I should not be here. I should not have come. For his sake. But the message perplexed me. If you were the same Tallis, I could not understand what information you could possibly seek; it never occurred to me you didn't know."

"Know *what?*" Tallis demanded, and then lowered his voice. "I've learned a few things, but not what and not why. I know Theseus is dead. I know Bion committed suicide. And I've heard about Kardus. I wasn't told why or . . ." He trailed off, because the name of Kardus incurred extraordinary response.

"Kardus," Julia whispered, and her face crumpled, her fist went to her mouth. Her eyes were stricken, and when she gazed at him, tears welling, he saw her heart laid out, baring anguish. It was an unveiled moment for a strong woman, and he could only look for a moment before decency made him look away.

Tallis rolled the goblet between his palms. Surely it came to one thing, and with his voice thin, distant in his ears, he felt his way and said, "Julia . . . tell me about Portia."

And Julia closed her eyes. A tear fell.

It was all Tallis needed. He closed his eyes too, as weighted memory tumbled down upon him.

He wouldn't believe his father; he had to see for himself. Father always said bad things about Mother; why should Tallis believe him now? Unless he knew . . . somewhere was dark truth in his words. Whatever truth was there, he had to find out for himself. So one evening he followed his mother into the woods.

Julia was saying something, bringing him back from the Theban hillside, the gully from which he had crouched and peered and lost all innocence remaining to a twelve-year-old boy. She was speaking to him. Whispering him back, just as Callimachus did. He stumbled out of the gully now as he did then, senses reeling. . . .

"How did you know?" she was saying. Those stricken brown eyes brought him back to a common room in Palestine.

You're wrong, Kes 'Elurah, there is a great deal of fear in her eyes.

"Tell me how you knew to name Portia."

"My mother was a Bacchante."

Memory bore down, and the prettiest face in all of Palestine could not have kept him out of that gully.

Brambles replaced the face, moonlight upon a hilltop clearing. The moonlight was silver, but he remembered in ghastly orange, the light of the bonfire around which the women danced. Silver had no part in what happened.

He had hidden in a thicket, peering through parted brambles to watch the dances of the Maenads. He watched his mother, flushed with loveliness, catch up her skirts and kick her feet in an elegant step he had never seen before. He saw joy that had never been, joy his harsh father would never have understood or allowed. His mother was laughing with it, drunk with it, dancing in a happiness that had never touched Tallis's life. He felt something like envy then, and a certain gladness for his mother.

He watched as a child, three or four years old, was passed from one celebrant to another. The child was fearful, Tallis could tell from where he crouched. It looked as if he were recently woken. There were blanket creases on his face. His dark eyes were wide, his thumb fast in his mouth. Every dancer received the child with joyous ecstasy, like a mother long away from her son. The child clung to each whirling celebrant with uncertain eyes now upon the bonfire, now searching among the dancers, perhaps for his mother. The celebration went on for a long time.

Dark eyes wide. Thumb in his mouth. Face bathed in an orange glow. The gods and the goddesses and all sacred under the sun, Tallis would have screamed then. He would have leapt from his hiding place, as he had in his imagining a thousand times since, he would have . . .

The women in the midnight dance fell upon the child like a pack of wolves, tore him apart before his eyes, and his mother, oh, gods, his mother, his mother had blood on her hands.

"Excuse me."

Tallis pushed up from the table and tugged down the sides of his toga. He left the common room, walking as straight as he could, woodenly aware of the stares from Julia and Kes. He had to get to his place by the water. He had to get to the sea.

Callimachus forbade him to remember, he forbade . . .

Callimachus would say it was old grief rolling over; it would soon go to sleep.

Callimachus had no orange bonfire memories. All of his work to keep a broken boy out of that gully came to nothing.

He went through the kitchen and paused at the doorway. He slowly raised his eyes to the hills of Kursi. Same feeling as in the Theban gully. He'd felt it the moment he first came from Hippos, an oddness in the air, a vague awareness, and he'd spent every moment since his arrival pretending it wasn't there. He knew what it was now. He never forgot the bonfire presence.

He studied the Kursi hills, smoky indigo with twilight. Alexander never did return home. Neither had Tallis; he'd not been home since he was twelve years old.

Kes`Elurah watched Tallis leave, his face white as milk. The lady remained at the table. Ordinarily Kes would make the lady pay for what she did to make Tallis look that way, but Zagreus said the lady had no fear.

Kes came around the counter and sat where Tallis had been. She took his goblet and took a long sip of wine, wiping her mouth with the back of her hand and resting the goblet on her cheek as she considered this lady.

The lady looked at her, surprise mixed with anxiety.

Kes set down the goblet and put her chin on her fist. "You were lovers," she mused.

The woman studied her, then said sadly, "We should have been."

The woman was lovely. Kes would never have enough money to buy her kind of perfume, let alone the lustrous fabric she wore. Nobody like her had ever crossed the threshold. But then, nobody like Tallis had ever stayed here.

"Is the boy his?"

Mild surprise crossed the woman's face, then mild amusement. She folded her arms and cleared her throat delicately. "Your question is forward, at the least; most would consider it rude. Ordinarily I wouldn't answer. But you—remind me of an old friend." Her gaze drifted in memory, and sadness descended. "He was just as plainspoken, never a thought for convention."

Tallis was like that. And he padded his plainspeak with humor. A gentleman with a joke, right from that first day. Mother would not have approved of him, and so Kes didn't, not at first. "Do you speak of Tallis?"

"No."

Such sadness in those eyes. Fine ladies had bad things happen too. No one was safe, didn't matter if you were fine and lovely and rich. Troubles put a connection between people, made them the same, in a way. Kes felt a twinge of pity for the woman.

The lady blinked and drew herself straight and looked evenly at Kes. "The boy belongs to my husband."

Kes glanced toward the kitchen. "I've not seen Tallis like this." Always so cheerful. It had been a long time since the inn had cheer living in it. "He was fine until you came." She didn't bother keeping resentment from her tone. "What did you say to him?"

"Now you are being rude. Where did he go? To his room?"

"No. To his place by the sea. I gave him a chair for it." She never knew a guest to enjoy the view as Tallis did. She had never thought of it as a view, and neither had anyone else. Somehow she knew it became more than a view for him. It became a place he needed. *Nobody like him has been here before, and now I fear he is going to leave.*

"How do I get there?"

"You're not going there."

Startled, the woman said, "I must speak with him."

"Not today. You've upset him enough." Kes rose and stood the way her father did over the whole common room—even when he was sitting down—with proprietary authority not to be questioned.

The woman rose, eyes bristling. "He posted a message in the forum, and I am answering that message."

"Answer it tomorrow."

Any other woman would have put up a fuss, at least the women Kes knew. This one merely regarded Kes with icy dignity, then turned and left in a soft wake of expensive perfume and graciously flowing fabric. She heard the woman call for the servant, heard the servant call for the child.

Kes rubbed a water spot on the table, until she noticed her roughened hand.

In the tombs of Kursi sat a man with his back to the sea. For a long time he sat with his back to the sea. Until it got uncomfortable, and he broke position.

Polonus rubbed his back and grumbled, "I don't know how you do it."

He had situated himself as Kardus did, bowing his back precisely against the lake of Galilee, forehead on his knees. He tried to make himself sit for hours, as Kardus did, but Polonus was sure he didn't make it ten minutes. His back muscles were cramped, his neck hurt for pressing his forehead on his knees, his back leg muscles were stretched to pain, his head pulsed with pressure from his blood. He looked over his shoulder and squinted at the glittering waters, wondering what the sea had done to earn Kardus's contempt. He looked to where Kardus lay, sleeping beside an ancient mound of rocks.

If sleeping it was. For the three years he had been observing Kardus, the man was never in what Homer called "the sweet grip of sleep." There was nothing sweet about his twitchings or his eerie half-lidded look, like a drowsy coma. Polonus had hoped at the beginning that sleep would afford Kardus reprieve from the waking nightmare in which he lived; sleep only trailed the nightmare along.

"I will be going away for a while, Kardus," Polonus said softly. "Don't worry, I'll be back. I won't be gone long. A few days."

Polonus gazed at the twitching form. He wasn't able to get clothes on him today. Kardus grew stronger all the time.

Dirt and defecation covered Kardus like his bruises and scabs, so that actually, from a distance, it looked as if he were indeed clothed, camouflaged in havoc. Havoc, covering havoc. Sometimes he allowed Polonus to pull a tunic over his head. A day later Polonus would find the tunic ripped to shreds or bedecking a gravesite in a horrifying fashion; Kardus once had laid out the tunic over a rock mound like a shroud, and had put a dead bird for a head and broken shackles for the feet and hands.

He hated to be clothed. It panicked him. Once Kardus had used a cast-off tunic to strangle a stray pig. A pig! He showed Polonus his triumph, then to Polonus's horror settled down to eat the pig raw. He couldn't stay for that.

"I swear to the gods and the elements," Polonus whispered, "I will see you whole again. If there is a way into madness, logic says there is a way out. I will give you that ladder myself. No human was meant to live like this."

It used to be he could chain Kardus up. He would then lead him to people who promised they could help. Some of the people were genuinely concerned; some were charlatans who only took his money. They put the blame on Polonus if the cure did not work.

Once he took Kardus on a four-day journey east to a revered wise woman of the Chambari tribe. Upon examining Kardus, she announced that she could help and prescribed a spell—which Polonus had to purchase from her at great expense—certain to chase away the "many evil ones" she was sure had come to reside in Kardus. He had to take Kardus to a place where great violence had been done (she recommended any place where gladiatorial spectacles had been put on) and conduct the spell just as dawn broke. In the dirt of the great violence, he had to write out the charm in blood from the womb of a sheatfish, mixed with the juice of the sarapis herb and the spirit Sisioth. Then he was to take the leftover mixture and place it in the mouth of a dead dog. If conducted at dawn, Kardus's healing would take place within the hour.

He took Kardus to Scythopolis, because Hippos did not have a Great Stadium. Neither did Scythopolis; their Great Stadium was under construction, but they had a large area where the spectacles were put on until then, by a steep hillside upon which the people sat to watch. He paid off the steward to conduct the ritual, undisturbed, at dawn. He had selected a dog he felt somehow was noble, and with apologies he killed it. He had no idea what the spirit Sisioth was, knew less how to mix it with the sheatfish blood, but he paid for the services of a local temple priest to come and invoke the spirit at dawn. The womb of a sheatfish does not have much blood, not for the script of the lengthy spell, so he had had to purchase many sheatfish to ensure he had female ones for the womb.

He wrote the charm in the dust at dawn as the priest, smelling of strange oils and looking like he had just rolled out of bed, invoked the spirit Sisioth. He put the leftover "ink" in the mouth of the noble dead dog, and waited for an hour with the shackled Kardus.

Nothing happened.

The priest, who had been mildly interested in the proceedings, shook his head and left. They waited all morning as the sun grew hotter, until the steward came and told him a spectacle was due to start within the hour.

Polonus squinted up at the man, whose sympathy was clear on his face. "Maybe it was the wrong fish." He held up a warm and smelly carcass to the steward. "Does this look like sheatfish to you?" The man had shrugged and walked away.

Polonus left, with a sincere apology to the dead dog, and made straight for the Chambari tribe. Four days after he sat in the dirt of great violence at dawn, he presented the wise woman Cosomatura with a bill of what the whole venture had set him back, and demanded reparation.

"Why?" she asked, sitting on that pile of animal skins, waving away a fly with a bangled hand. He stared at her, and deliberately swung his gaze to the chained and drooling Kardus.

"It didn't *work*, that's why. You're a fraud, and I want my money back. I want you to pay me the coin I spent on the charm itself and on all the things I had to buy to make it work. Do you know how much sheatfish cost? Do you know I had to send to Caesarea for them?"

She seized on it. "Caesarea?"

"Yes, Caesarea. Nobody is hauling in nets stuffed with sheatfish at the Galilee, let me tell you."

"Well, there's your problem. I *told* you the charm had to be absolutely precise for it to work. You were to use *fresh* sheatfish. Now if you had to send to Caesarea for them," she said, and shook her head regretfully, "they were not fresh."

And all his stupidity came crashing down upon him in one stunning inglorious moment. Polonus, who had once taught the most brilliant minds at the most promising school Palestine had to offer . . . Polonus, who had earned a name even the great Callimachus had taken note of . . . Polonus, captain of the academy and leader of the once-revered Decaphiloi, stood now before a fat and baleful huckster, brandishing before her a bill of his own foolishness.

He let the bill slip from his fingers and said, "Come on, Kardus," and led him home.

The event had not cured him of hope for his old student. He remembered the look on the young Kardus's face whenever he arrived at the inn with another scroll. How he loved that eagerness.

He remembered introducing Kardus to his friends.

He remembered introducing Kardus to Portia.

Polonus watched the twitching Kardus. That was the one thing he wished with all his heart he hadn't done. Antenor had warned him, and he did not listen. For by then, things had changed with Kardus.

The schoolboy became a young man, and the young man grew . . . tiresome. He was brilliant, and he knew it. He was bloated with his gifts. He had a startling acumen for battle strategies and tactics; he could pick up an entire language in the time it took Polonus to read a book. At the age of twenty, he was fluent in Greek, Latin, at least one form of Persian, and Parthian.

Was it his own fault Kardus ended up the way he did?

In the beginning, Polonus had to work against the negative forces at the inn, the boy's mother in particular. She was a viciously strange woman, furious with Kardus for learning from Polonus, malevolent with the father for allowing it. The child had a nervous habit then, always blinking his wide eyes, except when he forgot himself in the salvation of education. The blinking never failed to go away then, and Polonus knew he had to handle this child carefully. He was careful to praise him lavishly for any accomplishment, careful to employ positive forces to counter all the negative forces that had borne down on the child ever since that shrew gave birth to him.

Was it all a mistake? It was a question to haunt the days he watched Kardus writhing on the ground, screaming as if under a hail of invisible blows. Gods, the screaming . . . his own hell to listen.

Was it so wrong to convince the child that he was great—and he was—that he was gifted—and he was? He only spoke the truth, and how that child needed truth. How he needed someone to tell him he believed in him. In Kardus, there was never a doubt that greatness lay within.

Soon Polonus had dreams of presenting to the world his own Alexander the Great, from the hand of Aristotle-Polonus, he who tutored all of the bad out of the boy, tutored the good of life and the joy of learning and the breath of understanding into him. His was a rare intellect. If he told Kardus something once, he remembered. Once! And his intuitive grasp of Alexander's tactics was nearly as singular as the tactics themselves. He had to scour for more books because the boy ran him out of learning. He was glad to have rescued him from that godforsaken inn, glad to throw a rope into that dark pit. . . .

How prideful Polonus was. How prideful Kardus became. How insufferable.

He couldn't wait to give him a teaching position so he could talk all he wanted to, beguile those who truly wanted to listen to him. Yes, Kardus had charm; he had an irresistible effervescence—but his personality, so attractive at first, led the unaware to an encampment where none but Kardus was the object of illumination. Polonus grew sick of it, sick of the unattractive boasting, sick of Kardus's mission to endlessly inform the masses of all he knew.

He tried out a new observation of himself, not entirely certain this one would make it to parchment: "I was jealous. Yes—I was jealous of you."

The truth of the matter was this: That jealously had led to loathing, and loathing led to the game with Julia. They had no business foisting Kardus onto Portia, because in his heart Polonus knew what kind of a woman she was. The truth was this: They introduced him to Portia in hope that he wouldn't plague them anymore, in hope he would find romance so that Polonus could be left in peace . . . left alone in the knowledge that Kardus was more brilliant than he would ever be. One day, people would know the name of Kardus as they knew the name of Socrates. They would never know Polonus.

Polonus didn't like drink, so where could he find consolation? In another student? He was too old to raise another prodigy. He'd never find another student like Kardus. So Polonus feigned solace in new books and new ideas and new teaching methods, and Kardus found new pleasures in the arms of one of the Decaphiloi . . . the most dangerous woman he had ever met.

"You warned me, Antenor, and I did not listen," Polonus whispered, staring down at the filthy ruin of Kardus the Great. "I tried to get rid of him once, pushing him off onto her, and now I will never be rid of him."

Kardus once had light brown hair with a touch of copper, thick and waving and stylishly cropped. Now it was matted and stiff and dully gray, infested with vermin. He once had alert eyes, bright with confidence and interest and pride; he never looked at anyone anymore. Polonus had caught a staring moment only once, and tried to see if any bit of Kardus was in there. What he saw he could never explain, not even to himself. It was the look of an animal. If he had seen a void of nothingness, it would have made more sense, because Kardus wasn't there anymore. But he saw an animal look. He saw something.

Kardus moaned in his fitful unconsciousness, limbs twitching, sometimes jerking.

"You became charming and unbearable. Someone I didn't like very much. But I never wished this on you."

A flitting from the corner of his eye made Polonus look and see.

"Who's there?" Polonus looked around him. "Is someone there?"

He thought he had seen someone. Seen a flicker of yellow. Grimly he turned back to Kardus. Someone spying on them, that's what it felt like lately. Morbid freaks who wanted to enjoy someone else's anguish.

"Freaks!" he suddenly shouted. "I know you're watching!"

No response, just the echo of his own shout. He settled down to his vigil, eyes as watchful on Kardus as on the peripheries.

IV

Tallis didn't want to go to sleep. He didn't want the gods to communicate again. Especially now that Dionysus had awakened.

He sat at the writing table wedged beneath the small window, head on his fist. His eyes drooped, but he wouldn't lie down. What if he sat all night and watched the fires across the lake? Light from a half-moon shone softly on the Galilee, and tiny fires lit the cities on the other side. Tiberias was a little to the south, directly across from Hippos. A soft, ringed glow was about the city, making even darker the surrounding countryside with its occasional tiny fire pit.

He had left Dionysus behind a long time ago, a grim world he had managed to forget as eagerly as he learned the scholarly world of Callimachus. Each year that passed was a bandage laid upon the wound until, so buffered, it hardly caused him notice at all. Pain had surprised him today. He didn't realize how thoroughly he had forgotten.

A knock startled him from his drowse. He sat in the darkness, wondering who it could be. Perhaps Kes`Elurah, making sure the guests had their lamps lit. He took the small lamp from his bedside table and went to the door.

It was the servant girl, Arinna. She saw he had his lamp ready. "Oh." She smiled at him and lit the wick from her candlestick. "Mistress Kes wants to know if you're hungry. You didn't come out for supper."

She seemed so young to have a child like Zagreus. Rather, she seemed foolish next to his earnest little solemnity. She wore cheap perfume meant to entice; right now it only nauseated.

"I'm not hungry," he replied. He started to shut the door, but she slid her foot in the way. He followed the foot to her eyes.

"Would you like anything else?" she said lightly.

He let his gaze travel slowly down and up. Truly, a lovely form. Beautiful bright eyes. "I would. I truly would." *But Kes`Elurah doesn't visit the guest rooms.* He smiled tightly. "But not tonight. I have a headache."

She looked him up and down as well. "Anything I can do? I'm pretty good with headaches."

Yes—go away; take your sickening perfume with you. Do Kes and Jarek know what kind of woman you are? They seem like such a naïve lot. Grim and naïve, a disconcerting combination.

"No, thanks. I appreciate the offer."

She glanced past him into the room. "They say you're a scholar or something."

"Something."

"Do you have any scrolls with you?" She gave a little shiver, apparently of delight. "I just love—scholar things."

"Really."

"Oh, yes." She glanced into the room again. "Maybe you could read to me."

He studied her, trying to guess her game. Tallis was not an ugly man; he had an idea he was good-looking enough, but he was not handsome. Not the Demas kind of handsome, the kind that had women baking him things. Did she think he was rich and could pay her well for her services? Was she a common thief? Did she hope to find where he stashed his coins?

"Arinna!"

Arinna jumped guiltily. Kes stood at the hallway door, a hard look on her face. The jumping had put out Arinna's candle. Tallis smiled wryly as he lit it with his lamp.

"He's not hungry," Arinna airily informed her. She smoothed her hair and went to the doorway. She was just past Kes when her mistress, with her eyes on Tallis, spoke.

"See to the family in room three. One of their children vomited. Get some rags."

Behind Kes, Arinna stopped and stared at the back of her mistress with revulsion. Kes couldn't see the revulsion, and Arinna couldn't see Kes smile.

"But—where's Samir? He does things like that. He does vomit."

"Samir is busy." Kes continued to look at Tallis and smile. Tallis bit the inside of his cheek to keep his face straight.

Arinna's tone became wheedling. "You know how I am with things like that. . . ."

"Then do it quickly."

The wheedling changed to contempt, and Arinna flounced away.

Tallis smiled broadly. Kes did too, and said softly, "Is she bothering you?"

Tallis shrugged. "I wish more women would bother me."

"She didn't . . . invite herself in, did she? We've been after her about that."

Tallis leaned against the doorway. "Why do you keep her? She doesn't fit with this place."

"She'd take Zagreus if she left."

"Ah. You like that little fellow."

Kes nodded.

"I think you make the better mother."

A sweet smile came at that, a small one. They looked at one another for a moment across the hallway. Then Tallis scratched the back of his neck and said he ought to get some sleep, and Kes said she had to see to the common room.

"Good night, Master Tallis," Kes said as she closed the door.

"Good night, Kes," Tallis said as he closed his.

He set the lamp on his lamp stand and forgot why he didn't want to go to sleep.

It was late. The fires across the lake had gone out; the half-moon was on the other side of the sky. Tallis tossed and groaned on his cot.

Midnight orange. Black winged things in the dances, things the celebrants can't see. A huge tar caterpillar, flowing sinuously, weaving through the steps . . .

In Arinna's room, Arinna snored softly on her bed. On the other side of the room, Zagreus lay on his pallet, whimpering in his sleep.

Black dogs running down from the hills, snapping on his steps. He ran as fast as he could from the dripping fangs and glowing eyes. . . .

In the barn, the slave Samir lay on his pallet. Slowly he opened his eyes and sat up.

Tallis moved his head side to side, trying to wake up, *Gods, let me wake up. Dream. Just a dream. Just a—*

A crooning began. It was a painful sound, filled with an aching ecstasy, filled with promise—promise to what?

DON'T YOU WANT TO KNOW?

What—!? Who are you?

COME AND SEE.

I don't want to!

WE KNOW WHAT YOU WANT. WE KNOW WHAT YOU WANT TO KNOW.

The crooning intensified, calling to a place in Tallis. He writhed away from the crooning, knowing he could not give in, knowing from the very place they wanted to go.

LET US IN, they pouted. **TALLIS, OLD BOY, LET US IN.**

What was this draw? So irresistible, so full of promise to . . . know something. There was fear, though, a warning signal—fear of them, and fear of the bargain they would have. He could not swap the place for what they offered.

For what *who* offered?

They wanted something. They would trade for the place they wanted to go. They'd give him something in return, something he wanted.

The promise sucked at him, pulling him into a rushing, enticing torrent
. . . and the deep place within whimpered in dread.

COME AND SEE! IT ONLY GETS BETTER! LET US IN AND FIND OUT!

Tallis suddenly saw a flowing tar caterpillar, and he screamed.
Crooning faltered. Confusion came. Loud confusion. An instant
burst of discordant nonsense all around him, a few voices standing out
from many.

FOOL! LOUT! WHAT ARE YOU DOING HERE?
I THOUGHT I WAS SUMMONED.
HE KNOWS YOU, FOOL!

The bang of a door, running footsteps, and one voice shouting
clear: "Be gone!"
He heard a curse from a different voice—Jarek . . . ?
He heard Kes scream, "Tallis!"
"Kes . . . ," he slurred.

YOU FOOL, YOU LOUT! YOU'LL REGRET THIS!

"Leave him!" the clear voice rang.
The voices snarled, lifted, and tumbled off in an angry huff.
Sensibility crept back. Awareness. He felt . . . cold.
"Tallis!" Kes cried, but the other voice said, "No! Do not go near
him. Stay where you are."
Jarek's voice: "Look at him—it's just like the shaman. He can't stay
here anymore; he has to leave."
"Please, Samir!" Kes begged. "He needs me!"
The clear voice was no less authoritative, but was now weary. "I said,
stay where you are."
Tallis opened his eyes. Black starry sky. Cold night air. He stirred,
palms running over the scrabbly ground beneath him. Where . . . ?
Great gods and goddesses. He was flat on his back in the chicken
yard.
Kes was on the edge of the yard, Jarek beside her, clutching her.

Beyond them, the child Zagreus watched fearfully. And Tallis, their cultured guest from Athens, lay limp on the ground, plastered with dread, naked in the cold night air.

"Get up," said the clear voice, now farther away. Samir, at the barn door.

Kes started for Tallis, but Samir flung out his hand and put a terrible look on her, eyes flashing white in the darkness. Jarek glowered at the slave, but held Kes back.

And Tallis could not move. He lay helpless on the ground, his guts turned to water, his limbs without strength. He made feeble attempts to move, to lift his head. He still felt terror, as if he was dipped in it. He needed human touch after the—inhumanness. He needed humans.

"Get up, Athenian." The Parthian accent came thick. "Get up, you Greek dog!"

"Don't talk to my guest that way!"

"I said, get up!"

"Samir!" Kes gasped.

"I said get *up*, Athenian! When they push, you push back. They give you ears in Greece? I said, when they push, you push back. And let no one help you rise."

Tallis hauled himself to a sitting position. Nausea washed over him, but he held it down. Trembling, baring his teeth with effort, he rose to stand swaying, clothed only on his backside with ground-in chicken yard bracken, some of it shaking loose as he stood.

The slave stood in the light of the barn door. Tallis glared at him and clenched his fingers to fists. The ebbing fear ignited a new emotion, crazy fury. He wanted to rush the slave and beat him bloody for no particularly good reason. The slave lifted his chin and gazed into Tallis, and he suddenly felt the warmth of human touch.

Fear and rage began to recede.

Jarek came beside Tallis. "Don't call my guest a Greek dog. You looking for the strap?"

Unperturbed, Samir backed into the barn, pulling the door with him. "Weak good comes to no good, master. Have you learned nothing?" The door closed.

The line of light from the bottom of the barn door was enough for Tallis to see Jarek's face. It was blank at first; the dark and heavy eyes were staring. Then a distant knowing crept over the face. It settled into an awful certainty. Tallis saw the things that had plundered the man's good nature, despair and regret.

"What happened in this place, Jarek?" he whispered, but Jarek did not seem to hear him.

He did not want to go back to his room; he did not want to go back to his cot. He wanted to stay by Samir, the only safe place around.

Tallis had been gazing at the line of light when it vanished. He raised his chin, and if he weren't naked he would have tugged down the sides of his toga. He would go back to that room, he would lie down on that cot, and by the gods, he would go to sleep. If a Parthian slave could do it, so could he. Debris crumbled off him as he turned away, leaving Jarek in the chicken yard.

Tallis slept until late the next morning, and if he had any more dreams he didn't remember them. No one said a single word about last night's debacle. Kes pretended it never happened and was grumpier than ever. The slave was silent as usual, moving about the premises on his various tasks, and didn't look at him once. Jarek wasn't around. Zagreus was white and withdrawn, with dark smudges beneath his eyes.

"I had another bad dream," Tallis heard him say plaintively to Kes. "Did he come again?"

Kes didn't answer. Only Arinna looked fresh.

Tallis spent the day in his place by the sea, and it was late afternoon now, running into evening. His three favorite boats were coming back. He realized he'd been waiting for them, and felt a certain relief when they appeared. He was worried about Jarek. He hoped the innkeeper had returned from wherever he had gone. He wanted the fishermen to go to the common room and do their lift-his-spirits thing with him.

What had happened in this place? Did the fishermen know?

The old salt, Bek, threw a line to a lad on the dock, who roped it around a piling. This man drew his interest the most. He had a ruggedness Tallis found appealing. He'd spent all his life on this lake, hauling in scanty or bountiful catches. Doing one clear thing his whole life. The only thing that mattered to Bek was how much was in that net. He'd never woken up naked in a chicken yard or—

"You said your mother was a Bacchante," came a gentle voice. It was the voice he had listened for, for years.

Julia stood a distance apart, hands clasped in front of her, watching the three boats dock in the tiny harbor. The breeze fluttered her garments. Today she wore lavender.

"How much do you know about the *cultus* of Dionysus?" she asked.

He should have felt something at that. He felt only deadness, and he lifted a brow; perhaps the work of Callimachus wasn't in vain after all. He'd spent years avoiding a place that was perhaps, after all, dead.

"I studied it for years." *Studied it for vengeance.*

"Did Callimachus never see a single letter of mine?" She turned to him. It appeared she'd gotten about as much sleep last night as Tallis had. Her lovely eyes were darkened beneath. "What about Antenor's letters? He wrote too, asking for help, begging for it. I sent mine along with his. Most of all, Tallis, I want to know about those progress reports you say he received. And you'd better tell me quickly—the little mistress of the inn doesn't like me."

The breeze took her scent to him. He put his head back and inhaled with closed eyes. Lost to him. Lost long ago. Occasionally, over the years, he'd allow himself a rare indulgence to think on that back-porch conversation. Sometimes he fancied up the indulgence. There was first a springtime wedding on Cal's estate, then a few children playing in the garden. He'd see Callimachus with a child on his knee, telling him story after story. He'd see Aristarchus, walking and talking with a child. The only person he could never see was her. Her face had been blank to him all these years.

Her perfume, so different from Arinna's. They could wear the very same scent, and it would be different.

He leaned forward to rest his elbows on his knees and watch the fishermen. One of them, the dark young man who always had the suspicious look, regarded him from afar.

"I don't know about the letters; I never saw any. As for the progress reports, to my recollection they were always penned in the name of Polonus—what can I believe now that I've been here? It could have been Polonus, could have been anyone."

"It wasn't Polonus. He wouldn't have taken a copper from Callimachus. He loved him. That's why you posted the message, isn't it? Callimachus must have been sending operating expenses these past three years. You could have left last week—but you wanted to find out who stole from Cal."

He rubbed his forehead, then dropped his hand to glare at her. "What do *you* care?"

"*I* sent the letters! I pleaded for someone to come and set matters straight when everything had fallen apart! When we realized Athens had abandoned us, we took matters into our own hands—Polonus and I— and my husband—and we disbanded the school entirely."

"Athens did not abandon you—Athens never knew."

She was silent for a moment. "I know you have a great deal of affection for Callimachus. We spent half of that porch time talking about him. You told me he rescued you. You never said from what, but I have been rescued too, from something I thought I long left behind." Her lower lip trembled slightly. "I find it isn't behind me anymore. I don't think it ever left."

Tallis snorted softly at that. Sometimes he dreamed in orange.

"What are you doing here?"

Julia whirled around; Tallis rose from his seat. Kes`Elurah stood holding a tray, glowering at Julia. Wind whirled her dark auburn hair about her face, giving wildness to the look of an already angry woman. "You want to see one of my guests, you talk to me first."

Tallis couldn't help a half smile. "I knew it wouldn't last."

The angry look went from Julia to him. Kes balanced the tray on her hip and pulled hair out of her eyes to glare at him better. "What wouldn't last?"

"Your docile little servitude. You did well yesterday. But I knew it wouldn't last."

"Really?" she said icily. "And how would you like me to treat your next guest?"

He glanced uncertainly toward the inn. "What do you mean? I have another visitor?"

"Yes. And you can see him after *she* leaves," Kes said, tossing a look at Julia.

Julia and Tallis exchanged a look. "Who could it be?" Tallis asked her.

"I don't know." She turned a grim smile to Kes. "But nothing will keep me from finding out."

Kes glared at her. "I want you to leave. Just because you wear fine clothes doesn't mean you can— "

"Kes—I need her. She must identify someone for me."

Kes reluctantly took her glare from Julia. She considered his face for a moment. "Master Tallis, my father runs an honest place. He will not like it if questionable things are going on at the inn." Then her features softened. "But I will tell you this . . . Zagreus says there is fear in his eyes."

Julia watched them. "What does that mean . . . ?"

Gazing at Kes, whose face was now anxious, Tallis murmured, "It means she does not trust this new visitor. So neither will we."

The common room was beginning to fill. The fishermen were at the long table in the back. The old salt was making a joke at the expense of his boat companion. The young man glowered as the others laughed, the old salt loudest of all, but a certain affectionate toleration was in the grousing look of the young man.

A few more customers came in at the door, brushing past a short man who stood more outside than in. His arms were folded; he was leaning against the frame and gazing north at the hills. Kes had told Tallis the man refused to come inside, refused any refreshment.

He was mostly bald, and the rest of his hair, early gray, was very closely cropped. He studied the northern hills with a steady, wary eye. Without the man seeing him, Tallis slipped into the room and stood near the same place he'd sat with Julia. The man made Tallis think of a rope—he was compact, hard, and used. Even a little frayed. He had the look of a survivor.

"You have come in response to my forum message?" Tallis finally asked. The man pushed off from his hillside study. The light blue color of his eyes was surprising for these parts. And Tallis did not trust him at a glance.

Tallis took a long sip from his wine as he held out another goblet to the stranger. "Not bad, for a backwater inn. Come, refresh yourself."

"You are Tallis?"

"I am."

The man glanced at the offered goblet. "My master sent me. I'm not to dally."

Tallis took another sip and frowned at his cup. "Needs water. No wonder this place is so crowded at night."

The man scratched the back of his neck, looked over his shoulder, and came inside. He reached for the wine and took a sip, grinned at Tallis, and drank more deeply. Tallis slid a look at Kes, who worked at her mortar and pestle at the corner counter. She caught his glance and looked to the kitchen where Julia hid, then very slightly shook her head at Tallis. Julia did not know this man.

"They're asking for trouble," the man said, and wiped his mouth on his tunic sleeve.

Tallis nodded. "I don't know how it is here in Palestine, but in Athens there are laws against serving unmixed wine."

The man finished off his goblet and handed it to Tallis, who set it on the table and gestured for the man to sit. But the stranger shook his head.

"My master sent me," he said. "I am to ask you to accompany me to his villa."

"Who would your master be?"

"Polonus. He said you would know his name. He is most anxious to speak with you."

"Is he," Tallis murmured, glancing outside at the deepening twilight. Two men he recognized as customers came through the doorway, brushing past Tallis's stranger and looking about the common room. They saw Kes and greeted her. "How far is your master's villa?"

"Not far. A mile south, half-mile east. I have a cart and two swift horses waiting."

"It's getting dark out there." Only men looking for trouble wandered about at night. Others went to sip ale at cheap inns.

"The master just returned from Hippos with news of your note. He is most anxious to speak with you."

"Yes, you said that."

Kes was still talking with the men. Another customer ambled through the door. Jarek came through the kitchen entrance, mopping the back of his neck with a towel. He handed the towel to Kes and reached for an apron behind the corner counter.

"He asks the privilege of entertainment—the servants are preparing a meal for you. I am to tell you you are welcome to spend the night. Or if you prefer, we will escort you back to the inn."

Tallis set his cup down. He felt relief at the sight of Jarek. He hadn't seen him all day. "Very well—I'll accompany you, but I wish to be escorted back. I might receive other guests while I am gone and do not want to keep them waiting."

The man inclined his head. "As you wish." He went out the door.

Tallis looked at Kes, who was already looking at him while placing cups on a tray. "I'll be back in a few hours," he said as softly as he could over the growing din in the room. "If anyone comes for me—"

"Tie him up."

He smiled and glanced at the kitchen. "Tell her I said good-bye."

Kes nodded and watched him go.

The horses were indeed swift, and Polonus's servant seemed obliged to find every rut in the road. Tallis held tightly to his seat, trying not to lurch into the whipcord man at every dip. It was his first time riding the road instead of walking it. He glanced at the Galilee on his jolting right. The sky was particularly interesting this night; the last of the sun's rays striking wide shelves of cloud with crimson orange.

He didn't know what to say to the servant. "Lovely night—interesting sky" didn't seem right. Perhaps he was the only one to feel the awkwardness, and so he said nothing at all.

Where did Julia live? How would he contact her again? He hoped she left instructions with Kes. He wished she had come with him so they could speak to Polonus together, but he hadn't thought of it until now. She hadn't yet told her own story before he was whisked away to hear that of another.

How happily was she married?

Her husband had rescued her, she said. A certain bond existed between the rescuer and the rescued. He hadn't left Callimachus in twenty-five years, content to weed his garden and eventually run his estate without a thought of leaving, not permanently at least.

Tallis studied and wrote plays in his spare time. He'd studied Dionysus at first, until Cal put an end to it. Then one day he heard one of the teachers give a talk about Alexander of Macedon. He was Alexander's slave after that.

He combed continents—mostly through books—gathering lore. He did go to Alexandria in Egypt, with Aristarchus, to read a copy of Ptolemy's personal history of Alexander at the famous collection of books in the library. He went to Macedonia and spent a month there, wondering what a provincial place like Macedonia had done to produce a man like Alexander, or like Philip, Alexander's remarkable father. His material on Alexander grew, and he even started a scroll.

What did her husband rescue her from?

She hadn't needed rescuing eight years ago. She was like so many of the teachers who came to the villa of Callimachus that summer in Athens, full of enthusiasm and pride at being in the inner circle of Cal's domain—Cal had chosen the teachers himself.

He could see her dark silhouette in that chaise. She was gazing at the stars, a little tipsy, redolent with contentment. She confessed to Tallis she'd never worked harder than to get Cal's eye and gain a posting at the school in Hippos. While most of the mosaicists had produced copies from the masters, every mosaic template she'd produced for her entrance assessment had been her own design.

What if her husband died suddenly? How quickly could he win over her child?

"Do you know anything about Julia's husband?" he mused aloud to Polonus's manservant. "He's not, with any luck of the gods, an ancient dotard about to topple into his grave, is he?"

And suddenly, he realized the opportunity he had. Looking for information in the low places now seemed quite natural. At least he wouldn't have to pay out coin for this. "How much do you know about the academy?"

The man did not seem eager to answer. Perhaps a like-minded appeal would loosen him up. "Look, I'm a servant too," Tallis said dryly. "I know what goes on around my master's estate. What do you know about the Decaphiloi?"

The man did not answer. He leaned forward and peered ahead at the roadside, but his look was strangely obvious . . . like Tallis should look too . . . so he didn't. That's when Tallis noticed the man's fingers beginning to inch the reins into his hands, gathering them taut. A strange thing he was doing, inching those reins . . .

The blow snapped his head back, stunned him stupid. The crimson-shelved sky turned crazily, and he felt himself spilling from the cart. He clung to the side of the cart until he realized it had stopped, and then he slid to the hard-packed road.

He tasted dust and thought maybe the blow had rendered him deaf; he could hear only the isolated sound of his own pounding heart. He saw a man scramble out of the ditch and run toward him. Still stunned, Tallis waved his arm in a nonsense gesture to ward him off, but rough hands grabbed him and hauled him to his feet, slammed him against the cart.

The whipcord man bent down from his seat and gathered a fistful of Tallis's hair, jerking him upright. "Master says you are to leave for Athens in the morning," he hissed in his ear. "If you do not he will personally deliver you to Portia. Now my friend here will break your leg and you will make it back to the inn in an hour, on your belly, if you hurry. And you better hurry—the madman comes out at night!"

Clarity had seeped back with the rope man's speech—Tallis lunged upward, grabbing for his head to haul him off his perch, but the other man drove a blow to his ribs. He crumpled to the ground, clutching his belly, wheezing for air. The man grabbed him by the neck of his toga and dragged him to the side of the road.

Tallis heard a shout, and the man suddenly released him. Tallis instantly rolled away, clawing for the ditch. He reached the edge and tumbled in headfirst. He pulled back and pressed himself into the curve of the ditch, looking desperately about for something, anything, to defend himself with. He found only loose pebbles but grabbed them anyway, bracing for the man who had an appointment with his leg. He waited, tensed and panting—and heard nothing. Past the wildness of his heart, he heard only silence. What was this? Finally, he lifted up for a peek. The cart and the men were gone.

He slid back to his curve on the slope. He released the stones and put a trembling hand to his nose—it came away with blood. Rope man had slammed an iron elbow into his face. A swell of nausea came, and he suddenly rolled to his side, vomiting wine and the sardines he'd finally had a chance to try at lunch. He wiped his mouth and froze at a sound.

Cart wheels. He felt for another handful of stones.

He waited, flattened against the slope, panting and tasting bile and blood. But the cart wheels, which didn't seem in any hurry, rolled away. His stiff fingers finally released the rocks, and he closed his eyes, panting. This second cart must have scared the first away. He gingerly touched his eye. It pulsed as if about to explode from the socket. And if the man hadn't broken his leg, he had surely broken a few ribs. He looked down at his toga and cursed in dismay; so much for the brushing he'd given it. Even in the dusk he could see the blood. Another swell of nausea came, and he vomited himself empty, every heave now firing pain in his ribs. The tumult finally quieted, and he trembled on all fours, spitting the last of the bile.

"Sure. I'll come see your master." He spat. "We'll talk. Have some wine." He wiped his mouth. "Then I'll cut out his liver and roast it on a spit."

The thought came that he better get back to the inn as fast as he could, in case Polonus's men came back to make good on their promise.

He kept to the rocky ditch every painful step back to the inn, half the time looking over his shoulder. Soon he had to walk with his belly thrust forward to ease the pain in his ribs. He pressed his hand on his back, glad to be in the ditch; he walked like a pregnant woman.

Personally deliver you to Portia . . .

He came to the edge of the stable yard and waited by a tree while Samir led a horse into the barn. The guest rooms were in the back of the building, facing the lake; the window of his room was too high for him to climb into. He put his forehead against the tree, groaning softly. His room was the last one in the hallway off the very crowded common room, the same one he'd have to walk through to get to it. There was no way he could make it unnoticed.

He doused his face with water from the trough. He tried to brush off the bracken from the ditch, but his toga looked like he'd— got beat up and rolled in a ditch. His nose and eye would be difficult to conceal, felt like they had swelled double. He'd keep his head down and pretend to scratch his eyebrow all the way to his room. Maybe the place was so crowded he wouldn't be noticed.

He stood at the kitchen entrance, summoning the strength it would take to walk normally to his room, without sticking his stomach out.

Gods, all he wanted was his bed, just to slip into his bed. His nose had stopped bleeding, but clammy sweat made his toga cling to him.

He heard the murmur of conversation drift through the kitchen from the common room. He heard Jarek laugh loudly, heard someone start a song. He took as deep a breath as he could, held it, and straightened. He brushed past a staring Zagreus at the worktable and slipped into the common room.

He kept to the back wall, head low, rubbing his eyebrow the whole while. When he was three steps from the hallway, Jarek exclaimed, "What happened to you?"

The common room murmur came to complete silence.

Great gods and goddesses, all he wanted was his bed.

"Brigands," he managed, and waved at the front door. "Attacked us on the road."

Plates clattered, benches scraped. Everyone talked at once. Kes was at his side, helping him to a bench, Jarek was shouting for Zagreus to fetch a towel and water.

Tallis just wanted his bed. He could feel himself tremble with fatigue. And he was horribly thirsty. He grabbed the mug closest and emptied it before he knew what it was—a burning ale that slid like liquid fire down his throat. It set him to gasping and coughing, and he groaned at the fresh pain.

Jarek took the mug from him, saying, "Easy, lad, that's the wrong drink for you." He replaced it with a mug of water.

"Parthians?" a burly man demanded, his foot on the bench.

Tallis tasted blood on his lips. "Couldn't tell, too dark."

"How many?" said another.

"Couldn't tell."

"Probably that marauding band Lepidus warned us about."

"They wouldn't dare come this far west," someone scoffed.

"If it's that Shamash-Eriba, they would."

"I'm getting home, lads," called one over his shoulder, his tone warning others they should do the same.

The inn was mostly empty in a moment, men hurrying home with unspoken thoughts for their families. Kes went to see what was keeping Zagreus; Jarek went to the corner where a thick beam stood against the wall. He took it and set it near the doorway. He went behind the corner counter and rummaged about, finally producing a short sword, which he propped near the beam at the door. He came back to Tallis and said, "It's not often I have to bolt my doors, but if the devils come I'll be ready. Shamash-Eriba leads a bad lot." He squinted at Tallis's face. "How's that fella you drove off with?"

"He got away," Tallis muttered.

"You hurt anywhere else?"

"I just need to lie down." He ached everywhere, felt like he was going to be sick again. And all the while murmuring in the back of his mind, since he'd struggled out of that ditch, were the words of Polonus's servant. *Personally deliver you to Portia.*

Personally deliver you to Portia? Did he really say that, or was it leftover Dionysiac paranoia from earlier? How did he know to say the one thing Tallis could fear the most? He drank some of the water and wiped his mouth. "Jarek, I want to go to my room."

"Let Kes have a look at you first."

"By the *gods*, Jarek, I just want my bed!"

"She learned doctoring from her mother. Closest thing we got to a doctor, outside Kursi." The innkeeper gently patted his shoulder, started off to speak with the others, but hesitated. He scratched his head and, without looking at Tallis, said, "You're a good lad. I take it personal when a guest of mine is hurt." He went to join the others outside.

Personally deliver you to Portia.

Kes arrived with a bowl of water and some towels. She dipped a towel in the water and wrung it out. She dabbed at his face. He pulled away, shifting on the bench and arching his back to take pressure off his rib cage. It hurt to sit, gods, it hurt; no position gave relief. Kes looked questioningly, and he said, "I think I broke a rib."

"Arinna?" Kes called. "Bring an old bedcloth from the linen cupboard." With a quick glance at the doorway where men congregated inside and out, she softly said, "What happened? Was it that man? I shouldn't have let you go; Zagreus didn't like him."

Why a small boy should have a say in it was something he brushed aside for now. He didn't want to tell her what happened. He didn't want her involved. And why did she seem involved anyway? When exactly did that happen? When she volunteered to see if Julia had the mark of the Bacchantes.

"Is Julia still here?"

"No. She left after you did. She was angry with you. She didn't know where you were going or why. She wanted to come with you. At least—that's what I think. She didn't say much."

Julia's cart must have scared them away. "You don't even know why I am in Palestine, Kes`Elurah," he murmured. He suddenly felt the warmth of the ale moving along his blood. One eye was nearly closed, so he squinted at her with the other. "You don't know our business. Why did you help me and Julia? Don't tell me it's because of fear in my eyes. Or the lack thereof."

She did not reply; she simply washed his face and told him to take off his toga.

"You want me to take off my toga," he repeated carefully. He mused on this interesting piece of information. "That's a pleasant thing for a man to hear."

"I need to bind your ribs, you idiot." She fingered the sleeve of his toga. "Stupid garment. So thick."

Arinna arrived with a bundle of cloth.

Kes shook it out and began to tear it into strips. "Go get one of Kardus's old tunics," Kes told her.

After a lingering look at Tallis and his wounds, Arinna went to obey her mistress.

Maybe the blow had thickened his hearing. Maybe it was the ale. "You said 'Kardus'?"

"My brother. Come," she said, and tugged gently on his arm to get him to stand.

He pushed up from the table gingerly. He pressed his hand against his back. "Look at me—I'm pregnant. I think I'm having twins." Wincing, he said, "Is Kardus a common name?"

Kes`Elurah lifted the skirt of his toga, looking perplexed. "How does this come off?"

Yes, it would seem a complicated rig to people who knew only simple vestments like tunics. He showed her the way it wound from his left shoulder to his right thigh. She helped him shrug out of it. Because of the pain it caused, it reduced the embarrassment at being public in his smallclothes.

"Where is your brother?" he asked when the toga came off. "I haven't seen him about."

She gently probed the bruise at his ribs with her fingertips, her face in a slight wince. "I'll need aloe pulp. Some hot mint, mustard. Coralwart. I'll fix a poultice before I bind you. You won't like the smell."

"Kes . . . where is your brother?"

Her fingertips stilled on the wound. Many things stilled in that moment. He was holding his breath—seemed the whole place held its breath. Then she raised her green eyes to his, eyes with alarming elements Tallis recognized. Despair. Hopelessness.

"My brother lives in the tombs. My brother is a madman."

V

Kes stirred the pot carefully. The poultice would require more hot-mint than she had, so she sent Samir to old Shoshanna down the road. She was the only one in shouting distance who would have a large quantity of dried hotmint. With any luck she had it in leaves, not ground.

She had never had to tell anybody about Kardus before. They all knew.

Demas had never asked. She wouldn't have told him. And the first person she tells says the strangest thing, in the strangest way: with staring surprise Tallis had said, "Your brother is why I am here."

Kes frowned. He didn't seem like a shaman from the East. Father said he was a Greek scholar, or that he worked for a Greek scholar. He was on business from Athens; that's all anyone knew about the curious man who had been living at the inn for over a week. Nobody stayed at the inn for a week. They stopped over from the East, or from Damascus or Jerusalem, for one day only, sometimes two, to rest their horses; this weeklong guest came from Athens just to see her brother? Did his fame reach so far?

"He's not a shaman," she murmured doubtfully, then started when she realized she'd not been stirring the mixture.

Did they have a different kind of shaman out West? Someone who wasn't outlandish and did not smell bad and frighten people? Her father had hired a man from the East, a man renowned for his work in the dark arts. He was superior and strange. He brought his own food, even his own oil, and made Kes prepare strange things for his meals. He told her he needed to be one with the gods when he started his work with Kardus. His gods liked strange things.

He stayed at the inn for three days before he began his work with Kardus, and during that time, Zagreus would not set foot in the kitchen. He stayed in the barn, in such a state that she feared he was going the way of Kardus himself. He refused to eat; he could not sleep for the terror of his dreams. He begged and pleaded for Kes to send the shaman away. It made her angry with him, because Zagreus was never wrong about these things, because she had hoped with all her heart that the shaman could help.

In the end, nobody had to tell him to leave. After a single encounter with Kardus, the hill herdsmen carried the shaman back to the inn on a plank. It was days before he came out of his gibbering state. His eyes rolled wild, his speech was unintelligible. Then one day Kes went to his room and he was gone. Packed his things and left. Never asked for his money.

Samir came in with the hotmint, a bundle of dried stems and leaves. "Shoshanna says seven prutahs. She said she'll take it in eggs."

Kes nodded and glanced at him. He was acting perfectly normal. Perfectly Samir. He acted as though he had never defied her father. The strange authority that had risen in the yard had resettled to the docile man she'd known for twenty years. His familiar, plodding meekness nestled around him like his musty barn fragrance.

"Where's Zagreus?" she said briskly.

"With your father out front."

"Tell him it's time for bed."

"Aye, Mistress Kes." Samir went through the kitchen to the common room, passing Arinna through the doorway. Arinna flattened herself so she wouldn't touch Samir, and Samir had taken care not to touch her, though not as obviously.

Kes carefully scraped the mixture together. It was getting runny; she may have let it go too long. If it went too long, the pulp melted and lost its shape. It had to be just warm enough to hold together, so her mother taught her years ago. She pulled the pot from the brazier and set it to cool on an iron grate.

"Arinna, quickly"—she nodded at the bundle on the worktable—"help me strip the leaves from the stems. I want to get that swelling down before we bind him."

"Tallis is asking for you," Arinna said as she untied the bundle.

"*Master* Tallis," Kes said sharply.

Arinna shrugged. "Master Tallis. I never noticed how handsome he is. He's never around; he's usually gone to Hippos or sitting at the sea."

Their fingers worked quickly. Presently, Kes said, "He's not that handsome."

"No. Not like Demas," Arinna said with a demure little smile, and Kes was proud of herself—she didn't twitch at the mention of his name, and she knew Arinna looked for it.

The stems were thick but brittle, and the leaves pulled away easily. Kes tore a leaf and smelled it, tasted it. Good. Very potent. Harvested just before winter and dried properly. Mother had always counted on Shoshanna for quality herbs.

It was a pity Mother had not lived to see what she had done to Kardus.

Halfway through the job, Kes noticed Arinna's silence. Arinna was never quiet. Kes glanced and saw a small smile that tightened her stomach.

She couldn't tell her to stay away from him; it would only mount a challenge. She'd made that mistake with Demas. Arinna was prettier than Kes, and much more willing. It was Kes who had the eye of Demas from the beginning, wonder of wonders; but once Arinna found out about it, discovered Kes actually returned his favor, she'd slipped between them because she could. And the one man who had kindled Kes's interest, kindled her blood and set her to soft imaginings, was lost to her. Now she wished Demas was around. Arinna wouldn't look twice at Tallis with Demas around.

Demas was the man Mother would have wanted for a son-in-law—the kind of man she wanted for a son. He was once-in-a-lifetime beautiful, funny and smart, confident and arrogant, and could he sing? Oh, could he sing. Such a voice to match his strong handsome face.

Kes never forgot the day she stopped loving Demas. It wasn't Arinna, not even after Arinna's lazy boast one afternoon, standing right here while they chopped vegetables for stew—"The moon is full, but I'm not sure my flow will start." Even then she loved him, ignoring the hurt of Arinna's words, pretending she never saw the way Demas looked at Arinna. No. She didn't stop loving him until she realized he was everything Mother could have wanted for a son-in-law . . . or a son.

Demas moved on with his troupe to Scythopolis, and Kes went to visit a cousin in Caesarea for a time. How often had she longed to leave the inn? She left in defiance of the expectations laid upon her after Mother died.

She hadn't come back for Father's sake, he who never had the backbone to stand up to Mother. She blamed Father just as much for what happened to Kardus, because he was the man but never acted it.

Weak good comes to no good, master. Have you learned nothing?

Did Samir really say that? Did he know her father so well? She glanced at her arms—the words raised a chill on her skin. The truth of them astounded her.

Father should have stood in Mother's way; those years of cruelties and tyrannies, he should have stopped her. Samir saw that. Samir knew. The realization dumbfounded her. She could hardly believe he'd said those words, much less that he—

I should have stopped her.

She felt a clutch at her throat, but she swallowed it away. *What's done is done, Kes `Elurah,* she thought sternly to herself. *You're stronger when you remember that. You're stronger when you impart no blame. Don't hate your father because his fear of her was stronger than his love for Kardus.*

The thought squeezed her heart with pain.

"Look at me, I'm pregnant, he says," Arinna murmured with a chuckle. "I have twins. He's funny."

You could have stayed in Caesarea with Cousin Sazar. But you came back, Kes `Elurah. Never forget you came back, because your love is stronger than his. "Weak good comes to no good." The words dizzied her.

Am I weak?

"It's enough," Kes said of the mound of dried leaves. "Put Zagreus to bed."

Arinna dusted off her hands and left.

Father never said anything when she came back from Caesarea. She took up in the kitchen, and Father acted as though she had never left. Treated her coldly, like he'd never missed her and she shouldn't bother hoping he had.

Something Kardus said actually stayed with her, as many times as she'd ignored him—he told her something from the school he went to, something a man named Socrates said: Mankind will have no greater helper than love.

Your brother is why I am here, Tallis said.

She put the poultice pot level with the worktable and swept the hot-mint into the mixture. "Yes," she whispered as she began to stir, pulling back from rising vapors. "He's why I'm here too."

Kes pushed the door open with her toe, carrying a tray with the poultice dressings. Arinna had lit the candle on the small table near Tallis's bed. He was lying on his cot, half asleep but moving restlessly. She brought her tray to the candle table, but it wouldn't fit. She set it on the floor next to the bed and went to fetch the stool from the writing table, shoved beneath the windowsill. She frowned at that; likely the table edge would have scratches in it from the bottom of the sill. Didn't Tallis think of that, or did he only think of his precious view?

"Kes?" Her father stood in the doorway, looking unhappily at Tallis in his bed. "How is he?"

"I prepared a poultice for his ribs. If there is nothing else broken inside, he will mend." Then she asked about the "brigands," because he would expect her to.

"No, nobody saw anything. I don't fancy it was Eriba's band. Maybe a coupla drunken louts up from Hippos." He glanced at her directly and glanced away.

Kes understood. No, it wouldn't have been Shamash-Eriba's band of Parthian marauders; anyone leading a group of malcontents in these parts knew enough about the hills of Kursi to stay far away. It was an odd safety her brother provided for the entire village and its surroundings. Here there weren't any raids on herds. Here crops were left alone. Brigands gave the hinterlands of Kursi a wide berth. You could call it the safest place in Palestine.

But if the presence of her brother brought an odd safety, it also brought a pall; trade had suffered. Some families had actually moved away, families rooted in the landscape, their generations preceding Kardus's precious Alexander the Great. Kes and her father felt the onus of every incident tied to Kardus.

One man lost his daughter and claimed the madman in the tombs carried her off. It was later discovered the girl had run away with a trades-man. Well and good, but did the man come to apologize for the day he stormed into the inn and announced to the common room that Kardus had raped his daughter and probably killed her? No, but those were the last images the people had: Kardus the rapist, Kardus the murderer.

But Kardus *had* done terrible things these past few years. Every new report made Kes at first fiercely defensive of her brother and, as time went on, doubtful. Perhaps he really did some of the things they said he did—it was just so hard to believe. So painful to believe. Surely not rape. Surely not murder. Not Kardus.

Father was still looking unhappily at Tallis. "You think he's . . . ?" Her father whirled his finger at his temple. He was speaking, without speaking, of last evening in the chicken yard.

"It was only a bad dream. Zagreus has been having them too."

Her father turned to go, but Kes softly called him back. She hesitated, and glanced at Tallis. "He has asked for employment."

Jarek grunted in surprise. "You never know who has money these days. A man can be well dressed and speak like a politician . . ." He thought a moment, and sighed. He scratched the side of his head. "I suppose I can hire out Samir, when this fellow mends. I'd get some coin for it, at least."

"Thank you, Father," Kes said, and meant it. Jarek grunted again, for the bargain and for good night, and left. She watched him through the doorway as he stopped to pick up a scrap of something on the hallway floor. He went off examining it, probably heading for the trash heap out back.

"I've got the job?" Tallis croaked.

"When you mend."

Kes pulled the stool next to the bed and moved the candle table closer so she could see the wound on his chest better. She hissed at what she saw, a rising discolored mound, and glanced at his face. She reached and touched his temple, frowning. "I hope I have enough for this too."

"If you're talking about that evil-smelling"—he looked down with a curled lip at the pot—"mess, I'll be fine without it."

She picked up the pot and spooned the mixture onto a square of cloth, leaving some in the pot to treat the eye. "That's the coralwort. It's awful. I think Mother put it in because if it smells bad, it's bound to work." She folded in the edges of the cloth and tied the bundle. "I put it in because you never know." She let it drip over the pot a moment, then settled the pack on Tallis's wound.

He winced at first, then looked at her in surprise. "It's cooling."

"That's the hotmint."

"Why don't they call it coolmint?"

She pressed her lips. Always ready with a fast remark. She wanted to smile entirely too much around him. "I once looked into a pot my mother had just added a bunch of hotmint to—the vapors burned my face. Guess what Mother used to treat the burns?"

Tallis chuckled, then moaned delicately and went to hold his ribs, but remembered the poultice and clenched his fist instead.

Kes kept her sympathy hidden, something her mother taught her long ago—*Do not cry for him, you little fool, sympathy weakens; you will destroy everything I am trying to teach him*—until she remembered she was no longer under that old veil. She had to do that often, consciously remember that Mother was no longer around. She learned it was normal not only to feel sympathy, but to show it. It simply felt awkward.

Determined, she did what she wanted to and reached to brush Tallis's damp hair from his forehead with her fingertips. She liked how that felt, didn't mind so much the soft warmth in her cheeks, nor the flutter in her stomach. *No, we are not very pleasant around here; but I'm glad you did not go to Hippos and pay for pleasant.*

"Do you think your nose is broken?" she asked.

He gingerly touched it. "No. My eye took most of it."

"That little man did this to you?"

He looked at her indignantly. "I didn't see it coming. And he had another fellow with him."

Kes looked about and found a towel on the writing table. She tore it in two and scraped the rest of the mixture from the pot to the fabric. She bundled it up and eased it onto Tallis's eye.

"That feels good," he said, and added, "Thank you, Kes." He closed his other eye and sighed. "Cot feels good—room feels good. Feels safe. Safe makes me tired."

With his eyes closed she could watch him freely. His face was so pale, terribly pale. He was exhausted. He had lines near his eyes, as though he smiled a lot. She watched him guiltily; it felt uncomfortable, like prying. But she didn't want to look away.

He was not a man who could grow a thick beard; it was late in the day and there was barely a shadow on his cheeks. He had a little mole on his neck. Lines in his neck; with his chin tucked down like that. Blood at the corner of his mouth, inside his lip. She didn't see it when she wiped his face. She started to rise to gather the tray.

Tallis put his hand on her arm. "Which of us will talk first?" he slurred. He licked his lips.

"What do you mean?"

"Kardus."

She stilled, unsure what to do. He'd said he was here for her brother, but she had been taught never to speak of anything personal. Family matters were fiercely private. It was shameful to tell a thing from the interior. Shameful and weak.

But she had just gazed upon a man. Gazing was as bad as telling, she'd been raised to believe. Nosing into someone else's business was as shameful as telling your own, and looking at someone more than a few seconds, a disgrace.

She smoothed her skirts and settled on the stool, stiff-backed. A strange exhilaration twitched inside, as she'd felt when she gazed upon him. She never talked about her brother to anyone, not her father, not anyone. Except Polonus. It had taken a long time for her to trust Polonus.

"Did Polonus send for you?" she asked. "You don't look like a shaman."

That woke him up. His eyes flew open, and suddenly he lunged, tumbling the poultice into her lap as he seized her wrists. He shoved her sleeves up and examined her arms, front and back. Not finding anything, he pushed the sleeves up farther. Her face burned, but she held still. He examined her upper arms carefully, and not finding what he looked for, searched her eyes dubiously. He eased back into the cot, wary as a cat.

She picked up the dripping poultice from her lap. It made a dark stain on her skirts. She remolded the bag and settled it onto his wound. Her face still burned. "You were looking for those marks you told me about," she said lightly, fussing with the poultice more than necessary. "The ones you thought the lady might have."

He wasn't the way he usually was, open; his face was always open. Now it was closing with alarm, shutting away from her.

"You told me you were here because of my brother. If you came to help him, I am on your side, because I am on his side." Her voice softened. "I have always been on his side. In my heart."

He seemed to relax a little. "What about Polonus . . ."

"He is the only friend I have." She paused. "Besides Samir."

"Polonus wants to break my leg! His servant did this to me."

Her lips twitched.

"I said something amusing?"

"He'd laugh to hear he has a servant. And he'd sooner break his own leg than that of another."

Uncertainty came to his face. "What do you mean? He said I am to leave for Athens or he will personally deliver me to Portia."

"The man—he told you Polonus had sent him?"

"Yes."

"And you went with him because . . ."

Tallis blinked, and his face eased. Then he said grimly, "Because I knew the name. He was the leader of the academy, the name I would know best." He stared at the ceiling. "Then who came for me? Portia?"

"You wouldn't have gone to her?"

"Not on a bet."

"Polonus lives in the hills, just east of the tombs of Kursi. He has devoted his life to . . . righting a wrong. I thought he was done with shamans; I thought you were another he didn't tell me about."

"I've been mistaken for many things, never a shaman. A shaman for what?"

"Why—for Kardus."

They regarded one another for a moment, until Kes suddenly said, "You are a scholar?"

Tallis thought on it, then shrugged.

"What does *soma sema* mean? I've asked Polonus, and he won't tell me. I know he knows. I think it's Latin, and he knows Latin."

Tallis hesitated. "Why do you ask?"

"I've heard my brother say it in his fits."

"It means . . . 'the body is a tomb.'"

Silence. "Oh."

Gently, Tallis said, "Kes, what happened to your brother?"

The body is a tomb. Kardus always had a way with words. Isn't that what Mother despised about him, before the madness ever came? He had a way with many things.

"You have a natural pleasantness about you, so much like my Kardus . . . the way he used to be. It makes me fear for you." She plucked her skirt and smoothed it. *Talk, Kes! Just talk. Tell him about Kardus. Mother isn't here anymore.* "For Kardus—"

"There is a strange awareness of fear at this inn," Tallis broke in musingly. "I'm tired of it. It's beginning to rub off on me. I'm starting to *dream* in fear."

She clenched her hands to fists. Would he let her talk? "For Kardus, the way to the tombs started with fear. Other things too, but fear—"

Talk, Kes!

Tallis waited for her to continue, and not so patiently. "Before he what?"

She snapped, "Will you—? Don't you know I've never—" This stupid foreigner!

Tallis took her hand. The surprise of it flushed her cheeks, and words tumbled out.

"Nobody speaks truth around here. Nobody speaks." What was this? Tears! Tears, because of the compassion in this stranger. She pulled her hand from his and brushed the tears away.

Then the talk began to pour from her.

"There are people who call down curses on our place every time they pass. They make signs against evil. They take different routes to Hippos or Damascus. It didn't used to be that way. Jarek's inn was the place folks went to. They came for talk, for good wine, good company. They came because my father was a pleasant man. Kardus took after my father. And . . . I took after my mother.

"Shoshanna is an old woman who lives down the road. She knew my mother when she was a child. Recently, quite unexpectedly, Shoshanna told me something. She was teaching me how to stitch a wound, and said, 'Your mother didn't mean to be the way she was.' I never heard such plainspeak. I was so grateful for it. Shoshanna has tried to teach me things over the years. Ordinary things."

Suddenly she looked at Tallis and said, "Are you thirsty?"

Gazing at her, Tallis first shook his head, then nodded. She took a cup from the tray and filled it with water from the pitcher. He drank and handed back the cup.

She had never talked with Demas. Nothing like this. He would not have heard her.

"My mother thought it was wrong to be free with words. With expression. It was scandalous to her. That she had a child like Kardus was a joke straight from the gods. He was never meant for this inn. That's the joke to me. He was born for the courts of a king, not a family who didn't know how to handle a gifted child."

"I never thought Kardus would have come from around here," Tallis mused—then realized what he said. "I'm sorry. I didn't mean—"

Kes shook her head eagerly, whisking hair behind her ear. "No, no—you are right, you speak the truth. That's exactly the truth. He wasn't born for this place. I had such . . . secret pride for him." Her gaze drifted. "I adored my brother. When my father's friends began to tell him, 'Send Kardus to Hippos, educate him—he's been blessed by the gods' . . . my father ignored them, because he knew my mother. But all Kardus wanted was to learn. Some of the customers had taught him to read, which of course Mother tried to stop. My uncle brought him a few books, and how he devoured them. Writings of any kind. You couldn't contain him, he was so . . . And talk? Could he talk. Question after question, used to drive me mad. Such an imagination. Such a bright, sweet nature. He said the funniest things. You never knew what was going to come out of his mouth. Everyone loved him."

She wiped her nose on her sleeve. She was silent for a time. "No matter how much Mother tried to press him down, he squeezed out somewhere else. He was wild, I'll tell you that. You know—emotional. He'd get so angry with her, because he didn't understand why she— He'd get so frustrated, helpless, to the point of rage. And how could you blame him? He fought what she tried to do to him, putting him in a cage. It wasn't right and he knew it." Pain passed over her face. "We all knew it."

She looked directly at Tallis. "Isn't it funny how you know a thing?" She pressed her stomach with both hands. "You know it here. No matter what you're taught to believe. You know here if it's right or not."

"Getting down to that is what I suppose we're all trying to do."

She didn't continue for a while.

"I betrayed him. All my life, I betrayed him." She plucked the fabric of her skirt, only to smooth it down and pluck it again. "She made life miserable for us. I remember a time when I was very young, when she wasn't that way. It seems like a dream. I remember once, crying into her apron. Her arms were around me, and I remember the smell of the apron. Smelled like cooking. I don't know why I was crying, but she was holding me. I don't know what changed. Maybe life was hard for her."

Kes's tone had thinned.

"If something displeased her, she made home a miserable place to be, for as long as she saw fit. When she thought it was time for it to be over, it was over. Nothing we could do would appease her, no apology, nothing. Lasted days sometimes. We had to wait until it was over, and she said when. We were happiest when she wasn't around. She'd leave for market, and it relieved us for a time. Things got lighter; we all felt it. And when she returned, she returned fully. It came again, wrapped itself around the inn, and everything was back to normal. . . . We loved market days." She smiled a little.

"She hated noise. Everything had to be rigidly quiet. Today if I bang a pot, I look to see if she is angry. She'd rage at me, tell me the guests were sleeping, what an idiot I was, I probably woke them all up, even if it was a tiny little noise. Father did nothing. He saw everything, especially the way she treated Kardus. He knew it was wrong and he did nothing."

"How did she treat Kardus?"

"She hated that he was who he was."

Had she ever spoken such truth before? It was exhausting her.

"Hated he was different from her sisters' children. They were all the same, just ordinary boys, and she hated that he wasn't like them. He was . . . imaginative. He'd lie down by the sea and scoop up handfuls of shore and study what he found. Shells and muck and stones and tiny animals. Study it for hours. Everything delighted him and Mother hated it. She called it unnatural. She didn't like it when he studied anthills. She thought it was unnatural to sit for so long and watch ants. It made her angry . . . gods, it made her angry. But he loved nature. He loved everything; he was curious all the time. He'd ask Mother questions, and oh, she didn't like that. As Kardus grew older, her rages began. Awful rages. She raged at him for everything, and he raged back because he was so furious that she didn't understand him.

"She didn't do that to me. It made me superior to him. I didn't cause her problems; I was . . . ordinary. And I was smug with it. I was two years older but acted like I was younger, the way I treated him. When she was angry with him, I was angry too—for the simple reason that he had made her angry, didn't matter why. Isn't that stupid? I don't know why I did that. I began to wish he were like other boys too, so we could have some peace in the home. No matter what he did he made her angry, and I blamed him for it. And when he actually began to change . . . it hurt. He began to be mean, in small and petty ways that were not like him at all. He was mean to animals—he never used to be that way, he loved animals. Then one day I watched him strip a sapling of all its leaves. It horrified me, the sight of that bare sapling. Mother was winning."

Kes was silent for a time.

"What happened to him?" Tallis finally asked. "Something must have happened for him to find his way into the Academy of Socrates. Do you know he was the youngest to be admitted for a teaching position? The youngest to be *considered*? I remember talking with him years ago in Athens . . . even then I marveled at his knowledge of Alexander, wondered how someone so young could have such an accurate grasp on his life." He eyed Kes doubtfully. "He told me he was descended from Macedonian colonists. He showed me a trinket, a replica of Alexander's horse, Bucephalas."

"He still had that? I gave it to him when we were children."

"He said his father gave it to him. Said it came from his own ancestor, who was a general and a close friend of Alexander's—that Alexander gave it to him."

She shrugged. "Kardus fancied things up. We are indeed descended from Greek colonists, but many people around here are. We have Macedonian blood, but not from a general who was friends with Alexander. My father would have boasted of it." She held a handful of her dark auburn hair. "The red in it means I have Macedonian in me. My freckles too."

Tallis frowned. "Kardus's story evolved. I remember one report from the Decaphiloi. Kardus was telling his students that he was Alexander's blood relation. He was taken to task by Antenor, who made him retract it to the students. Polonus thought it noteworthy enough to include in the report. Cal mentioned it to me because I plan to write a history of Alexander. He thought it was interesting, because many people claim to be descended from him—he didn't expect one of his teachers to assert such a claim."

Kes smoothed the fabric on her skirt, plucked what she smoothed. "He changed a lot, in the end."

"What made him change?"

She sighed. "We all did, I think. We all had a part in what he is today. If there is blame to be had, then—"

"Kes. I didn't ask about blame. Tell me how he became a Decaphiloi."

"Years ago, a man came here whenever he went to Damascus. He saw in Kardus the things that should have been seen. One day he brought a scroll, and it changed Kardus's life. It ignited him. It was a fine thing, and a terrible thing because it infuriated my mother. She did not want Kardus to exceed the boundaries he was born to. But strangely, this time my father stood his ground and allowed Kardus to study with him.

"Mother made us pay for it, of course. Father had humiliated her, and she saved face by becoming—to herself. She stopped talking completely. And the more quietly she did something, the more of a triumph it was for her. It sounds crazy, but that's the way it was. She began to lose weight, and she wasn't plump to begin with. I hated her for it. But Kardus —he was so happy. I can see him sitting beside that man in the light by the window. Kicking his legs, twirling his hair, and he didn't know he was doing it. He was so happy! He loved learning. He loved the man, and my father was happy too. So glad for his son. So proud of Kardus, I could see it. . . ."

When she spoke again, her eyes were shining. "My father and I banded together. We two against Mother, for Kardus's sake. We became"—she rolled her hand as she tried to find the right word—"secret partners in the education of Kardus, without saying a word to each other. And do you know to this day we have never spoken of it? Not then, not ever. I was twelve. Kardus was ten. For five years, the man visited. As Mother became more withdrawn, Kardus . . . he was a like a ray of sun, shining out from thunderclouds. Everything Father and I did, we did for him. He loved us. . . ." Her cadence faltered. "I am sure he did—I'm sure he knew what we were doing. But . . . he forgot about us. We stood between him and Mother; we were a shield of protection about him . . . but I don't know if he saw that. I don't think he did. Doesn't matter, I suppose.

"He talked all the time about Alexander this, Odysseus that. Sophocles and Euripides and Plato, names I know only because he spoke them so much. He became a running stream of knowledge, and it began to wear away at me. He began to get smug with his knowledge. My father always listened to Kardus talk (in the barn, of course, because no one was allowed to talk around my mother), and Samir did, and at first I did too. I was glad to see something come of what Father and I did for him, taking his chores so he could study, distracting Mother when the scholar came. Putting up with all her misery." She broke off to look at Tallis. "You know who the scholar was, of course."

"Guessing wildly, Polonus." He grimaced. "Forgive me if the name is still unpleasant."

"Polonus taught Kardus everything. But—resentment began to form in my heart. When Kardus talked about Greek tragedies or comedies, it was like buzzing in my ears. When he spoke of the Roman republic or . . . Spanish gold mines . . . I only wanted him to shut up, because he knew I couldn't understand him, and that seemed to please him. I hated him for that. My father and I had tried our best to help him, but now I only wanted him to shut up." She absently scratched her elbow. "I should have listened to him."

"He should have listened too."

She glanced at him. "No. I was acting childish. I should have listened to him; he needed me to. It would have been kind to listen to him. It was cruel not to. If I had listened, maybe . . . things would be different."

"Sometimes it's hard, Kes," Tallis said, with a trace of impatience in his voice. "Who did you have to talk to?"

"He had so much to say. She bottled him up; she pressed him down all those years. He had a voice, and he needed so desperately to talk. She did her best, but in the end he won. So she killed herself."

Tallis froze. Kes smoothed and plucked. They heard the sound of settling in the next room—one of the guests had come in for the night. Kes saw the candle was burning down. She went to the writing table and took another candle from the drawer. She lit the new candle, snuffed out the stub of the other, and worked it from the candlestick. She placed the new candle in the holder and put the stub into a pocket in her skirts. She watched the burning flame for a moment, then came back to the stool.

"She used bristlebane. The days before she died were particularly quiet. Hardly knew she was around. She'd go and stand for hours and stare across the lake. Never sit, just stand. For hours. But because no one spoke around here, because she forbade it, no one asked her what she was doing. No one questioned it."

"Kes . . ." He reached to take her hand, but she pulled away. "Kes. I know what it's like to have a mother who is not well, in her heart, and in her head."

Kes lifted eyes of despair to him. "Did she make your life miserable?"

"Not until I was twelve. Miserable ever since."

"Did she hurt the ones you loved?"

Tallis did not answer. The poultice had rolled off when he went to take her hand. He eased back and put it on the wound again.

Kes said softly, "I used to think if she just went away it would answer everything. We could be happy. We could talk and make some noise. But what she did . . . it was her final way to wreck us. Not long after she died, Kardus left. He first went to Athens with Polonus, then came back, but not here. Never here—he was done with us. He settled in Hippos to start the school. That left me and my father. For the first time in our lives we could talk to each other, but now we had nothing to say."

"My mother killed herself too. But she didn't die." Broken ribs and all, Tallis rolled to his side and faced the wall.

Kes sat rigid, staring. His mother had killed herself too? What did he mean, she didn't die?

After a moment she took up the tray. She gazed at his curled form in the candlelight—his arm was over his head, his knees drawn up.

The lady Julia had troubles. This smart and compassionate man had troubles. Didn't matter if you were rich and refined, didn't matter if you were smart and the servant of a great philosopher. Didn't matter if you were an innkeeper's daughter. Troubles put a connection between folks; it bonded them as nothing else could.

Something bad had happened to this good man. His mother died, but there was more. He had been thrashing in the chicken yard at midnight, warding off unseen terrors.

She'd try and help him. Maybe she could talk to Polonus. Maybe to the lady. Tallis trusted her, and Kes saw clear through his eyes—she saw past the dignity down to the good.

She would put herself between Tallis and the unseen terrors. It was an old, familiar place. She'd try and help him, as she should have listened to Kardus.

She blew out the candle, paused in the doorway, and closed the door softly behind her.

VI

"Is it basket day, Mistress Kes?" Zagreus asked from his stool at the table.

Kes paused at her job. She was scrubbing out the pot she had used to make the poultice last night. "Yes."

"Do you want me to fetch bandages?"

"Master Polonus hasn't asked for bandages lately. No bandages today."

"That's good, isn't it?"

"Yes, Zagreus. That's very good."

Zagreus went back to turning the hand mill. Something more was bothering Mistress Kes. No bandages was a good thing for basket day; it usually made her more cheerful. Master Tallis had his ribs bound this morning, and Mistress Kes was pleased when she saw his wounds. She said the poultice had worked nicely. Then what could be bothering Mistress Kes—

Zagreus stopped turning the handle. His heart began to pound hard.

"Is it Auntie day?"

Mistress Kes stopped scrubbing. She would not look at him.

He put the mill on the table. "I don't want to see her."

"It's only for a little while, Zagreus," Mistress Kes said, her voice gentle.

"I hate it when she comes. I will to go to the barn."

Mistress Kes left the pot and came to him. She stood near him, and he could smell her apron. It smelled like cooking. It had a little bit of fresh in it from the clothesline.

She knelt in front of him and looked into his eyes. "I will be there the whole time, as I always am. She will not stay long. She only comes to see how you are doing. You are five years old today. She wants to see how you've grown."

Aunt Ariadne always came on his birthing day, and when he was exactly a half year older. Twice a year she came.

"I'm afraid of her," Zagreus whispered, and tears filled his eyes. "I don't like her."

"Neither do I."

Zagreus stared at Mistress Kes, waiting for her to take it back or to explain it. She did neither. He wiped his nose on his sleeve. "You don't?" he asked incredulously.

"Not a bit," she said crisply. "So we not like her together." She smiled at him, a real smile. "Do you think you can stay out of the barn?"

He pursed his lips as he thought on it. If they didn't like her together, he could do it. But in a very little voice he asked her, "Will you hold my hand while she is here? The whole time?"

"The whole time."

He sighed. "I won't go to the barn."

"Good boy." She began to rise.

"Mistress Kes?"

She eased down and looked at him. He liked it when he could see her eyes. He never saw his mother's eyes.

"Does it make you sad when I go to the barn if your brother comes?"

She did not answer right away.

"I am afraid of him too," he confided in a whisper.

She patted his knee. "It's okay if you go to the barn then."

"Just not with Auntie."

"Not with Auntie."

"And you will hold my hand."

She brushed his hair behind his ear, then said softly, "I will hold your hand."

Auntie never stayed very long, not even long enough to have refreshment. And Mistress Kes would hold his hand. He took the mill from the table and began to turn it again.

Samir came into the kitchen. "The lady Ariadne is here to see Zagreus."

Kes did not miss the slave's darkened tone; Samir was fond of Zagreus. She wiped her hands on a towel and kept her answer brisk—she would not let the slave see how she too regretted these visits. "Very well. Fetch Zagreus and Arinna."

"Mistress Arinna is already speaking with the lady in the common room. And Zagreus is in the barn." He lifted his chin and gave her a significant look.

Samir and Zagreus had a closeness Kes had subtly tried to encourage. She trusted Samir, a sun-dark Parthian born into slavery, as she trusted her own father. He was a good slave who looked after the family as if it were his own.

The only time her father had ever taken a strap to Samir was when he had hidden two-and-a-half-year-old Zagreus in the barn, the day Ariadne came to visit. The child had screamed to be pulled away from Samir, and Samir had wept like a child.

Kes had wept too, silently, when she later treated the stripes on Samir's back. She knew Father was right. A slave had to obey. And she knew Samir was right.

She put her hands on her hips as she regarded the unhappy man in the kitchen doorway. "Zagreus and I have worked a bargain. You go and see if he will not willingly come. You remind him about Mistress Kes's bargain."

"Yes, ma'am," he said doubtfully and left.

He returned, much mystified, with a reluctant but compliant Zagreus. Even after she washed Zagreus's face and brushed the barn sweetgrass from his clothing, she had to shoo Samir away. He clearly wanted to see what had made the child come, and clearly wasn't happy he came at all. He left for the barn with a scowl.

Kes straightened the child's overvest. She worked her fingers through his hair to smooth it out. She looked him over and gave him an encouraging smile. "It won't last long. You know she never stays."

He nodded miserably. She offered her hand, and he grasped it. The child's hand was cold and wet.

As they crossed the kitchen to the common room threshold, Zagreus hesitated.

Kes gripped his hand and whispered into his ear, "We won't like her together, Zagreus. There's nothing we can't do together." After a moment, they entered the common room.

Ariadne had been waiting anxiously for the child to appear. She was sitting at the table with Arinna, an impatient look upon her fine features. Her black hair was upswept and as lovely as usual, fastened under a brocaded red-and-black head covering, stitched like the finest tapestry. It matched a lovely red tunic stitched with black and gold; it had wide bell-shaped sleeves and an expansive amount of fabric in the skirt. A gold, braided belt was fitted about her waist, tied in front with the long ends dangling.

Two things Kes noticed at once: Upon seeing Kes, Arinna immediately slipped something from the table and hid it in her lap. And Zagreus gripped her hand with the strength of a man.

Ariadne rose in a rustle of fabric and clasped her hands to her bosom, gazing upon Zagreus with nothing less than rapturous joy. "My darling," she breathed, and went to her knees in front of the child. "My joy..."

The child could not speak.

Kes whispered in his ear, "Say 'Hello, Auntie.'"

The child said nothing.

Ariadne crooned over the boy, marveling how he'd grown. Her smile was wide and beaming; her teeth were white. Her brown eyes were filled with pure adoration, and her fingertips traced his hair, the lines of his face. She held his cheeks with wordless pleasure, and Kes saw tears rise in her eyes. Clearly she loved this boy, this child she saw only twice a year, and for such a short time. Clearly she loved him, more than his own mother, and Kes did not know why the woman vexed her so.

She wore expensive clothing—was it Kes's own feelings of inferiority that made her wish Ariadne wouldn't come? She didn't think so. Miss Julia wore expensive clothing, and Kes did not feel inferior around her. Not much.

The woman dabbed at her tears with a lovely embroidered handkerchief.

If you love him so much, why don't you visit more often? Kes always wanted to ask. *But I'm glad you don't, because he is going to squeeze my fingers off.*

Ariadne tenderly brushed a lock of Zagreus's hair with her fingers, smoothed it down on the side of his face. That is when the bell-shaped sleeve slipped back to reveal a mark on her inner forearm.

A small tattoo of twining ivy leaves.

Kes looked from the tattoo to the enraptured face. She looked from the face to Arinna seated at the table, picking at her fingernails, bored. She glanced at Arinna's lap and wondered what she hid there.

"I am so happy to see you, Zagreus, my joy," Ariadne whispered. "Soon, Zagreus. Soon."

Kes's voice cut like metal on the honeyed reunion. "Soon what?"

The woman dabbed her cheeks and rose. Her eyes turned on Kes, eyes interrupted of their adoration and not best pleased.

"Soon my Zagreus will come visit me, in my palace." She looked down on the child, and joy came rushing back to her countenance. Her eyes glowed as she gazed on him. She playfully flicked a lock of his hair. "Does it please you to know I am a queen, little Zagreus? I am *your* queen."

Ariadne had always been a little odd at these visits, bestowing upon the child such billows of affection that it never failed to make Kes uncomfortable. But she never once said she lived in a palace, though her clothing had the look of it, and never once said she was a queen. Was she only playing at some motherly game?

"Do you know anyone named Portia?" Kes suddenly asked.

Two things happened at once: On the periphery Arinna's attention snapped to Kes, and Ariadne's enraptured gaze upon Zagreus froze. A frozen look of rapture is not a pleasant thing to see, less so when it is turned upon you.

Kes felt something warm at her feet . . . Zagreus was wetting himself.

She did the only thing possible then. She swooped up the child and ran for the barn.

Motes of dust lazed in the beam of light coming in from the cracks. Kes had not seen the barn from this angle, tucked in the corner where she was, hidden from the doorway by the mound of sweetgrass. Not since she was a child.

Samir had started from a bucket of tools when she flew into the barn with the child, and he ushered her to the corner, throwing coarse sacks over them. He hurried to the barn door, then stopped and looked about. He grabbed a long-handled pruning hook for the olive trees, then slipped out the door and closed it. He'd stood sentry at the door for an hour.

Under the sacks, Kes had held Zagreus while he lay rigid and shaking. She tucked a sack about him and drew him close and whispered softly to him until his trembling stopped. He lay insensible for a time, staring with a horrifying blankness until at last he fell asleep. It got warm, and Kes pulled the coarse covering off her head and waited for Samir.

When had she last been in the barn? It was Samir's domain. There was living space for him in the opposite corner, blocked off by a hanging curtain. She could see a pallet beneath the curtain, and a table and a stool, and a small piece of rug in front of the pallet.

She and Kardus had sometimes played in the barn when they were children. They'd tickle the ears of the animals with long sweetgrass. They'd pretend there was an earthquake and throw themselves in a tumult around boxes and stalls, sacks of grain and piles of sweetgrass. They'd peek inside the saddlebags of the guests, wondering at the strange things they found. Once when Kardus stood guard, Kes had rummaged in a pack and found lots of little wooden horse trinkets. She took one and later gave it to Kardus.

The barn door creaked open. "They have not come back, Mistress Kes."

Ariadne had left the inn within moments of Kes's flight to the barn. Arinna had gone with her.

"Is my father back yet?"

"No, Mistress Kes."

"Fetch Master Tallis."

"Yes, Mistress Kes."

Her gaze wandered idly about the barn, until she noticed something hanging from pegs on the wall. Shackles. Sets of manacles for hands, shackles for feet. There must have been five or six pairs. A few of the sets had chains that looked newly forged. So this is where Polonus got the shackles; her father kept him supplied.

She'd wondered about that. Polonus didn't have a lot of money. She often wondered where he did get his money, because he didn't work. He only studied and roamed and tended her brother. Sometimes he was gone for days at a time, but he always came back. She never gave a thought to where he got the—

She bunched up a sack, pressed it carefully over her face, and cried soundlessly into it.

Tallis peered into the dimness of the barn. "Kes?"

The slave had summoned Tallis from a fitful sleep, the kind of sleep he should have woken from earlier to feel refreshed. But the only real plan he had for the day was to minimize pain, and he had lazed on his bed until he dozed again. Kes had bound his ribs earlier, and truly the support felt better. He should have gone to the lake then. He rubbed his face as he stood in the doorway of the barn, trying to shake off the grogginess.

"Kes?"

The slave beckoned and led him to the far corner of the barn. There he saw a strange sight indeed: Zagreus sleeping on a pile of sweetgrass with sacks tucked all about him, and Kes`Elurah in the pile next to him, gazing at the child. When she looked at Tallis, her eyes were swollen from crying.

Tallis didn't know what to say. She climbed out of the sweetgrass and brushed herself off.

"Is the child all right?" he finally managed.

She looked at Samir, who, as if answering a verbal request, came to the sweetgrass pile with his pruning hook and settled on the ground. After a long look at Zagreus, she whispered, "Let's go to the lake."

Tallis eased himself into his chair by the sea, and Kes sat on the ground in front of him. A breeze came from the lake, and she raised her face to the wind. She wasn't wearing her head covering; it was probably back in the barn. Her hair had sweetgrass in it.

It wasn't easy for this girl to start with her talk, and Tallis was learning to be patient. If he left off his own need to get the details as accurately and quickly as possible—something ingrained in him from Callimachus—he knew she would talk in due course.

It took a while this time, and he was beginning to fidget. Behind her back, he rolled his hand once—only once—as if to say "Any time, Kes." But he remained silent. Just when he had settled into musing on the waters and the surrounding hills, just when he forgot they were not here to take in the quietness and beauty, Kes began to talk. Her voice was nearly toneless.

"The council of Kursi came to the inn one evening. The people wanted to put Kardus down like a mad dog. They said we should put him out of his misery. My father and I, and Bek and Tavi, and Shoshanna, said no. Polonus kept telling us, if there's a way into madness, there's a way out. He gave us hope. He said Kardus was worth fetching back.

"But you know what?" Her lips trembled, and she shook her head. "I don't blame the people. They don't see any hope—it's been almost four years, and I don't have much hope myself, not as time goes by. Most know him as he is now." She clenched fistfuls of her dress.

"But I remember the way he was. He was just Kardus, and I loved him. I've told you some bad things of him, but there was good. There was who he was when he was a child. Who he was when he was learning." She released her dress. "When I look at him now I can't see anything left of him, except for the familiarity of his face. Even that is not what it used to be."

She fell silent and looked at her hands in her lap. The breeze lifted her hair, and she answered the breeze by gazing across the waters. Tallis started to touch her shoulder but drew back when she began to speak again.

"'The problem of Kardus,' they said. 'We're here to talk about the problem of Kardus. He scares our children, scares away trade. Something has to be done.'" She drew up her knees. "One man has affected an entire village. And the hills surrounding the village, and even beyond. This is the country of Gerasenes—the Girgashites. Long ago, they were driven out of their own land into this region. The name came to mean 'the expelled ones.' And I think of that with Kardus. He is an expelled one. Nobody wants him; they drive him away. Well, we told the council it would be murder to put him down like a dog, and that if anything happened to him we would bring it to the magistrates. We told them his violence was mostly upon himself. We said if they didn't like his screams to stop their ears with wool. That was a few months ago. The problem is, he is getting worse. How he grows in strength, I do not know. Maybe the evil inside him multiplies."

Tallis shifted in his seat. The evil *inside* him? Like grain in a sack? Madness and lunacy for certain. He'd seen enough madness in this world. He'd known lunatics. But *evil*?

"Polonus has tried to keep him in shackles so he will not roam about and frighten people. He tries to keep him quiet until there is a cure. But Kardus screams. And he breaks the chains because he doesn't understand; he hates the chains, and it—" Kes's breath caught. She tried hard not to cry. "It breaks my heart to see him chained like an animal. No human being was meant to live the way he is. I cannot go see him anymore; it hurts too much. That is weak of me, I know."

"It's not a weak thing to shackle someone you love," Tallis said.

Kes shrugged miserably. "Doesn't really matter anymore. The shackles won't hold him now. He tears them like they're made of cloth. Then off he goes into the hills. Bad enough to have him live in the tombs, the place of the dead. But he goes naked into the hills. Screaming, crying out."

Tallis's eyes widened. He remembered standing in the gravesite on that hill just south of Kursi, toeing a pair of broken shackles. His neck hairs came up—had a raving lunatic spied upon him at that very moment? The legendary Kardus?

"I went away from the inn for a time, after Kardus began to go crazy. I couldn't take it anymore; I had to be free from it all. Free from the guests and the silence of my father. But I didn't stay long. I *wanted* to come home. This is where I belonged. I realized I like taking care of things. Like my father.

"But it's more than that—I couldn't bear to be away from Kardus. He is my blood, no matter if he is cursing at me and saying the vilest things you can imagine. No matter if I am afraid to be around him. I remember the way he used to be. Around here they know him as the naked and unchainable. I remember a little boy. I know his face. He is Kardus. My blood."

After a few gazing moments, she seemed to come to herself. She looked over her shoulder at Tallis. "I certainly didn't mean to say all that. You bring out the talk in me."

Tallis folded his hands over his stomach, remembered his ribs, and changed position. "Good. You need to talk. And who knows? Maybe someday we will be able to talk about things not so grim." *Speaking of grim . . .* "Tell me about this Demas. Do you want to talk about *him* now?"

Startled, she said, "That's—not why I asked for you." She looked over her other shoulder, in the direction of the barn.

"Well, if you want my opinion, your Demas was a wharf rat. That's the impression I got from the people at the theater."

"Of course he was."

"You knew it? I'd expect better from you." He smiled a little. *Me, for example. I'm older and wiser and have no evil intentions for young maidens—not many. . . .*

"Remember when you told me about the tattoo the other day? Ivy leaves and vines? The one you looked for on my arm?"

She knew how to change a subject. "Yes . . ."

"Did you say her name was Portia?"

Tallis studied her. "What about it?"

Kes plucked at her sandal. "Five years ago, Arinna came to the inn with her baby. She brought a sad tale, how she had been turned out of her home by a drunken husband. She pleaded for work, said she'd do anything for room and board. Said her son could help around the place when he was grown. Father and I took pity on her, more for the child. He captured us from the start, perhaps because our hearts were wounded from Mother's death and Kardus's absence. Well, from the start, a woman came to visit Zagreus twice a year, on his birthing day and when he was a half year older. She is the boy's aunt. I always thought it strange that she never took them in. They were her blood. Well, today—"

She fell silent. She always fell silent just when Tallis strained to hear more.

She concentrated on fiddling with her sandal. "Zagreus—has always been afraid of her. He takes to the barn every time she comes, like with the shaman. It's strange because she reveres him. Today . . . she said she was going to take him home for a visit. To her palace. And that's when Zagreus wet himself, and that's when I took him to the barn because I saw the tattoo on her arm. The one you looked for."

The shock stole his breath for a moment. His gaze strayed to the horizon.

He'd never be free of it. He could go to the farthest corner of the earth and he'd never be free. He wished he had never sought to learn everything he could about the *cultus* of Dionysus. How he wished he'd stayed dumb as a rock. "Her name is Portia?"

"She calls herself Ariadne."

"Oh, gods," Tallis groaned. It had to be Ariadne, and she had to have the mark of a Bacchantes.

"What is it?"

He squeezed his eyes shut, but all he saw was an orange glow, and his eyes flew open. He got up stiffly from the chair. Hand on his ribs, he eased down carefully next to Kes and let his feet dangle over the rock. He gazed blankly upon the waters.

"Why do they call this a sea?" he muttered. "It's a lake. Have you ever been to the sea?"

"Yes. It's amazing."

"This is no sea."

"If you've been south of here, you'll know why they call it a sea."

He couldn't shut away the ache this time. There was nothing he could do but let it hurt until activities of the day covered over it; until life with its living breathed its busy mercy and allowed him again, for a time, to forget.

"Everywhere I look I see Dionysus, no matter how hard I try to stay blind. When Callimachus sent me here, I kept a vigilance to ignore Beth Shean, what the Greeks call Scythopolis. Any scholar of Dionysus knows the name of Scythopolis, and the name Ariadne. . . ." His voice dropped. "And the name Zagreus."

Kes looked at him, but he couldn't tell her that part. He went on.

"There is a temple in Scythopolis, and it is either an ancient one or it is built upon the site of an ancient one. It is the temple of Dionysus, and Scythopolis is one of the fabled places of Nysa. Nysa was a Maenad, one of the nurses of the god Dionysus, and Scythopolis is where he is supposed to have buried her. Every three years they have a spring festival.

He is supposed to be reincarnated then, during the rites. You know of the Festivals of Dionysus?"

"Of course. The celebrations are everywhere, even Kursi. Not every three years, but once a year, at springtime."

"But you've never heard of the practices of the Dionysiac *cultus*. Do you know of the Maenads?"

"The women followers of Dionysus. The Bacchantes. Kardus read to us from Euripides." Kes shrugged. "Everyone knows the Maenads."

Tallis put a hard look on the lake. Talk like this belonged to no part of the day. It was shameful to speak of such things, especially to an innocent woman like Kes`Elurah. Shameful to let his words put images into her head.

But the woman's name was Ariadne. And the child's name was Zagreus.

He remembered the fevered work he had done in his twenties on the activities of the *cultus* of Dionysus. He'd worried Callimachus with his single-mindedness. When Cal would ask when it would be over, he'd reply, "When there are no more Maenads left on the face of the earth."

And when his efforts actually changed something, passing legislation in the Senate that placed limitations on the activities of the Bacchanalia (which, in practice, only meant a watchful eye), Cal expected Tallis to set aside his pen. Cal said this had not happened since the senatorial decree nearly two hundred years earlier, that he should be proud of his work—it was time to put his heart to something else. And Tallis had replied, "Their activities are only limited; they're not banned yet."

Then the old scholar made sure Tallis had his eye. "All your efforts will never erase what your mother did. Your fight is not with the Maenads; it's with who drives the Maenads. I do not recommend you take your fight to him." Then he said, "If you cannot forgive her, imagine what it is like to be mad."

Not long after, Tallis set aside his pen. He never wrote anything else on the *cultus* of Dionysus. He would never forgive his mother, but he had put long thoughts to what it must be like to be mad. Only someone mad could do that to her own child.

How could he tell Kes about it? He could allude to the truth and let her draw the right conclusions, but the older he got, the more he hated allusion. If he spoke anything less than truth, he deserved to have his tongue cut out. Truth is what his little brother deserved.

Woodenly, Tallis said, "Ariadne was the queen of the Maenads, Dionysus's queen. Zagreus is the most ancient name for Dionysus. As Zagreus, he is represented as Dionysus reborn." He tried to say more, but his tongue stuck to the roof of his mouth. Truth was bitterly hard. "The Maenads are . . . the divine nurses, responsible to . . . rear the young god . . . participate in his revels when he has reached maturity."

Thumb fast in his mouth. He didn't have his blanket scrap with him. "They select a child. . . ."

Mother, so lovely in her joy. Kicking up her feet in an elegant step. "They rear him. . . ."

Tallis taught him how to whistle. He used to carry him on his shoulders.

"And at certain festivals the rites become mad. They look for his incarnate presence, and if it comes, the dancing and revelry is swept into chaos. Grown men have been killed in the most horrifying fashion, by the hands of mere women. But it's not until the"—he clenched his teeth, trembling with effort—"sacred ceremony at midnight . . . on a mountaintop . . . that a child is . . ."

Kes sprang to her feet. She stood with her fists clenched, breathing hard. Stones skittered as she flew off for the barn.

". . . sacrificed to the god of wine and comfort. They say they do the child a favor, and I'm glad you're not hearing this, Kes, because the horror doesn't stop there." He shook his head, and tears shook down. "No, the Maenads, the Bacchantes—they've been called cannibals, you know." His heart squeezed so hard he couldn't breathe, and he dropped his head with sorrow. He gasped for breath. "And it is . . . a shameful thing . . . to put on my lips . . . what should belong to legend and myth."

Except it was true.

He let it hurt because he couldn't stop it this time. He let it hurt as it had not hurt in years. And he wept, aching for his little brother, as he had not wept, or ached, in years.

He was lying on his side, and his ribs hurt. He pushed up and brushed off his face, imbedded with tiny rocks and little shells from the sea. He felt old and shook out and weary.

"I miss you. I've missed you for twenty-five years. I'm here, and I haven't forgotten you, little brother. You're not forgotten. Don't think I have. Don't think I have."

He looked over his shoulder, north, toward the tombs of Kursi. No longer did he feel hatred for his mother or for her friends. Something was there for them, but it was not hatred. More like despair. He felt a stirring in a place he thought long dead, not for the followers of Dionysus but for Dionysus himself. For the first time in his life, the hatred felt clean.

As he looked at the hills he remembered a bonfire night in Thebes. He remembered being laid out in a chicken yard, pressed down by a force from which he could not rise. And he remembered human touch, from the fiery eyes of a slave who had challenged the Evil.

A foe was in those hills, worse than the Maenads.

Was it time to take the fight to him?

How do you fight a god?

He found Kes in the barn, asleep next to Zagreus.

He hated to scare her like that. Hated how it made him feel when he looked about the barn and found things that belonged to the sane day and not mad nights. Sacks of grain. The smell of the donkey. A heap of sweetgrass. All an illusion. Thin comfort in the certainty of the Evil abroad on this land. This world suddenly seemed less real to Tallis than the other he knew existed.

The money stolen from Cal seemed like a vague wrong. His gaze stopped on shackles hanging from the pegs. More than he wanted to find out who stole from Cal, he wanted to know what had happened to the academy. Why Bion committed suicide, why Theseus was murdered. Why Kardus went mad. Did anyone try to bring the murderers of Theseus to justice? Or, as Tallis suspected, were they too afraid to seek justice for fear of unholy reprisal?

Tallis strolled to the barn door. Despite sore ribs and a sore face, he felt like some exercise. Kes said Polonus lived in the hills, just east of the tombs of Kursi.

He regarded Samir as he paused at the doorway. The dark eyes had been on him since he entered the barn. Tallis looked for what he saw in the chicken yard the other night, that authority, that presence, but saw only a slave's guarded impassivity.

"Do you know what day of the month it is?" Tallis asked softly.

The slave shook his head.

"Dionysus is called the god of many joys. He is also called Lord of the Souls. The god of madness."

The slave slowly nodded.

"The nones of the month is only days away, and it is the third year. It's the Day of Awakening; all of Scythopolis will be celebrating." Tallis looked over to the sleeping Zagreus, and to Kes with her arm across him. "Don't take your eyes off him."

And slowly the slave nodded.

In the tombs of Kursi is a man who is staring at his skin. For a long time he will sit, staring at his skin.

He sees scars upon scars upon thick and ridged scars. Gouges, where ovals of flesh have been bitten. Puffy lines of infection, the creases where maggots lived. Fingers with their blackened nails creep over this skin, inspecting this, their shell. Their possession.

Voices and voices and voices.

TURNAROUNDTURNAROUNDTURNAROUNDBITTERBITTERBITTER BITTERBITTERBITTERBITTERBITTERALEXANDERALEXANDER ALEXANDERALEXANDERALEXANDERRRRRR!!!

The voices crescendo, they waver, they descend, and they whirl. At his ear, across the clearing, in and out around his head. Ancient babble, endless babble. No rhythm, no cadence. A thousand will shout and a thousand will croon and a thousand will twitter and a thousand will hiss. Were there cadence and rhythm, even with the nonsense, he could tolerate it. It was better when they accused or blasphemed; it attracted him from the corner where he dwelled. Coherence of any kind took his attention. A well-formed sentence of accusation or blasphemy was better than catalogues of babble.

No rest, no quiet, no stillness. He doesn't know what it is anymore.

The madman slowly reaches for a broken shackle. He screams above the nonsense and plunges the shackle into the shell. Blood sprays his face, and the pain is victory; it tells him he is trying his best. He will break the shell and let the voices out. He will dig out the Evil. Never meant to be there. Wrong to let Them go there.

He will cut himself, gash himself; he will gouge and rake the shell. He will gorge on raw animal flesh and vomit hard enough to break blood vessels in his face; hard as he can, any way he can. He eats things no human would to make his bowels react with violence and expel Them; he'll eat bloody pig eyes, fistfuls of dirt, his own filth. He will tear at his eyes and ears, nose and mouth, rectum and navel. He will vomit, defecate, gouge, and gash—anything to expel Them. Hard as he can, any way he can.

He once assaulted a tall rocky cliff and launched himself headfirst. He did it fast to fool the tricksters, but They wouldn't let him kill the shell. They yanked him short and he dangled in the air, his head inches from the ground. They held him upside down for punishment, for hours and hours, until his face bulged and his mind left him for a time, a rare time of relief.

RUNRUNRUNRUNRUNABADDONABADDONABADDONAPPLLYON APPLLYONAPPLLYONAPPLLYONSOMASEMASOMASEMASOMASEMA SOMASEMASOMASEMASOMASEMAOMASEMASOMA SEMA!

The madman screams with every plunge of the shackle into the shell. Blood spatters his crusted body, mingling with old blood on his chest.

He suddenly hurtles backward and lies insensible against the rocks. His eyelids flutter; his face is ravaged by unnaturalness. Slowly he rises, and cunning comes to his eye. He flings the shackle away. He takes what he has closest and smears it over the newest wounds, protecting the shell, protecting the shell, protecting the possession. . . .

VII

A cool wind came down from the heights and made the climb more bracing, especially for a man with recently broken ribs.

Tallis left the road and the few travelers bound for Damascus when they came to the southern slope of the el-Kursi Valley. He'd gotten a ride in a peddler's cart when the peddler stopped at the inn for refreshment. The ride had saved him a few steps, to be sure, but the wind coming down from the heights would challenge what rest he had taken. There was no path up this slope, but at least the way wasn't difficult. Small rock croppings gave easy purchase, and otherwise tall spring grasses were trampled by the herd of pigs he'd seen grazing the other day.

He had smelled the herd before he saw it and had to press his sleeve on his face when he passed. Apparently the herdsmen favored this rocky terrain. He now caught the familiar smell on the wind, but mercifully, it wasn't as strong today. He hoped the herd had moved on, hoped it was nowhere near where Polonus lived.

East of the tombs of Kursi, Kes had said. Tallis tried to keep his course just that. He'd strolled the tombs once, in unwary abandon, and Tyche the goddess of fortune had favored him; he had had no encounter with the madman. The goddess could see fit to conceal him once more until he found Polonus.

When a sweat broke on his body, he stopped halfway up the slope to sit down and rest. He pressed his sleeve to his forehead and rested his arms on his knees to have a look around. He was actually quite curious to see Kardus—and wasn't sure if he was ready. He had a stout respect for the unpredictability in such a man. He'd read too much; he'd seen too much. Who knew what a madman would do next?

What if madness were passed on?

Tallis had long been haunted by a vagary that perhaps the madness of his mother had tainted his blood: madness, dormant in his veins. He never wanted to think on it, for fear the thinking would stir it up and lend it power. Nor could he look away, not anymore. Though his mother had been a rather inward woman, as long as he knew her, she had been kind and good, and that was the horror of it. In the end, she was mad. Didn't he suppose himself to be kind and maybe a little good? What prevented him from going the way of his mother? If only she were all bad. She *was* bad; she was also kind and good.

Did Alexander ever fear that the madness of his mother lay wait in his blood? For all the thoughts he'd had of Alexander, this was a new one. Olympias had danced at midnight on the mountains too. Had she ever participated in the sacred rite? The books never said she went that far, none that he had read; they said only that she writhed in the revels until the frenzies came and the spirit of Dionysus possessed her. What horror attended his incarnation then? How *should* the books have read?

Alexander, did you have a little brother? Was your mother mad, like mine?

Olympias's family claimed to be descended from god-men: from Pyrrhus, son of Achilles, and from Helenus, son of Priam—king of Troy. Perhaps to later explain the singularity of her son, Olympias had claimed to be impregnated by Zeus, at the clap of a thunderbolt during a storm. If this was true—and only the credulous would believe it—then Alexander was a son of the gods.

At times Alexander used the belief of the credulous to gain his own advantage, tactician that he was; mostly he worked to counter it, especially among the men with whom he fought his campaigns.

Though no one was likely to ask Tallis what he loved best about Alexander, he had an answer ready.

"He tried hard to be as one of them, accepted not as king, let alone the son of a god, but as brother," Tallis answered the nonexistent questioner aloud. "As fellow soldier." His efforts, like eating the same food, visiting the wounded, and comparing battle tales, had won their hearts. He never wished to be elevated in their sight, save for the respect necessary to command. Once when he was wounded in the leg with an arrow, he dryly commented, "It is no ichor I bleed." Ichor, the blood of the gods.

Things like this had come down through the ages and seized Tallis's imagination. The battle strategies alone were legendary. And though his brilliance was something to be admired, Tallis never thought it was gods-bestowed as much as learned from his remarkable father, Philip of Macedon. In studying Alexander, he had become fascinated with Philip. Philip made the magnificent army and handed it down to Alexander. Philip saw something special in his son and hired the great Aristotle to tutor him—maybe the smartest thing he had ever done. Philip once told Alexander, "My boy, you must find a kingdom big enough for your ambitions. Macedonia is just too small for you."

Tallis wondered, if the fever had not killed him at thirty-two, what sort of man would Alexander have been at sixty-four? Alexander, so passionate, he who wanted a taste of everything, who ached to see what lay around the bend. If not the fever, would his own zeal have burned him up? How would the world be different today if Alexander had lived?

Aristarchus, Callimachus's colleague, had long thought Tallis a fool for taking after Alexander so—he liked it better when Tallis applied himself to ridding the world of the Maenads. Called *that* a worthwhile obsession. Said it actually accomplished something, unlike pining for a leader who was probably as corrupt as any other king. Aristarchus said learn of Alexander, but not enough to teach him.

Why he steadily worked to chip at Tallis's respect for Alexander, Tallis did not know. He hated the way the pinched man lay in wait to pounce his opinions. Aristarchus was so cynical even his mouth was twisted in a permanent grimace. Why Callimachus kept him around was another reason Tallis loved Callimachus—the loved man felt sorry for the unloved man.

Cal tried to make Tallis see the good in Aristarchus, and Tallis told Cal he could see just fine and saw nothing he liked. Always dour, always stuffing the atmosphere with counterisms. Always happy to be contrary. True, Aristarchus had an odd acumen. He'd shuffle past a conversation, toss in one comment to make the ones he'd interrupted stare after him, and he'd change the course of their discussion entirely.

Tallis found himself smiling. "You won't cure me of him, Aristarchus. And I'll teach of him someday." The thought brought a pleasant flutter: Tallis of Athens . . . Alexander's historian.

He rose, wincing at the soreness in his chest, and pulled up his tunic to have a look. Kes had bound his ribs firmly; enough that breathing was a compact affair. But it did make mobility easier, and hopefully would make the bones knit—

Without warning, his senses leapt.

He gazed at the bandages, wondering why his stomach plummeted, who had thrown the damp on the sun. . . .

He let the tunic drop. *Turn around; look up the slope, it's right behind you.* Sluggish with inexplicable terror, he slowly looked over his shoulder.

A dark crouching form shut out the sun.

Immobile, Tallis stared at the backlit form. Then the form screamed, gusting fumes over Tallis, and his mind went blind.

Midnight orange. Cadent steps and moving skirts. Serene smiles, sharpening to bug-eyed grimaces. The celebrants did not know their faces had changed, one moment joyous and lovely—the next turn in the steps showed faces stupid and grotesque, with thick-lipped lurid grins and huge unequal eyes, drunk with evil nonsense. Black winged things moved among them in their dance, huge tar caterpillars flowing.

He heard the form scrabble backward up the slope, heard animal grunts of terror attend its retreat. The grunts crescendoed to an undulating scream, and it echoed in the valley. The scream paused at the top of the hill, then ran away, trailing jaggedly off, leaving behind a bruised silence.

Dampness slid from the sun. Sensibility crept back.

Tallis put out a hand as he sank to the earth. Gods, the scream. There was hell in it. And the smell— Ah, gods! The smell had rolled over him like a belch from Hades.

The man was covered in filth like he was painted in it. Filth is all he wore, not a stitch of clothing. He could not see the face—it was backlit

120

by the sun. Tallis only had an afterimage of wild hair. He couldn't see much for the roaring of the presence.

This was Kardus?

Tallis looked slowly up the slope. In the weak afterflush of terror, he panted, "I know you. I know you."

That was the force of the meeting, not the horror of the pathetic individual he had seen, but the primordial presence transcending him. He recognized it. He *knew* the presence. Everything he felt in the Theban grove, he felt in the man.

And gods, what was this? He felt for his stomach. Something had answered the presence. He didn't imagine it then—when he had wept on the shore of the Galilee, something had dislodged within. He felt more than terror at the presence in Kardus; he felt deep revulsion. Clean hatred. Whatever it was, it was grossly affronted by, and just as primordial as, the opposing presence.

"Follow pain to the truth, Tallis," Callimachus once said. "Let it hurt until it leads you to where it is."

Tallis had denied the pain because it was too much to bear. Today, he let it hurt. *Follow pain to the truth.* What was the truth? He rubbed his belly. He could not say what had answered the Evil. He wanted to define the clean hatred; he wanted to see it clearly so he could direct it, or obey it. But he felt it settle.

As Samir had settled.

Presently, when the remnants of his human fear had faded and strength had returned to his limbs, and that was a very long time, he rose and began to climb the slope again.

He found Polonus's home only when he had looked too far to the east and come back to the tombs. He had mistaken the home of Polonus for a tomb itself; it was built into the hillside like some of them. A short dark passageway, flanked with curved walls of rock, led down a few steps. A stone beam carved into the bedrock overhung the dark door, and over the beam grew long patches of untrimmed grasses. It probably *was* a tomb once, converted into a home. Tallis looked around the graveyard, at the rock mounds that served for Polonus's front yard, and at the other tomb against the rounded curve of the hillside just past this.

"Do you have the neighbors over often?" he muttered. He could think of a few other places he'd rather live.

He'd taken a second look at the place when he noticed the small shed, then again when he saw a cistern. Then he saw other evidence of habitation. A folded-up stool against the wall in the passageway, a cup on the ground next to the stool. He found a fire pit behind the shed with a grate hanging from a metal tripod. The fire pit was cold, though it looked recently used. The place felt as if the owner had gone away for a while. The shed door was closed; the door in the passageway was closed. People didn't close their doors unless it was night or they'd be gone for a time. They didn't let a fire pit grow cold. The herbs growing in a few pots behind the shed looked thirsty.

Tallis called around softly for Polonus, but no one answered. He stood in front of the door, debating whether he should go in. Before the debate was over he stepped down and nudged the door. It pushed easily inward.

"Polonus?"

The door began to swing back to him. He pushed it all the way open and found a stone doorstop.

It was a small room. When he stepped out of the path of light, the sun reached halfway in. The more the sun dropped west, the more the room would be illumined. Polonus likely did most of his work in the afternoon, and it was evident this former tomb was the home of a scholar. Tallis saw scrolls everywhere he looked.

The first thing he really noticed was the smell. It was earthy and stony and ancient all at once. It wasn't unpleasant, exactly, but disturbing; if this place had been a tomb, maybe he was breathing the dust of the dead.

The elevated recess carved into the bedrock at the back of the room had to be the place Polonus slept; it had in it a thin pallet and a flat pillow at one end. How could he sleep there? It was a bed for the dead. Did people once kneel there to honor their dead, to pray to them or to their gods? Did they imagine the place would one day become a desecration? Maybe Polonus had to clear out the remains of the former occupant to make his own bed. The thought made Tallis shudder.

A desk with a stool behind it was in the path of the sunlight, situated near the sleeping place. Polonus had arranged it at an angle to take full advantage of the sun's path. A wide woven mat went down the center of the room from the doorway to the bed.

Tallis slipped off his sandals at the doorway and stepped onto the mat. He went to the desk. Ink stains in the grain of the wood. Scratches from too sharp a pen nib, perhaps in an emphatic moment. He came around the desk and settled on the stool. He looked out the passageway, and knew why Polonus had put the desk here—not only for the sunlight, but also for the bit of the Galilee he could see through the narrow doorway.

The glance outside prickled his neck hairs. Kardus was roaming around out there, he with hell attending him. May Tyche be pleased to let him roam far from this place.

The desk was wide and solid, the surface smooth with a venerable patina. In the right corner was a trio of stoppered ink pots, a vase of styli near them. There were scraps of parchment with handwriting on them, placed in deliberate spots like reminder notes. A closed wooden tablet, a diptych likely filled with wax, lay on the left. Next to it was a half-unwound papyrus roll, the dowels askew to prevent the paper from scrolling up.

Tallis studied the room from behind the desk.

On the inside left of the door was a cylindrical container full of papyrus rolls. On hooks above it hung an old tunic, a pair of shackles, and a few leather scroll carriers. The left side of the room had a long shelf built into the wall, about as high as a man's sore ribs, loaded with scrolls. Beneath the shelf was a stone bench lining the entire wall. Perhaps this had been a family tomb, and the lesser members of the family had rested on the stone bench. Instead of desiccated bodies, and Tallis didn't much like the image, the bench was filled with an assortment of odds and ends. Crockery, a few sacks likely filled with grain or beans. Some small tools, leather lacings.

The shelf above was filled with neatly stacked scrolls. A smaller stack was apart from the rest, tight and fresh rolls of papyri without dowels, waiting for ink. There was a stack of tablets and a stack of parchment, likely from Pergamon by its trimmed, quality look. Why so many rolls of fresh papyri; why the quantity of parchment? Why so much for one man? It would take six months of constant printing to fill one scroll alone. There was enough on that shelf to supply a . . . school.

He realized he was looking at the remains of the Academy of Socrates. This place was still a tomb.

The smell of the papyri was part of the room smell, he realized. He loved the odor, though some did not find it so appealing. To Tallis, it was Homer and Sophocles, Plato and Menander. What notes would he find in the margins of the scrolls? There is where he would find Polonus. There is where a scholar dwelled, in what he wrote in the margins of the texts of great men. He had penned enough of his own outrages and agreements in the margins of such scrolls.

He looked at the pieces of papyrus bordering the edge of the desk. They were quotes, he realized. Passages. Meaningful sayings not to be forgotten. No wonder Tallis liked this desk; it reminded him of his own back in his apartment at the house of Callimachus. It even had a mound of wax the size of a coin next to the ink pots, stuck with a few nails. Tallis worked one out to look at the point. Polonus kept the nails filed to a needlepoint for picking out debris in the papyri when an un-suspecting pen nib ran into minute obstructions.

"My kind of finicky," Tallis murmured. He looked at one of the notes in his hand.

Call no man happy until he is dead.

"Cheerful."

If there is a way into madness, logic says there is a way out.

Tallis considered it and shrugged. "Agreed."

The next was longer. The first part of it was carefully printed, the second was scrawled. The first part read: *The man who fights the gods does not live long.—Homer.* Scrawled emphatically below it was *The man who does not fight the gods should not live.—Polonus.* The word *not* was underscored three times. *Polonus* was underscored once.

Tallis smiled. "I think I like this fellow."

The last note was written in smaller print. *How dangerous it is to solve a great problem with a small answer.* And below it in very small print, *All my answers have been small.*

Tallis carefully replaced the pieces of parchment.

He hooked his fingers on the edge of the desk, and his gaze slid to the wooden diptych tablet. How far would he go, prying into another man's business? He eyed the tablet, then pushed aside the scroll to clear a path for it. Finally, he pulled the tablet over and flipped it open.

He wasn't sure what he was reading at first. The left side of the diptych had a numerated feel to the lines scratched into the amber wax, like a list. The right side seemed a compilation—a gathering of thoughts, perhaps direct conclusions to the list on the left. He started with the left plate.

Chambari tribe, wise woman Cosomatura.

Referral to the shaman, Shamash-Adwar.

Trepanning.

Temple of Asclepius—enkoimesis incubatio.

Leeches.

Oracle at Delphi.

Reversal at Scythopolis. Disinvitation of the paredros.

Trepanning—drilling holes in the head. *Enkoimesis incubatio*—sleeping overnight in a temple to procure the favor of a god. Sometimes people chained themselves to an altar to wrangle a healing from a god for a loved one or for oneself. The temple of Asclepius on Cos was world renowned for its healing center. The physicians there were the best in the world.

Tallis felt a chill at the last line of the plate. Disinvitation of the *paredros.* And at Scythopolis, no less—surely at the temple of Dionysus. The *paredros* was like Socrates' *daimon,* it was a close enough comparison; Tallis had read enough old curse tablets to know some people actually invited evil to cohabit with them, for whatever purpose they wished to achieve.

He slowly raised his eyes to the entrance and the bit of Galilee. All he needed right now was a wild form resounding with hell to darken that entrance. He would be blocked in. "Fortune favor the terrified," he mumbled.

He began to read the corresponding lines on the right-hand plate.

Sheatfish. I'll say no more.

Should have paid attention to Zagreus. Lost no money this time.

Two gold staters—I should have my own head drilled. No infection, thank the gods. No change, either.

Blank space for the corresponding left-plate line of *Temple of Asclepius.*

He ate them. Tallis glanced for the corresponding line, found the word *leeches,* and groaned.

For *Delphi* was *Cost of trip prohibitive. Will speak with Jarek.*

For *Reversal at Scythopolis,* the bottom portion of the right plate was blank.

It was a long while before Tallis closed the tablet. He pushed it back into place and leaned on his elbows, rubbing a hand over his fist. Where was Polonus now? Off to Scythopolis, trying to fulfill the last line of the list? Didn't Kardus have to be with him to . . . disinvite the *paredros*?

He noticed a bit of parchment sticking out from beneath a small lamp, near the trio of ink pots. He picked up the lamp and carefully peeled away the parchment stuck to the bottom. It was stained with lamp oil.

If there is no hope for him, there is no hope for anyone.

He folded the scrap and tucked it into his pocket. He fell again to rubbing his hand over his fist.

What course to lay out? What was it now about? For Polonus, according to the tablet, it was all about Kardus. What did Polonus know about the murder of Theseus, he who had been found, as Lysias had said, in large chunks outside a disreputable bathhouse in Hippos? What of the suicide of Bion? The Greeks had long considered suicide an acceptable method to end matters on earth. (Aristarchus called it melodramatic petulance; Callimachus called it a shame—their thinking was fashionably un-Greek. Any kind of un-Greek thinking was fashionable—that's what made it Greek.) Did Polonus know why Bion did it?

There were new shackles on the hook, old shackles on the stone bench. And here was the tablet, with the list. The disintegration of the academy came down to Kardus for Polonus. Is this where Tallis's own path lay? Should he truly forsake any ideas of pursuing the mysteries of the Decaphiloi, not the least of which was who had penned the progress reports and stolen the money from Cal? Should he take his hand out of the adder's nest and simply try and help Polonus find a cure for Kardus? Wasn't there good in that? Callimachus, he sensed, would find it a worthy occupation. Maybe even Aristarchus would agree.

Callimachus, how I miss you. I miss you both. How I need your wise counsel.

His idle gaze fastened upon the opened scroll he had pushed aside. He tilted his head. What did Polonus read in his spare time? There was a circular tag attached to an end of the dowel. Tallis turned the tag over: *XV.* He took the handles and unwound the scroll with his right hand, rolling up loosely with his left until a portion was spread upon the desk.

He tilted the left portion of the scroll to see—it was tight. Puzzled, he unrolled more of that portion—it was blank. He unwound the right portion and looked closely. It was Polonus's handwriting, from what he'd read on the parchment notes. Tallis sat back in surprise. Polonus was writing his own text.

He hesitated. He had no right to read this. A text was a private thing until made public by the originator. He pushed it away. He studied it a moment more, then got up and went to the shelf where the large stack of scrolls was. He read the dangling circular tag on one of the scrolls in the middle. Number 8. Beneath it, in the bottom of the stack, number 4. They started at the right and moved left, 1 through 5. Next level, 6–9. Next level, 10–12. On top, 13 and 14. What was all this?

He debated, and before the debate was done, he had tugged out roll number 1. He unrolled the end to see what the name of the text was. Papyrus rolls were always titled at the end, the part least likely to be damaged.

No title. How odd. He brought the scroll to the table and unwound it to start at the beginning.

I, Polonus of Hippos, undertake to seek the restoration of Kardus of Kursi.

Two months I have dwelled in his habitation of the tombs, and have now set up a habitation of my own. It is preferable to a moldy tent.

A steady pounding began in Tallis's gut. He looked up at the other scrolls. These were Polonus's private journals, and this was only roll number 1. He had no right to read them, not without permission. It was like stealing.

Kardus will not come in here.

"Thank the gods," Tallis murmured.

I do not know what he fears. I have made it a pleasant place—as pleasant as one can make a former tomb—but he is beginning to abhor all things pleasant. It is neat, and it is orderly. This is the first observation I record, that Kardus no longer tolerates order. Not even the simple order of a line of stones to my doorway. I did it for decoration, and to remind my-self that I am part of a society far away, a society that will line their pathways with stone.

It was a clean line. Kardus came and kicked it out of order, made chaos of it, my simple clean line. Such a small thing, compared to the other things he's done. A small thing to make me sit on the ground and weep. I can't say why I did it; he's done much worse.

He destroyed many books of the academy, when I was still living in the tent, the books he loved so much. He destroyed histories and plays. I have desolation in my heart from it. What he did to a scroll of Jewish sa-cred writings still has me perplexed: He laid out the Hebrew text and urinated on it. Then he trampled the scroll with a glee I cannot compre-hend. The scroll was a gift from a Jewish friend. What perplexes me most is this: I cannot read Hebrew, therefore Kardus cannot. Everything he learned, he learned from me. Why, then, would he destroy that which he could not possibly understand? Gods, he even chose the scroll quite care-fully from the barrel. Unrolled and read parts of it out loud. He cannot read Hebrew.

This, the first observation, that he will no longer tolerate order. Not the order of the written word, not even the order of words he cannot un-derstand. Not the order of cleanliness, of relieving himself in a private place like a normal human being.

My clean line of stones is my first observation.

From habit, Tallis reached for his cup of watered wine, surprised to find it wasn't there. He felt like he was poring over a text on his own desk at home. He gazed at the roll in his hands, at all the rolls on the shelf, at roll 15 in front of him. He eyed the leather scroll carriers dangling from the hooks. Did he dare take the rolls back to the inn? When would Polonus be back? He didn't want to read in this place, maybe from guilt, maybe from fear that a madman lurked around the corner. He had a sud-den flash of his own blood spattered on these scrolls.

He loosely unrolled the journal, skimming through the columns of words. There was nothing in the margins, not on the sides and not on the top or bottom; every column of the text was margin—everything was Polonus.

Poseidonius attacked Chrysippus for denying the existence of an irrational element in the soul—moral Evil—though whether he was ready to concede a matching irrationality of moral Good is not at all clear.

He came to a drawing of three circles. The circles on the ends overlapped the one in the middle. The middle circle was labeled *Human*. The overlapping circle on the left, *Good*. The overlapping circle on the right, *Evil*. Tallis read the lines beneath the drawing:

I have formed a basis from what I've observed in Kardus: that perhaps the universe is made of three forces. What would Chrysippus think of me?

Tallis skimmed the rest of the scroll, set it aside, and went to get scroll number 2. He started for the table, then turned and took an armful of scrolls. He dumped them on the floor next to the table, went back quickly for the rest. There were only a few hours of afternoon light left, and no banked coals to light a lamp. He would have to read quickly. He was thirsty and would have to ignore it. Hungry, and would go without. Some lines were neatly printed, some scrawled in haste.

Scroll number 3.
Good day today. Not sure why. He is quiet and docile. He even ate bread today, real bread! Such hope in my heart for that. I thought he may have even recognized me. He glanced my way, I am sure of it. Most of the time he does not know I exist. It is strange, because he is aware of anyone else who comes by. He is aware of the herdsmen. He is aware if Kes `Elurah comes. He is aware of Samir, the slave—gods, he is aware of him. I told Kes `Elurah to keep him away; the slave vexes Kardus terribly.
But he is not aware of me. Never is. I lay out food; I replace his clothing. It is strange to be tolerated. It is strange—I do not exist to him. His old teacher is no more to him than a rock on the ground. I wonder if I am being used to . . . keep him alive. To keep him. Perhaps that's all I am to Them. A keeper. Maybe that's why he tolerates me.

Scroll number 5.
Not so much a releasing of inner madness, but inviting madness to the innerness. A granting of access to the depths. Invitation.

Soma sema. The body is a tomb. Prison of the divine spark.

Bled him today. Covered him with fifteen leeches. Poured on the salt when I realized he enjoyed it. He took a swollen leech and ate it; the blood ran down his chin. And I simply wiped the blood away. Before, I would have vomited. Nothing surprises me anymore.

Had to chain him today. Jarek wasn't happy. I got angry and said try living with him. He got me a pair of shackles.

Gods, I hate the shackles. Half the time he rages at them, the other half he stirs the chains in bewilderment, like a child. Ah, gods, I wish it would end.

Scroll number 7.

I made him drink a vial of the bathwater of a holy man. The water was gray. Cost me a silver drachma and did nothing. The holy man is rich, and I am a brokenhearted old fool.

He suffers as much from my attempts to help him as he does from what afflicts him. I would walk away, were his face not Kardus. You, whom I once knew.

Do you hate me, Kardus? I would if I were you.

Scroll number 10.

I don't know what I believe anymore. I used to believe in *ataraxia*, escape from the violence, chaos, and anarchy of the world around. What of the violence, chaos, and anarchy within? Escape from without to find it within. The gods are laughing.

I wouldn't believe in good anymore, save for simple things like a basket of food. Today Kes included my favorite pastry. Such kindnesses reduce me to tears. Such kindnesses are a mooring line, thinly lashed to a boat in a maelstrom.

Samir. He is a mooring line.

How clearly the smallest good stands out against evil. Samir looked at me today. Just a look, but I felt his strength. I felt a moment of . . . I don't know what to call it. Relief. Peace, perhaps, but I didn't recognize it as such. I have forgotten what it is.

Mooring lines.

I used to see a mooring line in the sunset. I saw mooring lines in beauty. I cannot see them anymore.

Scroll number 11.

Saw something today. Not sure what it was. A flickering of light, movement of some kind. It was behind me. I turned to look and it wasn't there.

Throughout the texts Tallis found various versions of Polonus's original diagram. Sometimes the circles overlapped, and sometimes they floated free. There were always three. He found the last version of it in scroll 11. This time the circles did not overlap, but were lined up, the middle circle touching the edges of the outer circles. At the places where they touched, Polonus had drawn a dark mark. He had circled each mark and written *doorway*. The left outer circle was labeled *Good*. The right, *Evil*. The middle was labeled *Kardus*. Polonus had drawn heavy dark arcs from the Evil circle through the doorway into Kardus. The Kardus circle was scribbled through with black. The Good circle had an X over it.

Heroes for the good and heroes for the bad. Kardus uncorked the tunnel from the bad and let the bad heroes inside. The good heroes, if they ever were, are no longer.

Must close the door. Don't know how. Must drive out bad heroes first. Don't know how. Told Them to go once—first time in a long time Kardus looked at me, and I was never more afraid. Such a baleful eye. Such dark glowing mirth. He said leave Us alone. Us, he said. I never did it again. No wish for that contact again. The smell came.

Ah, gods, I want to leave this place, I want to go. I am in hell.

Is the door already closed? Is there no hope to open it once again and drive Us away? If there is no hope for Kardus, what of the others who may open the door unawares? And why in the name of the gods and the goddesses can we not open the door to the Good?

Ah, gods, I wish it were over. Ah, gods. I wish it would end.

Is he still in there? Did They kill him?

Yellow light on the periphery. Movement. Flickering. Someone spying on me. Watching me! I turn to look; no one is there. I am frightened.

Tallis rubbed his lips. They were gummy. He was terribly thirsty. He glanced outside, gripping the edges of the scroll. There was a cistern outside. But maybe he would run into Kardus.

Scroll number 12.

You gave them a place to hang their cloaks, and now I am beginning to hate you. You brought it on yourself. I hate what you've done to the place.

I hate what she did to you. I'd kill her if I could. Give me the chance—I will kill her, for you and for me, and with relish I will do it! I looked at you today, and my stomach flamed with hatred. Why do you let Them stay?

She took you with flattery and lies. It's all you ever wanted anyway, and I despise you for it. I may hate you, Kardus. Let me think about it. I'll let you know.

Not a yellow light. A yellow face, I am sure of it. Corner of my eye. Gone whenever I look. But it's there. I know it's there. It is patient.

Scroll number 13.

They say there is a young Socrates on the other side of the lake. Yes, the place you hate to look. They say he does miracles, a regular son of the gods. I despise him already. He will assemble his pupils on the steps and stand in a colonnade. He will have great hope for one particular pupil, and I hope that one turns out like you. I hope he will learn what comes of sacrificing everything for one arrogant whelp with a dead witch for a mother and a living shrew for a sister and a milksop for a father. I hope the whelp destroys his life, like you have destr—

Kardus! Kardus, forgive me! I didn't mean it. I get it mixed up—I destroyed your life. I pushed you to her, because I wanted to be rid of you. That is poor love. And I loved you! You were a good boy. I was the one who knew better, and I was weak.

Curse my weakness! Curse the day I ever came to the inn! An ignorant you would have been better than this. You were a good boy. Forgive me, my son. Forgive me.

The ink was smeared in this portion.

I told it to go away. It was behind me again. Appeared at the corner of my eye. A yellowish face, stretched tight, like a lumpy barley sack. It flickers yellow. There is invitation in it. It wants something.

Always half a step behind me. It's slow. Slow and plodding, always there, relentless. I look, and it is gone. I spend more time outside, in the sunlight. Safe in the sunlight.

I am frightened.

Scroll number 14.

Maybe it's a hero of Good. Maybe one of the long-lost heroes of the Good, come to help me. I knew there was Good!

Then why am I afraid?

Barley face says he will guide me. Maybe to the mystery of Kardus, to the mystery of his healing.

Polonus, you fool! It says nothing, because nothing is there. It's your fancy, the fancy of an aging man who has long lived with a madman. Go to Hippos and visit the brothels. Get drunk. Wake up, man, and live. Go see a play. Go see Antenor.

I am attracted to Evil. It fascinates me. I do not know if this makes me a bad man.

I think you were invaded. Antenor thinks your mind snapped. But I've lived with you too long. I know about Them, and there is no explaining that to Antenor. I don't even try. I let him talk. It was good to see him again, but it amazes me how tiresome he has grown. I don't remember him that way. Were all the Decaphiloi so blind? Foolish people. So blinded to the Realms.

Barley face came today, and I screamed for him to go away. I saw Kardus, and he was laughing at me. I screamed at him. I don't like it that he looks at me now. He sees me, all the way through, searching for the secret place, and I hate his searching eyes. He told me it was only a matter of time. Told me I would be his. Gods, he frightens me. Never used to. Never cared about me. Now he has turned his eye upon me, and I am terrified.

Tallis slowly reached for the last scroll on the desk, the one he found next to the tablet. There were only two short entries in the last journal. The first one puzzled Tallis.

I don't like Across the Sea.

Tallis looked up at the blue waters now touched with waning rays of sun. Did he speak of the Galilee? Or the Mediterranean, the real sea far beyond the Galilee? What didn't he like across the sea? And why? Tallis's squint left the lake, and fell on the last line Polonus wrote.

They are coming for me.

Tallis stared a moment at the words, then slowly rose. He should roll up the scrolls, put them back neatly, arrange everything so that . . .

He hurried to the cylindrical container in the corner and gathered the scrolls. He didn't bother with the scroll carriers on the peg, and when he fled, didn't even shut the door behind him.

VIII

Tallis came into the kitchen from the back entrance. Samir had told him Zagreus was still sleeping in the barn, but Kes had gone into the inn.

He was glad to have had that half-hour walk from Polonus's home to let the flight-fear settle into something more manageable. He felt calm as he stood in the kitchen, comforted by the sight of dirty dishes on the worktable and the greasy charcoal smell of the brazier.

Kes hurried in from the common room, paused when she saw him. She went to the worktable and began to quickly slice a loaf of bread.

"Where did you go?" she asked, not looking at him.

"To talk with Polonus."

"You should have told me you were going; I'd have sent the basket with you." She arranged the bread on a plate and then took the plate to a large crock on the floor against the wall. She removed the lid and took a handful of olives from the crock, letting the brine drain through her fingers, then put the olives on the plate.

Tallis eased onto the stool at the worktable. His ribs had had enough for the day. "He's not there. Looks like he hasn't been there for a few days." Did she know about the record Polonus was keeping on her brother? "I would like you to tell me about him."

Kes unwrapped a block of cheese and cut a hunk from it. "What do you want to know?"

"Anything you do."

"I'll be right back." She arranged the hunk of cheese on the plate and took it to the common room.

She wasn't right back. Tallis leaned on his stool to see. The place was beginning to fill with hungry people for midmeal. Arinna was nowhere to be seen. Kes spoke rapidly with her father, who wasn't happy at her words. With his back to the customers, Jarek's face deepened to a glower as he listened. It cleared instantly when he turned to the guests. He spoke with them as he reached for his apron behind the corner counter. Jarek never worked in the inn during the day.

Kes flew back to the kitchen and pointed to the loaves of bread on the worktable. "Hurry, cut those loaves, not too thick. We have a delegation to Damascus from Jerusalem. Ten people."

It took a moment to realize she was speaking to him. He reached for the knife and pulled a loaf over.

"I don't care if she's gone," Kes muttered as she quickly took down a stack of bowls from the cupboard. "I don't care, I'm glad. She never acted like a mother to him. If she comes for him I'll—" But she left it unsaid, and stirred the stew in the pot on the brazier.

The brazier was a long narrow trough set into the wall, with a long grate over it. Half of the brazier was for grilling meat; a thick patina of many meals coated that part of the grating, with dried drips clinging to the underside. The other half of the brazier was for pot cooking. An extension at that end was a work surface. Kes quickly set out bowls on the extension and began to ladle the stew.

She had tied her hair back with a faded blue cloth since Tallis last saw her asleep in the sweetgrass. She still had a few bits of the grass in her hair. She was barefoot and rose up on her toes to ladle the stew. She wasn't markedly short, but the brazier was high, and the pot was tall. Perhaps her mother had been a tall woman.

Between slicing, he watched her work. She swooped to grab trays from under the worktable and slid them onto the surface. She pulled out a basket and rapidly rummaged through it for napkins. She inspected them for cleanness, tossing dirty ones in the corner. She layered the clean ones in a pile, smoothing each one she placed on top.

She knew this kitchen, she knew her work, and it was evident to see that she took pleasure in it. Not that she smiled, he rarely saw that—only when making Arinna clean up vomit—but in the swift, measured way she worked, he could sense the pleasure it gave her.

Tallis considered the thickness of his slices. He held one up. "Is this all right?"

She glanced and nodded. "Three each. One piece of cheese each."

"What about these little end pieces?" He held up a crust of bread.

"Not for the guests. We eat them or give them to the pigs."

"What will you do if she comes for him?"

She smoothed out the last napkin, picked at a dried something on it and brushed it away, then whisked the basket beneath the table. "I won't give her her son." She began to fold the napkins.

Jarek's anxious face appeared at the doorway. "Kes . . ."

"Two minutes," she replied.

She pushed aside Tallis's loaves and slices until they reached the edge of the table, then laid out the trays.

"Olives?" Tallis asked.

"In the crock, right there. Fill up two bowls from that cupboard."

Tallis fetched the dishes and went to work filling them. He popped an olive into his mouth. "Do you know about Polonus's journals?"

"The scrolls? Yes. He is keeping a record of his work with Kardus. He hopes it will someday help others who suffer from the same . . . malady."

"Have you read any of them?"

She snorted. "I cannot read. Kardus used to read to us. Sometimes I tear off a piece of his favorite scroll and put it in the basket. Polonus told me to stop destroying a good book, because it means nothing to Kardus. I keep hoping it might help him remember what he used to love. Maybe it will remind him of us."

"Kes—I read some of the scrolls." He hesitated. "I think you should know some of the things I read."

"We must speak of it later."

"Where do you think Polonus could be?"

"Probably out with Kardus. Tallis, I can't talk about it right now."

She took the bowls filled with stew and began to hurry them to the trays on the worktable.

"His door was closed. The fire pit was cold. Kardus was alone."

"You saw Kardus?"

"Briefly, yes."

"Were you frightened?"

Tallis glanced up from the crock. "Briefly. Yes." Now wasn't the time to tell her of the effect of that meeting, that for a few moments he went blind. He still did not understand it.

Suddenly she said in surprise, "Tallis." She looked at his nose and his eye, still slightly swollen. "You should sit, you should . . . you shouldn't have gone to see Polonus. What were you thinking?" She reached for the olive dishes. "How do you feel?"

He moved the dishes out of her reach and put them on the trays.

"I'm fine. You tied me tighter than an Egyptian mummy. Maybe my ribs are only bruised."

"What's a mummy?"

"A bound dead person."

"Tallis, why did you go see Polonus?"

"Let's get the trays out there." He helped finish loading the trays with bowls of stew, and added spoons, baskets of bread, and the dishes of olives. Kes took the napkins and a platter with sliced cheeses; Tallis took two trays and followed her into the common room.

For the next hour he filled cups with Kes and Jarek, he joked with a few of the customers, he fetched more bread or specially requested herbs. It felt like home. It felt like serving Callimachus. Well, and wasn't he now in the employ of Kes and her father? One customer asked what happened to his eye, and he hooked his thumb at Kes. She saw him do it, and for the first time he heard her laugh.

She refused to let him wash the dishes with her. Instead, she handed him an amphora of wine and a fine silver cup and told him to go to his place by the lake. She said she'd join him when the delegation for Damascus had left. When he glanced over his shoulder on the way out the kitchen door, she was watching him go.

It wasn't comfortable to sit slouched in the chair. After enjoying a cup of truly fine and undiluted rich wine, Tallis laid himself out on the sun-warmed boulder. The breeze came down from the eastern heights to sweep over the lake, and it was cool with leftover winter. Prickles rose on his skin, but the sun was warm. He couldn't relax, though; his middle felt too tight. He fought with the wrappings and loosened them a bit.

He felt for the piece of parchment in his pocket and held it against the slanting rays of the sun. *If there is no hope for him, there is no hope for anyone.* The oil stains made some of the ink smear. He rested the scrap on his stomach.

Kes had told him Polonus was devoting himself to righting a wrong. He was trying to reverse what had happened to Kardus, trying to make it right. He had left everything to dwell with a lunatic. Three years he had lived with Kardus. Gods, what was that like? How could he dwell daily with that presence Tallis felt on the slope? He'd be mad himself, inside a week. What sort of a man was Polonus to hold out against the madness for three years? Or was Tallis himself simply weak?

Tallis fiddled with the scrap. He knew that presence. It was enough to trouble him into next week. He knew Kardus from his force. He knew it from the Theban hillside, knew it from different times in his life. He had felt it in the chicken yard when he woke up.

He had been stained with it, like this parchment, stained in his studies when he learned of the deep atrocities of the Maenads. Every time he read of their horrors he felt an assault on the innocence first molested in the grove. Reading of it left him defeated at the depravity in the world. Tallis was not an innocent man, but encounters with the orange presence were always a lecherous lunge toward an innocent place within. If it went there, if it violated that one place, in that moment he would die. Worse, like Kardus, he would live.

Once he was in a marketplace in Athens, hunting down peppercorns for the cook. He paused suddenly in the press of the crowd, and a dread came upon him. It was unaccountable, illogical, this nightmare feel in the broad of day.

There was a distant confusion, growing in its babble. He had let the crowd jostle around him as he stood still. Then he began to look around, with fear seeking the source of daytime darkness, and finally saw across the marketplace an old man. He looked as unlikely as the fellow standing next to him, but Tallis knew this was the man, as if he were a single red poppy in a field of white.

So far away, he knew him. So far away, he recognized him. It was the stench. He felt the odor, felt vulnerable to it, this putrescence marauding his senses. He was assailed where he stood at an impossible distance apart. It was not possible to *feel* an odor, yet he did. He felt in the odor what he had felt in the Theban grove, and terror held him hostage.

It seemed the old man should sense Tallis the way Tallis sensed him, but he never looked his way. He picked his way through the crowd, and, yes, Tallis saw the way others turned troubled looks upon him. Some, confused, looked past him as if what they felt did not go with what they saw. Others were aware of the force then—if only a few—and in this Tallis had found great comfort.

As he lay on the sun-warmed rock, warmed without by the sun and within by the wine, he wondered about that old man. Wondered what was his end, if he ever came to it, and wondered what was his beginning.

Seabirds dipped and cried over the Galilee before a limitless blue sky. The breeze brought not a stench but a fresh smell of water and fish, and from the inn, the smell of the charcoal. Tallis drowsed into a stupor.

Distant confusion, growing in its babble.

I am here.

A dark form backlit by the sun. In a monstrous metal squeal it creaks open its cavernous mouth, and reveals within deep treacherous blackness. He hears pandemonium rise from the well, sees flashes of yellow-green light. He hears echoing torment, as if from a thousand beings slowly disemboweled, humans, animals, fell creatures; ragged voices blended into one hellish misery.

Dread images fill his mind, fair agonized faces and rotting corpses and black winged things, melded in sticky amalgam. The fair faces, hopeless with knowledge; the grotesque faces, surprised by suffering.

Tallis lay at the bottom of the slope, and Kardus slid toward him in a black boiling mass, his cavernous mouth open wide.

Help—!

The force lunged for the sacred place. . . .

Help me—!

Kardus could not touch him, could not touch him; if he did he would . . .

. . . the presence touched him, and Tallis went blind.

He knew rape. He knew invasion as dry scrabbling claws from the mouth of Kardus pried him open, tearing, gouging, frantic for the place.

He now heard voices in the bedlam from the black cavern, distinguished agonies. One voice rose above all, a crooning singsong of despair, and he saw his mother.

Tallis! Why are you here? Run, Tallis! Far from this place!

Black claws ravaged for the sacred place, and he lifted his head and howled.

He couldn't see. Couldn't move. Where was he?

"Wake up!"

WE WILL END YOUR AGONY, POOR MAN, POOR MAN, SAY YES SAY YES SAY YES!

IT WILL ALL END IF YOU JUST SAY YES!

HOW LONG WE HAVE WAITED FOR THIS! GIVE US YOUR YES, POOR MAN . . .

Say yes. The plunging will go away. The digging will end. The torment will cease.

The fight would be over.

"Tallis! Wake up!"

Pinpricks of pain, of awareness. He tried to speak; it came out slurred.

WHORE! GRAY SLUG OF A HUMAN, THIS IS OUR BUSINESS!

YOU'RE NEXT, SISTER OF MADMAN, DAUGHTER OF MAENAD!

Suddenly—shrieking. Wails of despair.

HE COMES!

WE GO!

The babble of voices retreated, angry and sullen.

"Tallis, Tallis!" Kes was shaking him. Jarek was beside her, clutching her shoulder, peering anxiously. Samir, with Zagreus under his arm, came striding up. The slave was chanting or cursing.

Full face slaps, one after the other, until Tallis fumbled for her wrist.

She saw him rouse and seized his face, looking anxiously into his eyes. Her own eyes were red, her face livid with emotion. She searched his eyes until Jarek pulled her back to look himself. Kes turned away to weep quietly into her apron.

Jarek was angry. It was the first honest emotion Tallis had seen in him. The innkeeper was alarmed, and the alarm angered him. After searching Tallis's face, the innkeeper turned away and went to look at the hills, the northern hills. He watched with his fists on his hips, and then dropped his head. Tallis heard him curse softly.

That's how I feel, Jarek, Tallis thought. *Once again, flat on my back, helpless and shamed. Don't I feel the fool.*

Samir, with a squirming Zagreus under his arm, squatted beside Tallis and took his chin. Tallis caught his musky odor, strange spicy oils and sweat, and the barn. He looked long into Tallis, dark eyes searching until he was satisfied.

What safety did Tallis find in those dark searching eyes? Only now did relief wash over him. Samir smelled like the barn. He smelled *human.*

The slave waited, and Tallis found he had the strength to nod. Samir rose then and left with Zagreus under his arm, softly chanting in a tribal lilt. It was almost like a song, but the dark look to accompany it was far from songlike. Jarek, after a moment, followed the slave.

Tallis tried to rise but had to lie helpless on the boulder. He felt naked.

Kes's weeping had softened to stillness. He was embarrassed to lie close to her, unable to move, and the embarrassment strengthened him. *Let no one help you rise.* Trembling with the effort, he pulled himself to a sitting position. Face pounding, inflamed with shame and fear, he stared unseeing at the waters of the Galilee.

"Kardus came, a few moments ago," she said in a soft trembling voice. "Some cannot be around him. He does that to Zagreus. He did it to the shaman. One of our guests, a little girl, had a horrible fit. He has put a cloak on the village, on the whole region. Some feel it and some don't. And I fear for Polonus, because he used to be so strong. He is beginning to change."

You have no idea.

His mouth was so dry he could not speak; he felt like he had chewed flour. He looked for the amphora. Kes saw and searched for his cup. She poured the wine, but instead of placing it in his hands, she held it to his lips. His cheeks flushed but he drank. She wiped his lips with her fingers, set the cup in his hands in his lap.

"You cannot be around him. He will hurt you."

Tallis knew it was so.

"I feel a lure to the hills," he whispered. "Since I've been here."

A lure stronger than the strongest sexual desire he had ever felt, stronger than the thing he had wanted most, the death of the Maenads. A lurid pull. He felt promise in it. He wanted it, foul as he knew it was. Wrong as he knew it was. Was he a bad man, then? Attracted to evil? Where was that stirring he felt, that indignation? Why had it settled to obscurity? Why didn't it rise to confront?

"Some come to see the lunatic because they are cruel and want to taunt him. They throw things at him, they hurt him, and I hate them." She was looking down into her lap, and her hair covered her face. It didn't sound like she was crying, but Tallis saw tears drip into her lap. "Some think they can help him, and they fail. Polonus will fail. I used to be terrified he'd leave. Now I can't get him to leave, and I'm so afraid for him. He's changing and he doesn't see it. Worse, he doesn't care."

He felt the warmth of the face slaps, and he looked at Kes. She pulled her hair behind her head and caught his look.

Dark brown auburn hair. Light brown eyes with their elusive green. Her face had freckles and strong lines. Honest lines. The furrow in her brow softened as he continued to study her while she retied her hair with the cloth. She was so pragmatic. Hard-nosed and sensible, not like a lot of the nymphy Greek flutter byes who came to Cal's estate to try and win his heart—they thought a vast depository of wisdom meant money. How different was this woman from those. He had a flash of Aristarchus, who rubbed the nose of nonsense into its own rot.

"What keeps you safe?" he asked.

"I've wondered that. Maybe it's because I'm his sister."

"What if it runs in the family?"

"I hope not."

He wet his lips. "How is Polonus changing?"

She sighed. She peeked in his cup, and he handed it to her. She took a long sip. "Have you ever had this warmed? With cinnamon and ginger? Some ground cloves? It's a fine drink on a winter night. The guests love it, even the big men with their ale." She circled her finger on the rim.

"I feel a distance in Polonus. Never used to. I try to let him know he has friends. I try to hold on to him. We used to talk, but he doesn't talk anymore. He picks up the basket and leaves. Kardus is changing him, and I wonder—" Her breath caught in a sudden gasp, and her tone went higher and fainter. "I wonder if the villagers are right. If it would be better to take him down with an arrow than let him take others. We're trying to rescue a drowning man, but we don't know how to swim."

Tallis could not answer, because he thought maybe she was right. The shackles said somebody loved him; they were shackles—hard and cruel, but they prevented him from hurting himself and others. And those shackles could not hold him anymore, maybe as their love couldn't hold him—no matter how much they loved him. Hurt was the only conclusion. Hurt to himself, and a world of hurt to others. Take him down—it sounded sensible.

He'd wanted to take the Maenads down so they couldn't hurt anybody anymore. Aristarchus had approved of it, and Aristarchus was sensible. He scratched his neck. On this, Callimachus and Aristarchus disagreed. The Maenads were capable of great evil, and in some cases were proved in it—while most eluded justice for lack of evidence or fears of reprisal; others had been executed for their crimes. Aristarchus called it a good end to a bad beginning. But Callimachus said it would not end. He said to challenge the Maenads was to spit in the wind; challenge, instead, what moved them—only then would real change occur.

How does a mortal challenge a god?

The man who does not fight the gods should not live. Fine, stout words— but Polonus was losing his god-fight.

How far does a person go before he calls it? When would Polonus know it was time to walk away? Would he walk away in time? Maybe Polonus had to go sooner than Kes thought. Or maybe it was time Polonus had some help.

"A rabid dog can do a world of hurt," Kes said softly.

"Yes, it can." He pinched his lip. Would Polonus welcome the help?

"You have to take it down before it kills. I understand the way they think."

Tallis dropped his hand to look at her. "Kardus is no dog."

She circled her finger on the rim of the cup. "I know. I know."

"It's a fight and you're strong. After all this time you're still strong."

Her finger stilled. "I wonder how that is. Maybe it's because I'm his sister, and I know who he really is. I know that no matter what he acts like, it isn't him. He would hate what he has become." She was silent. "I hope he doesn't know."

How could he help Polonus when he couldn't even be around Kardus? He crippled Tallis. "I want to tell you I will be strong for you. But I'm not like you."

"You have a strength you do not know of," she said with sudden earnest. "I know this. I feel it, and so does Samir. They wouldn't hate you so much. They wouldn't try for you so hard. This hasn't happened before. No one like you has been here before."

They? How did she know it was like that?

"You've seen how I am. You've seen my—weakness."

"Yes—that's where it is. Tied up with that very thing. Polonus said the same great capacity for evil is the same great capacity for good."

"He got that from Callimachus." He debated, and before the debate was over, he suddenly said, "I want to help Polonus. Maybe I'm meant to. I don't think I'm going back to Athens."

A whisper of a smile came, which she quickly suppressed. She looked to the waters. "What do we do now?"

Excitement began to stir. He went to rise because he liked to pace as he thought, but he was too stiff and sore. "I have no idea. I want to meet with Polonus. I want to know where it all started in the Decaphiloi— where did it go wrong? Cal has always said you won't find the answer at the end; it's in the beginning."

"Tallis . . . it started long before the Decaphiloi."

"Callimachus needs to know about this. I'll send a letter. Maybe he could come. He could come help us! Think of it. Maybe even Aristarchus." The thought of the two of them in the common room gave him a grin of joy. "Oh, Kes, you would like Cal. Samir would like him too. He is so wise. He said go back to where pain began. If you want truth, go back to the beginning." He clenched his fists. "If only we could meet with every member of the Decaphiloi."

"It didn't *start* with the Decaphiloi. Aren't you listening? It started with my mother, and with her mother. How far back do you want to go? Shoshanna knows about my mother's family. The Decaphiloi was only a jumping-off place for Kardus. It only went from bad to worse." She paused. "The evil was there, waiting for him, as it's there for all of us. The difference is, he made a place for it, long before he ever met Portia. She only completed what was started in him. Maybe it's Shoshanna we need to talk to. Maybe even my father."

"Were Portia and Kardus close?"

"He didn't speak of it, not to me, but from what Polonus has hinted at, they were lovers. Maybe the part of him that wasn't yet bad was look-ing for a place to *be* bad, and found it in Portia." She shuddered. "She is worse than Kardus. Kardus has lost his mind, but she hasn't. You don't think she would actually hurt Zagreus, do you? She loves him."

He rubbed his forehead. He felt at once agitated and ornery. "The question is when. And where. If they knew the truth of the human sacri-fices, all good men would rise up and put an end to the Maenads. Do you know what happened to a king in Scythopolis? In your Beth Shean, where Dionysus dwells? I read in Herodotus that the Scythian king, Scytes, became a devotee of Dionysus . . . and he was driven out and killed by his own people because they saw him dancing in a frenzy with the Bacchic rout. *They* knew what this unholy alliance meant—that the very office of the king now made way for the murder of their own chil-dren. And they rose up, like Lycurgus, in the *Iliad*. He drove Dionysus and his nurses into the sea with the oxgoad. And do you know? They went. They went, because one man stood against them. One man would not put up with them."

"A strong man," Kes murmured.

"It would have to be," Tallis said darkly. "And Polonus is not strong enough. Not anymore."

"The *Iliad* is story, some say."

"And Herodotus is *history*. Besides—there is truth in story."

"Truth or wishful thinking?"

"Both."

Tallis wanted to tell her, but he couldn't. He wanted to talk about his own beloved Zagreus, but he couldn't say what he had seen, couldn't say what his own mother had done. But the talk wouldn't stay in his head.

"I saw the mountaintop ritual, Kes. I was there. A child was torn apart right in front of my eyes. But everyone thought I was the crazy one. You see, I went to our village and screamed what I saw, but nobody believed me because it was too horrifying. Nobody believed me when I said my brother was dead—they didn't believe I had a brother. Mother had kept his existence a secret. No . . . they didn't believe me, because Apamea would never do such a thing. They thought I was the mad one. And truly, my mind left me for a time.

"Not even my father knew he had another son. He was in the army, on campaign. When he came home on leave, she hid Zagreus from him. Sent him to her friends until he left again. She had told me never to speak of Zagreus to him, because Father would hurt him. She told me he would believe he was from another man, and I believed her because she was my mother. It wasn't until later that I understood what she had done."

Kes took his hand and brought it to her lap.

"Now I know that Father, harsh as he was, would have saved Zagreus's life if he had known. He was good under the harshness. He brought me things from the places he'd been. He stayed on campaign because he didn't understand Mother. You know what the worst is? She planned it, Kes. I don't know how a mother could do that."

Kes gripped his hand.

Her face, flushed with loveliness and joy. Dancing the elegant steps. "She killed my little brother, and I couldn't save him. I didn't know what they were going to do. How could I? How could I think they would do something like that? How could it enter my mind? They were just dancing, and it was lovely. And then I tried to tell the world, and the world did not believe me, and it did not care."

She brought his hand to her face and held it against her damp cheek. She kissed his hand over and over, and he felt her tears run down his arm.

"That's how the Maenads got away with it—no one knew Zagreus existed. And they will continue to murder, and dance the beautiful dances of the Bacchantes, and hide behind the acceptable mask of Dionysus, good old Dionysus. And I only spit in the wind."

"Do you hate your mother?" she whispered against his hand.

"I don't know." He considered it. "I haven't thought about it. That part of me is dead."

She kissed his hand one more time, lowered it to her lap, and released it. She wiped her face with the end of her haircloth, and when she was done and rested her hands in her lap once more, Tallis took her hand to his own lap. He needed her touch.

"What about your father?"

"He died years ago, on campaign."

"Is your mother alive?"

Run, Tallis!

"I—don't know. I don't think so." He heard a slight hiss of breath from Kes, looked at her, looked at his lap—he'd gripped her hand so tightly her fingertips were purple. He instantly released her hand, then grabbed it back to gently rub away the hurt he'd inflicted. "I'm sorry."

He looked at her. "Kes, where is Polonus? We must find him."

She watched him gently knead her fingers. A little color crept to her cheeks, and she slipped her hand from his. "He'll be back. He always comes back."

"What about the basket for Kardus?"

"Samir will bring it." Her eyes, still shining with tears, now glittered. "They hate Samir."

He didn't like it that he knew exactly what she was talking about. He took the cup and drained it. "What about Samir? Why am I safe when I'm around him? What's his story?"

Kes shrugged. "Father bought him at the slave market in Antioch years ago."

"Where is he from? Who are his people?"

"He is Parthian. The Parthians are like nomads, only much fiercer. They have Persian blood—"

"I know about Parthians—politically, that is. What does he believe? Who are his gods?"

But Kes only shrugged. Tallis soon forgot about Samir as he paid attention to the new excitement within. Would he really stay and help Polonus? Aristarchus would take care of Cal.

"How are your ribs?"

"Sore. Kes—what do think about calling the Decaphiloi for a meeting?"

"You tried that, didn't you? Only Julia showed up, and one of the Decaphiloi wants you back in Athens."

"It would have to be something big to draw them out. Something— dire." He turned eagerly to Kes. "Let's do it. We'll summon the remnants of the Decaphiloi for a meeting in four days. It's perfect, because the Festival of Dionysus is in five days. Memories will be strong. They'll all be thinking about Portia."

"Tallis . . . what do you hope will happen at this meeting?"

"I want to stir up an adder's nest."

"What if Portia comes?"

"All the better. Well—if Samir's around." Samir, the living amulet. The mooring line lashed to solid land.

"How will we get them to come?"

Tallis frowned. "I'll post a message in the forum. Tomorrow morning. That will give them three days to find out. And, ho, they'll find out. I'm sure they all have friends. Post a message for the world to read, and the world will read."

"But what will you say?"

Whatever it was, it had to be good. "I don't know," he finally admitted. "But I'll work on it. Starting now."

"You—Tallis," Jarek called from the top of the path. "You work for me or not?"

It took a moment for Tallis to remember his recently humble state. He grimaced. "I guess I'll start later," he murmured to Kes. He rose slowly and stood as upright as he could. He called to Jarek, "I work for you. You need some Latin translated to Greek?"

Jarek squinted at him warily, and grumped something Tallis couldn't hear as he turned around. Tallis hurried after him, calling out that he was only kidding.

IX

Early the next day Tallis went to Hippos. He first went to the finest bathhouse. Then he visited a stall in the marketplace. Then he went straight to the message boards in the forum.

He put a piece of parchment in front of the scribe and told him to copy it in bold letters on the scraped leather. While the scribe carefully printed the new message, and it took a while because it was long, Tallis removed the old. He purchased six blank messages, so the empty pieces of leather surrounding the new message would set it off like a—red poppy in a field of white. Then he went to look up Lysias.

He found the slave in the public slave quarters behind the military barracks at the western gate, throwing dice with some soldiers. Lysias wasn't pleased to see him until he saw the coin. He listened to what Tallis had to say and tucked the silver coin in his belt—making sure the soldiers didn't see reason for another round of dice.

Tallis could not resist reading his message one more time. It was a good piece and had taken a long time to get right. If he stood in front of the boards to read it not once but three times, and if he stood off watching others read it, well, the piece deserved it. No one had ever purchased six blank messages to set off one; Tallis could see it from where he stood on the bottom step of the temple of Athena, in the very place where the Decaphiloi had met three years earlier.

He sat on the step and rested his arms easy on his knees. The sun warmed his bones, and the view from the top of the diamond-shaped mountain of Hippos was a fine view indeed. He'd just spent his last coin bribing a slave to spread the word among the subculture of Hippos that any member of the Decaphiloi had best check to see the new message posted on the forum board. He was utterly broke and wearing a tunic, and he thought maybe tonight he might catch Kes alone in the kitchen and tell her exactly what he thought of her. He felt lighter than he had in weeks.

A small crowd was gathering at the message board. He watched one young man, a lad from the theater, he guessed, read the message and run off. He watched another man read the message not once, but twice, and he too hurried off. Presently he returned with none other than the pie-faced magistrate who worked in the public rental offices.

Kes? Do you know how I feel when you dignify that child with work? You dignify me. Do you know how I feel when I see that basket, filled with food for Polonus and Kardus? It fills my own emptiness. Do you know how I feel when I see your guilt and grief over a brother you're sure is lost? Sorrow for you, because sometimes you love, and your love doesn't change a thing, and there is nothing you can do about it, Kes.

Do you know what I have learned from you and Jarek? I can't say it exactly, but I feel it when I see the basket, and the shackles hanging in the barn. You said your father was weak. It's not a weak thing to shackle your own son.

Tallis rose and went to the message boards one more time, and, yes, he enjoyed the astonished murmurs from the people who read. He was astonished too. It was the hardest thing he'd ever had to write. After vicious cursing that did not help, and inventive cursing that only distracted him, after whipping his sandal across the room, which took out the terracotta lamp, and after explaining to Kes what the ruckus was all about, he'd finally dropped, defeated, on the stool at the desk. He'd tried to come up with something big enough to draw the Decaphiloi out, and came to only this: the truth. And as he watched the crowd grow around the message board, he realized the truth was big enough.

THERE IS A MAN IN THE TOMBS OF KURSI, AND HE IS CAP-
TIVE TO MADNESS. THREE YEARS THE MAN POLONUS HAS
RISKED HIS SANITY TO HELP. AND I WONDER—WHERE
ARE THE REST OF THE DECAPHILOI, THE LEAGUE OF TEN
FRIENDS? WELL, ONE WAS MURDERED, AND HIS NAME WAS
THESEUS. ONE MURDERED HIMSELF, HIS NAME WAS BION.
ONE CALLED FOR HELP, HER NAME IS JULIA. ONE TRIED,
BUT GAVE UP, HIS NAME IS ANTENOR. THREE I'VE NOT
HEARD FROM, THEIR NAMES ARE LUCIUS, HECTOR, AND
MARCUS. PORTIA, YOU ALL KNOW. MY OWN NAME IS
TALLIS, AND THREE DAYS FROM THIS AT NOON, I WILL
MEET THE DECAPHILOI AT THE INN-BY-THE-LAKE, SOUTH
OF KURSI, ON THE ROAD TO DAMASCUS. THIS IS A FORUM
FOR TRUTH, FOR WHICH THE ACADEMY OF SOCRATES
ONCE STOOD—AS CALLIMACHUS ONCE CALLED YOU BY
NAME, SO I NAME YOU AND CALL FOR TRUTH. AS FOR THE
MAN WHO LIVES IN THE TOMBS? HE ALSO HAS A NAME. IT
IS NEITHER MADMAN, NOR LUNATIC, NOR DEMONIAC OF
THE GERASENES. HE IS KARDUS.
KARDUS.

Tallis adjusted his new ink pot on the writing desk. He liked two
kinds of ink but settled for one; it was all he could get for trading the
last of his expensive bath oil from Athens.

He had the good sense to take his unguent to the best bathhouse in
Hippos and the better sense to drive a hard bargain with an attendant
who knew quality. He bought another stylus and a waxed wooden tablet.
He didn't purchase picking nibs, but instead got a sharpened nail from
Samir, because he was now a poor man and would make do. He was
rather proud of this concession, and felt the fine glow of sacrifice.

He had no dowels to roll and unroll the papyrus, but he could make
those—couldn't he? Resourceful poor man that he was? Samir could
help him find the right wood, and he'd whittle them himself. This
thought pleased him, and the prospects of being poor did not seem so
abominable right now. He had a filthy toga but a clean tunic. He had a

mug filled with water, a plate with two slices of Kes's spiced bread, and the scrolls he'd borrowed from Polonus.

He idled with a stylus as he gazed at the waters of the Galilee. He had purpose again, and this time it was not to destroy but to heal. The purpose felt right, and when he looked at the scrolls laid out on his cot, he knew a gratitude so sharp it was almost painful. The chance to help another from a madness he had tasted . . . it made him feel spacious inside. The chance to help the brother of one for whom he was beginning to care, it felt good inside. And to do what Callimachus had set out to do when he founded his academies: to seek truth, to learn truth . . . it felt like a gift. Together he and Polonus would discover what had happened to Kardus. They would go back to the beginning for understanding; there they would find the truth, tangled perhaps in pain and lies, and they would carefully sort it out. Truth, then, would bring understanding and understanding, liberation. Logic says if there is a way into madness—

A knock came.

Tallis snapped, "Who is it?"

"You work for me or not?"

Tallis pinched the place between his eyes. "I work for you. You need some Latin translated to Greek?"

"That was funny once."

"You didn't laugh."

"You didn't hear me. I got some guests in from Sobol; they need their horses curried."

Tallis gazed at the fine setup on his writing table. He dropped the stylus into the vase. "Yes . . . master."

Having never curried a horse in his life, because Callimachus did not own horses and the only horse he'd petted was his father's military-issue nag, Tallis looked at the crusty sweat on the reeking mouse-colored hide, looked at the brush in his hand, and wondered what he was supposed to do with it. Maybe brushing horsehair was not far from brushing the dirt out of a good toga. He tried out different positions with the brush before he started.

Jarek came and gently took the brush from him. Before Tallis could protest, Jarek said, "Look—Arinna is gone and gods know when she's going to return, and"—he glanced about for Zagreus—"if she doesn't, we're glad. But Kes is the one who needs help running things inside, and it seems to me you're better at that. No offense."

"None taken. Believe me."

"You did good with the guests the other day. You've got a pleasant way about you. Folks like that. It's the most important part of running an inn, making them feel good to be here."

Tallis watched a moment as Jarek worked the brush over the animal in firm, fluid strokes. He liked the sound the brush made on the animal's hide, and it seemed as though the horse enjoyed the brushing. Jarek felt him watching and paused. He looked over the horse's back at Tallis, and his look was weary, as if to say *What now, Athenian?*

Tallis didn't remember looking in Jarek's eyes for long, except when he was flat on his back in a miserable state. The innkeeper's eyelids were saggy, and his dark eyes were large and had oldness in them. His face was heavy. His head was mostly bald, but for the black feathery fringe on the sides, like a low Olympic wreath.

"You're going to help Polonus, aren't you?" Jarek said, and added, "Kes says."

Being an innkeeper had to be a tricky occupation. On days you did not feel gracious, you had to be gracious. On days you did not care, you had to act as though you did. Maybe Kes thought her father was weak. But maybe the innkeeper part had bled over into the father and husband part, and maybe it was Kes's mother he'd tried hard to please and accommodate. It wasn't right, maybe, but looking in his eyes Tallis could understand the man a little. Maybe he'd tried to act like a husband when he didn't feel like it. Like a father when it was hard. Did it make him weak? Tallis saw strength. Maybe not the kind Kes wanted, but strength was there. Innkeepers had to be a tough lot.

"I'll try to help Polonus as best as I can. But you know I have a certain . . . weakness of mind. Or soul. I don't know what it is. I don't know how far I can go."

"I only know you want to help my boy. Nobody else does." He bent to his brush strokes again.

Tallis started for the kitchen and stopped. He couldn't get the image of those shackles out of his heart. Couldn't imagine what that must be like, shackling your own son. Couldn't imagine being that loved. Not quite turning around, he said, "I am honored to be in your employ."

He didn't hear anything for a moment, then heard steady brush strokes again.

Tallis kicked off dirt from the barn and washed his hands in the bucket outside. He wiped them on his tunic as he came in, and he stood in the doorway and looked long around the kitchen.

Drying herbs hung upside down over the kitchen window that looked out on the chicken yard. Across the room Kes had her back to him, arranging charcoal in the brazier with tongs. In the middle of the room was the good solid worktable, with a shelf beneath filled with kitchen things, and the right side of the kitchen had cupboards and shelves. The left side had more cupboards, and a shelf lined with crockery. Past the shelf was a curtained alcove filled with stores. It was no ordinary kitchen; it was the kitchen of a busy inn, and Tallis liked the smell of this place. It was becoming familiar to him.

Zagreus leaned on the worktable over little cups filled with different seeds. He was sprinkling sesame seeds over the flatbread that would go into the oven in the kitchen yard. He looked up at Tallis. That child would favor Kes more than he ever favored his own mother, and Tallis felt it was a gift from the gods. No wonder he'd taken the boy for Kes's son.

"Mistress Kes says you work for Master Jarek now," Zagreus said in his bright little-boy voice.

Tallis wasn't used to being around children. The tone was so small he first thought it an affectation, until he remembered he was a child.

"That I do. You have anything to say about it?"

"I'm glad!"

Tallis laughed in surprise and went to fetch an apron. He kept his attention fastened on Zagreus as he tied on the apron and said, "Well—do you think Mistress Kes is glad?"

"Oh, I know it."

They looked at Kes, who refused to turn around from the brazier. Tallis crept over and leaned to see, and said in a loud whisper to Zagreus, "Red cheeks. She's glad."

"It's the charcoal," she said flatly. "Don't flatter yourself."

"Too late," Tallis said. "Well, Kes, I'm officially assigned kitchen and guest duty. Jarek says he can't take any more of my incompetence in the barn. He kicked me out, threw the horse brush at me—he even swore at me."

Zagreus's eyes widened.

"You mean you didn't hear it?"

Zagreus shook his head, still wide-eyed.

Tallis put his hands on his hips and nodded grimly.

"What did he say?" Zagreus asked.

Tallis glanced at Kes and whispered conspiratorially, "I'll tell you later. Women shouldn't hear such things."

"Master Tallis?" He pointed to Tallis's mouth. "I like that little space."

Tallis stuck out his upper teeth. "This one? You know quality when you see it. I've won every spitting contest in Greece. People came from miles around to see me—even Emperor Tiberias came. He patted my head." Tallis nodded solemnly at Zagreus's stare. "I can even put out kitchen fires."

Kes laughed. "Don't believe such tales, little boy."

"Can you show me sometime?" the child said eagerly.

Tallis said, "Are you planning to start a fire?"

"No . . . I just want to see how far you can spit."

"Sure."

"Maybe we can have a contest."

"Wouldn't be fair." Tallis shrugged.

"I don't mind."

Zagreus suddenly smiled at Tallis, his little mind obviously wandering to something else. Tallis wasn't used to children, but he enjoyed being around them. Occasionally a guest at the estate would bring along a child. While the guest spoke with Callimachus, Tallis and the cook would entertain the child in the kitchen. Sometimes Aristarchus joined in. They had as much fun as the child. Tallis discovered the dour Aristarchus could make children laugh more than anyone else.

"I hope my mother never comes back."

"Zagreus," Kes gasped. She set the tongs on the sideboard and went to the boy. "Don't say that."

He looked up at her, bewildered. "Why not?"

"There's an honest child," Tallis muttered.

"Because she's your mother."

"I don't like her. I like you." He went back to his bread. He took a pinch of poppy seeds and sprinkled them on the flatbread. He wiped off his hands, then took a pinch of salt. "I like things now."

Seemed Kes didn't know what to do with him. She smoothed down his hair, then briefly hugged him to her apron. Softly she said, "A little more salt, lad."

He added more and tidied his flatbread, then eased it onto a baking stone. Carefully he lifted it from the table and carefully went out the kitchen door.

They stood in silence, Kes gazing at the seed cups.

"Is this a good time for a kiss?"

Still gazing at the seed cups, Kes grinned. "You say the craziest things." She slid a look at Tallis, and, oh, he liked those dancing eyes. "You'll have to work for it."

"What do I have to do?"

"It's a long list. Common room has to be swept."

"What else?" He moved a little closer to her.

"Porch has to be swept."

"What else?" He moved closer.

Her cheeks flushed and she laughed. "Give me a minute, you're flustering me. It's a *very* long list."

"Where's the broom so I can get started?" He inched closer.

"It's in the—Tallis, go away—it's in the . . . why, it's in the . . . why, I can't remember where it is. . . ."

He kissed her gently, but was so terrified of someone walking in on them it wasn't a long kiss; long enough, though, that when Kes did tell him where the broom was *he* was so flustered it took him five minutes to find it. When he did find it (in plain sight, propped behind the corner counter), he swept the common room with such vigor it kicked up a dust that settled on the tabletops and had Kes chiding him to dust the tables. He set about wiping them.

Kes presently commented in a loud whisper from the kitchen, "You're in debt, you know, kissing me before you earned it. Shameful thing to be in debt."

"I'll work it off."

X

The rest of the day that he had kissed Kes was the happiest day Tallis had known. Happiness is not squandered when it comes to people long bereft of it. They know what to do—hold it gently like a small bird, amazed the bird came to alight, and be pleased to let it stay as long as it will.

He didn't know when he went to bed that evening, shoving the scrolls off his cot, lying down with his hands behind his head to look at the ceiling, that it would be some time before the small bird came to rest in his hands again.

It had been a fine night, serving the guests in the common room, working in the kitchen. When he came into his room, he looked at his newly purchased writing things and the scrolls on the cot, and he felt the bird flutter in his hands. It was easy to forget his newly found purpose when Kes taught him the difference between charcoals—the cheap kind heated the pots; the good kind roasted the meat—or when Jarek put a pleased look on him after he shepherded laughing guests to the door.

Once the guests were gone, he noticed a settling on the house, a not-quite-sadness. Kes and Jarek had long lived and worked in silence, with only the guests to lift them from their taciturn ways with each other. If things were beginning to change at the inn—and they were—it would come slowly.

It had been a good day, the best of his life; and he thought over those good things, held them carefully in his hands, before he went to sleep. Today he had kissed a fine woman; today he made a friend in Jarek. Today he stood at the kitchen threshold and looked around, and felt like he came into purpose more at that moment than this, in looking at the scrolls and remembering the mission for the restoration of Kardus. He thought on Samir, how he protected this family. He thought on Zagreus, how the child would be raised safe and loved, and he felt joy for the child. He thought about the fishermen from the sea, was glad for the way they encouraged Jarek, and looked forward to serving them tomorrow.

Then the small bird flew away.

It was close to midnight, and Arinna bit back a yawn. She wasn't used to being up this late, but all the others were intent on the words of Queen Ariadne. The priestesses of the temple of Dionysus felt excitement in every duty performed these days, even in the midnight rites. Scrubbing pots, working the gardens, rehearsing the choruses, it didn't matter—they exchanged eager glances; they shared happy smiles. The Festival of Dionysus, their mighty god of intoxicated delight, was only three days away. All of Scythopolis prepared for it.

Sprigs of ivy and pine and fig leaves, things dear to Dionysus, began to appear in the homes. Old Dionysian vases were taken out for display; great masks of Dionysus were given pride of place on tables and in entrances. Taverns ordered huge quantities of wine, but the faithful knew Dionysus himself could provide *rivers* of it—Queen Ariadne told of a time when wondrous streams of wine flowed for *seven days* at a temple in Greece! So mighty was his incarnation at the festival that year, so shattering his appearance, that grapevines bloomed and ripened on one and the same day!

The only people who did not festoon their homes with Dionysian emblems were the religious Jews—but Queen Ariadne said they got theirs, many years ago, when Antiochus Epiphanes had enough of their sanctimonious ways. With dripping relish (Queen Ariadne knew how to tell a story) she regaled the initiates with the fate of those who dared defy the glorious incarnation of Dionysus Most Blessed. In righteous anger, King Antiochus stormed their temple in Jerusalem, threw down the affronts to his gods, and set up veneration for them. He introduced the worship of Dionysus and gave the Jews a choice: Worship Dionysus or be killed. He even made the Jews sacrifice *pigs* to Dionysus, right in their own holy temple!

Queen Ariadne could never help laughing at this, so rich the paradox. If an initiate of the Bacchantes didn't quite get the joke, her neighbor let her in; the Jews were forbidden by their God to even *touch* pigs—the pig was a symbol of uncleanness to their God. Then the initiate could laugh along with the rest. How droll was Antiochus Epiphanes!

True, times had changed, and the Jews were no longer forced to be part of the citywide celebrations. One of their people had risen in revolt after the pig incident and kept Antiochus busy with mild civil war. The feeling from that lasted two hundred years, and nobody felt it worthwhile to compel the Jews anymore. Did the smug Jews think to affront their neighbors by refusing to bedeck their homes with the emblems? Who cared? Surely they were made to feel ostracized when the processions frolicked past their homes, and they heard the gaiety and joy and the laughter and the choruses, and saw the dances of the beautiful Maenads. Let them stew in their piousness while the rest of the world celebrated the wild coming of the madcap god from whose presence springs forth—life! And *feeling*! And a torrent of epiphanies!

Arinna twisted a curl around her finger as she listened to Ariadne speak to the initiates. That she was an initiate herself, and not yet one of the venerable nurses, did not bother her in the least—for five years she had held a status not even one of the nurses had. For five years Arinna was spoken of in awed whispers. When she arrived with Ariadne, and when Ariadne introduced her to the women assembled for rehearsal of the choruses, so amazing was their awe of her, so unexpected their intake of breath that Arinna herself gasped. She saw, in that astonishing moment, wonder and veneration—*for herself*. And for the five years she'd spent slopping pigs and waiting tables and keeping on eye on Zagreus, she finally felt recompense, more than in the coin Ariadne gave her. She had lowered her eyes demurely at that first rush of admiration, and felt an intoxication no coin ever purchased, no wine ever stirred.

She never mentioned the coin to any of the priestesses she now met. Arinna was the Keeper of the Divine Child, Guardian of Zagreus Most Blessed, and incidentals like payment for her service seemed too of-this-earth. Money meant nothing to the devotee of Dionysus; all goods were held in common once a priestess entered the vocation. The goods, that is, that the others knew about.

She would not mention the coin, nor the arguments she'd had with Ariadne, nor the times Ariadne had to wheedle, threaten, bully, and menace her to stay at the inn. She missed Demas and others like him. She could never tell them her true divine purpose, and that was frustrating indeed. For five years she was stuck at the inn with no one to talk to, not about real things.

Arinna glanced at the women around her, whose rapt attention was on Ariadne. Of course, Ariadne herself would get the real glory. Arinna was only the Keeper of the Divine Child; Ariadne was his mother.

All the women knew of her sacred and secret, grand and glorious sacrifice. It made Ariadne better than Arinna, who had to change his diapers and wipe his nose, endure his prattle and his nightmares, and act like she loved him. But for Kes, she would have never lived through it; Kes's care for Zagreus made things tolerable.

Arinna was through with the creepy Samir, and with Jarek who never liked her, and most of all with Mistress Kes, whom she'd hated from the start. Maybe Kes had thought she could elevate her swampy little life by associating with a woman who had seen more of the world than the backwater "mistress" could ever hope to see. Arinna let her know right away that wasn't going to happen. If now she thought that maybe it wouldn't have been so bad to bestow on Kes the occasional gracious favor of her attention, as befitted her true and noble station of Divine Keeper, it didn't matter—that part of her life was happily over.

Ariadne had said to make them love Zagreus, and before he was a month old he had won them over. She said their love would protect her child, and it did. No child she knew had more protection than that one did, even, in a freakish sort of way, from Samir. She shuddered when she thought of him, but it was a delicious shudder because that part of her life was over.

Ariadne was adamant about where she wanted her child raised. She wanted him raised in the house of his grandmother, because his grandmother was a Maenad. Maybe she went crazy in the end and took her own life—probably because she was doomed to the life of an innkeeper's wife—but bloodlines were all that mattered to Ariadne. She chose Kardus to be the father of her child because, with his own mother a Bacchante, it surely boded well for his offspring. Well, and the child was a boy, wasn't he? Of course he was; it was fated to be. Dionysus could not come back as a girl.

Arinna shuddered again, and this time it was not enjoyable. Kardus had come to the inn a few times during her stay. Before the madness took him completely, she rather enjoyed the visits. He was good-looking and interesting and rather charming at first. She could hardly believe he was related to Jarek and Kes. He had a glittery way about him, like Demas, yet not like Demas at all.

Demas was gorgeous and seemed to spread his gorgeousness around the minute he walked in the door. Kardus wasn't like that. He was *intense*, a man of glowing secrets. He was certainly much smarter than Demas. He'd visit with his father and watch his own son play on a blanket in the common room. He never knew it was his son, of course; he thought it was simply the bastard child of the servant whom he never acknowledged.

But it wasn't long before Kardus began to change, and then Arinna didn't like it when he came. His face went from open to closed off. He didn't have the lighthearted-Demas look anymore. His intensity became something dark, something wrong, and his glowing secrets no longer interested her—they frightened her. He looked at her once and seemed to see right through her. She felt like she'd told him everything in that one glance. She hated that superior, knowing, *gloating* look. She hated it when he came. She hid behind the door to the guest rooms.

How goes the teaching, Kardus?

Kardus had eyed the common room, wary as a cat, then realized his father asked a question.

Fine.

You know how proud Kes and I—

Where's Samir?

Samir? Out back. Do you want to see him?

No. I feel him.

Are you . . . is everything all right, Kardus?

I miss Portia.

Arinna's ears had pricked at that, and she listened more closely. Part of her job was to make sure the child was never connected to his mother.

Portia . . .

The whore. She says I'm insufferable. She didn't think so before.

Arinna had peered through the crack. Kardus's look was sullen and black.

Sorry to hear that, lad—and watch your foul mouth. How is Polonus?

Insufferable.

Kardus, what is wrong with you?

Why do you say that? Why do I come here? I don't like it here anymore. You're all so small. Can't have a decent conversation with anyone— nobody knows what I'm talking about! I speak, and they look at me with tomfoolery faces, so stupid and dull. I could tear those faces off. There is no one intelligent to speak with anymore. I am alone. Alone.

I don't like the way you're talking, boy.

Most of the visits ended with Kardus storming out, incensed that his family could not understand him, convinced they did not care about him. And one day, Jarek threw him out.

Kes had invited him for supper, but Samir was there too, and had provoked Kardus somehow. Kardus leapt from the table, and when he opened his mouth at Samir it was as if Hades itself poured forth. Arinna shivered, remembering.

He had cursed viciously at Samir, cursed Samir's God with spittle flying and his face ugly crimson. Kes got angry and stood between them, shouting that Kardus was selfish and arrogant and thought only about himself, and why did he never thank them for what they had done for him all those years; couldn't he even say a simple thank-you? Why was he always so selfish?

Kardus went berserk at that. He overturned the table in one move; he heaved a bench across the room. Jarek was dumbfounded, and Kes cowered at his rage. Then he screamed things at her that turned her gray as ash. He claimed that Kes, his own sister, had tempted him to evil . . . he screamed that Kes, his own sister, was a whore, and Samir her lover. He said his own sister would lie on her back for anyone who looked twice, that Jarek likely profited from her trade and that, he, Jarek likely enjoyed it himself. Jarek grabbed him and threw him out then, told him never to come back.

For a time he didn't. Then one day Polonus rushed into the inn and told Jarek and Kes to come quickly. They ran outside and found Kardus in the back of a cart, looking like they had never seen him before. Arinna stood on the porch, and when Zagreus tried to make his way down the steps and see what Mistress Kes was crying about, Arinna snatched him back and watched from a safe distance.

Kardus had pressed himself into the corner of the cart. His face was gray with dark shadows in it. He looked at them all with a cornered animal gaze.

"I've been searching for days," Polonus had cried. "I found him in the tombs! Something is terribly wrong!"

Jarek cried, "Kardus! Kardus, my son, what's wrong?"

Then Kardus spoke, and abominable cold fell upon them.

TAKE US TO THE TOMBS!

Kes screamed, and Arinna backed away, holding Zagreus as a shield. Tears of horror streamed down Jarek's terror-struck face at this strange, strong, chorused voice coming from Kardus.

Polonus leapt into the cart and whipped the horse. The cart bounced away, and the exultant eye of Kardus was on them all. When the pall of his presence had left, and they stood in a wash of shaken relief, they heard a commotion from the barn. The animals were clucking and squealing, barking and braying, and one horrifying sound rose above it all. They found Samir in the chicken yard, flat out on the ground, arms spread wide as if embracing the earth . . . pouring forth such a lamentation of grief that Kes sat on the ground to weep, Jarek hung his head, and Arinna raced for the safety of her room, where she slammed the door behind her and dove beneath her bed.

"Keeper of the Divine Child?" a young woman whispered timidly to her.

Arinna blinked. "Yes—my dear?"

"What was it like?" she asked wistfully. She was about fourteen. Blue eyes in a thin face shone with wonder.

A few who heard the question leaned in for the answer, trying to keep attention on their queen while helpless to prevent attention from the Divine Keeper.

"I can't believe you lived with Dionysus all this time . . . ," one whispered, and she impulsively reached to touch Arinna's sleeve.

"Truly, you were favored. . . ."

"Handmaiden of the Lord of Souls . . ."

"I can't wait for the festival!" another put in with a shiver. "They say his presence begins with the midnight revels . . . I hope he touches me!"

"My friend's cousin fell to the ground in a trance for two days. She said it was like . . ." The girl put her fingers on her lips and glanced around coyly. ". . . Like *sex!*"

Gasps and twitters. They silenced themselves when disapproving eyes looked their way.

When it was safe, someone behind Arinna whispered in tragic awe, "I can't believe she's going to do it."

Pitying eyes fell upon the lovely Ariadne, who was listening to a question from one of the novitiates in the front row.

"So brave, to sacrifice her own child."

"Remember what she said? 'Sacrifice is giving up what you want for what you believe in.'"

"I wrote that down on a parchment."

"So wise . . . so brave."

"Of course—no one was closer to Zagreus than I," Arinna sighed.

Sympathetic murmurs, pats on the back. One put her arm around Arinna and hugged her close.

"Poor dear . . ."

"You poor thing!"

Arinna sniffed, then lifted her chin bravely. "I'll miss him . . . gods, how I will miss him. So beautiful in . . . radiance. So majestic in . . . in . . . majesticness. Sometimes he would sit for hours, perfectly motionless, as if he were somewhere else, in the presence of Zeus on Mount Olympus, maybe; and I, his humble servant, would sit at his feet and just . . . *listen* to his presence."

Some of the girls gasped. All eyes were wide.

"Five years with him. Five glorious years, and now . . ." She sniffed and wiped away a suggestion of a tear.

More gasps, this time of abject pity. Arinna felt their pity so palpably she began to feel sorry for herself. Yes. Yes, she *would* miss him, poor Zagreus. A real tear stung. Then, overcome, she covered her face.

"Don't cry, dear Keeper!"

"Be brave! Be courageous!"

"Think on the courage of our queen," said one initiate in a gently remonstrating voice, meaning to give stoutness to her heart. "It is *her* child the god will receive."

Arinna kept her face covered for a moment, then lifted her head in wan courage. They petted her and they patted her, and she felt comforted for all her years of toil at the inn.

Tallis was trying to adjust the grindstone in the kitchen yard, though he felt it was a task best assigned to Samir, who was a genius at fixing things. He did not completely understand what was wrong with it to begin with; Kes said the grind was off.

"Off," Tallis had repeated.

"Yes, off," Kes had said. "My flour is too coarse."

"Off," he muttered.

It wasn't easy to harness thoughts to off grindstones. Last night he'd had a nightmare that followed him into the daytime. Kes and Jarek and Zagreus and Samir were all in his dream, and their eyes were all the same: huge and oddly slanted and colored orange. Kes had been at the brazier with her back to him, then turned those shocking eyes on him. Zagreus had a thick-lipped leering grin with the eyes. Jarek laughed and laughed at him, with those huge slanted eyes. Samir was the worst; his eyes were not only huge and orange, they were dead; and when he smiled at Tallis, he showed rows of sharp teeth that went all the way around to the back of his head.

Terror held Tallis fast in his cot when he woke. He was drenched in sweat and breathing hard, wondering if he had cried out. It was the middle of the night, and he'd tried to go back to sleep but had to admit he was afraid to.

Fear felt palpable in the room. He thought he heard a door open and shut, and during the brief time it was opened he heard a chanting buzz, a swell of many voices. He was certain he'd heard the door when he was awake, but was also certain the door belonged to the nightmare. Even now, chills raised on his skin as he thought on it.

"You'll never guess who's here!"

Tallis jumped and cursed, then turned on Zagreus with very pained patience and told him *never* to sneak up and shout at a person like that, and never, *ever* repeat what Master Tallis had just said, especially to Mistress Kes.

"Master Tallis, you'll never guess who's here," Zagreus tried again in a loud whisper between cupped hands.

Tallis first looked at the recalcitrant grindstone. He glared at the awl in his hand, wondering what Samir thought he should do with it. He'd like to tell Samir what to do with it. "My grind is 'off,' she says. Who is here?"

"Master Polonus!"

He stared at the boy, then tossed the awl on the grindstone and followed Zagreus to the common room. He paused in the doorway to get a look at Polonus before meeting him.

An elderly man sat with Kes and Jarek at a long table, he on one side and they on the other. Perhaps they had been in conversation for a time, because now nobody spoke. Polonus glanced about at nothing in particular, idly brushing his lips with his fingertips. Jarek looked uncomfortable, shifting glances from Polonus to Kes, and Kes didn't take her eyes off Polonus.

He was the same man who had picked up the basket many days ago, the tall one with the intriguing aloofness. Yet a difference attended him, even from that brief visual encounter. Tallis scratched the back of his neck.

Tallis remembered his face from Athens. It had aged astonishingly in eight years. He remembered a composed, inquiring gaze; now Polonus's gaze did not stay in one place but flitted about the room. His color was gray, as though he hadn't seen the sun in an age. He had dark color beneath his eyes, making the rest of the gray almost white, and his fingers wouldn't quit their fiddling with his mouth. Every now and then his stare jerked to the left or right. Sometimes he looked over his shoulder.

Polonus was the first chosen by Callimachus to lead the academy in

Hippos. Where was the composure Tallis remembered? Where was that good-natured confidence? But then, Tallis had read his scrolls.

He came into the room and gave a small deferential bow when the trio noticed him. "Master Polonus, it is an honor."

Polonus's look was first suspicious, his eyes unnaturally vivid by the dark contrast beneath them, unnaturally lurid, with a strange *flickering* within—and just when a chill began on Tallis's neck, the scholar's face cleared, the eyes reduced somehow, and childlike recognition came.

"Why, Tallis! Tallis, of Callimachus! Kes told me you were here!" Polonus rose and came to embrace him as if he were Callimachus himself. He held him back to look on him with pleasure. "Tallis from Athens. Gods and goddesses, how I miss Athens. How is Callimachus?"

The grip on his shoulders was strong, and he was not letting go. Tallis smiled at him and cut a glance at Jarek and Kes. Neither smiled as they watched Polonus. Their faces were troubled.

Tallis discreetly pulled himself from Polonus, covering for it by seeing him to the table. "Callimachus was well, last time I saw him. He has the gout, however, and suffers at the ministering hands of Aristarchus."

"Aristarchus!" Polonus exclaimed joyously as he took his seat.

Tallis sat opposite.

"Good old Aristarchus! Oh—how I pity Callimachus—you know how Aristarchus is." He gazed eagerly at Tallis. His eyes were focused now, and he plied Tallis for information of Athens.

Tallis told him what he could, said Cal had a new young philosopher in the school by the name of Diomedes who was taking over some of the teaching. He told Polonus that Cal was growing too old to attend the forums, and at the time he left Athens, was getting about with a donkey and cart instead of his gout-troubled feet. When Tallis exhausted his supply of hometown news, even the trivial things for which Polonus seemed pathetically eager, a silence settled. Polonus's gaze began to drift, and he went back to twiddling with his lips.

Tallis had a plan to present to Polonus, and he even had rehearsed some of what he would say. He wanted to join forces with Polonus on behalf of Kardus, join this noble fight to help the man regain his mind. Somehow it seemed out of place to bring it up. There was an odd mood in the room.

Suddenly Tallis was no longer certain his plans for the redemption of Kardus were good plans at all. In fact, all at once they felt foolish. What did he know of the mind of a crazy man? He was no scholar. Look what it was doing to Polonus—there he sat, dazed and fidgeting.

"Polonus, where have you been?" Kes ventured.

Polonus slid a guarded look her way. "Why do you want to know?"

She didn't know how to answer. "I—we were worried."

"Worried," he sneered, his upper lip curling. "You weren't worried about me. You were worried about your precious Kardus."

From her astonished look, this wasn't a typical conversation. Tallis eyed Polonus carefully. "That isn't true, and you know it," Kes said defensively.

Polonus blinked at that, and the sneer lowered. He brushed his fingertips on his lips, then something at the kitchen entrance caught his eye. His hand slowly lowered.

And only because Tallis had been watching carefully did he see the reaction. He saw the pupils dilate, saw the leap of fear within. He saw revulsion, and it seemed Polonus fought. The pupils contracted. Then came relief. Relief in such amounts that tears came to his eyes. Somehow, Tallis didn't have to turn to know Samir was in the doorway.

"Samir!" Polonus cried and got up to embrace the man. "Good old Samir!"

Such gentleness and pity in the face of the slave. While Polonus held Samir's shoulders as he'd held his own, and regarded Samir with pathetic enthusiasm, Samir returned an apprehensive compassion. This morning when he handed the awl to Tallis, there was no emotion whatsoever, only a slave's passivity. No hint that, only a few days ago, he'd held Tallis's face and searched deeply, authoritatively, in his eyes, and before that, stood like a god come down from Mount Olympus in the chicken yard, warding off unseen terrors. Now the slave brought out new emotions.

If Tallis got *Get up, you Greek dog*, Polonus got compassion. Samir gently led Polonus to the table as if he were a feeble old man.

"It's always better when you're around," Polonus said affectionately, patting Samir's arm. He sighed. "Always better." They settled on the bench.

"How are you, old friend?" Samir asked, and his face was creased with care.

Polonus's eyes glazed for an instant, and with eyebrows high and his voice in a confessional hush, he said, "I am weary, Samir."

"Do not go back there, Polonus," Samir said, quietly pleading. "We have a place for you here."

Polonus gazed at him with a slight smile. Then the smile faded, and the lip brushing came. "No. No, no, my place is with him. It's my work."

"A wise man knows when his work is done. It is time for another." Samir indicated Tallis with a move of his head. "This man wishes to join the fight. Did he tell you that?"

Had Tallis told Samir that?

"He didn't have to." Polonus slid an odd glance at Tallis.

Tallis thought now was a good time to confess. He cleared his throat and said, "Master Polonus, I must tell you—I don't know if you've been back to your home yet. I visited when you were gone. I read some of your work—I'm sorry, I should have asked first." As long as he was confessing, he may as well tell it entirely. "I brought some scrolls back with me. Borrowed them."

Polonus didn't answer. He didn't seem to hear. He'd faded out and stared across the room.

"I'm sorry I didn't put the other scrolls away. I left them on your desk. I . . . left in a hurry."

The eyes focused and found Tallis. "Did he frighten you?"

"Oh—well, actually . . . what I read in the scrolls frightened me."

"Ah." Polonus smiled a horribly empty smile. "A sensible man. Only fools aren't afraid. I've been a fool much too long."

Tallis leaned forward on the table, and a ripple of the purpose came back. "Sir, I read things on your desk, on parchment scraps. I read things in your scrolls. I think it's good that you and I talk. I may have something to offer." It came to him as he spoke, and he felt his way for the words. "You see, my mother was a Maenad. I studied Dionysus for years, and I see things here in Palestine . . . tangled lines with a commonality—"

"Where do you think the word Maenad came from, my brilliant lad from Athens?" Polonus said sharply.

Tallis pulled back but noticed a subtle reaction from the others. Jarek and Samir exchanged glances.

"Well, from . . . madness," Tallis said.

"Ah. No intellectual slouch are *you*," Polonus said dryly. "Of course, a child on milk would know that."

"What is your point?" Tallis asked.

Samir seemed to relax. He was pleased when Polonus was rude.

"The word Maenad is rooted in madness. If you want an answer, go back to the beginning." Polonus looked for his cup and took a drink. When he tasted it, he took another sip and eyed Jarek over the rim. He smiled then, a crinkly eyed look. He licked his lips and lowered the cup, fondly regarding the contents. "You always served a good stout cup, Jarek. Where was I?"

"Madness," Tallis prompted.

"Yes. If you want an answer, go back to the beginning. It's what I always told Kardus—if you lose something, go to the place you last saw it. Start from there and minutely expand your perimeter."

"You learned that from Cal. Back to the beginning . . ." Tallis looked eagerly at Kes. "That's what I told you. We have to go back to the Decaphiloi."

"Do not waste your time." Surprisingly, it came from Samir.

"What do you mean? That's where Kardus went wrong."

Samir said gently, eyeing Polonus, "He went back to that beginning. It's not where it started."

"No. No, you're wrong. All I have to do is say her name, and you know where it started. She's a priestess of Dionysus!"

"It didn't start with Portia," Polonus murmured, and the sass was going out of him.

"It started with his mother," Jarek said thinly. "His mother was a Maenad."

Silence.

"Mother was—*what*?" Kes demanded of Jarek. "A Maenad? Why have you never told me this?"

Tallis sat back, faintly dizzy. It couldn't be. If the madman's mother was a Maenad . . .

"I'm sorry, Kes," Jarek said sadly.

"How could you not tell me? What else haven't you told me?"

"What good would it have done?"

"You never tell me anything!"

"And who can talk to you about anything? You're just like your mother!"

Tallis sat silent and still.

If Kardus's mother was a Maenad, then the blood of madness, from mother to son. Why did he think himself exempt? Tallis himself would one day wear shackles. No—no, he'd kill himself first.

Head in his hands, fingers working into his scalp, he stared at the tabletop. Why didn't he see it? He was weak around Kardus because of his blood. It was madness calling to madness, and it was only a matter of time. He could never have children, not with Kes, not with anyone. Never could he pass this blood to another. He looked at his wrist. Madness, coursing through these veins.

"Raise your head, you Greek dog!"

He touched his blue wrist vein. Why was Samir always kicking Tallis with words?

"Stop being weak," Samir snapped. "Alexander had a Maenad for a mother. Alexander!"

Alexander.

Alexander, who ate the food of his soldiers. Alexander, who compared battle wounds with the least of his men. Alexander, with his passion for new people and new cultures; Alexander, with his great heart that led men to places they never dreamed. Macedonia was too small for him the moment he was born.

He knew he bled no ichor, and he knew his blood was not mad. He acted not like the son of a Maenad, no—

He acted like the son of Philip.

And it seemed to Tallis, in that moment, that he had gone back to the beginning.

What did he know of his own father? Why hadn't he thought of his father all these years; why did he bury his father with his brother? How much good was buried with the bad? And why was Callimachus in Athens when Tallis needed him in Palestine?

He hadn't seen his father since he was twelve. He learned of his death about ten years ago. Cal was worried about how he would react, but Tallis received the news with true indifference. He had buried his father with his brother, long before he died.

Father was good. Beneath all the harshness, beneath his contempt and his misunderstanding of Mother, Tallis knew his father was good. Because whenever Father was around, it felt right. It felt safe. He clenched his hands to fists. By the gods and goddesses, he had blood from his father too. And he felt the first pang of sorrow then, that he had ever felt for him, not only for his death, but because he never knew him.

He looked for Kes, but she was not at the table. He heard Kes and Zagreus in the kitchen. He heard her ask Zagreus what he thought of her date bread.

"More dates?" Kes said, astonished. "You're going to run me out of business."

The men at the table were silent. He took his cup. What had happened after Tallis left Thebes? What did Father come home to? An empty house, or was Mother there? Did his father ever think of him? Did he miss him? Did he wonder what happened to him—did he try to find him? He saw his father in his mind, riding that military nag from village to village.

Another pang, this time of remorse.

"Polonus, your work fascinates me," he made himself say. "I've been thinking on something you said: Logic says if there is a way into madness—"

"Rhetoric!" Polonus bellowed. The inflammation receded as suddenly as it came. Polonus settled down to his mug, gripping it with both hands. "What if the way is shattered beyond repair? There isn't logic anymore."

"Polonus, listen," Tallis said. "I've called for a meeting of the Decaphiloi. Right here at noon, two days from now. It's a forum for Truth, and I'd like you to come."

"What good will it do? They haven't lived with a madman for three years. For them there is no great evil, not this kind. I know—I thought like them." Polonus wasn't happy. He began to shift in his seat. "It isn't right. It doesn't feel right." His fingers went to his lips.

"What does the meeting have to do with Kardus?" Jarek asked.

"It isn't right."

Tallis stared at Jarek, dumbfounded. "What does it have to do with Kardus? Everything! We're tracking backward, and our backward trail to the *beginning* goes *through* the Decaphiloi!" He lifted his hands and let them fall. "*Gods*, isn't anyone listening to me? I am *stunningly* alone on this!"

"Doesn't feel right."

"What isn't right, Polonus?" Samir asked.

Something in his voice made Tallis glance at him. Samir had a strange look of alarm.

Distant awareness came, barely perceived. Tallis stilled, his gaze drifting. A faint buzzing. A far-off humming, felt rather than heard . . . felt and heard at the same time. Tallis slowly rose and stared out the front door, about the same time Samir got a dread look and Polonus's face lost color.

Jarek stared at them all. "What? What is it?"

The atmosphere contracted, thickened.

A plate shattered in the kitchen.

"Tell Kes I went to Scythopolis to kill Portia," Polonus said bleakly. "But they wouldn't let me near the city. Big column . . ."

Tallis stared at the ceiling. Bright sunshine out there, but it felt like a storm was ready to burst on the inn.

And Samir did a strange thing. He planted one hand on Polonus's shoulder and twisted the cloth into a grip. Then he lunged for Tallis and snatched him by the throat of his tunic. He yanked him eye to eye over the table, twisting the cloth into a grip, and just as Samir shouted into his face, "You hold!"

The room darkened, his hearing dimmed . . .

Pandemonium crashed over the inn.

Silence engulfed him, and he went down, tumbling at the razor bottom of an ocean surge. Drowning, frantic, he clawed the thick dreadful soundlessness back to the surface—and underwater silence erupted to roaring. Blindly he tore at the grip on his neck; he reared violently from the hold, then lunged against the stiff arm for the face of the slave, the face he could not see in the torrent.

The singsong began.

HELLO, TALLISSS . . .

"Hold! They take only the ground you surrender! Surrender nothing!"

YOU THINK IT'S MADNESS, BUT THE OPPOSITE IS TRUE.

STEP INTO THE STILLNESS AND SEE. SPACIOUS STILLNESS.

"Look at me! They are trespassers! Do not let them have what is not theirs!"

Voices in and out, whirling around him, one moment at his ear, the next across the room.

WHAT DOES HE KNOW?
HAS HE SUFFERED LIKE YOU?
DOES HE KNOW YOUR PAIN?

"Whatever you hear is a lie!"

SHUT UP, WORM, YOU ARE NO MATCH FOR US NOW. WE ARE MORE.
YOU HAVE NOTHING TO LOSE, TALLIS. THINK ON ALEXANDER!
YESSSS . . . YOU THINK HE DID ALL THOSE THINGS ON HIS OWN?
THIS IS IT, TALLIS—THE HORIZON YOU'VE ACHED TO REACH. THE
BEND AROUND WHICH ALEXANDER SAW . . .
COME AND SEE!

"Give them nothing!"

WE PITY THE POOR SLAVE.
HE DOESN'T KNOW YOUR PAIN. HE ONLY INVITES YOU TO MORE.

"Hold!"

DREADFUL PAIN! IT'S NOT WORTH IT.

"Hold!"

IT'S NEVER WORTH IT, IN THE END.
YOU'RE TOO TIRED TO FIGHT IT ANYMORE.
YOU WERE BORN THIS WAY. CAN'T CHANGE WHO YOU ARE.
LET US IN.

"You can choose, Tallis! You can choose! You *can*!"

The crooning faltered.

LIAR! FILTHY SWINE LIAR! WE HATE HIM!
YOU HAVE NO CHOICE, TALLLISSS. YOU ARE WHAT YOU ARE.
LET US IN. WE WILL MAKE YOU STRONG.

"You can choose. Oh, Athenian . . . you can choose."

DID LITTLE BROTHER HAVE A CHOICE?

The voices went into consultation.

THAT WAS RISKY.
NO—CLEVER!
TRUTH IS DANGEROUS.
AH, DANGEROUSSSS . . . BUT POWERFUL. SEE HIM NOW, SEE HIM
NOW. YESSS . . .
HO, HUMAN SLUG—BROTHER-SON OF MAENAD HAD NO CHOICE!
WHAT MAKES YOU THINK YOU DO? UNFAIR FOR YOU TO HAVE A
CHOICE . . . AND NOT POOR BROTHER-SON!
UNFAIR, UNFAIR! the voices chorused in glee. *LET US IN—THERE*
IS NO CHOICE.
POOR BROTHER HAD NO CHOICE!

"No," Tallis slurred aloud, words coming thickly. "But my mother did."
Watery ripples stilled. The face of the slave grew clearer.
Soothing voices became shrill.

FOOL! BRING OUT TRUTH WHEN VICTORY IS ASSURED!
I THOUGHT IT WAS!
YOU WILL ANSWER FOR THAT!

Voices scurried off. Dimness lifted. And Samir and Tallis stood in a
frozen grapple.
The slave had scratches on his face where Tallis had dug for release.
Several scratches beaded with blood. Sweat shone on his brown forehead.

He dropped his arm from Tallis as if he could hold on no longer and looked down the other arm to Polonus.

Tallis dropped to the bench.

Kes rushed in from the kitchen. "Kardus is here!"

"We know," Tallis said hoarsely.

The slave's dark eyes were wide. He was staring not at Polonus but at his own hand. He withdrew his hand, fingers stiff, twisted in the shape of his grip. He brought the hand to his stomach, and cradled it with his other.

"According to Parmenides, the world as we know it is merely illusion." Polonus's voice was chillingly toneless. "It doesn't exist." His face was gray, his lips darker gray. "It means we're all in hell."

"Polonus!" Kes cried. "What's wrong with you?"

"POLONUS!" Though it came from outside, it shook the room, a many-timbre'd voice.

"I have to go," Polonus murmured. He rose from the table.

Tallis gazed at Samir. "Don't let him go."

But Samir was staring at his twisted hand. "It's over."

"He can choose," Tallis whispered.

"He has chosen!" Samir shook his head in sorrow, tears falling on the cradled hand. "The way has closed. I cannot help him anymore."

Polonus moved slowly to the door. He paused in the doorway without turning. "Tallis. They want me to tell you your little brother was delicious."

Polonus drifted away, and the swell of the storm receded. Silence engulfed the room.

"Samir? What's wrong with Tallis?"

"Tallis! What's wrong?"

His nose ran, and tears flowed, and his mind staggered because nobody knew, nobody knew, not a single person knew. Not Callimachus, not Aristarchus. He hadn't told Kes. They knew how his brother had died, torn apart in the Bacchic frenzy. They didn't know what happened after.

Samir's voice cut clear. "You think he will play clean? Look at me. You think he will play clean? He plays for keeps." If the slave's face was newly aged, if he held a crippled hand, his eyes blazed with a terrible light. "And so does the Most High."

The madman in the tombs listens to Their laughter. They have gotten away with something dreadful. The madman doesn't know what.

Portia used to laugh like that, without making a sound.

And the medium he went to, seeking information. For he knew he had more in his blood than that of a mere innkeeper. He knew his blood came from Alexander the Great, and he spent money, and paid other prices, to confirm the truth he already knew, that his blood was unique. He knew he was a descendent of Alexander. He knew he was the son of a son.

SONOFASONOFASONOFASONOFASONOFASON . . .

The wise woman told him much. Offered him more than he asked, revealed to him secrets lodged beneath mountains, knowledge past the black of the universe. She poured into him the rich wine syrup of truth, and after it settled into the last crevasse, after the headiness receded, there came a disdain for mankind.

He needed no one, then; he was attracted only to the newfound, vast desolation. It was a place of great relief, and he learned how to get there without her help. It was an arid place, a comely place, and silent. So silent. So empty. A place where he could be still, locked away from the noisome interference of humans. He went there more and more, aching with an agony to stay forever, loathe to return to loud and painful discourse, the banality of mankind. Humans had become small in his sight, diminishing to insignificance, save what they could do for him.

But They tricked him. And once he couldn't leave, it wasn't a quiet place at all. No longer arid and desolate. What was once attractive and soothing now crawled with jagged filth. The spacious place within became a dark hole clogged with endless torment.

They're laughing. They've gotten away with something, the tricksters, and he doesn't know what.

He remembers the sound of confusion that came from the medium, like a buzz about her. It had puzzled him, and he was wary. The small place within had recoiled at the sound and sent up a warning to flee. But the lure to knowledge was greater than the warning, and the small cry went unheeded. Then, after They came, They made him plaster over the place to shut it up and make it interfere no longer.

He doesn't know what the place is. Maybe his name is in it. But he can't get to it any longer. It's closed off. They think it funny. They always think it funny.

He stays near the plastered-over place, at the dark end of his being, from familiarity alone, dwelling beside it like a bewildered dog next to its dead master.

XI

A nd so does the Most High.

Most who?

Tallis sat at his place by the sea but not on the chair. He wanted to be closer to the water, so he climbed down the short drop and went to the shore.

It was twilight, and the darkness concealed and comforted. He listened to the water gently lap the shells and the rocks. Closer to the shore meant close enough to smell the fly-ridden piles of yellowish, rotting seaweed, but the wind was on his back and took the stink across the waters.

He watched winking fires begin to appear on the other side of the Galilee. It was a quiet, clear night, and getting chilly. Kes said it had been a mild winter, and the heaviest rains had stopped a few weeks before he arrived. Enjoy the cool evenings while you can, she'd said. The heat would come all too soon. Come? he'd said. He thought it was already here.

It was a comfort to see familiar star formations in a foreign land. It was not a comfort to have Callimachus so far away, not when he had a hundred things to sort through.

Most High. Though the two words meant one above the rest, Samir spoke the words with a curious sense of singularity—a sense of dismissiveness. As if his god naturally blotted out the other gods. Of course, "My god is better than your god" had been around since time began; but there was that implication of singularity. Maybe his tribe believed as the Jews, in one single god, not Zeus and not Cronus the father of Zeus, but simply Creator. This was not new to Greek minds, any more than the commonly held belief in the pantheon. It was not new, but it was not believed. He had an idea what Cal would say if he seriously suggested the possibility of only one god: "It's up to the gods if there is only one." He could almost hear Cal chuckle.

He thought of the diagram in Polonus's scroll. Good. Evil. People in between. No circles for gods or goddesses. Of course, this brought it back to the tired old questions ringing the colonnades: of Evil, who made it? And who made Good? Who was responsible for it all? Why didn't Polonus make circles for the gods? After three years with a madman, did it come only to Good, Evil, and Human? Where did Most High figure into this?

Callimachus never troubled himself overmuch with the gods, and neither had Aristarchus. If anything, Aristarchus would take after Samir, for practicality's sake. One god uncomplicated things, though, of course, one god was much less interesting. Whom could you blame when things went wrong? Only one god? Whom could you supplicate for help? Only one? Life was too uncertain to place all your bets on one god. What if he—or she—was busy? Tallis felt it took more faith to believe in one than in all of them.

Good. Bad. Humans in between. The question was, did all three have equal footing, or did one rule above the others? Most important of all, was Samir's Most High *Good*, and was he stronger than Bad?

How could Polonus have known about Zagreus?

His nose tingled again, and his skin rose with prickles. He thought it over carefully: He'd told no one about Zagreus's death; that he died, yes, but he gave no detail. He'd tried to tell Kes, but she had run off for the barn. And he was glad. He hadn't wanted her to hear it.

When he had first learned the name of the child at the inn, a haze came. Blankness had settled with the name. Now he could see Zagreus clearly, the boy of the inn, and in his mind, he saw another. A smaller child with darker hair and more solemn eyes. He could see the soft bit of wool he carried with him and held to his cheek; he could see the thumb in his mouth. Tallis hadn't been able to see him for a long time.

He used to tease him about the thumb. He'd ask him what it tasted like, and Zagreus would smile, breaking the suction, and with the thumb in his mouth he'd say grapes, or mint, or blackberries. Sometimes Tallis would act astonished and grab for the thumb to taste and see, and Zagreus would laugh. Once Zagreus asked Mother if he could have honeycake for dinner because that's what his thumb tasted like. Mother laughed, and said so we shall. And they had nothing but honeycake for dinner.

He remembered he had loved his little brother; he remembered how much he loved him, because the blankness was gone and he could see him again, a dark-haired little boy with the thumb in his mouth, standing behind the fair-haired boy of the inn. And he felt pain, and the aloneness of grief, and he felt human again.

"Which is better," Aristarchus had once asked, "blindness or refusing to see?"

"Hear me, Good, if you are there, and any heroes for Good," Tallis suddenly said to the waves on the lake. Then he waited for a while, because he didn't know how to say it. "I suppose I'd like to know if Good is there at all, because we all know Bad. We're smoked through with it, if a woman can kill her child."

Most High plays for keeps. That had a good heartening sound to it, coming from Samir. He couldn't prop it with logic before Callimachus, because Callimachus would not understand it. He hardly did himself. But it had a good sound.

He turned a mocking tone on the waves: "Most High plays for keeps; sounds nice, Cal, don't you think? I'll serve myself the hemlock now. . . ."

They made Socrates drink hemlock because he led the youth of Athens astray with his truth nonsense. Not soon after, they revered him. They had to kill him to revere him, and Callimachus and Tallis had a private joke when the world went upside down and called truth, falseness, and black, white: They answered absurdities with "I'll serve myself the hemlock now. . . ."

"Do you wish to be alone?"

Tallis looked over his shoulder. The soft call behind him had come from Samir.

The slave stood on the drop, an eerie stalk of white capped in white in the indigo twilight.

"No. Not anymore." He turned to the waters. He heard the slave drop down, heard the gristle of the shore under his sandals.

Samir settled in an easy squat not far from Tallis and gazed out on the lake. "Winds are dying down. I'm ready to put in my garden."

"You haven't planted yet?" Tallis asked.

"We wait until the strong rains stop. I should have planted weeks ago."

"How long have you been at the inn?"

"Perhaps twenty years."

Tallis studied him. The sight of his hand, still twisted in the shape of his grip on Polonus, sent a silent shock through Tallis. Yet his contented gaze on the lake and the sky belied any concern for his hand. "Who are your people, Samir?"

"I am come from a Parthian tribe. The Charaxi."

"I don't know whom you remind me of more, my master, Callimachus, or my aggravator, Aristarchus." He glanced toward the inn. "Who is with Zagreus?"

"We moved his pallet to Mistress Kes's room."

Tallis nodded. Two days until the festival. He didn't have to look at a calendar, not since he'd arrived in Palestine. He wore the calendar inside him. He felt the date approaching.

"Tell me about your people," Samir said.

"Cal and Aristarchus?" A warmness came. "Yes, I suppose they are my people. My tribe." His first memory after Thebes was not Callimachus but Aristarchus.

"I was twelve, and I woke up after a bad dream. How I got from Thebes to Athens is still a mystery to me. I awoke on a porch, a fancy colonnaded place, to a man who was shaking me and telling me to shove off." He smiled. "That was Aristarchus. He thought I was a vagrant. Callimachus came, and he is my second memory. He did a strange thing; he took my chin and looked into my eyes—" He broke off to look at Samir curiously. "As you have done—and looking into those eyes, I began to cry. I don't know why I did it. It was the first real conversation I ever had.

"Cal took me in, and he helped me to . . . repair. Aristarchus helped too. I heard them once, when they thought I'd gone to sleep. 'The restoration of Tallis,' Aristarchus said. I didn't hear anything else, just that. The restoration of Tallis." He chose a place on the horizon to be Athens. "This is my tribe, Samir. Aristarchus and Callimachus."

"I knew you were fortunate."

"Yes." Then Tallis lifted an eyebrow. "Well—we could argue that." Eyes still on Athens, he said, "I never told Polonus what happened after they killed my brother. I never told anyone, not even Cal. How did he know? What happened in that room today?"

Samir grunted an affirmative. "I also knew you were wise."

Tallis squinted at him. "Why are you a slave? Because you are not."

"I am a slave because I am a slave." There was a shrug in his voice. "In this, I do not have a choice."

"Would you have chosen something else? Are you a slave because it is your *fate* to be a slave?"

Samir smiled. His teeth shone in the dark. "We could argue that."

"Samir . . . why is the way closed for Polonus?" He couldn't help a glance at the crippled hand. "What did you mean by that, that he has chosen—why did it sound awful? How did he know about Zagreus?" He added, "My Zagreus—my little brother. He died when he was four."

Samir sighed and regarded the far shoreline for a time before he answered. "I will tell you what a person must learn for himself, if the learning will have strength." He lifted his head, and his eyes traveled the sky. "Time, we do not have. My fathers and my mothers will understand." His troubled expression said he wasn't so sure about that. "Master Athenian, my tribe teaches this, that there are two truths. The first truth: You can choose. The second truth: You cannot choose for another."

Tallis realized he'd been leaning for the words; he remained motionless for a moment, then made his withdrawal as discreet as he could. He scratched the back of his neck. "So that means . . ."

The slave sighed deeply. "It means you are not weak."

"Talk plainly, please," Tallis said, unable to keep the sourness out of his tone. "Tell me how Polonus knew my brother died, explain what happens to me when Kardus is near—I don't see Kes and Jarek on the ground like a couple of jellyfish. Just don't give me philosophy. I've had it all my life. You want philosophy, you want rhetoric? I could debate you senseless. And I'm only a servant."

"Polonus tried to talk plainly to the Decaphiloi, and those wise people would not understand. They refuse to see great evil, just as they refuse to see great good."

"Which of them tried to hurt me?" Tallis said, more to himself. "Who forged the reports?"

"It doesn't matter," Samir snapped. Then he muttered sullenly under his breath, probably complaining to his solitary Most High.

"Gods, you sound more like Aristarchus every time I listen."

They sat in stiff silence, the gentle rhythmic lap of the water the only sound. Just when Tallis was ready to get up and leave the uncomfortable wedge that had dropped down between them, Samir spoke.

"The greatest trick of the Lord of the Souls is to convince a man he is weak. Weak against drink, against rage. Weak against any form of evil, middling or not. Too weak to change things." Samir rummaged in the sand. He held out his palm, upturned, with a pebble on it. The palm was a floating light patch in the twilight, the pebble, a dark dot upon it.

"If a man knows that good lies plain as this, that all he must do is choose to take it, Lord of the Souls is defeated. But he is a master of deception. Good appears impossible." He closed the pebble in his fist. The light patch disappeared.

"Kardus chose to be weak, and do not despise another for weakness, or you ally yourself with Shaitan. To believe we *can* make a good choice is hard work." The patch appeared again as he displayed the pebble. "Even a free man fights every day to know good choice is there. And without choice, there is no such thing as love. Only shackles. All of this, Athenian, belongs to the first truth. The second truth is that we cannot choose for another. And that is all that belongs to the second truth."

"Then how do we help people? How do we help Kardus?"

Samir let the pebble slide out of his hand. His voice was gentle. "I am trying to help you."

"This is about Kardus, not me."

"You cannot help Kardus until you help yourself. We do our best for others by always choosing the good for ourselves. It starts there. Flows out in ripples, like a stone dropped in a pond. Our choice for good will always aid another. Always! We may not see it; it may not be ours to see. Not in this life."

Tallis didn't know what to think, how to feel. He couldn't answer.

"What should have been costly for you to obtain, by pain and struggle, I have given freely, and I did you no favor." The slave rose and dusted the shore from himself.

Tallis heard his footsteps retreat, the shore rustling under his feet.

This is why the world was in such a mess? Nobody choosing for themselves, but always trying to choose for another? He looked for Athens on the horizon.

"Cal, we have two new truths, file these under Charaxi. Truth number one: You can choose. Truth number two: You cannot choose for another. Pass it on to Aristarchus; he may be impressed. He may think more kindly of me."

Well and good, Samir, well and good.

"What if there's hell between you and the pebble on the palm?" Tallis shouted over his shoulder. "How do you make hell go away? You have another truth for that?"

No answer, save softly retreating footsteps.

"Is there another truth for that, Samir?"

What if despair fills you for the choices others have made? Aching came for the little boy with the thumb in his mouth. What if their choices cripple and blind you, what if their choice was not a pebble dropped in a pond but a planet smashed in the sea, and the waves have laid you out on the shore and they keep coming and coming and you cannot stand up for their crashing?

What then, Samir?

"Curse you for your truths, Samir! You *idiots* who reduce life to two truths!"

If it weren't for the message in the forum, he would leave right now. Samir had said it with such dreadful finality: *Polonus has chosen.* Well, so had Kardus, and now Polonus was out of the picture, so what was Tallis still doing here?

"Polonus has chosen," Tallis muttered darkly. "So what are you going to do, Samir? Keep taking your good pebble, and that's going to help them both?"

Louder, over his shoulder, he said, "You know what? I hate philosophy. I hate maxims and two truths, and I'm going back where things make sense. This time I swear, I swear by every god known or unknown, I swear by them all or I swear by the one—I'll stay out of the colonnades."

He settled into a brood on the lake. "I'll stay in the kitchen this time, Cal. The only thing that makes sense is a well-made sauce. I won't venture to the portico again, not ever, not unless it's to serve myself some hemlock—and wouldn't the colonnades be the perfect place for that? Alexander hated rhetoric. Hated debate. Said it was insidious to play both sides equally well. And I am talking out loud to myself on the shore of the Galilee."

Tallis kept to himself as much as he could the next day. He had woken from yet another nightmare to sit on the edge of his cot, rubbing away the clammy sweat on his neck. He saw the scrolls from Polonus on the floor. He noticed the serene writing desk with all the pristine writing supplies. He didn't have the strength, because of the cursed nightmare, to sweep it all to the ground and crush it to rubble.

Heavy on him for the duration of the day was the meeting of the Decaphiloi at noon the next. It was too late to go to Hippos and post another message, saying he didn't care anymore and please don't come, unless it's to bring money for his passage home. He'd made a fool of himself with that message, with the inn folk, and with everyone else. An utter and complete fool.

Everyone else seemed in as morose a mood as he. Kes was quiet, and snippy when she did speak, wearing an unflattering scowl. Samir kept to the barn. Jarek had Zagreus help him work on the roof of the inn, making repairs after the winter rains. Jarek didn't say a word to Tallis all day, acted like he didn't even see him. Tallis had to tidy the guest rooms and clean the common room, then finish repairing the grindstone. He worked on it all afternoon and finally stalked into the barn and threw the awl at Samir's feet and told him to do it himself. He ended up in the kitchen chopping onions.

Yes, he'd made a fool of himself and took great satisfaction in knowing he'd put this place behind him as soon as he earned enough money for passage to Athens. If a couple of dinars didn't get him to Athens, it would at least put him on the next ship out of Caesarea and get him to a port closer to home. The itch to go was on him, however, and if could pack enough provisions, he'd walk to Athens.

That would be a small adventure, backtracking Alexander's route, and the thought cheered him a little. He could visit Tyre on the coast and see the place that had defied Alexander (and earned his respect) on his southern march to Egypt. He could visit the battleground at Issus, where the Persian Darius first met the young Macedonian in battle and had a taste of his tactical genius. The Persian army outnumbered the Macedonian army ten to one: Alexander made it look the opposite.

Alexander had been in the latest nightmare. He had those huge slanted orange eyes. He was laughing at Tallis because Tallis was full of fear. And when he awoke in another nightmare sweat, he swore he could hear—actually hear—laughing. Thought he'd heard a door close again, a door in the air in his room.

"Too coarse," Kes said, inspecting the pieces of his chopped onion. "They're going in my lamb balls, not a salad."

He scraped the onion pieces together and attacked viciously with the knife.

"You don't look like you're getting much sleep," she added quietly. "You're still mending, you know."

It was on the tip of his tongue to say something crude, like *I'd sleep much better with you in my bed.* Then the thoughts went from bad to worse, as images flickered in his mind. Bad images, memories from a sleazy public bathhouse in Athens. Tallis had gone on a dare from his friends. The bathhouse was only a cover for its real doings. He'd seen things there to shock him to his core. Aristarchus said there were things a whore would never dream of doing, and things a wife would do on a bet.

What was wrong with him? Battering thoughts came like a hail of stones. If she knew the perversions roiling in his brain at that moment, she'd send him packing herself. He reached for another onion to chop— and an insane thought came to rush at Kes with the knife.

He could understand a few thoughts of Kes to warm his cheeks, but the sleazy bathhouse kind? And running at people with knives? He couldn't help an incredulous chuckle.

"I'm going mad," he muttered, and froze. This was not the thing to say in the hearing of the sister of Kardus. Thank goodness she had plunked a small iron skillet on the brazier at that moment.

She glanced at him. "What did you say?"

"I—regret calling the meeting tomorrow."

She took a small sack of seed and poured some into the skillet. In a few moments he knew the seed was cumin, as the aroma filled the kitchen. They used a lot of cumin in Palestine, even more than they did in Greece. Kes stirred the seed carefully with a wooden spoon.

"Why do you regret it?" she presently asked.

"Because everybody seems to. That makes me uneasy." He wondered how many would show up. "Do you think you can make some of that date bread for tomorrow?"

"Of course. Chop some dates when you're done."

"I'm going back to Athens."

Kes shook the pan over the grate. She smelled the toasting seeds, stirred them over the brazier a few more moments, then emptied the seeds into a stone mortar.

The longer she did not answer, the worse he felt.

"I can't help your brother." *Not without Polonus, and Polonus is going the way of Kardus.*

She stirred the seeds, cooling them. "Then don't stay for him." She took the pestle and began to grind the seeds. The aroma was spicier than ever.

Why did I kiss her?

Tallis, you fool. You made it all the harder to leave. You've gone and made someone care for you, a stunning feat, and now you're going to leave her. Just who is the wharf rat?

What about me? I care for her too.

You know where caring gets you.

"In a whole lot of trouble," he muttered.

"What?" Kes asked.

"Where are the dates?"

XII

Antenor had hired a man to drive him to the Inn-by-the-Lake. He left Hippos early to arrive before the other Decaphiloi, if any dared to show—he snorted softly; knowing them, they all had the same idea, and Tallis's meeting would begin an hour early.

And which of the Decaphiloi remnant would show?

Not Polonus. He'd visited Antenor at the theater the other day. Acted like Kardus did before he took a nosedive into insanity. That plucking of his lips and the paranoid glances. His initial gladness at seeing his old friend quickly diminished.

Half the time Polonus said nothing, seemed to forget why he'd even come. The rest of the time he mumbled randomly, apparently trying to remember whatever he and Antenor had in common. It hurt Antenor to see him this way; it angered him, and he felt relief when he finally left. Score another ruination for Callimachus.

Julia? She'd show. Good, clean Julia and her handsome, forthright husband. Antenor couldn't think of anyone in the Decaphiloi—Portia included—who did not secretly or openly yearn for Julia, body, soul, and spirit. Yearn for her sweetness and her kindness, her gaiety and loveliness.

Julia, shot through with goodness and naïveté, equal parts, so that she could not see how desperately a man could love her. Julia with her buckets of tesserae and her goodwill cases, students who couldn't pay, but she managed to plead them a spot in the academy because nobody could say no to her.

Nobody could say no to Portia, either, because she was the opposite of Julia, twisted through with treachery and deceit. Would she dare show her face? Antenor gripped the fabric of his toga, enjoying the sensual swell of rage that thoughts of her brought. He hadn't seen her in three years, not since the very last meeting of the Academy of Socrates in Palestine. Not a single word was spoken in that last meeting, and of course, not everyone was there: Bion was off killing himself, and Theseus was already dead. Kardus had abandoned the academy and taken to the hills.

The mesmeric plodding of the donkey jostled him gently in the cart.

It was the day after the Festival of Dionysus. The students had not yet arrived. They were sleeping off the revels of the previous evening, but the teachers were there. The teachers were there.

They had arrived one by one, Polonus first, Antenor second. The two stood in the cool of the portico, Polonus with those stricken eyes, Antenor, horrified and finally believing, with no words to tell Polonus how sorry he was. Julia arrived next, rushing in, stopping short. By the horror on her face she too had heard the news. She gazed from Polonus to Antenor, tears in her eyes, hands pressing her mouth to quiet her convulsive gasps. Lucius and Marcus arrived together, shock and disbelief etched deeply on their faces. Hector came next, staggering into the stoa as if under a great weight, leaning heavily on a column. His horror was the greatest: He was the one who had found Theseus.

Portia came last, strolling into the stoa. Antenor could still hear the soft click of her sandals on the marble, and the dreadful emptiness that sound brought. It was interesting, looking back, that it was not rage he had for Portia at that moment. Rage did not come until later, and it grew as each year passed. At that moment, for the first time, he truly feared her.

Her hands were clasped in front of her, and her face was the only one without incredulity. Her mouth was slightly turned up at the corners, her brows were lifted, eyes bright with an unnatural glitter. Those of the Decaphiloi who had learned to look away from her, in cowardice or in revulsion or in mere uncomfortable avoidance, now stared in open shock.

It was her moment of complete triumph over the Decaphiloi, the moment of its destruction. Antenor could feel it splinter and crack, crashing down around him as one by one the Decaphiloi left the academy, never to return. Polonus, his face heavy and gray, left first. Julia, bursting into sobs, ran away next. Then Lucius and Marcus. Hector shoved off from the column, stumbling away. Only Portia and Antenor remained in the portico.

Polonus had warned them. And Antenor had led the rest in not believing. He saw his own folly as he looked into her eyes and realized she had used him all along.

He had disbelieved Polonus's frets about Kardus and his suspicions that Portia's teachings with her students were going too far. He'd dismissed the rumors of secret meetings where strange things were happening. Some of her students had left the academy entirely, and Polonus claimed he had proof that she was proselytizing them to the temple she attended in Scythopolis. And Antenor had disbelieved. He'd never liked Portia, but never dreamed what lay beneath her coolness.

He disbelieved the fears Polonus had for Theseus, who openly mocked Portia and her Dionysus. He disbelieved the whole bit about Portia's proselytizing. The only one of the Decaphiloi who had believed Polonus was Bion. They would later learn that the same night Theseus was murdered, Bion had hanged himself.

Portia had gazed at him across the way, with those unusually bright eyes. He felt her supersedence then; he had a strange sensation of looking up at her, though she was shorter than he. And then she turned and strolled away, sandals clicking. Hatreds began then. Hatred for the sound of clicking sandals. Hatred for himself for not believing Polonus, hatred for Polonus for being right, hatred for Portia who had the power to deliver a man to a heinous death, simply to prove that she could. Hatred, most of all, for Callimachus.

The cart stopped in front of a low-roofed building. A little boy appeared on the porch of the inn, regarded Antenor for a long moment, and then ran off.

He sat in the cart for a few moments. He hoped Claudius had posted the schedule for the new performances, hoped Master Quirinicus showed up to craft another scathing review. Wearily, he climbed down from the cart and wondered if Portia would really have the guts to show up. He wondered what he would do when he saw her.

The light curtain of the sedan fluttered in the wind, giving Julia glimpses of the eastern hills, glimpses she did not see.

Her stomach had been in twists since Philip told her about the message posted in the forum. He sat beside her, gazing out his open window at the Galilee, as silent as she. He had insisted on coming, and she could not protest. She couldn't tell him she wished she could go alone. If she told him she should face it by herself, he would nod gravely and say he understood. And he would come anyway. She smiled a little.

Oddly, it was Philip who first thought she should go, and Julia who did not want to. It was hard, being in the place where Kardus used to live. And it was hard enough seeing Tallis again, without seeing him with Philip by her side.

Philip had asked her once if there had been a lover in her past, and she said yes, but they never had the chance for love. He had clasped her hands and kissed her fingertips and said he was glad.

She'd fallen in love with Tallis before they ever exchanged a word. What was it about him that had attracted her attention as he served the smug crowd at the house of Callimachus? The gap-toothed grin that had flashed after he'd made a side comment to a pompous scholar? The scholar had forgotten his pomposity for the moment and laughed hard enough to attract attention. Everyone looked, bemused, upon the famous scholar, but Julia had watched Tallis and his small satisfied smile as he turned away with his tray, delivering a quiet instruction to a slave, swooping to pick up a napkin from the floor. He'd attended the noisy room with immaculate attention to detail, and all the while managed to keep a subtle eye on Callimachus. While everyone couldn't help a constant regard of the infamous Callimachus—glances strayed to him, no matter what the activity—she couldn't take her eyes off Tallis.

His face wasn't smooth and strong and handsome like Philip's. It was rugged and went with a gap-toothed grin. His dark eyes glinted with amusements. He was unperturbed by fretful outbursts from the cook or the crooked little man named Aristarchus or haughty scholars. He had held the entire gathering together, yet was invisible. He acted more like the great Callimachus, affable and gentle, ready with good humor.

"Are you nervous?"

Julia broke from unseen glimpses. She smiled at Philip.

He reached and squeezed her hand.

"A little."

"Who do you think will be there?"

"I don't know."

"Do you think Portia will show?"

She squeezed his hand back. "I don't see how she could."

His face became grave, and he searched her eyes. "She isn't like you, Julia. She isn't like most people—she doesn't have a conscience. She could easily show up. Who knows how she thinks."

She studied his gray eyes, remembering a time when they were filled with worry for her. A time when his earnest pleading made her think differently of the son of the Hippos market controller.

Can't you see what she is doing to your precious group? How can all of you be so blind?

Philip, please . . . She is wise, she is trying to teach us a new way of—

She's a sham! Do only a few students see it? Or outsiders like me? No one will listen because none of you could possibly be wrong! You're all so full of pride; you think you could never be taken. Julia, I thought Polonus ran your group—open your eyes; look and see who holds the reins.

Polonus has had misgivings about her lately. . . .

Misgivings. She's a sorceress witch, and he has "misgivings."

Antenor never liked her. And Kardus has been acting strange. So strange . . .

Julia. One of these days you're all going to wake up and see what she really is. I hope to gods it isn't too late.

Philip—

Don't let her ruin you, Julia. Not you. Not you . . .

"Philip," she said suddenly. "Thank you for coming."

He smiled and took her hand to kiss her fingertips, then looked out the window once more.

Who would show? She'd seen Antenor only once. They saw each other in a wineshop and pretended not to. By then he had grown a beard and went by his second name, Patroclus, and he was the master of the theater. She thought she'd seen Hector once, when she was out on an evening stroll with Philip, but that could have been her fancy. The rest she had not seen since that awful last meeting in the colonnade.

Antenor—she remembered how her heart had crushed at seeing his face, so betrayed, so bewildered. So broken. She remembered Polonus and his despair. And Hector . . . poor Hector. Theseus's best friend. Most of all she remembered Portia and her wordless coup.

As Philip had wondered, how could they have been so blind? It was mystifying, how they seemed to give Portia more and more control over them. Utterly mystifying. The things she said in the end that had made sense would never have made sense in the beginning.

Julia missed the way it was at the beginning, the camaraderie with the teachers, the respect she felt from them, her happiness when she took out the templates and the buckets and began to teach of mosaic. She missed the way it felt to walk through the colonnades on a beautiful day and see Polonus and Antenor seated on the steps with a group of earnest-faced students, deep in conversation. She missed the way Antenor acted the good-natured antagonist, the way Polonus parried his jabs, the laughter of the students. She missed the way Antenor teased her. She missed Hector and Theseus, Lucius and Marcus, and Bion. Sweet, shy, stuttering Bion. He brought her a posy one day, tied in a lavender ribbon.

And Kardus. Kardus thought he was in love with her.

Tears came, and she let them slide down her cheeks so she wouldn't catch Philip's eye by wiping them away.

She and Polonus had entered a whimsical pact, to push Kardus away from themselves to Portia. Julia would be free of his increasingly sticky bids for attention, and Polonus would be free to "be," he had laughingly said.

Kardus, honest Kardus, so effusive with learning and teaching, so earnest and direct. How expansive he was with the dreams of Callimachus; how he loved to teach his students, most of them his own age. Kardus was so dramatic he would actually act out some of the scenes he told of Alexander the Great. The other teachers would gather discreetly behind the columns to watch, bemused and entertained, as the talented young man regaled the students on the steps. He even attracted the attention of shopkeepers and passersby, and they applauded when he was done. He would grin and bow with a flourish, and once leapt down the steps to fleece the crowd with an upturned palm. All the teachers had laughed and clapped at that.

At the same time Kardus thought he was in love with her, she began to notice the son of the *agoranomos*, the market controller of Hippos, the handsome man named Philip who collected the shopkeepers' rent. He collected the rent each month from Antenor, who was in charge of the academy purse, and Julia soon had occasion to be where he was at every collection.

Kardus was younger than she was. It was hard, at first, because she *had* been interested in him, despite the gap in their ages. He was charming with his enthusiastic ways, handsome by those ways. She was just beginning to return his interest when she noticed the son of the market controller.

Was it her fault? Did she sense the danger in Portia before she pushed Kardus her way? If so, she was guilty of murder, because Kardus was the living dead. Everything bad happened after Kardus became involved with Portia. And once Portia controlled Kardus, it seemed she controlled everything. Kardus, the greatest tragedy of the Decaphiloi demise. So winsome and bright. Just as dead as Theseus and Bion.

Could she have been happy with him if she tried? If she had tried, then Portia would not have ruined him. Then Theseus and Bion would be alive, and Polonus would still be teaching; they would all be teaching, and—

"I don't want to go!" Julia cried. "Please, Philip, I don't want to go!" She seized his arm. "*Please*, Philip! Please take me home!"

Philip called for the driver to stop, ordered him to turn around. He took Julia into his arms and held her tightly as she wept into his neck.

"It's all right," he whispered into her hair. "We won't go, my darling. We won't go. Oh, Julia . . . don't cry, my love."

Hector never made it out of Hippos.

He'd seen the message in the forum. Seen it every day since it was posted. Read it so many times he had it memorized. He sat now in the back of a comfortable wineshop, under an awning of green vines. He was unused to the daytime and had a slight headache, but he couldn't sleep. He lifted the mug to his lips and took an absent sip.

He thought about going. Had thought about nothing else for the past three days. He'd visited the baths and gone to see the comedies three times, brooding all the while on whether he should go. His nighttime job as watchman at the western gate gave him much time for introspection. None of the Decaphiloi knew he was still around, at least he didn't think so. A former teacher at the Academy of Socrates in Hippos surely had fled the debacle in Palestine and landed at Asclepios on Cos to pursue a career in the growing science of medicaments. Surely he did not lose himself in the obscurity of a silent nocturnal life on a workman's wage.

Sometimes things were interesting. He had to investigate the occasional nighttime ruckus in the marketplace, a thief plundering a stall, a drunkard raising laments. Mostly, things were quiet. He patrolled the dark and empty streets, duly checking out every storefront and stall, making sure the rare drunken sprawl did not become a brawl. He avoided the bathhouse on the northeast side; it was the only place he did not patrol. There, he had found Theseus. Theseus, his best friend. It was Portia's particular cruelty to leave Hector the note of where to find him.

The dismemberment had not occurred at the bathhouse, this half his brain informed him as he observed the monstrous scene; the other half of his brain was occupied in shock. He had come upon the scene thinking he saw a man spread-eagle on the bathhouse steps, wondering why he lay with his arms outspread as if to embrace the sky, wondering why ivy leaves were sprinkled over him, and why he wore a mask. It was a mask of Dionysus, a typical mask used for home decoration or for parading the streets. It was early morning after the festival, and Hector thought it was a reveler sleeping off his celebration.

As he approached, the scientific half of his brain thought the arm span oddly long; the other half of his brain recoiled. The scientific half thought the man on the steps the tallest man he'd ever seen; the other half shook. The scientific half saw, when he came close enough for the other half to make him halt with dread, that he was not an extraordinarily tall man with a very long arm span, but a man who had been dismembered and reassembled, with several inches between the severed limbs. The scientific half knew instantly the violence had been done elsewhere, for the lack of an ocean of blood on the steps; the other half remembered the words of Portia's note, and they beat upon his breast: *You will find the mocker on the altar of the ruined.*

The mocker—Theseus.

Altar of the ruined—it was Hector and Theseus's joke. They once had kidded that the ignorant gathered on these bathhouse steps to glean wisdom on the altar of the ruined. This particular bathhouse was known for dark deeds, and they joked that no man of repute would be found dead upon its steps. Portia had listened, had laughed along with them.

The scientific half said don't look, you know it's him. The other half with shaking hands lifted the mask and saw. Theseus, eyes garishly staring, flaccid gray face drained of blood, head a few inches from his neck.

Hector lifted the mug to his lips, set it down before he took a sip. The scientific half wondered if she had wielded the knife herself, and how did she know exactly where to separate the limbs, and did she simply drain him or did she cauterize the wounds, and could wounds like that be cauterized.

The other half ached whenever he saw the widow of Theseus and his orphans in the marketplace. The same half kept a secret and silent vigil to protect the woman and her children for the rest of their lives. The same half left her money where she could find it, not much, only a workman's wage, and the same half wished this Tallis well on his quest and hoped he would not end up on another altar of the ruined. To this Tallis, and his forum for Truth, Hector lifted his mug.

The man named Tallis sat at the other end of the long table. He had stopped looking anxiously for any other Decaphiloi to attend his little forum. Antenor had watched the sister of Kardus give the man concerned looks when Tallis did not notice. As the hours went by and no one else came, Tallis sank into a stupor over his mug and no longer attempted to make Antenor feel like a guest.

Well, and it was time for him to leave. He knew this would be an exercise in futility. He wondered how Claudius fared with the troupe. Anything could happen with Claudius in charge.

Tallis hadn't seem surprised when Antenor appeared at the door. He'd even greeted him by his surname, not Patroclus; Antenor wondered how he knew. The servant of Callimachus was cordial, if tense, and looked like he could use a good night in a reputable brothel. He had a fading bruise at his eye and looked as if he hadn't slept in a week.

"Did you ever put on something from Sophocles?" Tallis now asked, scoring his thumbnail in the grain of the tabletop.

"I tried." Antenor sighed. "The government, with its meager stipend, now has suggestions for all of our performances. None of the suggestions include Sophocles."

"A pity."

"It is. Fortunately for the arts in Hippos, Lepidus is now in control. I have hopes his sensibilities are of a more tragic nature."

"I liked that fellow the other day—what was his name? Claudius?"

"Claudius," Antenor said, chuckling fondly. "I can send him to the market with a page to post the performances, and he'll return with a bundle of nut pastries and the page stuffed in his pocket. He can't remember to put his sandals on in the morning, yet the man can play Achilles—gods, can he play Achilles."

"Patroclus is your . . ."

"Forename."

"I should have recognized you."

"You were pretty busy, if I recollect, that summer so long ago. That was eight, nine years ago? You had a lot of people to look after." Now that they were talking, he couldn't resist. "So . . . how is Callimachus these days?"

"Well enough. He has the gout."

"Does he."

Tallis finally looked over at him.

Truly, the man appeared haggard, not the amiable fellow he'd met at the theater a week ago. But then, this was all about Portia and truth finding, wasn't it? Haggardness went with it.

"I'm sorry to have wasted your time. It appears the others are not coming," Tallis said.

Antenor touched the rim of his mug. "Ironic that I'm the only one to show up, don't you think?"

Tallis looked at him uncertainly.

"Well . . . considering your message. 'Antenor . . . the one who tried but gave up.' An eloquent description. I wondered how you could have known me so completely."

Tallis flushed and looked away. "It doesn't matter anymore."

"Doesn't matter? I thought this was a forum for Truth." Antenor narrowed his eyes. What had happened to the fellow? He didn't seem like the vibrant soul who had posted that message. It rather disappointed him.

"Don't you want to know who forged the reports and stole from Callimachus?" He pushed on to the next: "Don't you want to know why Theseus died?"

"Not anymore."

"Why not?"

Tallis rubbed his face, then snapped, "Because it doesn't matter anymore."

Antenor studied him. What had changed? He'd read the earnest (if perversely naïve) message and felt for the first time in a long time a jostling within. It was the cursed swell Callimachus used to bring when he inspired hearts with fine words.

Antenor was old and wary now. Portia had twisted the good, sucked it dry from him until he no longer believed in good, no longer trusted the motivations of others. But when he read the second message from Tallis of Athens, he felt a rustle of the dryness within; a wind skittering dead leaves along. It wasn't much, but it was something. A hope blowing.

If he let himself, and he would not because he was too old and wary, he would see one impossible and unexpected chance for his own redemption.

"I did not believe Polonus," he said suddenly, startling himself. He raised his eyebrows.

Tallis had been absently rubbing his hands together and now stopped. "About what?"

"That Kardus was—being overtaken—" He hesitated. "By Evil."

Tallis turned such eyes upon him, such dreadfully despondent eyes. He said dully, "And why was that so hard to believe?"

Antenor slowly shook his head. "I don't know. I knew he was right all along. I didn't want to believe it. I betrayed Polonus, my dearest friend, by allowing him to face alone a monstrous, a moving, a very real Evil. An Evil I could not understand with my head, but knew with my heart.

"I had warned Callimachus, in the beginning, and against all logic, not to take Portia on. It's all his fault, don't you see? I warned him, and he asked me why, and I could not tell him how she managed to put cold in the room by walking into it, how the light of day dimmed when she was around. I could not explain this to him. The gods on Mount Olympus will witness that I tried. He ignored me." Antenor snorted sadly, shaking his head. "The dear old fool ignored me. He made me feel ungracious and uncertain for not seeing the good he saw in her. She bewitched him as she bewitched everyone else. I could not understand how I was the only one to see it. The only one, until an unlikely fellow that Julia eventually married. Philip, son of the market controller. A most unlikely candidate to fill the shoes of a seer. As unlikely as myself."

"Seer . . ."

Antenor shrugged. "I saw, he saw. Call it what you will. By then I was embittered, and I denied everything I felt by defying Polonus when he began to notice the changes in Kardus. Philip, this uneducated outsider, was the only one to do something about it. But by the time Julia woke up, Kardus was gone and Polonus had been shut out—by me, and by the others because I led them. Except for Bion. Bion believed Polonus. And I soon began to warn Theseus about his mockery, from some foreboding within. He said, 'You defy her; why shouldn't I?' I said, 'Theseus, there is a difference between defiance and scorn. She will not bear your scorn.' He laughed at me. Much as Callimachus had."

"Cal's great downfall was to believe in people."

"Yes, isn't it funny—that's what we loved most about him. His tragic flaw." Antenor eyed Tallis, who now seemed less withdrawn. "I wasn't the only one to warn him about her, at the beginning."

"Don't tell me—Aristarchus."

Antenor nodded and smiled a little. "I never liked him."

"I still don't. Creepy little man." Then Tallis said, "He saved my life as much as Cal."

Antenor folded his arms, remembering. "Aristarchus was watching Portia regale a group on the lawn one day. I noticed, because I watched for anyone who looked on her with other than admiration. She was an Egyptian, from Alexandria. She had an accent, a charming accent. It drew attention to her, and she used that accent. Just when I lost interest in what she was saying to the group, I saw Aristarchus. He was shuffling past, and he'd paused to regard her for a moment. He had the most amazing look on his face: astonished disgust. Like he just stepped in a pile of fresh dung.

"I caught up with him and had the shortest and most engaging conversation I ever had in my life. I said, 'Why don't you like her?' He stopped and looked at me, like he couldn't believe I asked such a foolish question, and he said this: 'Same reason you don't—she stinks.'"

Tallis laughed. It was unexpected, a pleasant sound. "That's Aristarchus," he said fondly. "That's surely him."

Antenor's smile soon faded. "I watched her after that, for the whole summer. Sometimes I thought I was being ridiculous, but certain things she did waved a flag at me. It was as if she tried hard to be normal, but didn't know what that was. It put my attention on her as on a scorpion. No one else noticed the way she tried to fit in. Soon I developed an odd awareness of her. I knew if she walked into the room even if my back was to the door." He looked at the other man. "What happened, Tallis, between the posting of that marvelous message and this moment?"

Tallis did not answer right away. He went back to absently rubbing his hands. "Polonus has been taken. I'm not strong enough to replace him."

Polonus has been taken. The words fell heavy upon his heart.

"Then don't replace him. Listen to me, Tallis: Go back to Athens, now. I'd ask you to stay, because I like you. I'd ask you to run the theater with me. I have indeed read your play, and you have talent. But I knew Polonus was right, though I didn't want to believe it. If you say you are not strong enough to replace him, I believe you. With all my heart, I believe you. I would fear for you if you even tried."

"How do you know I would try?"

"Because you remind me of Callimachus." A pang caught his heart. "He doesn't give up on people, to his own hurt and to the great hurt of others." He leaned forward. "Tallis—fly from this place. Polonus was my friend."

Antenor and Tallis were locked in a look that took some persistence to break. They finally became aware of a small shy voice.

"Master Tallis?"

In the kitchen doorway stood the spitting image of Kardus. And Portia. He had her nose; he had the set of her eyes. But the brown hair touched in copper belonged to Kardus, and the way his ears stood out.

Antenor had wondered what became of the child. What great fortune had placed him here, in the safety of the innkeeper? He couldn't even imagine the child with Portia. Couldn't imagine her as a mother.

The child came through the passage with a tray. "Mistress Kes wondered if you would like refreshment now." On the tray were plates of cheeses and olives, sliced date bread. He went to Tallis and carefully put the tray in front of him.

Tallis, despite the mood, smiled a weary but true smile at him. He said to the child, "Are you taking over my job?"

Antenor remembered Portia's pregnancy. Remembered the looks she gave Kardus, looks meant to be affectionate, but which in reality were chillingly possessive. Savory with triumph.

Kardus didn't notice—or did, and enjoyed it. He'd changed after he became intimate with Portia. He had been proud of her growing belly, defiant, because he knew what they all thought of her.

Antenor had warned Kardus too. It was exactly the wrong thing to do with Kardus. They all had to watch his disintegration and, from heartbreak, pretended not to see. How Antenor missed that boy . . . he was as fond of him as he was of Claudius.

"No, Master Tallis."

"Spill something for once, will you?"

Pleased, smiling self-consciously, the boy withdrew to the kitchen.

"Does he know he has a son?" Antenor asked sadly.

Likely he was not even aware of him, from the state Polonus described. What a sad and tragic thing, to have a son and—

What look was this? Tallis was staring at him. And what was this? Kardus's sister, the woman named Kes`Elurah, had obviously been listening—she now peered through the kitchen doorway with an incredulous face.

She slowly came out of the kitchen, abandoning pretense at eavesdropping, clutching her apron with both fists. "Does who know?"

Antenor was confused. He glanced from the girl to Tallis, whose face was just as shocked.

"You said 'Does he know he has a son?'" she said very carefully. "Does who know?"

"Why—Kardus, of course." Antenor sat back. "Oh, gods—you didn't know. Why, that must be a bit of a shock. Yes, he belongs to

Kardus—Kardus and Portia, though you may not know that either—say there . . . are you all right?"

Antenor rose quickly, because the woman looked ready to faint. He hurried over and helped her to a bench.

She fanned her face, then pressed her palms on her cheeks. Tallis offered a mug, but she pushed it away. Suddenly the woman locked eyes with Tallis. She froze, and Antenor feared she'd drop at that instant. Instead, she began to smile. Then she began to laugh, and Antenor feared worse than a faint: He feared hysterics.

"He's ours," she finally cried. "He's ours!" She drummed her feet on the floor, laughing and crying at once. "He's ours!" And she bolted from the bench and ran for the kitchen. "Zagreus!"

For the space of a heartbeat, Antenor and Tallis stared at one another. Then they ran after her through the kitchen, and out the back door.

"Zagreus!" she called.

The child was standing near the donkey and cart Antenor had hired, feeding the donkey from his palm. The woman flew at him, skidded to her knees in front of him, startling the donkey. She caught the child in a fierce and laughing hug.

"Zagreus, you're ours, you're ours!" she cried.

A dark servant hurried out from the barn, alert and wary. The man Tallis had introduced earlier as Jarek the innkeeper, Kardus's father, came running from around the inn.

"What's going on?" Jarek demanded.

"You're ours, Zagreus!" Kes`Elurah was on her knees, holding his shoulders, then his face.

His cheeks puckered with the hold; he eyed her first, then the other adults.

Kes snatched him again in a fierce embrace. "*I'm* your auntie, not Ariadne! I am! Arinna is not your mother—she's not your mother, Zagreus! We didn't know it, child. We didn't know it!" She looked about wildly, then pointed out Antenor to Zagreus. "See this man? He came all the way here just to tell us."

"What's she saying?" Jarek demanded, his face incredulous.

"So Portia never told you," Antenor said grimly. "Of course not. Vicious shrew."

"You are my nephew, Zagreus," Kes`Elurah breathed, tears coursing down her face. She took his hands to her heart. "You are my blood. It means you never have to go away. You'll never see her again; you'll never see either of them because you are ours." She turned to look up at Jarek. "Father . . . this is your grandson."

"Kes . . . don't tell him who his father is yet," Tallis murmured at her ear. "Not yet."

Antenor noticed the dark slave nod in agreement.

Kes gazed at her father. "Haven't we always known, Father? Haven't we?"

Jarek looked at Kes and Zagreus, Jarek's dark brown eyes unreadable, his face firmly mistrusting. Then the eyes began to soften, and his lip began to quiver. Finally he said, "We have." He blinked rapidly. "We have, haven't we? Well, just look at him—can't you see him in the boy?"

Antenor watched the scene, maintaining the proper detachment of a stranger because to them he was a stranger. But in his heart was joy, because something good had come to an unfortunate family, through an old and corrupt master of the theater.

The only one who did not seem surprised was the dark servant who soon withdrew to the barn. Antenor thought he caught a wry expression on his face. If the slave would have spoken, Antenor felt quite sure he'd have said, "Well—now you know what I've known for years."

"It isn't Master Jarek anymore, and it isn't Mistress Kes," the woman was saying to the child. "It's Grandfather and it's Auntie. And nobody will take you from us because you belong to us now. We're blood, we three. We're family."

Antenor knew, then, that the forum for Truth was over. He allowed himself one more moment. Then he caught the eye of his driver and nodded.

Tallis sat on the edge of his cot, gazing at the yellow flame of the lamp he held in his hands. The cool clean light would not go out tonight. He made sure the wick was long and that there was plenty of oil in the lamp. He carefully placed the lamp on the table, on the same ring of oil so it would not make another ring.

Zagreus did not understand it all, but was happy because everyone else was happy. He couldn't make himself say Grandfather today, and couldn't call Kes *Auntie* because the word was not pleasant to him. But his shining face constantly looked from Kes to Jarek. Tallis tried to be happy for them, and turned in early because he couldn't keep it up.

Tomorrow was the Festival of Dionysus. The festivities would last all day, and escalate in gaiety come evening. They surely had formal activities planned in Hippos. In Scythopolis, one of the holy places of Dionysus, it would be a day off from work. It was an official holiday in Greece and in Rome. He didn't know if Persia, in the East, celebrated Dionysus. He knew the Jews of Palestine did not. He felt a kinship with them, even if their reasons to shun the day were different from his own.

For most, the Festival of Dionysus was a celebration of spring, a time to get together with friends, drink their health, and while you were at it, lift your mug to good old Dionysus as well. For the religious, it was a chance not only to celebrate their god, but to proselytize the unbelieving. This was their day, and they were in charge. Everyone knew it; everyone respected it.

The nightmare would be about Zagreus; not his little brother this time, but the son of Portia and Kardus. If the others rejoiced to know his blood, Tallis felt unrest. All they had to do was get through the next two days; then he would be happy for them.

He made sure Zagreus was asleep on his pallet in Kes's room before he turned in. He noticed that Jarek barred the front door after the last guest had left, and that Samir made up his pallet on the floor of the kitchen. They knew what day it was tomorrow. And now they knew more about the dark history of the festival, told to them by a certain Greek dog from Athens over cups of wine in the common room after Zagreus went to bed.

Soon you will come to live in my palace. Kes told them what Portia had said, and Tallis told them a male child was sometimes chosen for their sacrifices to Dionysus. That's when Jarek bolted his door for the second time in a week.

Tallis watched the flame as he slowly lowered himself onto the cot. Sleep would come—he knew it and he feared it—and he would gaze on the flame as long as he could.

COME AND SEE.

He stood on the top of the ridge, bitter wind urging him forward. The light all around him was a cold grainy light, as though the air was salt and pepper. It made the landscape surreal, made the new green of spring mouse brown. He looked for the sun, but there was no sun. Only cold grainy light.

Ahead of him were the tombs.

COME AND SEE. . . .

Laughing chill wind herded him.

He stumbled into the clearing of Polonus's home. He braced against the wind urging him forward, for he began to hear the laughter. Mocking laughter, one moment at his ear, the next a distance apart. In and out, whirling around. Triumphant laughter.

The wind shoved, and he fell on his knees. He stayed on the ground because he could not turn that corner, could not go past the shed for the mounting dread.

COME AND SEE, SON OF MAENAD. . . .

Kardus stood before him. He wore broken shackles like bracelets on his wrists and ankles. He was naked, save the shackles. His body was covered with cuts and scars, scaly with filth. His eyes were livid orange and slanted. He grabbed Tallis by the hair and dragged him forward.

Flies everywhere, buzzing about the doorway, crawling on the door.

COME AND SEE!

Grief struck him, and he cried, "I don't want to see!"

Kardus spoke with a many-timbre'd voice. *YOU WILL SEE.*

Kardus dragged him even with the kicked-apart line of Polonus's stones. They were chalky in the grainy light. Tallis reached for one, but

Kardus picked him up and dropped him on his feet in front of the fly-swarmed door. The laughter was louder.

Kardus threw the door open, and chaos burst.

Tallis clamped his ears. Whirling screams rushed into the room, a coursing pandemonium of voices, a bucking tide of filth. He could feel the air move as They passed. Glee, such laughing glee. He could almost see the tumult in the air, shimmers here and there, brown streaks, black hair and wings. Horrible enough, what was happening in the air in front of his eyes. He tried as long as he could not to look at the man on the floor. Tried, but at last his eyes fell upon Polonus.

He lay spread-eagle upon the mat that lined the floor, dismembered, reassembled with space between the ragged limbs, arms wide as if to embrace the sky. His mouth was open. His eyes were gone, black caverns of gore left behind. Blood, oceans of blood everywhere. The room was dragged over with it.

Laughter, shrieks and screams of delight, everywhere.

He was in the chicken yard, driving his head into the ground.

A trampling of feet—Samir threw himself into Tallis.

Tallis lay panting, bewildered, trying to understand why he was in the chicken yard again. His knees were bloodied and filthy. He put his hand to his hair; it was ground down with chicken yard filth; the top of his head felt raw. Then he stopped breathing. He got to his feet and looked for the northeastern hills. Samir came beside him, peering too.

"Zagreus?" Tallis panted.

"Safe," Samir said.

"I must see Polonus today. I can't go without you."

"I will come."

"What about . . ."

"His grandfather will look after him."

After a moment Tallis nodded, the movement jerky. Morning light began to crest, illuminating the ridge. The sun was rising on the Day of Dionysus.

XIII

I'm glad you asked me to make date bread. Kardus likes date bread—
he used to. Polonus once told us if we didn't feed him, he'd resort to
foul things."

She was too chatty. While Tallis sat at the kitchen worktable trying
to rub away a headache, Kes packed the basket.

Was Polonus as bad as Kardus now? How long would it be before he
was just like Kardus?

"How long will Jarek be gone to Kursi?"

Jarek came in through the kitchen door at that moment. "I'm not
going. Not until you and Samir get back."

Tallis kept his relief to himself.

Kes paused at the basket. "Samir is going with you?"

"I have some scrolls to return, and I don't want to damage them.
He'll carry the basket for me." It was an easy way to explain the two of
them going. "I want to tell Polonus that Antenor came. He might like to
hear that." He exchanged a look with Jarek.

However he tried to hide it, his relief, knowing that Jarek would stay
to look after Zagreus, must have been evident: Jarek produced an iron

key from his tunic fold. He smiled grimly and said, "Don't worry, Zagreus will be fine."

"Father!" Kes said, astonished. "You didn't lock him up. . . ."

Jarek shrugged. "Just until they get back. Baraan is coming to discuss a shipment from Tiberias, and I don't want to wonder where that rascal is flitting about. How long will you be gone, Tallis?"

Tallis slid off the stool to reach for the basket, and cheerfully gave the back of Kes's head covering a firm tug. "About an hour. She couldn't last an hour without me."

While Kes glared and readjusted the head covering, Jarek said, "What's an hour, Kes? He's in the barn. He's comfortable. I gave him things to occupy his time. I gave him some cinnamon sticks."

Kes turned her glare on her father as she tucked up her hair into the covering. "You *shackled* him in the barn and bribed him with sweets."

"He is not shackled," Jarek protested. "He is protected. For his own good. Master Athenian says it's not a good day for him to wander about."

Samir appeared in the kitchen doorway. "Master Baraan is here."

On his way to the common room, Jarek said in a low tone to Tallis, "Not more than an hour, please—Baraan can talk the hind leg off a donkey." He ambled into the common room, where despite his complaint they heard him volubly greet his guest. Tallis wondered who the donkey should be more afraid of.

Kes threw her arms up. "He shackled his grandson in the barn."

"It's not going to kill him. What's an hour?"

Kes sighed. She frowned and fingered the edge of her head covering. "Well . . . maybe I can tell him stories for an hour." She eyed Tallis. "Don't be gone long; I have a lot to do."

Suddenly there was nothing else to distract him from the reason he was going to see Polonus. He wondered if somehow Kes knew about his dream, wondered if she'd heard a ruckus in the chicken yard this morning. He handed the basket to Samir. Kes followed them out the doorway, and Tallis gathered the scrolls he'd propped against the wall.

It wasn't even close to noon and the day was already hot, felt more like midsummer than spring. Kes walked with them along the short turn-off down to the road. "I thought you were going to read those scrolls," she said.

Didn't she understand that he was leaving and that returning the scrolls was part of it?

"One is a Euripides play. I've already read it."

Read it? He had it memorized. It was *The Bacchae*, the tragic tale of King Pentheus and his murder at the hand of his Bacchantes mother. How was it that Polonus had a scroll of *The Bacchae*? Was it simply a literary work in the library of a learned man?

"The other scroll is written in Aramaic, I think. Or Hebrew. I can't read either. Besides, I wouldn't have time to read them before I leave."

They stopped at the road. Samir turned toward Kursi with a glance behind him at Tallis. Tallis told him he would catch up.

Kes fussed with the edge of her head covering, glancing now and again at the barn.

"I'm glad Zagreus is your nephew," Tallis finally said.

He watched her fidget with the cloth. What was he thinking, flirting with her like that, tugging on her head covering. And his brilliant comment. *She couldn't last an hour without me.*

Tallis, why do you say such things? Wharf rat. Then suddenly, because he was learning of her, he realized what all the cloth fidgeting was about. She was trying to say something to him. He looked in panic toward Samir, who was not walking toward Kursi, but waiting for him.

It was painful to watch her try and wrest words from a lifetime of silence. Her words came so haltingly, he felt a sting of compassion.

"I—don't want you to go," she managed, not looking at him.

Tallis, don't say a word. I swear you'll regret it.

Her next plainspeak was not any easier. She stayed intent on the head-covering hem. "I like it with you here."

Could he live so close to Polonus and Kardus without helping them? Could he live here with his soulish infirmity? He was strong in Athens, weak here. And Tyche favored him at that moment, because he noticed movement at the corner of his eye. An old woman was coming up the road from the south. "Who is that?"

Kes peered under her hand, then gave a little gasp. "It's Shoshanna, coming for the eggs. She won't understand Zagreus being locked up."

"Don't let her see him."

"Are you coming, Athenian?" Samir called back to them.

"She'll expect to see him; she always brings him something," she fretted. "I hope she's in a talkative mood; maybe she'll forget Zagreus."

"Athenian?"

"I'm coming!" Tallis snapped.

Kes looked to Samir. "Why is he so impatient? He hasn't been himself lately." Her tone softened. "I suppose none of us have."

"Kes—"

"You better go." She trotted off to meet Shoshanna.

An hour did not give them much time. It would take half that just to get there. Well, all he needed to do was drop off the basket and scrolls, give his regards to a lip-fiddling old man and maybe a foaming-mouthed freak, and make sure the lip-fiddling man still had eyes.

He'd leave for Athens day after tomorrow. Day after, because Tallis knew the lore of the Bacchantes. Today was the Day of Dionysus, but tomorrow was the nones of the month. His brother died on the nones.

"I've been thinking about Polonus. Do you think he's as bad as Kardus yet?"

"Not yet." Presently Samir asked, "What did you dream?"

"You knew I had a dream?"

"You were screwing your head into the ground."

"There is that."

He needed Samir like a cripple needed a walking staff, and he resented that fact. Maybe he was still annoyed over Samir's exalted Two Truths. If Samir had remained mysterious, if he'd kept his philosophy to himself, Tallis would have liked him better.

With the bright sunshine and the heat of the day, the glitter of the Galilee and the exertion it took to keep up with Samir's long steady stride, the horror of the dream began to diminish. Maybe being away from the inn helped.

"How is your head?"

Tallis grimaced. He must have looked ridiculous. "Sore."

"What did you dream?"

"The usual. Bad things."

Samir was silent for a time. "Do you always have nightmares?"

"I had them a lot when I was a child. All the time after my brother died. Then . . . I don't know when it was, my late teens, they simply went away. Since I've been here, they've started up again."

The slave was silent once more, and Tallis fell to thinking about home.

He missed Callimachus. He'd never imagined he would be gone this long. Aristarchus had accompanied him as far as Alexandria to visit the academy there, then sailed back to Athens. He wondered how they both fared. Wondered how the house was running without him.

How had he come to depend on Samir as he depended on Callimachus? What was it about the two of them, so very different, and yet . . .

He thought about what had happened in the inn with Polonus, when Kardus came. Nobody had said anything about that. Samir had handled it, somehow; he had taken care of them. A bizarre, freakish encounter, and a Parthian slave had kept them safe. He had a twisted hand to prove it.

"How's your hand?" Tallis presently asked.

"Not very useful," Samir admitted. "It will mend. The last shaman we had was in a state for days. But he came out of it."

"That—encounter—was like a nightmare, except in the day. I haven't heard from Kes or Jarek about it, which makes me wonder if what happened was commonplace, and that makes me wonder if you're some sort of a living amulet."

No answer.

"What happened at the inn when Kardus came, Samir?"

"What do you think happened?" Samir said testily. "Evil happened. Bad happened. Zagreus could have told you that. Don't make things so difficult."

"But—it happened during the day. With the sun." And it was much worse than when he first met Kardus.

"I wonder how you can be so thick at times."

"You're cheerful today."

They walked in silence for a time. Then Samir spoke quietly. "I too had a dream."

Neck hairs prickled. "If you say it was about Polonus . . ."

"No. Kardus." After a moment, the slave said, "I never dream."

"Was it bad?"

"Yes. Bad."

Tallis wet his lips. "Was there . . . blood? And laughing?"

For an answer, Samir slid a look at Tallis. Tallis saw startled fear in his eyes.

They gained the top of the ridge and followed it west toward the Galilee. The herd of pigs they smelled had trampled the grasses on the top of the slope. He looked northeast, from where the wind brought the smell; in the distance he saw the brown backs of pigs grubbing in the new spring grasses, and a couple of shepherds looking under their hands at them. Yes, two men heading for the tombs would give them something to talk about.

His sandal suddenly slipped in pig dung, and he went down to a knee. The fall made him crumple one of the scrolls. Cursing, he examined it in dismay, then realized he was pushing the end of the other scroll into the filth. He cursed again, louder, and struggled to his feet to search out a clean patch of grass to wipe off the scroll.

"Gods, what a stench," he muttered. He found no clean grass patch and looked unhappily at his tunic. There was already a knee-sized patch of pig filth on it. He groaned and sat on a rock—splotched purple and white with bird droppings—to clean off the rest of the scroll with his own clothing. "Kes is going to have a fit. At least I wasn't wearing my toga."

He took the edge of his tunic and carefully rubbed at the smears on the scroll. He frowned dubiously at the result of his work, and sniffed it. He gagged and recoiled. "Polonus is not going to be happy with me."

He spat on the smear, then carefully worked at it some more. When he heard nothing from Samir, he glanced in the slave's direction.

Samir had the basket hooked through the arm with the injured hand, the hand pressed against his stomach. His lost gaze was somewhere across the Galilee. The sun picked up the oils in his complexion; a satin sheen glistened on his forehead. The forehead drew Tallis's eye, because he'd not seen it bunched like that.

What was worse, the memory of a butchered Polonus or the stricken look of a living amulet? If Samir, a man who could stop a tidal wave, could look like this . . .

He took a few more swipes at the scroll, then rose and carefully arranged the scrolls under his arm. He came and stood near Samir. The wind had a mountain chill in it when it blew strong. Seabirds called and circled and bobbed in flecks upon the water. An indigo range of snow-crested mountains capped the north of the Galilee, many miles distant.

"I'm writing a letter to Cal and Aristarchus. I told them about you. I told them the thing you said. 'When they push, you push back.' In Latin, it is *Quandocumque impellunt, repelle.* I made it a little different, I hope you don't mind. *Quandocumque* doesn't mean 'when,' it means 'whenever.' Whenever they push, you push back. And I see you do that all the time. You don't take it. You push back. For you people strong in head and heart, you people like Callimachus and Aristarchus, the choices seem plain." Tallis shook his head. "Not for people like me."

He looked at Samir's brown crippled hand and found himself blinking back unexpected tears. "People like me need people like you to help us see past hell. You don't have to make the choice for us; just help us see that there is one."

When they came upon the clearing and he saw the shed, dread came in a trickle, buffered by the cry of the seabirds and the heat of the sun. When they passed the shed, the dread picked up force, not a trickle but a stream. They stood at the edge of Polonus's "neighborhood," regarding his tomb home. Samir put down his basket, and Tallis set down the scrolls.

Tallis looked all around for Kardus, but Kardus was nowhere to be seen. He looked for flies on the door. There were no flies. The buzzing from his dream was not there, and neither was the laughing.

Leaving Samir, he moved forward. He felt like someone else, walking slowly toward that door. He felt pity for the dread-filled man who put his hand on the door and slowly pushed it open.

There was no blood, that backdrop of his dream, and the Polonus who sat at his desk, waiting for him, had both eyes and was very much alive.

Tallis sagged against the door.

The place was bright with lamplight. Two small lamps burned on the desk. Another burning lamp was on the stone bench lining the wall, another on the mat in front of the bed.

"Where is Samir?" Polonus asked. "I know he is here."

He seemed in perfect repose, hands folded on his desk. He looked at Tallis from beneath hooded eyes. There was no repose in the eyes. His lips were as dark gray as they were the other day. He looked as if he were cast as a specter in a play, heavily painted, ready to whirl out on the stage.

"Looks like you're getting as much sleep as I am," Tallis said uneasily. "By the way, forgive me if I can't move—had a bad dream, thought you were dead. Is Kardus okay?"

"Of course not." The hooded gaze was unwavering. "Is he alive? Yes."

At least he wasn't fiddling with his lips, but that unearthly repose was almost as disconcerting.

"Do you know what day it is, Polonus?"

The repose faltered. His gaze shifted. "Day of Dionysus."

"Maybe that's why I had the dream." Tallis glanced over his shoulder. "Samir? Everything is all right."

But Polonus was slowly shaking his head.

Tallis studied him. "What isn't right?"

"I'm sorry, Tallis," he whispered.

"What are you sorry about?" Tallis said, alarm rising.

Tormented eyes went to his. "I had a dream too."

Samir was at Tallis's side. He glanced anxiously at Polonus and looked around the rest of the room. His face had not lost any of its fear.

"What are you sorry about?" Tallis repeated.

Polonus's dark staring eyes widened. Tears welled and one spilled.

Tallis went rigid. "What did you dream?"

His face contorted with anguish. "I'm sorry," he cried, and fell on the desk to weep upon his arms.

Samir gasped, such a shrill intake of breath it stopped Tallis's own. Eyes wild, Samir clutched Tallis's arm and breathed, "I left him."

All of him went still. "The old woman on the road," Tallis whispered.

"What old woman?"

"The one who came to see Kes—did she look like Shoshanna to you?"

But Samir was shaking his head. "What old woman?"

"Don't say that, Samir, you saw her just as we were leaving. You saw the old woman; she was on the road. I saw her, and Kes did, and Kes went to—"

"There was no old woman!" Samir cried. "There was no one!"

They stared at one another a moment more. Then Tallis pushed past Samir and stumbled up the broken-stone path, as an eerie shriek from Polonus followed.

"The Day of Dionysus!" the old scholar wailed. "The Day is come!"

Tallis was in a dead run before he left the clearing.

He leapt over rocks; he slid in pig dung and righted himself at a scramble. He raced along the top of the ridge and descended the slope to the road in a tumbling run. He fell, skidding on his hands when he hit the bottom. He staggered up and ran.

He heard only his own hard breathing; he didn't realize Samir was on his heels. When he stopped for breath, bracing on his knees, the slave ran past him. Gasping for air, he lurched after him.

The alarm of the nightmare rang strong upon him when the inn came into sight. Cold grainy light came to his heart. He stopped where the road turned into the inn, breathing hard. All was silent. He did not see Samir, who had run on ahead; he saw no one. All so silent, and everything wrong. He started for the barn.

He didn't know why he did not see her when he first came upon the inn. She was lying on her side in the chicken yard. Her head lay on her arm in a graceful form of repose; she looked to be asleep upon the grass, not in the dirt. She wasn't wearing her head covering, the faded blue head covering with the hem she'd fingered as she tried so hard to talk to him. The wind gently lifted a few wisps of her hair; they lilted in the wind. Her lovely form was so still. So graceful.

He moved slowly toward Kes, aware of sound, finally, of a wail so saturated and true it split open his heart. It came from Samir in the barn, a long undulating cry.

Tallis sank beside Kes. He captured a wisp of her hair and rubbed it between his fingers. He took her shoulder and gently pulled her toward him, easing her to her back. He brushed the hair from her eyes. The eyelids fluttered, and his breath caught—

He looked her over quickly, felt along her limbs. He didn't see any wounds. He brushed the rest of the hair from her face. Her cheek was red, creased where it had rested on her arm. She didn't open her eyes, but moaned slightly, as if deep in sleep. Kes . . . oh, Kes, thank the gods. Kes . . .

He gathered her in, his face in her hair. He held her limp form fiercely, unwilling to answer the wail from the barn.

The wail did not stop. It began again after it ended, rasping now. Gently Tallis laid Kes down.

Samir had torn his tunic down the middle. He'd torn off his head cap and heaped his hair with straw. The wail did not end when he saw Tallis; he only took another handful of barn dust and threw it over his head. Tears streaked the gray dust upon his face.

Jarek was dead. He was not dismembered; his eyes were not put out. Tallis did not see the blood of his dreams. Jarek lay on his back, mouth open, eyes empty. His face was scratched and beaten, and there was some blood, yes, but not much, not the blood of his dreams. Tallis felt for the wall and braced himself on it.

Zagreus was gone. He could see a place of fresh splintering in the wood where the shackles had been hacked from the wall. They had no key to unlock him, because Jarek died to keep it from them. There was no blood where Zagreus had been. Only broken cinnamon sticks.

Zagreus was still alive; Tallis was sure because he knew the lore of the Bacchantes. Unless they were fully engulfed in the frenzies, unless a hapless mocker stood in their way, they did not sacrifice humans to Dionysus on the day of the festival; they saved that for the nones, the day after. While the world put away their festoons and masks, the Bacchantes prepared for midnight.

Tallis's dull gaze fell upon Zagreus's grandfather. He did not see the blood of his nightmare, but he felt it, like the cold grainy light.

The blood was in the air, dragged over with it.

XIV

The common room was filled with the people of Kursi within a few hours. The old salt and his fishermen were among them. Those who could not fit into the inn milled about outside. Children played, happy to be with other children, unsure of what event had called them away from daily chores. Some did not play, but watched the adults, wondering at whatever mystery had happened in the barn.

The authorities from Kursi had been notified of Shamash-Eriba's raid on the inn and had sent a rider on to Hippos. Hippos had jurisdiction over Kursi; any incident had to go through Hippos, especially incidents like this, of a marauding political nature. Leave it to fanatics like Shamash-Eriba to wait for a festival day for a raid.

The Kursians speculated on this brutal attack. Did Eriba believe Jarek was in league with the Romans? Jarek was a loyal Kursian; he'd not willingly deal with the Romans other than to pay his taxes and take their coin for ale. He often joked that Romans were his favorite customers because they were paying back his taxes.

Why would political fanatics target their own loyal Jarek? Why would they steal a child?

Shoshanna had come, a plump old woman swathed in dusty dark purple, first seeing to Kes in her room, then taking over in the kitchen. Other women were there, working silently. They sliced up whatever they found in the kitchen and set it on the table in the common room. They folded their arms and watched their men outside. Everyone waited for the authorities to arrive from Hippos. They kept a constant vigil on the southern road to give themselves something to do. Some figured it might be awhile; it was the Festival of Dionysus, and Hippos was busy.

Samir had not left the barn. He was quiet now, thank the gods, the eerie wail spent. A few Roman soldiers kept watch on the hills, as if Eriba and his men would leap from cover and descend upon the inn at any moment. A few trackers had been dispatched and had not yet returned.

Tallis was in a far corner of the common room, seated on the floor with his back against the wall. A cup came into his sight. He looked up; it was the old salt from the sea.

Tallis took the cup as the older man eased down next to him and folded his hands over his stomach. His sun-darkened face was creased and grizzled. He had the same look as everyone else, that heavy shock.

"I am sorry for your loss," Tallis said quietly. "How long have you known Jarek?"

"All my life." He glanced about to see if anyone could hear him, then said quietly, "They're not going to find anything, those trackers. Shamash-Eriba wasn't here."

"How do you know?"

"Eriba is a patriot, but he is no murderer. Too much is laid at the feet of the Parthians. You don't have to be a murderer to want independence."

"What is your name?" Tallis asked, though he already knew. He had served him wine just the other night, but it was too busy to be officially introduced. He'd only said, I've seen you on the water. And the man had eyed him and replied, I've seen you too; no one stays at the inn more than a day.

"I am Bek`eshan. I am called Bek."

"Bek, I need to get to Scythopolis. I have to pick up some people along the way. I'll need a cart large enough to carry four or five men. I need to leave as soon as possible."

"Is this about Zagreus?"

"It is."

"He has been—taken, then?"

"He has. And we have to find him before the sun goes down, or it will be too late."

"So . . . if we are going to Scythopolis," Bek said carefully, not looking at Tallis, "then this is not the work of Kardus."

Surprised, Tallis said, "No."

A wave of emotion came. For a long moment, Bek covered his eyes with his hand. Then he sniffed and rubbed his nose. His lips trembled, but he kept control. He gestured at the people in the inn.

"These good people don't want to believe it was Kardus. They don't want to believe he could do this to his own father; they don't want to believe he took the boy. So they talk about Shamash-Eriba. They need to believe it was him, and we must not take that from them." He looked at Tallis with weary sorrow. "I will come with you to Scythopolis, and I will bring my son. We will bring Zagreus home to Kes."

When Shoshanna found out where they were going, she made them wait in the common yard with the cart and horses, and hurried to the kitchen. She came back with a bulging water skin and a covered basket and handed them to Tallis in the back of the cart. "There are cinnamon sticks in there; he is fond of cinnamon sticks." She gripped Tallis's arm then patted it. "Bring him back, lad." She went to say more but pressed her lips and patted his arm once more, and turned back to the inn.

Samir had said nothing, merely leaned his head on the barn door and watched them go, his brown face dreadfully vacant. The cart pulled away, and Tallis had looked at him as long as he could, hoping for something, anything. The piercing look that imparted strength. A bid for good fortune, a blessing, a wave. Nothing.

Bek`eshan's son was named Bahat`avi. He was called Tavi. He sat behind his father in the cart and said nothing to Tallis. His features were darker than those of his father, his curly hair and his beard, his look. He stared hard at the other side of the cart and didn't even look up when his father introduced them.

Tallis gazed on the eastern ridge of hills as the cart bumped on the road. Scythopolis was some twenty miles south and west from Hippos. It would take several hours of brisk travel to get there. In Hippos, he hoped, it would not take long to rouse as many—any—of the Decaphiloi as he could find.

Bek stopped the cart at the bottom of the traversing lane to Upper Hippos. "I don't want to take the horses up, not with Beth Shean ahead of us."

Tallis had learned many of the locals referred to the city as Beth Shean, not by the Greek name of Scythopolis. He jumped down from the cart. "I won't be long."

He started up the slope. To his surprise, Tavi was right behind him.

The two men were silent on the way up and through the western gates. Tallis glanced at the ivy draped from the archway as they went under it. He caught the scent of roasting food and heard snatches of instruments and choruses from within the city. The Day of Dionysus was in full swing.

They wove around happy festivalgoers in the streets. Fathers carried small children on their shoulders, mothers kept the rest of the clan together; vendors sold sprigs of ivy and pine, clusters of grapes and figs, tiny souvenir *thrysi* sticks twined with ivy, the sacred wand of Dionysus and the Maenads. Jugglers and acrobats could be seen in glimpses through the people that ringed them. Choruses paraded the streets, singing the praises of Dionysus.

They were halfway through the crowded forum when Tavi spoke. "Who are we fetching?"

"A man named Antenor. He runs the theater."

"What about Polonus?"

Tallis looked at him sideways. "You know Polonus?"

Tavi dodged a group of laughing young men who had suddenly pushed into them. He hurried back into step with Tallis. "I know him. Kardus and I grew up together."

"Polonus can be of no help to us now."

After a moment Tavi said darkly, "Then he goes the way of Kardus."

"Yes." Tallis hesitated. "Did you know Zagreus is Kardus's son?"

"It is true, then?"

"Yes."

"Everyone suspected it. Except Kes and Jarek."

"They know now. They found out yesterday. They found out from the man we are going to see." From the side of his eye, he noticed Tavi's glance.

"Jarek knew before he died? He knew Zagreus was his grandson?"

Tallis nodded.

After a moment, the young man said softly, "That is good."

"It's what I heard Jarek call him this morning. My grandson."

The theater spilled over with revelers. Wine stalls had been set up outside the building. Hawkers sold their trinkets, and vendors plied them with figs, the favored food of Dionysus. Tallis shouldered his way through the crowd to the stone arch, Tavi close behind, where on either side of the arch two young men dressed like Dionysus sold tickets to the performances.

"I need to speak with Anten—with Patroclus," Tallis said to one of them.

"He's busy." The tall young man was counting coins in his box. His cheeks were reddened apples, his lips were reddened slashes. Kohl darkened his brows, and glittery purple-pink painted his eyelids. A fake beard of corkscrew curls dangled from his chin and jiggled with his counting. String tied the beard around the back of his head. A wreath of ivy with clusters of grapes fastened to it adorned his head.

Someone from the crowd called out his name and hooted at him, and he glanced up with a grin, mouthing the count of the coins.

"I must see him. I have grievous tidings."

The young man glanced at Tallis and at Tavi behind him. He finished his count and looked at the other costumed man on the other side of the arch. "Gracchus—I'll be right back." He closed the lid and picked up the box. "Follow me."

He led them through the arch and picked his way down the stadium stairs, clogged with people waiting for the next performance. He led them down to the stage itself, up onto the platform, and over to the side curtain; here the young man held his hand up for them to wait, then ducked behind the curtain. After a moment he reappeared, with Antenor behind him. The young man left.

Antenor wore heavy stage makeup and a wreath of ivy on his head. "What is it? What tidings do you bring?"

"Jarek is dead. Murdered."

"Jarek." Then recognition came. Stunned, he said, "The innkeeper?"

Tallis nodded. Antenor held aside the curtain and beckoned them in, but Tallis said, "She took Zagreus."

For the first time, pain swelled to his throat. He ground his teeth to keep the grief down, but it swelled mercilessly, and as he gazed on Antenor, tears rose. Too long he had leashed grief; seemed the release of the old had made him weak against new. Angrily he dashed at the tears, kept his look down in embarrassment.

Jarek was gone. He'd held long vigil at that inn, waiting for the day his son would return whole. Waiting for a miracle, seeking desperately for it in a shifty shaman from the East, in an old philosopher now broken; providing shackles and baskets, tirelessly keeping up a fake smile, watching over an orphan he finally learned was his own grandson.

Fury rose, and the swell quieted the grief. The thought of vengeance steadied Tallis. He raised his eyes to Antenor.

"I'm going to Scythopolis to fetch Zagreus, and if I get the chance, I will kill her. There will be no justice for Jarek, same as there was no justice for Theseus. Or for my own little brother." He felt the questioning stare on him from Tavi. "Come with me, Antenor. This is what you've wanted."

He became aware of the crowd noise, of backstage chants from the rehearsing chorus. The play today would be from Euripides, *The Bacchae.* Tallis looked at Antenor's makeup and the ivy wreath, the silver brocaded vest. "What part do you play?"

Antenor's made-up face was still, his look distant. "Cadmus," he said absently.

Cadmus, father of Pentheus the unbeliever, killed by his own mother in a Bacchic rout.

Antenor pulled off his ivy crown, let it slip from his fingers. He shrugged off the vest, let it drop to the ground. Tallis turned and went the way he came, Tavi and Antenor following.

The pie-faced magistrate wasn't in the public records building. A different, younger man was at his desk. He looked up when the three came in. "Servos has gone to the theater."

"We are looking for Philip," Antenor said.

The man looked them over as he rose, in particular at Antenor's face, which had not been washed clean of the makeup. "Last I saw he was in the back. He may have gone with Servos, but I'll see if he's still there."

He came back a few moments later with a tall man who had to duck to clear the doorway.

Julia's husband was younger than Tallis had expected. He was a markedly handsome man, Roman-soldier tall, with a smooth, strong face and clear gray eyes. He nodded at Antenor, lingering briefly on the makeup, and glanced at Tallis.

Antenor drew him aside and spoke quickly to him, softly enough to prevent the young man at the desk from hearing—and it was evident he strained to listen. Tallis slipped casually between them to make sure the clerk didn't hear.

Philip's face grew dark, color rising high in his cheeks. When Antenor finished speaking, Philip drew himself tall. He regarded Antenor first, then Tallis and Tavi. Tallis got the feeling he really didn't see them. He unbuckled the pouch about his waist and laid it on the young man's desk.

"Tell Servos I had to go to Scythopolis. Tell him it's a follow-up to the Shamash-Eriba incident in Kursi."

"What Shamash-Eriba incident?" the clerk replied indignantly.

"He sent Marcus an hour ago to check out a raid on an inn near Kursi."

"They never tell me anything."

"I believe we passed him on the road," Tallis said.

"Send a messenger to Julia; tell her I will not be home for dinner. Tell her—" Philip paused. "Tell her I'll be late."

He disappeared through the doorway and returned with a light cape about his shoulders, fastened at his neck by a brooch with some emblem Tallis did not recognize. The cape did not conceal the short sword fastened about his waist.

Hector groaned at the shaking. He cracked his eyes open, noticing first that his window shade had the glow of daylight behind it. They knew better than to rouse him before dusk. Then he remembered: Today was the Festival of Dionysus. Likely some revelers had already drunk the health of Dionysus too enthusiastically, and reinforcements were needed.

"All right, I'm awake," he growled at the man shaking his shoulder, then looked again. He squinted. "Unless my eyes trick me, it is Antenor."

"It is."

"Antenor with garish makeup." He sat up. "This is not a pleasant way to wake up."

Antenor settled on the end of his bunk. "Are you on first watch?"

Hector snorted. "All watches, today."

Antenor folded his arms. "How would you like to lose your job?"

"And how would I do that?"

"By not showing up."

Bek had waited at the bottom of the slope, gazing at a vessel at the Lower Hippos harbor. They were off-loading a shipment from Tiberias across the lake. He glanced up at the western gates of Upper Hippos, from whence his gaze did not stray long, and looked again. At last, Tallis and Tavi came down the path, leading three other men. He gathered in the reins and clicked at the horses.

To quicken their journey, Philip and Hector had insisted on riding their own horses, stabled at Lower Hippos. They rode on either side of the cart as they all listened to Tallis.

Tallis stood to be heard well, hanging on to the back of the driver's seat. "We are bound for the temple of Dionysus in Scythopolis. There will be services and ceremonies. Today initiates become priestesses, and the curious seek answers. The lore of Dionysus will be taught by his faithful to any interested. It will be crowded and busy. Saving those things, I do not know what to expect. I've only seen the temple from a distance; I've not been inside. Have any of you?"

No one had.

"The temple is on the northeast mount," Philip said. "We'll see the back of it as the road nears the city. We will not have to go around to the main city gates; we can take the northeast gate; it won't be as crowded."

"I don't know where they will be hiding Zagreus," Tallis said, "but he is considered holy to them. They killed to get him; they'll kill to keep him. Going to the temple is risking your lives." He looked at everyone in turn: Antenor at the back of the cart, Tavi behind his father. Philip on one side of the cart, Hector on the other. "You must know that."

"Why would they kill a little boy?" Bek said over his shoulder. "How could anyone do such a thing?"

"A male child is reared by the nurses of Dionysus, and when he is five or six, he is offered in sacrifice on the holy day. At the moment of the slaying, Dionysus is supposed to appear. The child is regarded as his human host. A mere possession of Dionysus, nothing to him, just an earthly container. The Maenads believe killing the child releases the god. If they do not release him, they believe they will suffer consequences for it."

"I hate this world and all it contains," Antenor muttered. "I hate religion, and I hate the gods, and I hate the ones who revere them."

"How do we know he is still alive?" Hector asked.

"I have been a scholar of Dionysus," Tallis said. "The day most sacred to him is the nones of the month; any human sacrifice is offered on the nones at midnight, upon a mountain or hilltop."

"But there are hills all over," Philip said, frustration in his voice.

"Which is why we must find him before dark. He's sure to be in the temple."

"What is the plan?" Hector asked.

Tallis glanced at him. He could not remember this man from that summer at Athens. If he did, he remembered a slighter version, wearing a toga, not garrison garb, toting a tablet—not a sheathed sword.

He was now a watchman, employed by Hippos to police the city; he wore a leather vest and a hard leather helmet. Add hobnail boots and a cape and a few more inches of height, and you'd have a Roman soldier. This man seemed twice the size of the scholar in Athens.

"Medicine," Tallis said suddenly. "You studied medicine."

Hector did not reply.

"Didn't you?"

"He was brilliant," Antenor said, eyeing Hector. "Sought after. He chose our little academy over a position they offered him at Asclepios—another diplomatic feat wrought by Callimachus, curse him forever."

"What's the plan?" Hector repeated, his tone unchanged.

"I have no plan," Tallis admitted, "except for rescue."

"And justice," Antenor put in. "Remember justice?"

"What justice?" Philip asked.

Antenor looked at Tallis, and Tallis did not reply.

Philip looked warily at both of them. He guided his horse around a hole in the road. When he neared the cart again, he said, "You told me this was about the child, Antenor, not vengeance. I will have no part in lawless retribution."

"What about you, Hector?" Antenor asked. "Given the chance, what would you do with Portia?"

For answer, Hector took his gaze from the road ahead. It slowly swept past Tallis on the way to Antenor, and Tallis felt its chill in the passing. Hector kept the dead stare upon Antenor, then looked back at the road.

"The authorities are handling this," Philip announced, warning in his tone. "They will investigate, and justice will be brought to its conclusion."

"As it was for Theseus?" Antenor twisted in the cart to look at Philip. "Ask Hector if he thinks there was justice for Theseus. Or even an investigation. Ask the widow of Theseus; ask his three children if there was justice for a father literally ripped apart and—"

"We're not talking about what happened three years ago, Antenor," Philip cut in. "Marcus says Shamash-Eriba and his band raided the inn."

"Shamash-Eriba would do no such thing," Bek said over his shoulder.

"Why would you go to Scythopolis if you didn't believe it was Portia?" Tallis asked Philip. "You think Eriba's camp is in Scythopolis?"

Philip did not answer.

Antenor said clearly, "Philip—if I get the chance, I'll kill Portia without hesitation or guilt. I have been around this *cultus* of Dionysus long enough to know there will be no justice for the innkeeper. And why? Because no one will interfere with the gods. The authorities will execute a cursory examination, find out it leads to Dionysus, then call it a mystery and consign the matter to the dust in the archives. Just like Theseus.

"She wasn't stopped then, and look what has happened for it.

Another man murdered, and if we fail today, a child will die. Call it justice or call it prevention, Philip. Kill her now, and you'll save someone
else later. Maybe someone you love."

"How do you hold a god responsible for the death of a mortal?"
Tavi wondered with a frown.

"At last, some logic!" Antenor exclaimed, raising his hands and
dropping them. "Refresh me, what is your name?"

"Bahat`avi. I am called Tavi."

"Tavi, you don't hold the gods responsible—you hold the villain
mortals with the dripping hands responsible, despite their filthy protes-
tation, 'The gods required it!' Abominable cowards. Hades is too good
for them."

"Do you have proof that Portia killed Jarek?" Philip demanded.
"Any witnesses?"

Eyes went to Tallis, and Tallis could not answer. Anger flashed within
him, recollection of the same helplessness he felt when he had returned
to his village to seek justice for his brother.

"That's what I thought. Neither could they prove that Portia killed
Theseus." Philip's tone was far from satisfied in its rightness. "Don't
think they didn't try, and try hard—and try for a very long time. But
there were no witnesses and there was no proof. I believe as you do; I believe Portia had a hand in Theseus's death, and yes, in the death of the
innkeeper, given all I know of this *cultus*, and of the circumstances of the
inn. But we cannot condemn a man or a woman without witnesses, or
proof, or the word of a king. If we do, we are lawbreakers. I ride with
you to help a little boy, because I have a boy of my own—but I'll have no
part in the shedding of more blood. By the gods, if you raise a hand to
another in my sight, I will strike it down. Only the boy matters."

"Let me tell you of a boy and of blood," Tallis said, his own voice
hollow in his ears. "They tore apart my little brother before my eyes."

Silence, save the sound of the horses and the cart.

And the thing, that thing, monstrous beneath the surface, now crept
into his heart. He couldn't save his own Zagreus, the gentle boy with the
thumb in his mouth, smiling to break the suction, telling him his thumb
tasted like honeycake . . . how could he be sure of saving this other
Zagreus? He didn't want to doubt, for fear the doubt would lend power
to the evil at work, but doubt was the monster, and Tallis knew fear such

as a nightmare had never invoked. If a mother could kill her child, if *his* mother could do it, anything could happen to the fair-haired Zagreus of the inn. The very calamity he had witnessed assured him it could happen again.

He spoke thickly, hushed, to keep control. "I was twelve years old. *I* witnessed it. I was proof. Not only their hands, but their mouths dripped blood. But nobody listened to me because I pointed in the wrong direction. They were Maenads: devout women, pious and chaste in their behavior. They were women my village had known all their lives. Good mothers. Good wives. Fervent in their devotion to their god, and their fervency was respected and admired. No one could believe such a thing of them. And if this child, this other Zagreus . . . if he dies too, all is lost. Everything is lost."

Silence, save the creaking of the cart.

"For years I would spit in the wind, trying to get the Senate to outlaw the Bacchanalia. The only law on the books is two hundred years old, and it never went far enough. It sought only to 'limit' their activities, and it never spelled out the limitations—a broader invitation to disregard the selfsame 'law' you will not find. All my effort did only one thing: It only dusted off that old law. And when I think on this child torn from his home . . ." His breath caught. "And when I think on the good man who died to protect him . . ." When he could, he finished, "I say you won't find justice in the law books."

They rode in silence for a time, until a quiet remark came from Tavi. "Master Tallis? I am sorry about your brother."

The cart jostled on toward Scythopolis.

In the tombs of Kursi are two men with their backs to the sea.

One is newly come to madness. He is acquainted with rape and knows invasion. He is aware that a chasm now lies between himself and his former hope. He is aware, now, that the hope had been sufficient. He chose despair because he was weary of the fight, not because he could not fight. He knows he has been cheated, that there is no going back to his weak fight. He knows, now, with shattering surprise, that even his weakest swing had been enough. This, then, his madness.

The other is old at madness. He has been lashed and driven to the furthermost part of his soul, and he cowers near a plastered-over place. His intellect is his possession no longer; it belongs to the Others. For him there is neither despair nor regret. Despair and regret are rungs, and the luxury to climb, whether up or down, is no longer his. He knows one single directive for preservation: Keep his back to the sea.

For both of them, the way is closed.

XV

Something bad happened in the barn. Zagreus could not remember what it was.

Master Jarek—no, it was *Grandfather* Jarek now, Grandfather brought him cinnamon sticks. He said Mistress Kes would come to tell him a story. It was the last thing he could remember.

After that, something bad happened.

Bad enough that he was in a place far away, without Mistress Kes, and without Grandfather, and without Samir. He wanted Samir first, because this place frightened him worse than when Kardus came. It went down deep into the cold stone floor like roots from an enormous tree, went down very deep, and it was very, very bad.

He wanted Grandfather next, because Grandfather was sometimes gruff and the gruff was good. After Samir, he felt most safe around Grandfather. And he wanted Mistress Kes so he could smell her apron when she hugged him. So he could look up and see her looking down on him, and feel her hair tickle his face. He'd smell fresh air in her hair, like she'd hung it on the clothesline.

The room was small and high and cold. They put a fine rug in the middle of the room and a little golden chair upon the rug. That's where they wanted him to sit, on the little golden chair with the cushions. The golden chair had pictures carved on it. A man with a pointed beard and grapes for his hair. Dancing ladies with long sticks.

He sat on the chair when they came. He didn't like it when they came. He shook when they did, for the ladies had guests with them they could not see, black furry guests. While the ladies crooned over him and offered him wine and grapes and figs and lots of things, he watched the black guests and they watched him. And when the ladies left and took their guests with them, he crept from the golden chair into the corner and sat as small as he could.

Mistress Kes needed him. He knew she needed him; his own deep-down roots told him so. Mistress Kes would worry about him. Grandfather Jarek would be angry, him being gone so long. He had to go home. He wanted to go home.

Arinna declined to see the Divine Child after his arrival. She was busy in preparation for the sacred dance at midnight.

She did not know the choruses like everyone else did. She didn't even know the order of events. Five years ago, she had been an initiate only for a few months before Portia whisked her away with a baby, a pack filled with baby things, and a story for her arrival at the Inn-by-the-Lake.

The least Portia could have done was inform her of festivity procedures. Portia clearly had not expected Arinna to return with her, the day Kes had snatched Zagreus and fled for the barn. Portia stayed in a simmering brood all the way back to Scythopolis. And no one there had expected Arinna. One would think, with the Day of Dionysus at hand, that they would expect his Keeper to arrive.

Today Portia had sent a first-level initiate to teach her the choruses and dance steps. First level! The only thing to make up for that particular humiliation was Arinna's own station.

The girls seemed to accept the fact that Arinna had fulfilled her part of the long plan, and that a consequence of the plan was ignorance. Things had changed in the five years she'd been gone, and they were eager to teach the Keeper of the Divine Child. Even the temple disciplines had changed. And what little she did remember had been altered over the past five years by ever-evolving epiphanies.

Strange, that the nurses of Dionysus were surprised at her appearance with Portia.

"Turn, and *lift*, and turn and—Divine Keeper, when I say 'lift,' I mean you must raise your leg and give a short kick. See? A short kick, like so. Just enough to ripple your dress."

"Semele, what did Portia—Queen Ariadne—tell of me?"

Semele stopped in midstride. She lowered her arced arms and brought her hands together in prim repose. "I'm not sure I understand your question, Divine Keeper."

Arinna adjusted the gold belt at her waist and twisted to see how the long tasseled ends lay in the back. She smiled and gave a swish to watch the long ends flow with the rest of her skirt. Such lovely fine linen. She hadn't worn something so fine in five years. All of the girls had dresses like this; they were specially designed for the parade late this afternoon on the plaza. And for the private ceremony at midnight.

"One of the priestesses moved out of her cell to make room for me," Arinna said, watching another swirl of her skirts. "She seemed surprised and not entirely happy. Why didn't any of you expect me? Didn't the queen say I was coming too? With Zagreus?"

Semele hesitated. "I—well—not really."

"I wasn't mentioned at all?"

"Well . . . no. Not if you mean for participation in the revels." Then Semele brightened. "But you were always—well, sometimes—mentioned in the prayers for the protection of the Most Blessed."

"Doesn't it seem a little strange to you that the Keeper of the Divine Child would have no place in the revels? That not a single part was left to me, and that this dress was only made for me yesterday?"

Semele didn't know how to answer. Finally she offered hopefully, "I know where they took the Divine Child. Would you like to see him?"

"No."

No, she didn't want to see him, because she should have been the first to know he had arrived. Portia should have sent for her the moment he came. She wasn't included in the venerations Semele spoke of, when he first set foot in the temple. No, the Divine Keeper was completely forgotten. She'd found out about his arrival only when Semele came to her cell, babbling herself into a swoon over it. He'd been here for two hours before she knew, and that from a first-level initiate.

Things here, Arinna discovered, were not much different from the inn.

She caught sight of herself in the bronze mirror set into the wall. She lifted her chin, pleased. Well, some things had changed. She smoothed down the front of her dress and admired the fit. Only the finest dressmakers in Scythopolis were hired to make the garments of the entourage of Dionysus.

"Are they really going to—"

Arinna glanced at Semele in the bronze reflection. She stood too far away, and her expression was blurred. Arinna turned to her. "Are they going to what?"

Semele was still in that stiff position, her arms delicately curved, her hands fitted together like pieces of a mosaic. Her face was a curiosity. Her eyes were bright and slightly widened. "Nothing, Divine Keeper."

"Tell me," Arinna said, her own eyes bright. She held her breath, not realizing it. For all it would take was one falter, one misstep.

She did not know she looked for the misstep.

What Arinna hoped for, without knowing, was one dissenting voice in the array. One voice to call it something less than sacred. Maybe even call it madness. For Zagreus, whom she had known for five years, was in one of the rooms in the corridor past the grand, echoing vestibule. Zagreus, son of the madman, whom she'd fed and dressed and tolerated for five years, whom Kes and Jarek and Samir loved.

All of the women who attended Dionysus in his temple, and Arinna had counted fifty-seven, all of the women called it sacred. And if she, the Keeper, named it anything less, then Dionysus would fall upon her as he had fallen upon Kardus. She had only the remembrance of the Many-voiced One to know it. And she had the vicious assurance of Portia, who told her if she failed Zagreus, then Dionysus would tear her apart and stew her soul in the Styx for all eternity. And Arinna believed her, because of Kardus, because of the Voice that once came out of him.

So she did not think of betrayal, not consciously, lest she betray her own skin. What looked for the misstep, then, was a part of her so vague she didn't even know it existed.

Semele blinked. She frowned a little, then smiled. "Why—I don't remember what I was going to say, Divine Keeper; it flew right out of my head. Forgive me—I've been intoxicated since his arrival." She broke her pose to resume the dance, but, disoriented, paused. Her face grew dreamy. "I wonder what will happen when he is unleashed from his earthly confines. The blood releases the power, and from the abyss of eternal night springs forth new birth, the renewed cycle . . ."

Semele was taken in a murmuring trance, and Arinna waited, listening to her dazed babble until she suddenly felt confused. She seemed to be waiting for something from Semele, she didn't know what. She turned to the mirror and smoothed down her dress, and looked again to see how the gold tassels lay. She frowned. She felt sad, or disappointed, and didn't know why. She wished she had an amphora of Jarek's good wine.

The Galilee was long behind them now. Bek kept the horses at a brisk pace, and the constant hard jostling, with the shine and the heat of the sun, soon gave Tallis a headache. He tried to remember what little of Scythopolis he had seen on his way from Jerusalem a few weeks ago. He remembered construction. Rome was busy turning Scythopolis into a decent Greek metropolis. The plaza in the middle of the city had bases set for columns. The columns would line the long street, both sides. He'd like to see that someday; the bases themselves promised quite impressive architecture. But at the far end of the city, the plaza ended in wide steps to a mount, and upon the mount was an ancient temple of Zeus, connected by a walkway to the temple of Dionysus. He'd looked once, and could not look again.

Tallis had been traveling with a group of merchants returning from a trade trip in Jerusalem, bound for Bethsaida, a city a few miles north of Kursi. They were anxious to get home and did not wish to stay any longer in Scythopolis than it took to water the horses and buy fresh food. He did not have to ignore the temple long; even the ignoring was a strange chore. Felt like eyes upon his back.

After several miles, Bek pulled up where the road crossed the Jordan River. The men climbed out of the cart, and Bek drew the horses aside to water them. The Jordan wobbled all over the place like a schoolboy's scribble. Tallis could tell when they were near it by the winding green foliage at its banks. Springtime was on the land, but already in the Land of the Sun the grasses of the plains were browned.

He remembered a text from one of the treatises on Dionysus: *Ancients preferred to look to the Land of the Sun for the Nysa in which Dionysus grew up, and from which he made his entry into the realms of men.*

Tallis gazed about at the austere landscape. It was an ancient land with layered histories. Long before Antiochus Epiphanes . . . Antiochus Epimanes . . . Antiochus, Madman . . . long before he sacrificed pigs to his beloved Dionysus, and forced others to do the same, Dionysus was here. He was right here in Scythopolis, the fabled Nysa, right here, all about this very land.

As Tallis climbed back into the cart, he wondered about the man named Maccabee, who had defied Antiochus Madman. He wished he knew more about him.

No one would question an all-male contingent to the temple of Dionysus, not today; a pilgrimage of any gender on the holy day of Bacchus would seem perfectly normal. Men chose Dionysus to be their god too; they simply did not fuss about it as much as the women did. Tallis's eyes fell on the water skin in the cart. They could take the water skin and say it was a special libation. A libation for the god of wine on his holy day was perfectly natural, only good sense; a nice ceremonial placation for nonreligious men—just in case.

Philip and Hector rode side by side behind the cart, in low conversation with one another. Philip looked like someone in authority, with his fine clothing, the short sword at his belt, that fancy clasp for his cape. Tall, handsome, perfectly erect in the saddle. Good looks and confidence could convey much.

He considered Hector. Shorter than Philip, more solid, with hardened features, and a way about him that said he'd put his sword to use with grim cheer at the first provocation.

Both men served local government; neither was military, but either could easily pass for it. Throw on rust-colored Roman capes, add a swagger, and it wouldn't be so hard to feign a legal inspection of the temple, if a guise of piety failed them entrance.

"Jarek said you were going to help Kardus," Tavi said. The young man still sat opposite Tallis, in the corner of the cart behind his father. He had a naturally thin face, now drawn with worry and sadness. "How are you going to help him?"

Tallis felt for the dirty sack wedged between himself and the cart side. He shook it out and swathed it over the top of his head, tucking it into the back of his tunic to protect his neck from the blistering sun. He didn't care what he looked like; the sun was roasting him alive. Then he considered the question and sighed. He glanced at Antenor in the back of the cart, who had bunched up sacks and rested his neck on them on the cart edge. His arms were crossed, eyes closed, and his face was open to the sun, as though he enjoyed the scorching. Tallis knew he could hear every word.

"I want to help him," he finally said to Tavi. He didn't like it that Antenor could hear. It wasn't any of the man's business if Tallis stayed or left. "I don't know if I can. When I am around him—it is hard to explain."

"He needs to go home to Athens, Master Tavi," Antenor announced, eyes still closed. "His own master needs him. He's been away long enough."

"It is not your business, Antenor," Tallis snapped. "Besides, Aristarchus is there."

"I didn't believe Polonus about Kardus and his invasion of Evil." Antenor opened an eye and squinted at Tallis. "I was wrong. Remember? Polonus is the most intelligent, compassionate human being I have ever known. If he has failed, then—no offense, Tallis—you don't have a chance. And Polonus loved him."

"'Mankind has no greater helper than love,'" Tallis murmured bleakly.

Why couldn't it be true? Why couldn't Samir's Two Truths be true? Didn't Polonus choose Good? Wasn't it good to help Kardus? Then why did his good choice ruin him?

"That's a much-battered philosophy I no longer believe," Antenor said bitterly. "And I regret the time I wasted subscribing to it. Socrates was wrong—Polonus loved Kardus, Jarek loved him, and look where their love got them."

"Evil is upon the land," Bek said over his shoulder. "Great evil. Only great good can defy it."

"There is no great good," Antenor said, and settled his neck on the cart edge once more.

"That is a singularly depressing thought, Antenor," Tallis muttered.

Antenor opened one eye, kept the other squinted against the sun. "I would presume that if great good was anywhere at all, it would see, and hear, and intervene. Great good is blind, and deaf, and cares not about the suffering of mankind, by its lack of intervention. And if it cares not, then it is neither good nor is it great. Therefore—there is no great good." He closed his eye and settled in again, as if comfortably, for the ride.

Arinna poked the figs about on the plate. She took one and started to carefully peel it because that's the fussy way she liked her figs, then realized she didn't want it and tossed it back onto the plate. She licked the stickiness from her fingers and glanced at Semele.

Semele was across the room curled on a many-cushioned couch, now quiet, released from her murmuring trance. She had a wan way about her that irritated Arinna. Her face was soft and serene, distant and rather—wispy. Like the wheat-colored curls of hair that escaped her fine blue hair ribbon. She'd never cleaned up a pile of guest-room vomit in her life.

"Where are you from?" Arinna asked.

Semele took her gaze from wherever it had been, focused, and found Arinna. "Pella."

"Why did you come here?"

"To become a nurse of Dionysus."

Arinna snorted.

Semele blinked and focused again.

Arinna poked at the figs on the tray. "That's what they all say. That's what I said." She picked up a fig and scrutinized it. "What's the reason you left Pella?"

"That . . . was the reason I left." The serene look faltered. "Mostly. I suppose the reason doesn't really matter. What I have now is all that matters."

Arinna frowned sourly and dropped the fig. She pushed the plate away and pulled a large cushion into her lap. She wrapped her arms around it and looked about the room. There were a few hangings on the wall and an ornamental bronze grate in the fireplace pit. It was the luxury of a palace compared to the inn. She sniffed the cushion—it smelled like sweet spicy incense, not a greasy kitchen brazier. She didn't smell sweaty men and their ale, either; all day long today she'd smelled pastries baking, made just for the Day of Dionysus.

She wouldn't mind the smell of Demas once again. She missed

Demas. He'd told her he was heading to Caesarea to perform for Pontius Pilate in the Great Stadium. She wondered what Caesarea was like. Demas said it was a miniature version of Rome. She sighed. What she wouldn't give to see a place like that. Demas said he would take her there someday.

"I miss my mother," Semele said.

Semele was staring again, this time without that distant look. Arinna regarded her thoughtfully, and Semele began to speak.

"I've been watching children all my life. I was the oldest of thirteen. I've never known my mother not pregnant. And do you know what? She never lost a single child. Never miscarried, never lost one in birth, never lost one to sickness. When I left, she was due by the next new moon." Semele looked down at the cushion she was holding and smoothed its satiny cover. "We have two sets of twins. Father and Mother joked about how the gods saw fit to bless them. Mother would say any more blessings would kill her, and Father would say try feeding these blessings."

Arinna let Semele talk, and listened carefully.

"It was time for me to be married, but Mother wanted me home to take care of the children. She always said I was the better mother to them, and in part, it was true. I loved being their mother and their sister."

Arinna held her breath; the look on Semele's face was changing.

"When I saw that child in the room, sitting on the golden throne . . ." Semele blinked rapidly. "I could not help but think, what if it was one of the babies. That's what we always call them, Mother and I, the babies. Even Jessup, who is only two years younger than I." She stopped speaking. Then she said, in a very small voice, "He was frightened, Divine Keeper."

She lifted her eyes to Arinna. The two regarded one another for a long time.

COME AND SEE, TALLIS, YOU WORM.
THEY WON'T REVILE US HERE. NOT WHERE HE DWELLS.
YESSSSS . . . EVEN THE MIGHTY ONES ARE AFRAID. THEY ARE NO
MATCH. NOT HERE.

"Scythopolis," Bek called over his shoulder.

Tallis opened his eyes. He'd sunk into the cart to hide from the sun under another dirty sack he'd found. Somehow the cart had jostled him into a stupor, and for the past hour he'd drifted in and out of not-quite-sleep. A strange state of consciousness, where he felt caught between this world and another. He'd felt a growing nausea, a strange—alarm. He suddenly pushed the sack aside and sat up. And saw something impossible.

Ahead on the road, to the west, he saw a great column rising from the city, as if of solid smoke, rising, not ending, swallowed into the sky. He dug his eyes with the heels of his hands, shook off the last of his ill rest. He looked again. His eyes followed the great form all the way to the heavens, where it disappeared because Tallis could not see farther up.

"What is it?" Tavi asked him anxiously.

"What is *that*?"

Tavi looked ahead at the city and back at Tallis, perplexed. "What?"

"That . . . thing." His mouth fell open as he gaped skyward.

"What do you see?" Antenor said slowly, straightening, searching the horizon ahead. "Because whatever you see, I feel. Like Portia walked into the room."

Tallis rose from the cart, steadying himself with a hand on Bek's shoulder. "Stop the cart," he said suddenly.

Bek pulled the horses up. Hector and Philip rode up from behind.

Hector looked from the city to Tallis. "What is it?"

Tallis put out his hand toward the city and felt a resistance in the air, a warning not to continue. The feeling came from without and from within, an instinct of great peril.

Briefly he thought himself a fool for not bringing Samir along, limp as they had left him. But not even Samir, his amulet, could withstand this . . . and he knew with dread certainty that he could never enter the city.

NO YOU CAN'T, NO YOU CAN'T.
NOT WITHOUT SAMIR!

But—Zagreus!

YOU ARE NO MATCH FOR US. NOT HERE. NOT WHERE HE DWELLS.

What you say is true. But I choose to help. Try and hide that choice from me. Blind, I will reach for it.

"Go, go!" he urged Bek. "Hurry!"

Bek whipped the horses, and the cart lurched forward. Tallis fell backward, tumbling into Antenor. He scrambled upright, and on his knees he held fast with both hands to the side. The cart bucked and bounced at the speed of the horses.

They were still a mile from the city, but he could easily see that the smoldering column rose from the acropolis at the end of the plaza. The city wall and a rise of trees on a hill prevented him from seeing the base of the column. He didn't have to see to know it rose from the temple of Dionysus.

"What do you see?" Antenor asked again, straining to see himself.

"I see a great column," Tallis breathed. "It reaches to the heavens, and I cannot see its end. It goes down deep. It is—gray. And moving. Up and down, it is moving."

The cart did not get very far before Tallis began to slump, gripping the cart side as the forces pressed him down. What a fool he had been. He should have known. The infirmity in his soul, his taint of madness, madness calling to madness . . .

. . . and yet . . .

. . . that which transcended the madness, that *place*, the sacred place They wanted, and Tallis fumbled for it on his stomach—it knew of the Evil, and it bade him to reach for the Good. A little farther. Just a little farther.

ARE YOU CRAZY?
YOU CAN'T GO THERE; THAT PLACE WILL KILL YOU.
GO BACK, TALLIS, GO BACK!

Madness, to ignore madness. But the place sent up signals of assurance, and instead of feeling vanquished with dread, though great dread was in the going, he felt an assurance that all would be well, he had nearly finished his part; it was soon time for another.

Another?

Who was the other?

XVI

Quite suddenly, the whole thing was ridiculous.

She didn't want to languish in this godforsaken temple the rest of her life. A figure like hers? Condemned to rites and rituals, when Demas himself told her that famous sculptors would pay money just to gaze on her? How could Arinna deprive the world of—what did he call it— statuary? Well, it seemed selfish at any rate, holing up here when she had a lot more to offer someplace else.

When she came to the temple, what seemed like a lifetime ago, she was just like Semele over there, running from one bad thing only to jump into another. The vocation wasn't what she thought it was, a few months into it. Portia had rescued her with her proposal of a special assignment. It gave her a chance to breathe again, if only in a place like the inn.

It was time to breathe again for good. The only thing that could possibly trouble her was Portia's promise of stewing in the Styx for an eternity of anguish if she didn't comply with temple edicts. She could even go mad like Kardus. If she doubted the Styx, what happened to Kardus was as real as it got.

But Caesarea was a long way away from the cursed inn and those cursed tombs, and this stifling temple. She brightened—and Rome was even farther. On the other side of the earth, she was sure. A long way from women who seriously considered taking a knife to the little boy in the chamber down the corridor.

"Go home to your mother and the babies, Semele. Better yet, get yourself a man. I'm going to Caesarea." Arinna set aside the cushion. She folded her arms and smiled deeply, with a delicious glitter she'd not felt since the last time she saw Demas.

Semele, with a pathetic wistfulness on her face, a not-quite-hope because she wouldn't allow it yet, gazed first at Arinna, then at the closed door of their apartment. "Divine Keeper, what are you saying . . . ?"

"I'm saying, let's get out of here. The sooner the better. And let's take Zagreus with us, eerie little brat that he is."

When Semele blanched and looked like she would faint from the blasphemous references to Dionysus, Lord of the Souls, Arinna quickly amended.

"I mean, ah, let us take Zagreus Most Blessed, and let us . . . ah . . . gather his sacredness into our unworthy arms, and—"

"You mean so he won't die?"

"Ah—yes. Your Divine Keeper has spoken." Though what they would do with the child was another matter. She would certainly not take him to Caesarea. Maybe Semele could take him home with her. She seemed to like him, and what was one more child when you had thirteen? Semele could tell her parents he was another little blessing.

Semele blinked, considered—and said quickly, "Okay." She set aside her own cushion.

"What's your real name?" Arinna asked. Every woman changed her name when she became the possession of Dionysus. It symbolized that they had left behind all earthly ties. She supposed she had never really cast off her attachment to the world. Though Portia had renamed her Thyone, one of the names for the mother of Dionysus, Arinna had never liked the sound of it. It was too stout, too *matronly*. From the first, the people at the inn knew her as Arinna.

Maybe that helped keep the detachment. Maybe keeping her own name kept *her*.

Semele was the name of one of the daughters of Cadmus, Arinna remembered from her early lessons of the play *The Bacchae.* It too was one of the names for the mother of Dionysus.

"My name is Devorah." A very small smile. She looked at Arinna. Her small smile faded, and her eyes were huge.

"Do you think we'll stew in the Styx?" Arinna said softly. "Do you think he'll hunt us down?"

"I don't know," Devorah whispered. "I'm frightened."

"So am I."

"I wish my father were here."

"How long have you been here?"

"Almost two months. If he knew where I was, he'd be here. He wouldn't fear Dionysus or Queen Ariadne or anything. He'd bash the door down. He'd come and get me, no matter what." Her voice dwindled. "He doesn't know where I am, because he would have come by now. Divine Keeper—"

"Don't call me that again. My name is Arinna."

"Arinna . . . what are we going to do?"

Arinna felt for the large cushion and took it into her lap. She wrapped her arms about it and fell into hard thought.

They could wait until the evening revels to slip Zagreus away under the cloak of darkness, but that is when he would be most watched. And how could they know where they were going in the dark? She didn't know these hills in the daytime, let alone at night. The only thing to do was to get him out of the temple before the parade.

The public parade would commence late in the afternoon, when all the women dressed in their finery would dance the choruses and make merry and herald the coming of the god. They'd wave their ribbon-bedecked *thrysi* and throw figs into the crowd. The parades, more than anything else, gathered new initiates; young girls gazed, enraptured, at the beautiful women making merry in the streets, and they too wanted to be beautiful and make merry and wave the sticks with the streaming ribbons.

After the parade the Maenads, drunk with gaiety and goodwill, would return to the temple for a great feast, after which another parade would take place at midnight. A very solemn and secret one.

Zagreus was to be dressed in a specially made gown, borne upon a special funeral bier. They would take him in procession to the northeast gate, the gate closest to the temple, and carry him to the place of sacrifice. The place was known only to Queen Ariadne and her eunuch, who had gone to the grove the day before to sanctify it. It would be somewhere far enough away from the city that no one would notice if the unpredictable Dionysus did indeed bring his famous reveling madness. Portia told them they needed to be more careful these days . . . something about a new law with a closer eye on the Bacchanalia.

Arinna set aside the cushion. "We must go now."

Semele—Devorah—started from the couch. Her hand flew to her throat. "Now? You mean—*now?*"

"We can't get him away in the dark, and the public parade starts soon. Likely there's a crowd on the steps already."

The moment the Bacchantes burst from the temple was a grand moment indeed, and many waited for hours to have a good spot for it.

"I must—gather my things," Devorah said, rising from the couch. Confusion was on her face.

"What if you see Portia?"

"Portia?" Devorah said uncertainly.

"Ariadne," Arinna said impatiently. "Devorah—we have one chance at this, and it's now. If you go to your cell, don't bother coming back. I'll be gone."

"But . . . I have a necklace from my mother. . . ."

"Leave it." Arinna took a small cushion and ripped a hole into a corner of it with her teeth. She worked her finger into the hole and tore the cushion open along the seam. She took out the stuffing and refilled it quickly, grabbing anything she could against an uncertain journey. The figs, a few sweets given her by admiring initiates, a wedge of cheese from the platter, a little basket of pistachios given by the woman whose cell she took over. (Not given, actually—left in the cell, hers by right.)

"Where do they have Zagreus?" Arinna looked ruefully at the few coins in her palm; if the color of her coins was silver instead of copper, she could get more than a loaf of bread and a skin of watered wine—she could get an armed escort out of the city, and safe passage to Caesarea. She put them into the cushion bag.

"In a cell, in the corridor on the west side of the entrance."

"Is it locked?"

"No, but it's guarded by two nurses. They cast lots for the privilege."

Devorah anxiously searched Arinna's face. "What will we do? How do we get him out of there?"

Arinna didn't answer. She went to the door and put her hand on the iron pull. Suddenly, her heart began to catch up. It began to pound so furiously she could feel it at the bottom of her stomach. What was she thinking? How could they get him out without anyone knowing?

Was she crazy?

She took her hand from the cold touch of the door pull. And even if nobody saw, which was impossible in a small temple filled with fifty-seven women, Dionysus saw; Dionysus would know.

"Divine Kee—Arinna?"

If they escaped the temple, could they escape Dionysus?

"Arinna?"

Would he track Arinna down? All the way to Rome? Sure, she had a body blessed by the gods, or so Demas had told her one starry night in the grasses by the Galilee; but Demas had left her at the inn. It was all because of Zagreus—Demas thought the child was hers, and the day Demas left, Arinna screamed at Zagreus that she was sorry to be stuck with such a leg iron as he, and why on earth was *she* chosen to be his mother? Why couldn't someone else have been chosen? And his face had gone white, and he sat small in a corner of their room while she raged at her misfortune. Handsome Demas with his glorious voice was gone, and she couldn't go with him, and it was all Zagreus's fault.

The pain on his little face made her more furious than ever, and she'd spent herself in a tantrum, screaming into her bedding so Kes wouldn't hear. She cried herself empty for the loss of Demas, for losses long before Demas, before she had ever arrived, broken, on the steps of the temple. She cried into the bedding the sorrow of a life used up at age twenty, until she felt a small hand on her back, patting, caressing. And she knew he'd never learned that tenderness from her, and she had wept a little longer.

"Arinna . . . ?"

Her hand was on the iron pull. She was terrified to go, and she was terrified to stay.

But the door was pushing slowly into the room by itself, and she stepped back. Arinna expected someone taller—when she dropped her eyes to the little figure who pushed the door, she did something she never thought she'd do, not of her own free will. She dropped to her knees with a cry and pulled the child Zagreus into her arms, as she'd seen Kes do, and held him fiercely. He smelled like home.

She held him back to look him over. "You look tired. Are you all right?"

The child nodded, and after five years of minding him, Arinna saw his eyes for the first time. Such dark, beautiful eyes, like Kardus's eyes, before the madness fully came. Tired eyes. He cupped his hands around his mouth and said in a hush, "I want to go home."

Devorah came behind Arinna. She put her hands together in a prim, nervous pose. "How did you get out of the cell, Zagreus Most Blessed?" she inquired formally, not quite allowing herself to believe he was a mere mortal.

"The big bright man," the child said. "He says we must hurry. He says we must take the kitchen entrance."

The three stole down the dark, narrow corridor into the east side of the building. Arinna saw no big bright man, but Zagreus had always been an odd child. She didn't know how Portia managed to get him away from Jarek and Samir and Kes, and Master Tallis too, but it couldn't have been easy. The trauma of his taking likely made him fancy an imaginary helper.

Zagreus led the way. He'd often consult with a look up to his left. It made Arinna's skin prickle. The quicker they got out of this eerie place, the better.

The aroma of many feast-day smells grew stronger as they hurried along. She could smell fresh bread and roasting meat and savory vegetables. But the closer they got to the kitchen, the more her alarm grew. Surely, they couldn't think to leave the temple from there.

"Zagreus, the kitchen will be crowded," she whispered.

"He says not to worry."

"Fine for him, he won't get caught," Arinna hissed.

Zagreus paused when the corridor ended at a more narrow cross-passage. Arinna nearly bumped into him. Devorah was on her heels, and did bump into her.

"What are you doing?" Arinna whispered to the child.

"He says wait."

So they pressed against the wall and waited. Arinna finally rolled her eyes and was about to take the lead herself. Suddenly voices came down the cross-passage, and she pulled back, pressing Zagreus and Devorah against the shadowed wall.

"My feet are killing me. I've been on them since dawn."

"And I haven't? You know, I don't think there's nearly enough nut pastry for the feast."

"That's because you've been snitching it."

"I have not!"

"What's in your pocket?" the other voice challenged.

"It's only because I won't get any if the other pigs go first!"

Two novitiates walked by, inches from Zagreus. Arinna felt the air move as they passed.

"Did you see the eunuch? Queen Ariadne's helper?"

"Yes, he's rather handsome. Well—from a distance. Up close he looks like my brother. Does a eunuch really . . . ?"

"Really what?"

"Oh, don't make me say it. *You* know."

"I have no idea what you're talking about. . . ."

The voices faded down the corridor, where they turned a corner and were lost completely.

The three slipped into the passage, going where the two novitiates had come from. The odors grew even stronger, and now Arinna heard kitchen sounds. The clatter of a lid on a cook pot, the rhythmic chopping of vegetables. Voices.

When they came near the kitchen entrance, from where light spilled into the dim corridor, Zagreus halted and consulted up to his left. He reported in a whisper to Arinna, "He says wait."

They waited. Then Zagreus crept to the kitchen entrance and peeked. After a few moments, he beckoned.

Arinna and Devorah exchanged anxious looks. What would they say to the kitchen workers? From the voices, there had to be five or six. They would inform Portia, and Portia would know they had gone.

Arinna thought quickly. She could tell them some nonsense about a Divine Keeper ritual she had to perform with Zagreus before the commencement of the ceremony tonight. She could tell them Devorah had to help with the ritual. Yes! She could say his ties to her needed to be cut, else catastrophic things would happen. And if anyone questioned her, she would say this, that Dionysus had appeared to her himself and had required it. Didn't others claim a visitation? Why not the Divine Keeper?

Zagreus beckoned more urgently.

Arinna swallowed convulsively. Devorah clutched Arinna's sleeve, and they crept to the entrance and peeked in.

One worker chatted amiably with another at a breadboard. One worker stirred a huge pot at the hearth. Another chopped vegetables at a worktable in the corner. Another stirred a sauce at the brazier. She dipped the spoon into the sauce, tasted it, and frowned. She took a handful of dried leaves from a bowl. She put the spoon in her teeth and rubbed the leaves between her palms over the sauce, and dusted off her palms.

And Zagreus was walking straight down the center of the kitchen, and not a single person noticed him. He got to the door on the other side, turned, and waited for Arinna and Devorah.

Feeling giddy, as in a dream, Arinna started stiffly across the kitchen with Devorah inching behind, clutching the back of her dress the whole way. Once the cook at the brazier turned and looked directly at Arinna. Arinna froze and felt the blood drop from her face and swoosh into her legs—but the cook looked right through her to the girl at the worktable in the corner and called, "I need a few more onions, chop 'em fine." The cook turned back to her sauce and, frowning, sipped another taste from the spoon.

Devorah's fingers dug into her lower back, and they crept across the kitchen, unseen by the five workers. As they passed the breadboard, Arinna slipped a flat round loaf from the board and hid it in her skirts. The bread makers carried on their conversation as if completely ignoring her, so she leaned over the terrified Devorah and snatched another. Zagreus opened the door into late afternoon, and all three left the temple, closing the door behind them.

"Quandocumque impellunt, repelle. Quandocumque impellunt . . ."

"What's wrong with him? What's he saying?" Tavi asked Antenor, warily watching Tallis. "I do not know this language."

Antenor regarded the servant of Callimachus in the bottom of the cart. Tallis lay curled on his side, his arms wrapped about his head. He was muttering, sometimes coherently, sometimes not. The closer the cart got to Scythopolis, and they were less than a half-mile away, the more the man shriveled up.

Antenor scanned the horizon where Tallis had looked; whatever it was, it was doing Tallis harm. Antenor feared to go any farther. "Stop the cart," he finally called to the driver. He gazed down at Tallis. "Something's wrong. We cannot take him there."

"It's time for another?" Tallis slurred. "Who's the other? *Quando* . . . easy for you, Samir, you've done it all your life . . . *impellunt* . . . certainly —and if you can stand upright to do it, why then, *repelle* . . ." He chuckled. "The gods are laughing."

"What's he saying?"

"It is Latin," Antenor said slowly to Tavi. "When they push, push back." He looked at the horizon.

"When*ever* they push. *Quandocumque.* My contribution. Can't let them get away with a thing."

Tavi watched Tallis. "It has to do with Kardus, doesn't it. It always has to do with Kardus, anything strange, anything bad." He looked where Antenor did, perhaps now as uneasy to continue as Antenor himself was. "He never used to be that way. Nobody believes it."

Hector pulled up his mount beside the cart. He took off his leather helmet and wiped his forehead on his sleeve. He gestured with the helmet at Tallis. "What's wrong with him now? We don't have time for this."

"Nothing is wrong with me," Tallis snapped, his voice muffled beneath his arms. "Why has the cart stopped? Are we there yet?"

Philip's horse nosed in beside Hector. "We're about a half-mile from the northeast gates." He glanced at Antenor, then at Tallis. "Are you well?"

"*Yes,* I'm *well,*" Tallis growled, still beneath his arms. "Stomachache. Bad fish. Gods and *goddesses,* keep going, will you?" He muttered a bit more.

Antenor didn't quite catch it, something about serving himself hemlock. He rose, looking for what he could not see in the air above the acropolis, then climbed out of the cart. Hector and Philip dismounted and joined him at the roadside.

"He cannot go into the city," Antenor said, keeping his voice low.

"He can make that decision himself. I think he just did," Hector replied, and the older man eyed him.

Had Hector learned nothing from the days at the academy with Portia? Had he so tidily put behind him all that happened? Hector himself had found Theseus. How could he not believe in . . . great evil?

Antenor saw in Hector's face great defiance; he defied Antenor to tell him Tallis was vexed not by last night's supper but by Evil, Evil emanating from the place they approached. Briefly, as Antenor searched the familiar face, he felt a twinge for the old days. Hector, and that old defiance. It used to be good-natured. They used to love to argue together, everything from the theorem of Pythagoras to Aristotle's forms; from what Socrates thought of women, to what women thought of Socrates —with Julia in on those discussions. Theseus would sometimes join in, usually taking Hector's side. They were best friends. They met each other at Cal's villa, were inseparable after that, Hector and Theseus.

Antenor glanced toward the city. He could feel the darkness, like cold shade on his heart. He could put a hand out, as Tallis did, and feel it on his palm. Hector did not believe in the resistance from the city, or refused to. And Antenor wondered, sadly, whether Great Good was indeed out there somewhere, was it in a place he could go, and did it put up a shield against Evil, as this Evil did against Good.

Movement on the road ahead drew his eye from the city. The sun was falling west, shining directly in his eyes, and he put up his hand against it. Through the filtered rays he saw two women with a child between them, coming this way. As they came closer he saw that, intriguingly, their dresses were the current fashion of the Bacchantes: the faint gleam from gold tasseled belts, the generous fabric in the skirts that allowed for dramatic movement, the color. He'd had the old theater costumes replaced this year, thanks to a grant from a pitying rich woman who loved *The Bacchae*, and who had been scandalized by the condition of last year's garments. The dresses of the girls on the road were even the same shade as the theater costumes, a rich ivy green.

The driver rose from his seat, shielding his eyes. Tavi looked up from where he crouched beside Tallis; then he stiffened. He leaned forward to grip the sides of the cart, gazing intently at the three, then swung down for a better look.

"Father . . . ?" he asked, squinting beneath his hand.

"I don't know, lad," Bek`eshan answered uncertainly. "I can't tell from here."

"But I can," Tavi answered, and he lowered his hand. "Look and see how his ears stand out. Looks like Kardus when he came from the inn, done with his chores. It's Zagreus, Father. It's Kardus's boy."

Bek`eshan sank into the seat and put his head in his hands. After a moment, his shoulders shook as he began to weep.

The young man went to meet the boy against the lowering sun. If Antenor did not have enough to take in at that moment, the little boy standing small before the young man, the young man looking long upon him, touching his hair, then gently picking him up to carry him back . . . Tallis, that conundrum of Callimachus's, dragged himself white and haggard from the bottom of the cart.

Tallis saw the young man with the boy, saw the two women, and said, "She's the other? Arinna?" And he laughed until he groaned, and flopped back into the cart.

Arinna sat on the ground next to Devorah, gripping her skirts. They didn't have time for this. Zagreus sat on Bek`eshan's lap in the driver's seat of the buckboard. As the adults spoke, Bek would occasionally slip a murmur to him, as if to say, Just listen to them—you and I better stick together. Once Bek grinned and gently roughened up his hair, but the grin died when Zagreus did not respond.

The sun was setting on the Day of Dionysus.

Arinna watched the two younger men and the old one as they argued across the road. Master Tallis sat not far from Arinna and Devorah, but he didn't look well and had his back hunched against the city of Scythopolis. Once he peeked over his shoulder, and his eyes went up to the heavens; he looked as if he would sick up, and turned away, hunching even more. Arinna glanced to see what he saw, but saw nothing.

Bahat`avi, Bek`eshan's son, paced near the driver's seat with his arms folded, a grim guardian over Zagreus. Arinna didn't like the looks he gave her, as if the whole thing were her fault. She made sure, once, that he got a full look of her own, one of disdain and scorn. She'd soon be done with this lot. Not soon enough.

"What are they arguing about?" Devorah whispered fearfully.

Arinna didn't like it that she didn't know, because she'd gotten used to the superiority of her station as Keeper of the Divine Child, and she ought to be the one in charge. The tall and very handsome man with the gray eyes let her know she wasn't, when, after she'd told them the story of their flight from the temple (leaving out the big bright man part), he ordered her and Devorah to sit until they figured out what to do.

"I don't know," she finally admitted. "I hope they get it straight soon. Looks like the shorter one in leather wants to go to the city, very badly, and the tall handsome one doesn't, and the old man . . . I can't tell whose side he's on. I think he's with the leather one."

"The leather one looks angry. They all do. But we're wasting time." Worriedly, Devorah cast a look behind her at Scythopolis. "They'll find out we're gone and maybe come looking. I want to go home." She looked eastward, longingly, at the hilly horizon. "This isn't the way to Pella. We took the wrong road."

Arinna knew they had but couldn't argue with Zagreus, to whom, incredibly, she felt she owed some debt. Zagreus had insisted they take the north road out of the city, not the east road. He said the big bright man told him so.

"No, and you can't argue with the big bright man," Arinna muttered with a sour look at Zagreus. They'd be in Pella by now. She'd be rid of the wan simpy girl and Zagreus as well, on her merry way to Caesarea, free and happy as a Bacchante in a parade. Her eyes widened—Bahat`avi did not like the sour look she gave Zagreus, *gods,* he didn't, and she dropped her eyes.

"Has the child spoken of Jarek?"

Arinna glanced at Master Tallis, who did not look so handsome now. What had she ever seen in him? You work at the inn for five years, you get desperate.

"No." She studied the arguing men. Maybe she could slip away if the argument got out of control, which is where it appeared to be heading. Let them deal with Devorah and Zagreus. Then she looked again at Tallis. "What about Jarek?"

He was watching the argument too. He looked older than she remembered.

"You don't know? He's dead."

"What do you mean?" she scoffed.

"He's dead, that's what I mean. Murdered." He looked at the child. "If Zagreus didn't speak of it, I don't know if that's good or bad. I wasn't as young as he when I . . . witnessed a murder." His voice softened. "At least it wasn't as violent for him. There is that."

The bald head with the black fringe, the large eyes. His thick hand scruffing up Zagreus's hair, shooing him to wash up.

"That's ridiculous," Arinna snapped. "Jarek isn't dead."

Tallis looked at her with dull, miserable surprise.

She rose quickly, smoothing down her skirts. "Stop talking nonsense. I'm sick of it all. I want to get out of here. I want go to Caesarea. And then maybe Rome, because Demas said they would pay me to sit for them."

"Sick of it all?" Tallis spoke as if the words tasted bad. "You're sick of it all? Like it was a game? Samir said they play for keeps."

"And don't speak to me of Samir. That's *all* I need right now."

Tallis rose, and Arinna avoided looking at him. She folded her arms and fumed at the three men, but Tallis came close.

"They murdered Jarek to get to him."

She backed away, but he followed.

"He died protecting him, and you . . ." He nodded in disgust. "You kept him safe for slaughter. You knew all along what they planned for him."

He caught her arm, and she tried to twist away from him.

"What did she promise you, Arinna? What was worth the innkeeper's life? What is worth a little boy?"

"You're lying. Get *away* from me with your lies!" She tried to push him away, but his grip only tightened. "Let me go!"

"Am I lying? *Think*, Arinna—how do you suppose Zagreus got to Scythopolis except over the dead body of his grandfather?"

"Jarek is not dead!" Arinna screamed.

Her voice echoed, and silence roared in after. And into the silence crept a very small sound.

She looked to see; Tallis, still holding her arm and breathing murder on her face, looked too. Zagreus, small on the lap of Bek`eshan. Zagreus, his little face stricken in horror, mouth open wide and dark eyes huge, as though he saw before him unspeakable atrocity. Small stuttering gasps attended his horror, until, finally, a wail, a wail so different from her own scream. It was the anguish of a child who knew, who had known, and it drew deeply upon all those in earshot. It was a dreadful sound of innocence lost.

Tallis groaned and started for him, and Devorah did too, and the three men stopped their arguing. Bahat`avi went blindly to a horse and hung his fingers in the bridle. He put his head on the horse's head and began to weep. And the eyes of the wailing lost child searched, searched, found Arinna, and from bewildered instinct, he rose trembling from Bek`eshan's lap, such a thin little thing, and put his arms out to her.

Tallis and Devorah were nearly at his side when Arinna leapt in like a cat, clawing them away, screaming at them to leave him alone. She took him down from the buckboard and gathered him in safe. She took him to the roadside and settled him on her lap, and she rocked with him. She murmured to him soothingly, and she held him close, and kissed the top of his head over and over. And soon she felt his small body let go and felt his small and weary sigh.

By the gods and the goddesses and all that was holy, she would never leave him again, not ever, not if they killed her to get to him.

There was no pursuit from Scythopolis, and the party traveling back to Hippos had watched hard for it. Watched for an anxious hour, until the darkness was thick enough for them to ease their vigilance.

Arinna sat in the corner of the cart, Zagreus asleep in her arms. She refused to lay him on the bed of sacks Antenor had made for him. She hadn't let him go since Scythopolis. Hector was gone, escorting the girl Devorah to her home in Pella. Zagreus had ended the argument of pursuing justice, for that day anyway.

Hector himself, who thirsted like a desert for Portia's blood, had gazed on Arinna and the child rocking on the ground and told Antenor and Philip he had a family to take care of in Hippos, the news of which surprised Antenor—he didn't even know the man was married. Hector said he needed his job, he'd talk to them later about justice—in a forum for Truth, he said with a glance at Tallis—and he walked away, leading his horse with the girl on it. Antenor had called after him, on impulse, "Let's meet for a cup of wine sometime." And Hector had replied, "If you're buying."

Bek`eshan stopped the cart at the bottom of the small mountain of Hippos, and Antenor climbed out. They'd seen Hippos from a long distance, glowing with the late-night fires of those for whom the revelry had just begun. Antenor wondered how the plays had gone. The Day of Dionysus was always their biggest moneymaking day. Perhaps they had enough in the coffers to set aside the comedies and put on a quality performance.

Tallis climbed over the side of the cart and dropped down beside Antenor. "Thank you for coming, Antenor."

"Not that I did anything significant."

"It was significant to me. Please thank Philip for me. I didn't realize he'd left; I must have dozed off."

"He left when Hippos came in sight. Couldn't wait to get home to his son, I suppose."

"I'll come and see you before I leave for Athens." Tallis's tone went wry. "There is a curious matter to discuss, after all, of certain reports forged to Callimachus."

"I have no idea what you're talking about."

Tallis smiled. But his smile soon vanished, and Antenor did not envy his return to the inn without the innkeeper to greet him.

He said, "You are welcome to stay here for the evening. It's very late."

Tallis shook his head. "No. I want to get Zagreus home to Kes." He glanced at the dark road ahead. "Brigands are toasting Dionysus right now. We'll be safe."

Antenor studied him, couldn't help but feel some surge of emotion for the man. To have lost your little brother like that, to have witnessed it. To be helpless with Kardus . . . same as he felt with Polonus. To have to scuttle back to Athens because the truth was more than he could stand up to. There was strength in this younger man, and frailty as well. He was an innocent man, that much Antenor knew. A good man.

"When are you leaving for Athens?"

"I don't know. Soon," Tallis said, gazing at Zagreus, sleeping in the arms of the girl.

The girl glanced up, and for a moment she and Tallis shared a look.

"Callimachus is lucky to have you."

"It's the only place I'm any good." He looked away from the girl. "I'm no use here."

"You tried, as Polonus did. You tried to stand against Evil. That's a good thing."

Tallis didn't answer, and Antenor didn't know what else to say, so he patted the man on the arm and told him to come see him before he left.

The old scholar watched until the darkness swallowed up the cart. He could still hear it on the road, gravel crunching beneath the wheels, and he listened until a raucous whoop drifted down on the wind from the flat mountaintop. The revels would last long into the night.

He wondered if Gracchus, his understudy, had remembered his lines for Cadmus in the play. He wondered how the whole day had gone, what had happened during the play—something crazy always happened, whether on the stage or in the audience. Claudius would be the one to tell what had happened; he always told things well.

"*Quandocumque impellunt, repelle,*" he said thoughtfully, hands clasped behind as he began the traversing walk to the city.

XVII

To Callimachus
At the Academy of Socrates, West Stoa
The Acropolis
Athens

From your servant Tallis
At the Inn-by-the-Lake
And that lake is the Galilee
In Palestine

Greetings.

Much has transpired since last we conversed, Callimachus, dear friend.

It's been a month since I wrote to you of the death of Jarek of Kursi. I know I said I'd be home soon. I find it difficult to leave.

You are dearer to me now than you ever were, you who took in a broken boy. You and Aristarchus could not erase from my mind things that had happened, but you made me strong against the day I should remember once more. I did not expect to be far away from you when the day came.

I should be home by now, but for a debt I have a chance to repay. I cannot erase from the mind of Zagreus what he saw, witnessing the murder of his grandfather, but neither can I leave him, not yet. I can do nothing for his father, Kardus, as I foolishly fancied I could, nor for his former protector, Polonus. Nothing for them, save grieve, and bring a basket of food now and then. But for Zagreus . . . I have a deep pity for this boy that goes beyond natural sympathy. I have a chance to throw down a ladder, as you did for me.

Yet I don't know what to do for him. I don't know what it has done to his mind. I want to make him strong against the day it visits him—but what do I know? Perhaps he lives with its visitation. Perhaps it is, after all, a reality he has accepted. He always seemed wise to me, for such a little fellow. He's had a teacher since birth, the man Samir. I will tell you of him someday.

The child is quiet. Day after day. He misses Jarek dreadfully, they all do. Kes `Elurah, Samir. The customers. Especially Bek and Tavi. But the child saw it happen.

Wickedness won the day Jarek died, and there is a new pall on this place. It's rather like a submissive bleakness. A capitulation. I feel it everywhere, from the inn folk, the villagers, everyone. Evil has pushed, and no one has the strength to push back. Not this time. They fear to, for repercussions more heinous. Patronage of the inn has dwindled, especially from those who used to come daily for a meal and a mug of wine. It is as though Jarek's death was the final proof of a place cursed.

Well, and I suppose the evidence is substantial: The mother committed suicide, the son is possessed by demons, the father murdered. The people are afraid, Callimachus. Can you blame them? And Samir is different. He is not afraid—no, it is much worse than that. He is defeated. Only the servant girl seems to defy the shroud on this place, and that's only because she's unaware of it.

There is a stretch of road between here and Kursi where people now fear to pass. It is the road near the tombs, where Kardus dwells. Travelers circumvent it, taking a lengthy detour east through rocky, uncleared terrain, extremely difficult to navigate with carts and wagons. The new route goes up the hills through the grazing grounds of the pig herds. The herders are not happy about it, but of all people, they know what it is like to be near Kardus.

I don't know why I presumed that if only we could get Zagreus back, if only we could save his life, that it would change things entirely, that somehow it would make things right. It did make things right; it was a triumph over Evil. But, and I know you'll think me melodramatic, we will be made to pay for it.

Yes, we have Zagreus; but They have Kardus, and They have Polonus, and since the murder of Jarek, They have the dread of an entire region, which fears now to push back. And because no one resists, I fear for this region, not only for today, but also for tomorrow, and the years to come, and for decades after. Evil has set-tled here, as if it colonized the place, and it will grow, and it will spread, and it shall not be dethroned, and if anyone tries he will be shattered.

I raise my own skin with this talk. I am being melodramatic. I hope I am.

I will return when I can leave the boy. I will see the both of you into your dotage. (I hear you say, I'm there already!) But I know you, dear Callimachus, and you would not have me leave this family to a despair I feel constrained to ease by helping the boy.

How madness plays out, long after the Maenad is gone. Her son, a mad-man; her husband, murdered; her grandson, nearly——

He almost used the word *killed*. But *killed* only softened it. His own brother deserved truth, and if Truth itself galled, it galled worse if less-ened by vicious euphemism.

——slaughtered. Slaughtered, like a pig. A human sacrifice to Dionysus. That we live in a world that does such things . . .

He didn't know he had stopped writing. When a small vessel with a square sail caught his eye, he came to himself. He wiped off his stylus and dropped it into the vase, and worked the squeaky cork stopper back into the ink bottle. He'd finish later. He had coaxed Zagreus into a spit-ting contest when he was finished with his chores. If the child wasn't en-thusiastic, to Tallis's surprise he didn't decline this time.

He held the letter at an angle to see if the ink had dried, then laid it carefully aside. Spring would soon run into summer. The days were cloudless and hot. He should take Zagreus across the lake to Tiberias for a day, on a little square-sailed vessel like that one. He might enjoy that.

Zagreus asked who his father was the other day.

He had been sitting on his stool at the worktable in the kitchen. Kes was chopping parsley and onions. Tallis was filling the coal box under the brazier with chunks of charcoal.

Zagreus had rested his head on his hand, looking out the kitchen doorway to the Galilee. He looked a little sleepy, like he was ready to doze off. Suddenly he lifted up from his hand as if he saw something on the waters, but instead turned to Kes.

"Who is my father?" he asked. "Jarek was not my father. He was my grandfather."

Tallis added a coal chunk to the box and glanced at Kes. She had stopped chopping. She brushed the onion and parsley into a pile with the knife blade.

"Jarek's son is your father, Zagreus," she said lightly. She did not look at him as she put the vegetables in a bowl.

"But that is Kardus."

"Yes, it is."

"But I am afraid of Kardus."

"Yes. I know."

Zagreus laid his head on his hand and went back to studying the lake once more. Presently he asked, "Does he know about Grandfather?"

When Kes did not answer, Tallis said gently, "He doesn't know, Zagreus. He is sick in his mind."

After a moment Zagreus said, "He would be sad, if he knew."

XVIII

Nearly a month since Jarek had died. Life at the inn somehow fell into routine.

Kes and Arinna ran things in the daytime, Tallis ran them at night. He served food and ale and tried to make the few customers smile. Every day he met Bek and Tavi when they came in from the lake, and they'd sit and talk. They'd ask of Zagreus, and Tallis would say the same thing, that he was closed off and quiet, hadn't cried since Scythopolis. Zagreus stayed close to Samir, who was busy with his garden and the two olive trees on the northern border of the property. Samir didn't seem to want the child around. Or, rather, he seemed indifferent to his presence.

One day Bek brought the most shocking news: Portia had been found dead in the temple. Her priestesses claimed she had been consumed by the presence of Dionysus, and had simply left her earthly confines. Her eunuch had left his too. Novitiate enrollment was consequently lower this year, and many of the priestesses had sudden epiphanies to take up other occupations; apparently, early death was not an enticement to the vocation of Dionysus.

If this news brought great relief from any southern threat, and indeed it had lightened their hearts for a time, the northern threat of Kardus soon resumed its rule.

Samir kept a distance from Tallis. Tallis would have liked to talk with him, as they had done on the shore of the Galilee that evening. Two Truths were not exactly what he had in mind for distracting conversation, but it was better than the bleakness permeating the inn. The only good thing Tallis could see, coming slowly, was that Kes and Arinna were beginning to talk to each other.

Arinna had gained a proprietary haughtiness Tallis found amusing to watch. She had ideas for rearranging the common room that at first had Kes doubtful, then interested. She came up with different menu ideas, or, perhaps, presented ideas long there but never broached. Without either of them realizing it, Arinna began to take charge of the inn. Kes began to defer to Arinna in small matters. It would not be long before Arinna wore Jarek's nighttime serving apron.

Once Tallis came upon Arinna braiding Kes's hair in the kitchen. Kes seemed embarrassed, or guilty, as if caught enjoying a cup of refreshment with the enemy. She also seemed to have been caught doing something she'd otherwise scorn, a womanly thing no busy innkeeper had time for, but Arinna insisted she stay put until she was finished.

Tallis couldn't help but linger and watch, and this did not please Kes in the least.

At last Arinna threaded the last bead, tied off the braid, and stood back with folded arms. A pleased smile came, and she tilted her head. She said to Tallis, "What do you think?"

He saw a self-conscious blush as Kes determined not to look at him. But when he said nothing, she did look—and blushed again at his gaze.

He saw a loveliness forged not from artfully arranged beads and braids, but from grief for her father, and sorrow for her brother, and worry for her nephew; from an incomprehensible courage to face it all over again, fresh every day, and run this place despite it all. And it brought an ache to his heart, and he could only give Arinna a fake smile and push off for the barn.

And it seemed as though a wait had fallen upon the land. Tallis felt an itch he could not get to. Sometimes it felt as though a lion lay in wait, sometimes like the day Polonus was taken over, when the tidal wave had hit the inn. He felt as though the inn were at the bottom of a cone, and the cone walls threatened to burst in at any moment. Nothing to hold them back anymore.

Then one day, Antenor visited.

They sat in the common room with a pitcher of watered wine between them. (Arinna had informed him that until the inn made more money, the wine would be watered. Tallis took the news stoically and managed to rescue a small amphora of the good stuff for his personal reserve.)

"I came because I feared you'd left without saying good-bye," Antenor said, eyeing his mug of wine suspiciously. "Then I came because I feared you hadn't left." He rolled the mug between his palms and looked about the common room. "It's different in here."

"Arinna's touch. And I apologize for the wine."

"I'm not talking about the decor," the master of the theater said with a frown. "Or even the wine. It *feels* different." His tone strayed to something more reflective. "Perhaps it is the absence of the innkeeper. Amazing, isn't it? How a single soul affects a habitation."

"It does feel different," Tallis agreed. "It feels . . ."

But he let it go. He couldn't tell Antenor how the air felt so thick he thought he could take a handful of it and rub it between his fingers, sniff it, study it. What the thickness was, he could not exactly say. Sorrow and loss, surely. But also the pall. The capitulation, as though a revolt had been put down. A failed insurrection.

"Feels as though we've been taught a lesson," Tallis muttered.

Antenor did not seem to hear, or chose not to answer. "You've heard about Portia?" he presently asked.

"Yes, a few weeks ago. Bek told us." Tallis observed him for a long moment. "Any idea what happened?"

He had his own theory. No one seemed more bound for justice on that road to Scythopolis than Hector. He remembered the feeling Hector had had about him, so chillingly implacable, as if justice for Theseus were an inescapable conclusion.

Antenor returned his observation with a knowing glint in his eye. Then he shrugged. "How should I know what happened? You must have heard the same thing I did."

"Yes. Seems once again a deed is laid at the feet of a god. Are they investigating?"

"Without question. I expect it to be consigned to the archives soon, filed under 'mystery.'" He lifted his hands. "What can you do with the gods?"

"Yes." Tallis first made sure no one could possibly overhear him. He leaned on his elbows toward Antenor. "Even if this one is perhaps a bit more corporeal. . . ."

"Do you mean to say he may wear a hard leather helmet and vest?"

"And patrol third watch in Hippos?"

Antenor lifted his mug. "To the god of the third watch."

Tallis raised his own. "His first libation."

It was good to be with Antenor again. He was a fine companion, interesting and droll. He brought welcome relief from Tallis's efforts to get conversation out of Kes or Samir.

For the first half hour, Antenor told Tallis how things were going at the theater, told him of Claudius's latest escapades. They conversed for a time on small needful things. Then Antenor asked about Zagreus.

Tallis shook his head. "I don't know how he is, Antenor. Maybe I'm watching him too closely. He spoke the other day, the most he's said since Jarek died. But it wasn't light—he asked who his father was. And Kes told him."

"How did he take it?"

"I can't tell. I don't know what it means to him. He was such a cheerful little fellow. A bright little boy, so eager to please. And now he is . . . older."

"Is he the reason you haven't left?"

"They all are, I suppose. With Jarek gone, and Samir . . . lost . . . , and Kes just as quiet, I can't leave. Not when everything feels defenseless." He couldn't help a sigh. "How things would change if Kardus did. Can you imagine?"

Antenor sat back, appraising Tallis. "If you stay, come to Hippos and run the theater with me. Become a playwright. Dream with me about reviving the academy. But don't stay here. Polonus did, and look what happened to him. By no means harbor a single misbegotten thought of saving Kardus. Don't even go near him. The Kardus we knew is not there, Tallis. He's gone."

Tallis gave a hollow chuckle. "Oh, I failed Kardus before I ever tried. I wish I could have known him before he . . . became what he is."

"I can tell you a little of him. He was a winsome lad. He was engaging and very clever. Very witty. Confident and so driven. He had much zeal." He sighed. "Such a tragic waste."

"Maybe it's best just to keep your head down and mind your own business," Tallis muttered. "Zeal for anything seems to bring nothing but grief." He vaguely thought on the diagrams in Polonus's scrolls. "Perhaps zealous qualities open doors. Bad doors."

Antenor raised an eyebrow and grunted. "Well, that's an interesting thought. The qualities I just mentioned were his good qualities, and they opened good doors. He was not only the youngest teacher in the Hippos academy, but in all the satellite academies. I will say he had other zealous qualities, not so good; he had a nasty temper, he mocked people—he was very good at that. He was also very impatient. And sometimes he had an unattractive imperiousness about him, when he remembered himself overmuch. We don't talk of those things, of course. We make more of him than what he was, as we do for the dead."

"But he *isn't* dead. If I could help him, Zagreus would have a father." Tallis pinched his lower lip. "And Kes, a brother. Imagine it."

"Do negative qualities *attract* evil?" Antenor mused to himself. "Evil to evil? Good to good? Interesting. Very interesting." Then Antenor eyed him. "Tallis, Kardus will not replace Jarek. Kardus reclaimed will not make up for what happened."

"No. But the inn would come into its own again. If Kardus were healed, the inn would become whole. The curse of the Maenad would be broken." He glanced about the common room. "The air around here, made right."

Antenor grimaced. "This is an old path gone down too many times. What more can you do that has not been done? Polonus spoke to me of shamans and exorcists, expensive cures, cheap cures, desperate and crazy cures—they all *failed*."

"Polonus had a list," Tallis said, more to himself. He watched the wine move in his mug as he gently swirled it. "He meant to try everything on it. Exhaust every possible measure, everything he could imagine. He didn't get through the list."

"Tallis . . . ," Antenor warned.

Tallis put down his mug. "What if it's the list keeping me here?" He raised his eyes, searching Antenor's. "Everything *hasn't* been tried, because Polonus never finished the list. I know; I saw it. And I know how dangerous it is to be near Kardus, to even try. But logic says if there is a way into madness—no, wait! Hear me out, Antenor, I believe this! Gods help me, it's one of the few things I do believe. It's because I *know*. I was in horror, and I wasn't left there. Cal and Aristarchus soft-spoke me out. And Kardus lives in hell every day. You think he's the living dead, but he's not. He's a prisoner. He's somewhere near the door to the bad." He made his hands into fists. "It's where I was. Antenor, he's there. He's sane. He's in a pit, and I want to throw down a ladder."

"You *can't*. Polonus—"

"He thinks he's been abandoned. He thinks all hope is gone, or maybe he can't think anymore. He's alone, because Polonus is not company in his madness. They're both alone. Weak as I am, if I don't try to help them, who will? There's nobody left."

Silence, for a very long time.

"Why do you do this?" Antenor said softly.

Surprised, Tallis glanced at him.

"Polonus, my dearest friend . . ." The old scholar lifted anguished eyes to Tallis. "You're just like him, you know. Yanking the leash, trying to drag me where I do not want to go. He wanted me to see what was happening with Kardus, and I did not want to see. From a broken heart, I did not want to see. He would have had an ally, but I left him to it." Tears filled his red-rimmed eyes. "I cannot see him that way, Tallis. Don't you understand?"

"Go with me," Tallis said, gazing intently at him. He reached to grip his forearm. "Let's find the last things Polonus did not do. Help me do those things, though we fail."

"If I see him, it will tear out my heart."

"It probably will."

"I wish you'd gone back to Athens."

"Antenor . . . both of us have unfinished business. This is what I must do. I know it now. Only then will I be free to return to Athens and all that is familiar. I've been lingering here, like that maddening feeling on this place, and I thought I had reasons to stay. I know now I have to do one thing. I have to finish what Polonus set out to do. I'll try, and when I fail, I'll go home knowing I did all I could. It's a good way to live the rest of my life. It's the only way."

Silence.

"When would we go?" Antenor asked quietly.

"What prevents us from going now?"

"I was afraid you'd say that."

"All we have to do is get that tablet, and we'll plot our course. We'll get the tablet, we'll get everything—we'll take it all back here. You'll find his scrolls quite interesting."

"I have no desire to read them," the old man said.

"Of course not."

"I don't know why I came here," Antenor grumbled. "You not only remind me of Polonus, you remind me of Callimachus. Curse him forever."

Impulsively, as Tallis rose from the table, he gripped Antenor's shoulder. "You remind me of him too." He patted his shoulder and headed for the kitchen. "I'll have Kes get up a basket."

Zagreus was slouched on his stool at the worktable, head on his hand in the same daydreamy position Tallis had often seen in the past few weeks. He was watching the Galilee, idly kicking his foot against the worktable leg. It was late afternoon, and the sun was lowering in the sky. Sunlight glanced off shimmering waters.

"Where is your Auntie Kes?"

"Clipping herbs."

"Where is Arinna?"

"Clipping herbs."

Tallis watched the Galilee with Zagreus for a time. He leaned against the wall, let his head rest, and for the first time in weeks, felt a great loosening in his chest. He knew exactly what he needed to do, and he was going to do it. He'd likely lose every sensibility left to him, going near Kardus, but he never did have much sense.

He tried to remember the things Polonus had left undone. Some of those things might take months—did Polonus ever take Kardus to Asclepios, on the isle of Cos? One of the unfinished things, he remembered—and it was the worst one—was to take Kardus to the temple of Dionysus in Scythopolis for the disinvitation of the *paredros*. What about that enormous column rising from the temple? Would it still be there? Would it *let* him disinvite the *paredros*?

"I don't want my name anymore."

Tallis pulled from his thoughts. "And what shall we call you?"

"I like the name Baraan. Grandfather's friend. I like the sound of his name."

It was the second longest conversation since Jarek died. Already, things were feeling better.

"I like it too. Perhaps we can have some sort of naming ceremony, or whatever it is you do around here. Though it might be a good idea to find out what it means first. What if Baraan means 'little boy who cannot spit far'?"

Tallis looked for a smile, but none came. When would he see that smile again?

"Baraan is a fine name, Zagreus," he said gently. "We'll have to get used to it, but . . ." He trailed off, because Zagreus saw something on the waters again.

The child straightened and stared at the lake. He slid off his stool and went to stand in the kitchen doorway, one hand on the door frame. His silhouette was dark before the blue backdrop of the sea.

"Thunder's coming," he said.

Tallis pushed off and came beside Zagreus. There wasn't a cloud in the sky. He looked down at the child. "You mean rain? Looks pretty clear out there."

The child, transfixed, gazed across the sea. He shook his head. "No. I mean thunder."

XIX

K es searched the kitchen for things to put in the basket for Kardus and Polonus. She'd made no bread today. She only had day-old loaves from what did not sell yesterday. They used to make twenty loaves of bread a day. Now they made ten, and even that did not sell every day.

Arinna helped her fix the basket, while Tallis and Master Antenor waited out back. For once, Zagreus wasn't slouched at the worktable. Tallis said he'd gone to the lake because he wanted to watch the storm. Ordinarily, Kes would have been relieved that the child was finally doing something besides brooding in the kitchen. But he'd said he wanted to watch the storm, and there would be no storm. There wasn't a cloud in the sky.

"He said he wants to change his name," Kes commented to Arinna.

"Why would Tallis want to change his name?" Arinna wondered. She took a handful of olives from the large crock, shook the brine away, and put them on a cloth. She wiped her hand on her front and wrapped up the olives. "I like his name."

"Not Tallis—Zagreus."

"Oh." Arinna tucked the olives into the basket. "Well, I can't blame him. I'd change it too. What does he want to change it to?"

"Baraan."

Arinna shrugged. "That's a nice name. I knew a Baraan. He picked his teeth, but it's a nice name."

Kes was not used to this new Arinna. For the first time in her adult life, she had a friend—someone she had lived with for five years. Someone who . . . but no. She refused to think of it. Arinna came back, that's all that mattered. It was brave of her to come back.

But things were awkward around her. Half the time Kes didn't know what to say, now that there was an avenue for talk. Like with Father, when they finally had the chance to talk. But that chance came and went, and it had been a very long chance. Why did she think it would last forever? Why hadn't she made the effort? Always wanting him to talk first. Resenting him for not. Such a long chance, it had been.

"Do you want me to get a piece of that scroll?" Arinna asked as she surveyed what they had put in the basket. "I've seen you put it in the basket."

Kes was surprised she'd noticed. "Well . . . Polonus didn't like it when I did. He said it ruined a good book. He said Kardus couldn't understand it anymore."

"I wasn't thinking of Kardus. Maybe Polonus can still read. Maybe it would be good for him."

The basket suddenly blurred. Blindly, Kes put in the day-old loaves and turned away from Arinna. She found a bunch of dried herbs to fiddle with. "Yes, get a piece of the scroll."

Arinna left for Kardus's room.

Kes dropped the herbs and dug her eyes with the heel of her hand. It didn't take much to put her into tears. She cried all the time, it seemed, and for the most part kept it hidden. Strange to cry so much when all she felt was numb.

It felt like Father was on a trip for supplies to Hippos. He'd show up any moment, hot, sweaty, and complaining. It felt like he was visiting relatives. It didn't feel like forever. She kept wanting to turn around. Maybe she thought she'd find him if she kept turning around.

And sometimes it wasn't Father at all who brought the tears, but unexpected things, like Arinna's compassion. Kes had not thought of Polonus, that a scrap from the book might be good for him.

Much had changed with Arinna. She treated Zagreus gently now, not with a stiff tolerance. She put attention to the common room, shaping it into a truly pleasant place to be. She did things like fix Kes's hair, and pinch her when Tallis looked at her like that. She offered to make the sweetbread one day, because she had an idea to combine different spices with, of all things, date juice. The bread was surprisingly delicious.

Arinna was telling Kes how sorry she was without saying a word. She was sorry Zagreus had been nothing more to her than a cause in which she found, in the end, she did not believe. She was sorry she had lied to him for five years, letting him believe she was his mother. She was sorry for Kes, that she lost her brother to demons long ago, and lost her father in that wake. For all of this she did not speak a word. She didn't have to.

Kes would never forget that morning after Tallis brought Zagreus home. She'd slept with the child curled beside her, clutching one another in their loss. When she rose to make bread the next morning, stepping over Shoshanna, who had slept on the pallet, she found Arinna at the breadboard in the kitchen. Kes stood uncomprehending in the doorway, because Tallis hadn't told her Arinna was back.

How could she show her face here, how could she . . . ? But fury mingled sharply with an odd compassion, for on Arinna's face was a defiance that dared Kes to tell her to go. Her chin was high, her jaw firm. They stared at each other for a moment, and then Arinna dusted off her hands, strode deliberately across the room, and deliberately took Kes into her arms.

Kes went rigid, because they had never touched each other before. But Arinna would not let go, even when Kes tried to pull away, and by then a fearsome swell leapt in Kes; and she clutched Arinna, and began to cry, crying as she'd never cried before. And by the time Arinna did release her, both faces were wet with tears.

This, the worthless servant girl who had lived with her for five years.

Arinna never explained why she came back, or why she stayed this long and dreary month. Kes did not know if she would leave—and couldn't bear the thought of it. One thing was clear: She was no longer a servant and never would be again.

"I don't know what this says," Arinna said, frowning, as she came into the room with a large piece of broken-off parchment. "They could be bad words. With my luck, Polonus will read it and it'll say, 'Why not take bristlebane and end it all.'"

When Kes smiled, Arinna grinned. "With my luck." Then she shouted to the back doorway, "Tallis! Come here, quick!"

Tallis ran in, alarmed, the old scholar on his heels. "What is it?"

"Read this to us." Arinna held out the parchment.

Tallis snatched it from her, glowering. "Don't do that to me!"

When Master Antenor saw there was no emergency, he first eyed Arinna while straightening his vest in a huff, and then told Tallis he would let the slave know they would be gone.

"We don't know what it says." Arinna went beside him to watch him read. She looked at the words, then anxiously at him. "We want them to be good words. It's for Polonus."

Tallis looked at the scrap, front and back. "You're wrecking a good scroll. It says . . . *But Patroclus, nerved for battle, dressed him down: 'Meriones, brave as you are, why bluster on this way? Trust me, my friend, you'll never force the Trojans back from this corpse with a few stinging . . . taunts.'*"

Tallis paused. He read on silently, until Arinna nudged him.

"*'Earth may bury a man before that. Come, the proof of battle is action, proof of words, debate. No time for speeches now, it's time to fight.' He led the way as Meriones followed, staunch as a god. And loud as the roar goes up, when men cut timber . . .*" Tallis stopped reading. He held it for a moment, then handed it to Arinna. "It ends there."

She took the scrap and held it in both hands, very pleased. "Those are *grand* words. Don't you think, Kes? They remind me of Demas. I have no idea what they mean, but they're good enough for me."

Tallis watched Arinna carefully fold the parchment and tuck it into the side of the basket. The words on the scrap had upset him somehow. He was lost in his thoughts, and Kes wondered what those thoughts were.

"Can Polonus still read?" Arinna asked. "Kes said he's not like he used to be."

Tallis didn't hear her, and as Kes allowed herself to look on him, she drew up in surprise. Why hadn't he gone back to Athens? Why was he still here? Portia was dead; everything was over for his investigation. Since her father died she hadn't really noticed him. Not until now. And there he was.

278

Had she been turning around for him this long month? Felt like she was coming out of a long thick drowse. He had been here all along, and so had she, but as she cast about the kitchen and saw Arinna fussing with the basket, and Tallis with his thoughts, she felt as though she were not flailing blind in the dark anymore. She felt as though she had stopped turning around.

"Tallis," she suddenly said.

He left off his thoughts and found her. And as her eyes searched his and traveled his honest face, over reposed smile wrinkles and freckles from the sun, a conversation crept into the look.

At first, as they labored up the southern slope of the el-Kursi Valley, bound for the tombs—the place everyone else skirted—Tallis couldn't keep his mind to Antenor's words. Not that Antenor expected a response; his was a long soliloquy of rhetorical comments, and he seemed to be enjoying himself. So Tallis left him to his speech, and as it rose and fell, he thought on Kes. That moment in the kitchen had stirred within him something unexpected, and not at all unpleasant. He wished Arinna hadn't been there, that Antenor was not waiting for him.

She called his name. She pulled him away from a moment of doubt, to an extraordinary moment when she gazed on him, surprised, wandering his face with those eyes as if reacquainting herself. It was a surprisingly intimate moment, like she was touching his face.

He shut Kes out of his mind, for his thoughts had taken an interesting turn indeed, and he hoped Antenor took the flush in his cheeks as exertion from climbing the slope.

". . . a floating pigsty. What a *stench*."

He sniffed the air. "What, this? You haven't smelled anything yet. This is a field of almond blossoms compared to Kardus."

Antenor slid an uncertain look at him. "What do you mean?"

"Actually, it's an interesting phenomenon. He smells bad enough, for neglect, but something happens when the—Evil is stirred up."

He couldn't say *demons* as easily as Kes did. It still seemed fantastical to him, the notion of netherworld entities lodged in human residence. But weren't the gods themselves netherworld entities? Wasn't he raised to believe in the gods? Or at least to believe in the belief of them?

"It's the craziest thing, like a window to Hades is pried opened. A stench comes, like nothing you've experienced. It invades your senses. It's the essence of decay. Swampy and fetid. Pure rottenness. It's hard to describe."

"I think you just did," Antenor said with a curled lip.

"Oh, it's not only the smell. You get thoughts you've never had before when you're around him. Horrifying thoughts. Sometimes you feel a fury for him that leaps out of nowhere, an utterly illogical fury. You want to hurt him. And sometimes you see things. Hear things."

"This encourages me?"

Tallis glanced at him and smiled wryly. "I guess I want to prepare you."

"Doesn't sound like that's possible."

Smoking column high into the heavens. Mounds of water.

Tallis jerked his head.

Orange slanted eyes. A coursing tide of filth.

Antenor's arm was on his. He shook him a little.

"Tallis? What's the matter with you?" Antenor nodded to where Tallis found himself staring, the east. "What's over there?"

What was wrong with him?

"I don't know. I . . . thought I heard something." He searched the east, both the earth and the sky. Nothing was there, not a glimpse of Kardus—the only thing to account for crazy mind flashes. "Antenor," he said uneasily, "don't be surprised if Kardus suddenly shows up."

With a dubious look on Tallis, Antenor said, "What do you say we rest for a moment. I'm not as young as you." He looked about and found a suitable rock.

After settling down and observing the hillsides and the Galilee, Antenor said, "It's a brave thing you do, bringing them food when the tombs are the last place anyone will pass. Did I tell you his fame is far afield? We had a group of actors in from Alexandria the other day— Egypt! I heard them ask about the madman from Kursi. It's rather sad, actually. Polonus once boasted of Kardus, that he'd be famous one day."

His tone darkened. "The young fools wanted to come up and see him. I said, certainly, go ahead—and ask anyone around here if they'd do the same." He eyed Tallis curiously. "Aren't you afraid? Has he ever harmed you?"

Tallis wasn't finished being unsettled by those mind flashes. Was Kardus lurking about? He didn't see him anywhere. After warily scanning the perimeter, he finally looked about for his own rock and sat with the basket in his lap.

"No, but I never come alone. Samir comes when he can, but more and more it's been Tavi. We bring stout sticks, and we leave the basket at the edge of the clearing. It isn't safe to linger. You feel violence in the air." He glanced about. "Can't you feel it already?"

"Why don't the authorities do something about it?" Antenor wondered.

Mounds of water. Blasting snatch of voices.

He jerked his head.

This was Kardus land. Paranoia sometimes accompanied him on the way to see the madman. Tallis resisted the urge to look east, over his shoulder. A sweat broke upon him.

"You look like a man trying not to show he is sick." Concern was in Antenor's voice. "Do you feel well? We don't have to do this today."

"I'm fine." A version of truth would likely make Antenor leave him alone. "My last encounter with Kardus is still fresh. All my encounters with Kardus are fresh."

"Ah. Well, as I was saying, why don't the authorities around here do anything about him? Travel isn't safe, people are frightened. I've heard reports of brutalities. . . ."

Something pressed for his attention, threatened the sense of well-being he felt in the companionship of Antenor. Antenor had a way about him that made Tallis himself feel capable. Being around him brought confidence, even a renewed sense of self-respect. He felt like a sane man around Antenor, which is why he resented this sensation, like someone incessantly tapping on his shoulder. Like Cal shaking him from a good dream.

He finally looked east. He saw nothing. Not what he felt. Looking seemed to diminish it, the way lighting a candle diminished noises of the night.

". . . grossly bizarre incidents. Since they speak of the Kardus I once knew, I scarcely believe the tales."

Tallis turned west and fixed on the sun, just now touching the horizon. The evening was serene. A yellow glow was on the lake; it was a lovely sight, like a golden footprint spun from the sun. It made the rest of the waters indigo purple. A few boats were out on the lake. It was a perfectly tranquil scene. What he saw contrasted sharply with what he felt, a distant hum.

"Didn't Polonus used to shackle him, so he could do no harm? Is Polonus so bad he can't even shackle Kardus anymore?"

"Polonus . . . ," Tallis murmured, resting his wrists on the basket handle as he watched the lake. He determined to keep his mind to Antenor and his words. "Polonus is bad. Not nearly as bad as Kardus. He still converses, though his speech has gained a . . . sharpness. A dissonance. He may want to talk, but I don't want to listen anymore. Not to him. He has nothing good to say. What's in him scares me."

"*In* him . . . ," Antenor said doubtfully, shifting on his rock.

"I know. I used to think the same way. You have to be around them to understand it. At least I can *be* around him, if for a short time. I couldn't do that before with Kardus."

"What changed?"

Tallis was still looking on the lake. "*Quandocumque impellunt, repelle.* Don't take it. Push back. Especially when you don't feel like it. Especially then."

Antenor's face grew quizzical, and his brows drew together. He grasped his chin and said, "How do you push back at Evil?"

Tallis snorted. "Any way you can" would seem a prosaic answer to a scholar of the academy. Antenor would require more than—

He lifted his head, eyes blank on the lake. "It isn't right."

"Tallis?"

"It doesn't *feel* right," Tallis murmured, fingers going to his lips.

A cold wind gusted, lifting the linen cloth that covered the contents in the basket. Before he could push it down, another gust snatched the cloth and lofted it in front of him. He lunged for it, but another gust swept it off, and it tumbled down the slope. Sand swept up from the path and colored the surge of wind, a tan ribbon swirling the cloth away. Tallis rose and trotted a few steps, watching it go. He wasn't about to dive after it. Basket in hand, he turned back to Antenor—and found himself bracing into a strong current of northeast wind.

Antenor rose, looking with Tallis to where the wind came. "Must be the Sharkiyeh," he called over the rising howl.

"The what?" Tallis yelled back. He held the basket behind him to protect it. Grit stung his face as he squinted at the eastern sky, expecting thunderclouds—strangely, he saw only the first hint of twilight.

"It's an eastern wind that can rise quite suddenly," Antenor called, his toga rippling. He raised his arm to cover his face. "This is a strong one indeed!"

"What was that?" Tallis cried suddenly, staring this way and that.

"What?"

"I heard something!"

The wind howled, whistling through rock clefts and rushing through brush. Tallis stood frozen, poised to listen, heart wildly pounding. He'd heard something, he knew he had. He listened hard and heard nothing at first except the strong sound of the blowing. Then . . . a groaning on the wind. Much more than that. A *monstrous* groaning, a titanic sound of movement like the creaking of a great ship. Tallis slowly looked east, and his eyes tricked him, then, for what he saw was not possible.

There came from the east a tempest, borne low upon the wind.

A great floating mass, like thunderheads come down, the height of a man its distance from the ground. Pigs ran wild and screaming beneath it. The ground churned with its coming; stones and grasses and bracken kicked up in a foamy boil. It came straight for Tallis. He felt a sudden freezing spray on his face, the forerunner of the storm, and from horror he could not move. Only at the last moment did he stagger aside from its path.

Heaps of water shaped the mass, rank on rank of roiling mounds. It was a fierce gale marching by—and his ears tricked him, then, for he heard voices in the gale, wailing and thrashing like the waves he saw. And in those mounded waves he saw flashes of birdlike faces, feathered elbows, black pumping knees. The ground trembled like an earthquake as the wind thundered its forces past. And the voices . . . the voices shrieked and groaned in watery rage, rising, whirling, falling, a sound to numb his heart.

Hell was passing.

Hell was passing, and for once, Tallis was neither its destination nor in its way. He looked ahead to where it marched—the lake. There was a boat on it, heading this way, for the eastern shore of the Galilee. Other boats followed the one, and Tallis knew they'd never reach the shore for the storm heading their way.

He could neither help nor warn, and if he did, he would die, run over and kicked aside, an utterly worthless death. Better to die their target than a mere incident of war. For war went forth to the golden footprint on the sea, to the boats on the lake, and there was nothing Tallis could do but watch.

He dropped the basket and began to run alongside the tempest on the wind.

In the tombs of Kursi is a man who is raising his head.

He knows better than to turn around and see; he knows he'll pay for it, but he does anyway, from his curiosity and from Their own. His is an animal visage turned upon the lake, eyes like a wolf with no wolf-shine in them, dead black and feral only. His face contorts in a snarl, and he rises from his crouch. A boat comes. Death is in the boat.

HE COMES!
WE PERISH, WE PERISH BEFORE THE TIME!

Pandemonium breaks loose within.

The madman leaps. He plunges down the slope of the tombs, reaches the bottom, and races across the road. He scrambles over large beach rocks, thumps down to the gravelly wet shoreline. He races to the water's edge, and in a many-timbre'd voice he roars at the boat, the scream of a monstrous bellows. In the scream is the knowledge of judgment, the certainty of damnation. He has rushed the waters like driving his belly on the pike of the enemy.

Deep within the cavern that is he, a man trembles beside a plastered-over place.

Sudden coolness above. The madman looks up. A low floating continent moving inexorably toward the boat. Help comes on the wind. Help, for Them.

His own help is in fragile wood, the destination of the tempest.

He is jerked from the sight of the boat. He capers about on the shoreline, reeling drunkenly, flooded with Their glee. For Hell has gone forth, and the boat will never reach the shore.

Despair takes the man within, and he howls beside the sacred place.

The tempest fell upon the lake. Tallis watched from above, in the place of the dead.

He grew aware of the presence of others, mustered as he was by the passing of the gale. The hill shepherds stared, struck dumb at the sight of the phenomenon descending on the Galilee. Antenor drew up beside him, panting hard, then gasping insensible cries of alarm. And Polonus. Polonus appeared, and he paced, gazing wildly on the scene, his face ravaged by such conflict of emotion it seemed as though it would burst.

Below them, the madman of Kursi jerked about on the shore in a caricature of a dance.

Then they could see the boats no longer for the obstruction of the gale. It gathered and rose, looming like a gargantuan animal, and then fell upon the boats like the fisted arms of Zeus come down. They strained to glimpse the hapless vessels.

And Tallis knew a grief he could not understand, as if he were witnessing the death of Alexander the Great. It was a great confrontation of ancient malice and unknown good, for surely malice would not go forth unless to challenge good. He looked away in sorrow, for soon he would see not glimpses of the boats and of frantic men, but kindling wood, and no bodies, for the sea would swallow them and take them down to murky depths.

Polonus broke from the onlookers with a desperate wail. He ran down the slope, and the wail swept off, sucked into the tempest's roar.

Tallis put his back against the tragedy on the sea.

Then suddenly—the earthquake tremble in the land ceased.

Wailing arrows shot past them.

The roar behind him abated, and Tallis turned just in time to see a great curtain of water drop, as if snipped from on high, and melt into the sea.

The tumult diminished, blanketing down to vast, sparkling silence.

Instead of wreckage, they only saw a few displaced boats. Not the fore boat. While the boats behind oared themselves about, the fore boat dug for the eastern shore . . . more relentless than the storm.

Deep within the shell, at the bottom of cavernous depths, the man beside the plastered-over place knew more torment than he had ever known. At last, he beheld what They long forbade, for Across the Sea had come, and come for him. He sat in the back of the boat, the man with searching eyes come for him. Hope lanced like lightning. And They knew it.

> *YOU ARE OURS!*
> *YOU THINK IT'S OVER? WE WILL NOT LEAVE. YOU GAVE US YOUR YES.*
> *HE KNOWS YOU ARE OURS, AND THERE IS NOTHING HE CAN DO ABOUT IT.*

Despair rose, and blocked Across the Sea from view. The darkness was greater for the shutting out of golden light.

He huddled in the corner. Did he see me? For just that instant when I saw him in the boat? Does he know I'm here? Past Them, I am here. What if he doesn't know?

Oh, gods—does he know I'm here? Did he see me?

> *HE DOESN'T EVEN KNOW YOU ARE THERE, MAGGOT.*
> *HE CAN'T EVEN SEE YOU, HUMAN SLUG. WE ARE TOO MANY.*
> *IF YOU LOOK HIS WAY, WE WILL KILL YOU. RAPE AND TORTURE YOU FIRST. ALL OF US, ALL AT ONCE.*

Beside him, the plaster on the place began to crumble. He stared at the falling bits.

> *PAY NO ATTENTION TO THAT!*
> *IT'S HOPELESS, YOU KNOW! WE WILL OBSCURE IT ONCE MORE!*

But They did not come near it. Before, They helped him smear it over.

Then the man froze—a long way off, outside, he heard a voice. The demons screamed louder than they ever had before, and he thought it was to deafen the voice; but it was pain he heard, and instead of his own, it was theirs.

And he saw across the room for the first time. He saw Them. A multitude of them, and more on top, and more yet, a column of filth all the way up past what he could see. And they were hideous to behold.

Unbodied voices now had form. And before he could fully realize the deception, before he could connect one clear thought to another, again, the voice outside called.

And he raised his head to answer, but one of the forms flew across the room and clamped his mouth. He fought, frenzied out of mind, to tear the thing from his mouth and answer the man, but far away, somewhere on top, another answered for him.

WHAT DO WE HAVE TO DO WITH YOU, JESUS, SON OF THE MOST HIGH GOD? HAVE YOU COME TO TORMENT US BEFORE THE TIME?

I am here! Do not leave me, I am here!

He saw them dig in. The base of the column thickened, bearing down. Talons launched low, and seized, and held fast. Malicious looks, triumphant jeering faces were bared at him as they linked, and gripped, and braced.

WE'RE NOT GOING ANYWHERE.
YOU GAVE US YOUR YES!
WE LOVE TO OUTSTAY OUR WELCOME.

Hideous eyes bulged with mirth, until—a few looks jerked to his left, bulging not with mirth but fear. The demon clamping his mouth yelped and fell away from him, and dry-scrabbled back to the safety of the horde. The plaster over the place was falling off in chunks. Wonderingly, the man began to reach for a fallen chunk.

YOU'LL DIE IF YOU TOUCH IT!
YOU THINK YOU'RE MISERABLE NOW?

Suddenly, a great trembling in the cavern—and the entire column of filth began to sway. Shrieking and wailing, a few of the forms lost hold. Instead of dropping down, they dropped *up,* wailing as they went, as if to a torturous death.

Then a great shaking seized the tower. Forms fought for a hold, and way off, on top of the pile, the man heard one of them shout, *"LEGION! FOR WE ARE MANY!"* and there was great vaunting in the words, as if to say, You waste your time, you are only one!—we, a multitude.

Still the column shook.

More demons lost hold and flew off, and more, and larger, pieces of plaster fell. He lunged for the place and began to pull away the pieces, frantic now, as the column shook in a blur and the entire cavern groaned, ready to fall in on itself. He had to get to the place; he had to see what had long been hidden. He tore away chunks and flung them aside; he dug and ripped, and he saw, revealed . . .

. . . the Truth.

That he could choose.

That he had chosen.

And terrible had been his choice.

Grief struck him, and he staggered. All his loss, all his pain, all the years of torment . . . the truth was, it never had to be.

And the man outside asked through this sacred place whether he wanted them to go. And the man inside looked across the room at the faces fixed on him. They were screaming, but he heard no sound. For the first time, he heard no voices. For the first time he saw before him choice, no force telling him which way to choose. No good telling him, no bad. It came down to him and the choice, laid excruciatingly, *excruciatingly* bare.

He knew these faces. They were familiar faces. He'd lived with some since childhood. He did not know the man outside. Did not know his price. Should he fear Across the Sea? Could he make it out there without them? They were all he knew. He did not know Across the Sea.

He turned from the faces to the sacred place. He reached and touched it and met with grief, and something like joy, met with what he had looked for his entire life. Concealed and denied and there all along. And he knew the man outside had something to do with this very place. He splayed his hand against it. Through this place, the man showed him—he could choose.

He gave the man his yes, and knew, then, his own name.

"I am Kardus," he sighed, and the demons began to go.

Some were so deeply entrenched it felt as though they tore talon streaks all the way up. They came up, and they came out, and they were not happy to leave. They fought all the way to stay. They never once stopped begging Kardus to let them stay. They cajoled, threatened, and screamed. And Kardus was shocked these *things* had indwelled him, and they kept coming up, kept coming up; it was ugly and horrible and wrong, these rodents within him, wriggling up his being as through a tunnel.

Hundreds, thousands—a horde pouring forth from his mouth, a black-winged stream issuing from the bowels of his being, for their domain had been down deep. And for a bargain struck, they flew coursing up the cliff. What happened next, Kardus was unsure; he was trembling on all fours, coughing mucus. It dripped from his nose and his mouth, and he—belched! He laughed a little, and belched again for the insane joy of hearing himself do it. For his ears had been unstopped. He hadn't heard anything outside of his body, not the sound of his own belch, or a little bit of his laughter, for . . . years.

And he knew the feel of the shore beneath his palms, wet and cool, coarse with sand and tiny shells. And he made fists in the shore, and took a handful to stare at it.

His mouth was dripping. He went to wipe his mouth with his sleeve, but he had no sleeve. And he stared, in growing horror, at what must be his arm—an arm he did not recognize. He gazed at the scars, horrifying scars, thick and ridged; and the sores, livid, stinking sores . . . crusted filth all the way up, all on his chest and—gods, the stench! Was it *him*? Before he could wonder long at his astonishing appearance, he felt a cloak draped over his shoulders, and one of the men from the boats was helping him up, and another was wiping his face. He stared at them, bewildered . . . such faces. He couldn't help but reach with trembling fingers to touch one of the faces, the bristly chin, the humanity. He saw tears in the eyes of this human face. He had not seen a human face in . . . years.

So many sensations came to him that he had to go slowly. He felt . . .

Light. Like he'd surely fly off if he didn't anchor himself to the ground.

Clean. Scoured inside with the most ruthless brush.

Huge inside. He took a deep, unencumbered breath for the first time in years. He took many deep breaths, for the great wedge within was gone.

He felt wet shore soothe the soles of his feet. A soft breeze on his face, with—oh, gods! Fragrance in it! Fragrance! He closed his eyes and lifted his face to the caress of the wind. Salt from his tears stung his face; his face felt ruined. But of all the sensations assailing his senses, one was most pervasive—the voices were gone. All gone. He'd stepped out of pandemonium into a great relief of dewy silence.

He opened his eyes to beautiful human faces around him—so achingly beautiful—some with fear, some with tremulous smiles, and some, tears. He looked at them, searching for one face. At last he found the man outside. He was smiling at Kardus, eyes glistening. He didn't just smile; the big lively grin lit his whole face. It was he. It was Across the Sea.

Down the shoreline, a half-mile south, a little boy whooped and danced on the beach.

XX

Tallis did not know when he had raced down the slope with the others. Maybe when the boat had landed, maybe when the man got out of the boat. At first the men from the boats went nowhere near Kardus, not the raging glint-eyed madman with the unholy voice and the dripping chin foam, not the naked and unchainable, the local legend. Most stayed in the boats, gripping their oars as if for weapons; a few got out but didn't leave the boats, as if to assure themselves of a quick escape if things turned out badly.

But the other one. He strode easily toward Kardus, unafraid, and with terrible purpose. There was an exchange between the two, which Tallis did not understand—the thing in Kardus shouted Jewish Aramaic, and Tallis knew only Greek and Latin.

Then Tallis witnessed a thing that later he told to Callimachus in a letter.

> *What I saw made me want to run away, but I was transfixed. All the evil in Kardus now manifested fully, and we would have perished if it weren't for the man—for once, it wasn't Kardus who had things in hand. The man*

confronted the evil with such anger, I knew not of whom to be more afraid. He wouldn't back down, as I despaired he would.

Yes, what was happening with Kardus was insensible to behold—he roiled with a grotesque convulsing, vomiting things I couldn't see. It was a horrible sight. And I thought I had smelled the worst from him—Cal, you have no idea. But the man . . . he wouldn't back down.

I soon heard a commotion on the slope above, and I didn't want to look because all of a sudden, the sight of Kardus was a wonder like no other, like a brutalized child whose long dark night is over. Sensibility had returned, and he was bewildered, and innocent, and childlike, and I was crying, Cal, I admit it. Crying at what he must have endured to have such a look on his face.

Others cried too, in my defense; some hid their faces. Some met him with such compassion: a cloak over his shoulders, a gentle kind word. For the very first time, I saw the real Kardus. He came into his face. That's the best I can tell it.

Of the commotion up the slope, to which I was sorry to put attention—the ground trembled, and there came an unholy screaming. And down the slope thundered a brown-black mass, leaping and frenzied. At first I feared it was a pack of demons, maybe we all did, it gave us a terrible fright; I'm sure you understand our frame of mind. But the hill shepherds cried out, and we watched as the pigs drove themselves into the water. The pigs! All of them! They swam as far as they could, and they drowned, all of them, rumps going down first, their snouts grubbing above water as long as they could, snorting and choking. A terrible sight, Cal.

I could write much more, but I want to get this dispatch off as soon as I can. And this, I suppose, dear Callimachus, is my final account. This ends my investigation into the mystery of the Decaphiloi. Its present accounting: Lucius and Marcus—whereabouts unknown. Antenor, Polonus, Hector, and Julia: whereabouts known. Portia, Theseus, and Bion—dead. And the madman from Kursi—mad, no more.

I later told Samir one thing, when he asked, wistfully, of the man who came. He said, "Master Tallis, who was he?" And I said, "Why, Samir—don't you know? He is the Third Truth." And Samir gazed at me for a moment, and he eased back with such a smile, Cal. Such a smile.

Time had passed, maybe an hour, maybe more. The sun was setting, and the cool of evening had come. A crowd had gathered on the shore, more coming by the moment. White tunics stood out lavender in the gloaming. People murmured with one another, arms folded, warily watching the two men converse in the boat.

Polonus sat in his newness, enjoying a serenity that sometimes had tears coursing down his cheeks. Kardus and the man sat in one of the boats, talking. And Polonus was content to merely watch them. He had lost Kardus to Across the Sea.

He could see that straight off, but all was well. Across the Sea could have him, and do better for him than had Polonus. Here was a philosopher who had the wherewithal to underscore his philosophy, whatever it was. Polonus would learn of him one day. He'd find his way across the sea and slip into a vacant step on his portico. He would hear what this man had to say, for he had his ear like no other. He'd like to speak to him now, but it was apparent that he and his entourage would soon leave this shore. He had no welcome here.

Antenor found Polonus, and settled beside him in the companionable silence of old. They did not speak to each other, but sometimes Antenor patted his arm, as if to tell him how happy he was for his old friend. No, they would not speak now, but watch as long as they could, listen for what they might, for Across the Sea would not be here long. The crowd itself ensured it.

Polonus looked over the crowd on the shore, growing larger by the moment. Who could blame them? Some faces were angry, likely the owners of the pigs now settled on the bottom of the lake. The pigs would rise eventually, bloated and bobbing, a great loss of thousands of silver dinars. It would be a huge undertaking to clean up that mess.

Other faces were resentful and fearful. This man had done what no one else had; they all knew of Jarek's efforts, and even of his own, especially the hill shepherds. Many looked over at him, as if to share an affront that Polonus did not feel. But he understood. Kardus was theirs. Their own, their blood, their problem. Who was this stranger to interfere with one of their own—to clean up their own mess?

Polonus understood their fear for two reasons: Who was this man? What did he want?

He was Jewish, and his friends with him—they came from the other side of the lake, and the other side was primarily Jewish. What did they have to do with this region? Jews did not live here. Some of the more cosmopolitan of them lived in Hippos; a few of his students were Jewish in blood, if not exactly in spirit. (He'd dealt with the outrage of a few Jewish parents, appalled to see their youngsters join a pagan academy.) Jews were one of many peoples subjugated in Palestine by the Greeks, who had formed the Decapolis against them all, and now the Romans carried on where the Greeks left off. Was this some Jewish stunt for attention? The beginnings of another Maccabbean revolt?

Who was this man? How came he to do in one confrontation that which Polonus could not in years? What other designs did he have? Someone with that much power, to subdue what could not be subdued —and to dismiss a gale like none other Polonus had seen as if dismissing a slave; someone like that had motive. What could it be? Why would he cross the Galilee to do a great kindness for one—well, two men? What claim had he on this place? The Jew looked them over at times, and the air above them. He considered this region of the Gerasenes like a rich man considering a weighty purchase.

A man like no other had landed on the shore, a Jew, and perhaps by sorcery or some other device, he would lay claim here. Another philosopher-king scouring for support to take back what the Greeks and Romans stole. The people on the shore feared fetters and chains. And they feared what they could not understand. Defiance with their fear lifted up against the man in the boat. Was this the first from a bagful of sweets, tossed to them to win their interest? These people had been taken before, by winsome words in treaty—they'd not soon cast their lot with this man and his tricks.

"How are you feeling?" Antenor commented. He had pulled up a long blade of sea grass and idled with it as he watched Kardus and the man.

To this Jew, this stranger whose motives no one could trust or comprehend, Polonus owed a debt he could never repay. "Oh, Antenor. I can breathe again. No effort in it at all, and I didn't know there had been. I feel . . . capable, again. All the dark is gone."

"I'm sorry I left you to it."

Kardus was pleading with the man, gesturing widely. Laying out a case to the man in the boat.

Polonus looked at Antenor. "What are you doing here?"

Antenor pointed the blade of grass at Tallis, who sat alone a short distance off. "He wouldn't leave you to it." He looked to Kardus and the man in the boat, and shook his blade of grass at them. "Oh, I'd love to be in on that conversation."

"Who is he, Antenor?"

"Well, well, well now. Isn't that the question. I may know his name. He may be the one I've heard scraps about. Jesus, from a town called Nazareth. He has something of his own academy over there. A traveling academy, and his disciples go with him. But *who* is he? Well—that's the question."

"Another Diogenes?"

Antenor squinted. "Perhaps less morose; and I never heard of Diogenes doing things like this. Wouldn't Callimachus love to be here right now."

"And Aristarchus."

The two did not speak the questions they wanted answers to most; their mouths couldn't even form the words. What power could a man wield that can calm a tempest and send demons fleeing? How did he do it? What would he expect of Kardus? What was his price?

Who was this man?

Maddening questions, drumming at them both—and they were teachers with no answers.

Something was happening in the boat. Kardus was begging now, loudly; his voice came even to where they sat near the boulders where the beach began.

"I only want to come with you! Please! Let me come with you; I'll do anything you ask. Just let me come. Please—I'm begging you."

Polonus straightened, and he gripped Antenor's arm. "Did you hear that?" he breathed. "Kardus's voice! His own voice! Oh, to hear his voice again . . ."

They did not hear the man's response, for his back was to them. But they saw Kardus's face, and Polonus instinctively rose to his feet. Kardus had been his responsibility much too long, and Polonus saw on his face great disappointment.

Anger rustled. The man said no to Kardus. How could he do that? How could anyone say no to this pitiful man with such ravaged features —scabbed hands holding the cloak together, a weather abused face, burnt and cracked by the sun. The man had other disciples—why not

Kardus? Was it because Kardus was not a Jew? Did the man think this pagan would offend his other Jews?

The man spoke to Kardus, and another look came: As Kardus turned the words over in his mind, he slowly took his seat again. Polonus watched intently, and sat down himself only when Kardus's face had finally smoothed. It wasn't happy but smooth. With his head down, eyes on the bottom of the boat, Kardus listened to the man. He nodded occasionally, and Polonus saw a tear drip from the end of his nose.

Kardus dashed at the tear, then looked in amazed disgust at the back of his hand. He put both hands in front of him, his face dismayed—then a sudden smile broke on his face. He glanced at the man and laughed.

Polonus's heart ached at the sound, such a sorely missed sound. He wondered what the man had said to make him laugh.

They spoke a little longer; then Kardus climbed out of the boat. The man stayed in, and the man's friends pushed the boat off from shore and climbed in. As they oared the boat about, the man kept his eyes on Kardus, the former madman of the Gerasenes. Though the man himself had done what no one else had, he seemed as joyful for Kardus as if he long knew him—as if he were Polonus or Samir. As if he were Jarek or Kes. As if someone else had done the deed, and he marveled along with the rest. He watched over his shoulder as long as he could. The boat paddled away, the other boats following.

Don't go, Polonus said to him in his heart. *I wish you wouldn't go.*

Antenor rose and brushed off sand. "Well. Perhaps Mistress Kes has heard by now, and perhaps not. I haven't seen her in the crowd. I think I'll take myself to the inn and tell them to set an extra place for dinner tonight. I like bringing good news to that place. Polonus . . . I'll see you again soon. And I am so—"

But emotion choked what he wanted to say. Antenor patted Polonus's shoulder and gripped it, and then he left.

Polonus recognized Bahat`avi, Kardus's friend from the inn. Tavi was the first to leave the crowd and go near Kardus. They watched the boat for a long time, the two of them, until it was far away. Then Kardus saw his childhood friend. Tavi said something Polonus couldn't hear, apparently about Kardus's appearance.

Kardus looked down to survey the mess that was him, and before he looked up Tavi suddenly embraced him, filth and all, nearly knocking him off his feet. Bek`eshan came and stood near.

Cautiously, one by one, many people on the shore began to creep forward and close around Kardus, and soon Kardus was obscured from his view. Many patted him on the back, and Polonus heard exclamations and laughter. These would be the people who had long known Kardus, known his family, had connection with the inn.

Others were not so interested in Kardus. Some dark looks followed the boat. Some people, perhaps the owners of the pigs, began to debate with one another, gesturing angrily at the place where the pigs had gone down, where bubbles still rose, wondering whom to hold responsible—perhaps they dared not wave the bill beneath the nose of a man capable of such things while he yet remained on their shore.

Some, who had not a vested interest in the pigs, nor in Kardus, stared at the retreating boats and at the former madman speaking with his old friends. They shook their heads, as if at a loss of what to make of it all. They spoke in low tones, the first discussions to play out for generations. They knew they were a part of something extraordinary; they already imagined telling it to their grandchildren. *I was there the day the man came across the lake. . . .*

What they did not know was how it would end. If he would come back. And how his coming would be. They didn't even know his name. They did not know if the miracle with Kardus would stick, and they would watch him; oh yes, they would watch him for a long time, for they had known him long. They did not know the rest, yet, of what they would tell their grandchildren.

I wish you would stay, Polonus said to the distant boat.

Polonus watched Kardus speak with his old friends for a time. After a long, last look at the boat, he slipped away.

Polonus stood before his tomb home, trying to decide what to take with him before he went inside. He noticed the stones lining the path to the door; someone had straightened them. He gazed at their smooth curve.

"Where will you go?" said a voice behind him. It was Tallis.

"I don't know. I hadn't got that far."

"It's good to see you again, Master Polonus," Tallis said. "It hadn't been."

Polonus twitched a smile. "I think I remember that sense of humor."

Tallis came beside him and regarded the stones as he did. He looked at Polonus. "How do you feel?"

"A little ridiculous. Like I'm floating. Do I look like I'm floating?"

Tallis looked him up and down, looked at his feet. "You're not floating."

"I feel like I could fly. Like I need to hang on to rocks because there's nothing to hold me to earth anymore. And if I feel like this . . . I can only imagine how Kardus feels. I also have a dazzling headache."

"I wonder if you're hungry. We brought a basket, Antenor and I. I don't know what happened to it." He scratched the back of his head and chuckled. "Bit of a storm on the ridge."

Polonus looked at Tallis, surprised. "I *am* hungry. Very hungry. I can't remember the last time I ate. Maybe the last time you—" He suddenly grasped Tallis's shoulder. "Thank you for that," he said earnestly. "Thank you for all the times you brought the basket."

"You remember?"

His eyes misted. "I do. Dimly. And I remember saying vile things to you."

"How about you come back to the inn with me, Master Polonus?" Tallis said gently. He looked at the doorway to the tomb home. "How about you don't even go in there."

"All my research . . ."

"Well . . . I'd say it pretty much comes to nothing now." He turned to survey the Galilee. "We were like scholars working out a theorem in long debate. Along comes this fellow, like Aristarchus, and he says a word and walks away. Solves it, no matter how hard you worked, or how close you got."

"Or didn't get." Polonus looked at the darkening waters. "I suppose it is like that. Solves it. Walks away."

"You did the best you could until he came. For that alone . . . I have a great deal of admiration for you, Polonus. So do Kes and Samir. How about you come back to the inn with me?"

"Do you think Kardus will want me around?"

"He'll need you around. He'll need an old friend."

Who had straightened his line of stones? He'd promised himself he'd not touch them until Kardus was whole again.

Tallis put an arm about the older man's shoulders and led him away, Polonus looking over his shoulder. Such a small detail in this array of events, scattered stones made straight.

XXI

The inn received its own again; the air, at last, made right.

The Parthian slave felt the repair; he sometimes studied the sky to ponder it. The dancing boy knew of it, and he didn't study the sky, he played. Kes knew; Jarek no longer felt so sharply absent from the place. Instead, all felt secure; shorn up, hemmed in—made whole. The air made right, generations back.

In the three weeks since Kardus came home, the inn became not a wayside resting place, but a destination. Never before had the inn been a destination, save for locals who came for good food and wine. It made more money than it ever had, and Kes and Arinna couldn't keep up with the baking. Tallis helped, when he could, and Shoshanna came. Samir added a makeshift oven to the kitchen yard, and the inn folk talked about building an addition. There wasn't any talk, yet, of Tallis returning to Athens; they were much too busy for that. And Kardus . . .

Kardus presided over the inn as no innkeeper had before. Not Jarek, and not Jarek's father. For no one had ever come to the inn to hear the innkeeper speak; but they came now, bursting the place at the seams. They had to lodge guests in the barn, but the guests didn't care. They put up tents near the garden; they strung their wash between the olive trees. The landscape became colorful, like a little tent city. Like a festival.

New wind blew in this region of the Decapolis. Oppression was gone, beaten way back east. One day the oppression would slither back to challenge the new lodger at the inn. It would challenge, and would prevail, but for Two Truths, and *Quandocumque impellunt, repelle*, and most of all, the one Kardus called Across the Sea. For across the Galilee dwelled one who would not put up with it, and it gave Kardus and the people at the inn great courage. He was powerful enough to dispel thousands of demons, and he was on *their* side; it was all they really knew about him, and all that really mattered.

Fear lost its torment and was soon forgotten.

There were so many people at the inn that Kes never knew if she served a paying guest or a visiting stranger. Arinna knew; she always seemed to know if someone had a meal coming or not. There were so many people constantly in and out that the inn folk occasionally made a dash for the shore, to gulp fresh air and feel empty space beside themselves, to gaze on the waters and wonder flittingly about the other side of the lake, until guilt trotted them back to the clamor at the inn. And they didn't mind it so much when they got back; it was a party atmosphere, bustling and joyous, the best kind of madness.

Polonus and Tallis went constantly for supplies. Samir helped Kes hire two new hands to work outside, and Arinna hired two to work inside. Bek and Tavi helped when they could, keeping an eye on the place, watching Kardus to see if they thought he needed a rest.

Truthfully, Bek and Tavi spent more time in the inn than on the lake; nothing like this had ever happened before, not these crowds of people, not this kind of miracle—not in these parts. For the novelty of seeing all the people, and being a part of it, for their propriety share in this family, Bek and Tavi stayed around.

People came one by one or ten by ten to hear Kardus speak. Most of the day, and all evening long, he sat on a stool in the corner, telling his story. Arinna made him a cushion for the stool, and Zagreus often sat at his feet.

The stream of visitors did not abate. If anything, after three weeks, it increased. People who had already heard Kardus's story came again with a friend, and later, the friend brought a friend. Antenor came one day with the group of Alexandrian actors. Hector came with the widow of Theseus. And Philip with Julia, who cried with joy when she saw Kardus. The whole place threw up its arms the day Shamash-Eriba came with his men, just to hear Kardus speak.

Rich and poor, educated and ignorant, notorious and law-abiding, from places close and places very far away they came to hear the former Gerasene demoniac. Some brought charms and amulets, in case a few demons had remained. Some brought relatives who needed the same miracle.

And all who lived in the region watched, and they waited.

They watched to see if the miracle would stick, and so far, for three weeks it had; they waited to see if the man would return, and so far, he hadn't. And the amazing idea came, then, that perhaps his motive was pure: He came, and he helped, and he left without asking a price. There *were* people like that in this world, they told each other, selfless people who would do such a selfless thing. There *were* people like that, you know.

Yes, an extraordinary thing had happened, like nothing else in these parts, and to the people belonged a singular dignity—for Kardus had remained to stay a part of them. It wasn't in his nature to stay, it never had been. But stay he did, telling his people what great things God had done for him, how he had mercy on him, and the people listened because he was Kardus, *their* Kardus, their own local legend whose ill fame was ill no longer. They listened too because much more had happened with the former demoniac, and the people who knew him came to ponder it.

"He's different," some speculated, not happy they couldn't say how.

"He's content," others noticed, not sure if good would come of it. The old Kardus had never been this content. The old Kardus couldn't stay put to save his life; it seemed this one wouldn't budge. Seemed like he didn't want to go. Seemed like he wanted to stay, and be a part of . . . them.

Night after night, for three weeks straight, Tallis heard Kardus tell his story until Tallis could tell it himself. He did, sometimes, to folks like the dockworkers at Lower Hippos, when they saw he fetched supplies from the warehouses much more often. He'd tell what had happened, that the lunatic was no longer lunatic, and told them to come to the inn for themselves; nobody could tell it like Kardus, and he never tired to tell his story. Not even at the third watch of the night, when a man came far from the north with his cruelly vexed son.

Tallis had third watch that night and had, at first, refused to rouse Kardus; but there he was behind him, belting his tunic, and he softly told Tallis that all was well, he would see to them.

The man was in the doorway, and a small figure was behind him on the porch. "Are you the one?" the man asked anxiously of Kardus, lowering his voice when Tallis informed the man they had sleeping guests. "Are you Legion?"

"I am Kardus," the young man said. "I am the one you seek."

The man's face, already tight with worry, now crumpled in anguish. "My boy . . . I don't know what to do. I've tried everything. He suffers terribly in his dreams at night; he is terrified all the time—something is wrong with him! He doesn't act like our boy anymore, and we only want him back. His mother is beside herself. Please—" The man impulsively clutched Kardus's sleeve. "I've heard of you. If you can do anything . . ."

Kardus told Tallis to shut the door behind him, and he went outside with the man and his boy. Tallis shut the door and barred it. He didn't like it when things like this happened. Bad enough when he sometimes heard it.

The story was compelling, and Kardus knew how to tell it. But when people actually came expecting Kardus to do for them what the man had done, it made Tallis uneasy. The man was the one in charge, wasn't he? The way Kardus spoke, the man Jesus was everything: liberator, protector, helper. An instrument of Samir's Most High.

It somehow bothered Tallis to see Kardus take things in hand with these people. It made him nervous. He spoke these things to no one, not even to Polonus, with whom he now shared an easy friendship. Polonus would tell him to explain why he felt the way he did, and he couldn't. He sat at a table, uneasily listening for what he might hear outside, until he finally went and fetched himself an amphora and a cup.

Arinna had taken to leaving a few oil lamps burning in the common room every night; with all the rooms constantly filled, a guest was bound to have his lamp go out and have need of a ready light. Tallis took one of the lamps and set it next to the one where he settled with his wine. The twin flames gave a soft glow to his space. It was pleasant at night, so quiet; Kardus's stool with its colorful cushion stood in the corner of the common room, casting a tall, wavering shadow. This was a nice change from a clogged room.

He poured himself a cup of wine and savored the first sip. Arinna, luckily, had amended her former decree, since the inn was making more money, and they served the good stuff once more, ordering twenty times as much as they did from a wine seller in the Gaulanitis.

Tallis rested the cup on his cheek as he looked at the stool in the corner. He wondered if this was how it had been at the academy. Only now, Kardus had a stool for a podium, the common room for his temple steps. He wondered if any of the former students of Kardus had been here yet. It was good to talk to Hector the other day. He thought the woman who was with him was his wife, and Hector had *blushed* when he asked—Hector! Tough, hardened Hector, corporeal god of the third watch. The pretty little woman had blushed too, and Tallis had to suppress a smile. Hector quickly informed him that—

His eyes widened as an unholy scream cut the air, and he gripped his cup reflexively. He hated this part of it. It couldn't be civilized. It was always . . . untidy.

He liked the festival atmosphere prevailing at the inn, but he didn't like the mess that sometimes went with it. Once, when Kardus got to the part about the boat coming, a woman near the door threw herself on the floor and began to writhe like a snake. Kardus calmly went to the woman and uttered a terse command—Tallis couldn't hear what he said, something like "Go" or "Begone"—and the woman shook like someone had taken her feet and was rattling her violently on the ground. Then she lay as if dead. If the others gaped at her in consternation, Kardus merely went back to his stool. After a few moments, the woman sat up, looked around, and slid back into her seat.

If something happened, it was always at the part where Kardus talked about the boat coming. And Kardus could tell it as dramatically as if he were on Antenor's stage, in a hushed tone and with rhythmic timing: *The storm was hellspawn, a malevolent masterpiece . . . still the boat came. They blocked him from view, all hope had fled . . . still the boat came.*

Tallis got uneasy around that part. He'd scan the crowd for possible interruptions. Why at that time did disturbances occur?

"Still the boat came," he murmured beneath his breath, rubbing his brow. A soft knock came. He went and lifted the bar and let Kardus in.

"Will the man need accommodations?" Tallis said in a low tone.

"No. He wants to get home as soon as possible to bring the boy to his mother."

"He is . . . well, then?"

"He is well." Kardus flashed him a smile. He noticed the cup and amphora on the table, and said, "Do you mind if I join you?"

"Not at all." Tallis took his seat and watched Kardus fetch a cup from behind the corner counter.

His face was beginning to heal. Kes put ointment on it every day, to soften years of exposure. The sores were going away, cuts were healing. Kes sometimes wept when she applied the ointment.

Her tears would annoy Arinna, and Arinna would snatch the jar from her and take over. Tallis couldn't help but smile; that girl had a pragmatic way about her. He wondered why she cared that Kardus sat on a hard stool.

"We haven't had a chance to converse, Tallis, it's been so busy." Kardus took his seat across from Tallis.

Tallis noted the apology in his tone; perhaps the lad had the blood of the innkeeper, after all, and felt the need to see to all who stayed beneath his roof.

"You have an important undertaking, with your talks," Tallis said, with a nod toward the corner stool. "I see how it affects the people. It's a grand thing. Perhaps a little more gratifying than teaching of Alexander."

Kardus rested his head on his hand as he looked at the stool. The pose made Tallis think of Zagreus—Baraan. The child insisted on being called Baraan.

Kes fretted to Tallis that Kardus was not paying enough attention to Zagreus, his own son. Tallis told her to give him time; it seemed Kardus had enough to take in, learning of the death of his father and the dissolution of the academy. Now he had a son, a son madness made him forget. Likely the last time he saw the child, knowing it was his own, was just after he was born, before Portia took him to the temple.

Tallis wondered briefly if Kardus had been at the temple too, and had absorbed whatever was there. The memory of the column of evil was no different from what he had felt from Kardus, whenever he used to be near.

It was still very hard to believe that this man at the table was the foaming-mouthed freak, the man around whom Tallis could not even stand upright, who once had a presence to crush everything about him. Now, it felt no different being around Kardus than being around his cheerful little son.

"Tavi and I have grand plans," Kardus said softly as he gazed at the stool. "We're going to start a different sort of academy, right here. We're at the beginning stages of drawing up a charter for it."

He glanced at Tallis, and Tallis averted his gaze.

"Do you wonder if any are still in here?"

Tallis looked back, and the lad had a grin. "Other people do. I've seen their amulets. Sometimes I want to roll my eyes at them, just once. I'm not sure they'd think it funny."

The cuts on his face were nearly healed. Most of the scars would fade, but many would remain. Were there any scars on his soul? What had the experience done to him?

"No, but I do wonder many things. If you're up for talking about it someday—"

Kardus spread his hands. "Why not right now?" He leaned forward. "You don't have to treat me like Kes does."

"How does she treat you?" Tallis already had an idea but wanted to see what Kardus thought of it.

Kardus didn't answer. His mind already leaping to something else, he said, "What do you think of Arinna?"

"Well, there's a subject for you. She reminds me a little of your sister; she likes to rub the nose of nonsense in its own rot. Just like Aristarchus."

Kardus shrugged. "Aristarchus? Oh—you mean from . . ."

"Cal's place, back in Athens. I think Arinna is remarkable. She hadn't struck me so, a few months back."

"I used to come and visit from Hippos, but I hardly noticed her. She wasn't interesting then."

"What changed?" Tallis mused.

Something had happened to her in the temple in Scythopolis. He thought of her holding Zagreus. He had never seen that tenderness before. Never suspected it. *Leave him!* Tallis remembered. She'd leapt in like a lion.

"She came into her face," he murmured in surprise. He glanced at Kardus. "Like you did."

Kardus returned the look with deepening eagerness. "What do you want to know? I'll tell you anything. I'll bet you'll ask more interesting questions than the others. I wish Polonus—" He broke off. He worked his thumbnail into the table grain. "He doesn't talk to me much."

"You don't talk to him either."

"I don't know what to say."

"He was your teacher. . . ."

"I know." Kardus sat back, restless. He leaned forward again, chin on fist. "You have to understand . . . I woke up from a nightmare that lasted years. My father's gone. I have a five-year-old son. Things are so different." His gaze strayed. "Portia's gone. I'm glad about that—I think I am. The academy is gone. Bion killed himself. Theseus was murdered—"

He shot an incredulous look at Tallis. "Did you hear about that? Hector told me. I didn't like him, and he didn't like me, but . . ." He shook his head grimly. "It's all so hard to believe. So much is lost, and changed. And some things haven't changed at all."

"What hasn't changed?" Tallis asked.

"Kes. The way she treats me. And Polonus. Things are different with him . . . but I don't know, he may still think of me as Kes does, and that—" Kardus clenched his fists. "It's my own fault. I let them treat me that way."

"What way?"

Kardus picked up the terra-cotta amphora, looked over the stamp from the vintner in the Gaulanitis, and set it down. He found a piece of twig, broken from the broom, and poked it at the flame in the lamp. His actions were no different than any other restless young man having to face something unpleasant; perfectly sane little actions, and Tallis couldn't help a small smile. No wonder they came to sit and stare at him.

His face was shaved clean, Roman-style, and Arinna had cut his hair because Kes cried when she tried. It was so matted and filthy and crawling with vermin Arinna had to cut nearly all of it (this, the girl who couldn't clean up vomit), leaving only a few inches. She did a pretty good job, giving it what style she could, and after a profound scrubbing, what Tallis had thought was bracken gray was actually a soft light brown, touched in copper.

The color of his eyes was no longer indeterminate, superseded by what had indwelled him. Tallis saw now they were light brown, and their shape was a little like Jarek's. He was a handsome lad, and the few scars would not detract from it. If anything, the scars gave his face a certain appeal for his utter unconsciousness of them. Tallis had watched as Kardus and Tavi spoke together, huddling over parchments at a table; the eagerness he saw in Kardus, the passion, were indeed elements to attract attention.

The end of the twig caught fire. Kardus watched it burn, then pressed out the tiny flame on the edge of the lamp.

"Kes stood between me and my mother, and I never thanked her. Polonus opened up the world to me, and I never thanked him. I came to expect what they did for me—Polonus, Kes, and Father. I took it as a right, not as a gift. I was so arrogant. So ungrateful. And it's too late to tell my father how sorry I am. And the last time I spoke with him . . . I can't even remember what I said, but I'm sure it was awful." Kardus did not speak for a time.

"I hardly know how to start a conversation with Polonus. And it hurts to see Kes treat me the way she used to, with a veneration I don't deserve. I don't want her to wait on me; I don't want her to fuss over me —and I don't know how to tell her. Sometimes I can't be near her, for the guilt. You have to understand—for years she put herself between me and my mother, and I let her do it. I knew what hell she was getting, and I didn't care. Then I went off to Athens that summer with Polonus, and when I came back I lived in Hippos. I hated coming here, even after Mother's death. I hated how much Kes and Father still loved me— I didn't deserve it."

He rubbed the ash off his charred twig. "Felt like chains on me. I hated that their love required something of me, and because of that, I began to hate *them*. Samir, most of all. He loved me exactly as he did when I was a child, without expectation, and that infuriated me. Worse than Father and Kes. Love without expectation has the greatest expectation of all. And by this time . . . I'd met Portia."

He frowned. "She opened new thinking for me, but . . . strange . . . I can't remember why she was so insightful. That's all gone. I have only memories I'd rather forget. She was . . . bringing me to a place I thought I wanted to go, so very badly. An empty place. My life depended on going there. There, I could forget everything. Forget Mother and the things she did, forget the way she was. Forget what I owed everybody."

Kardus noticed his wine and took a slow sip. What he had to say next seemed difficult.

"I get . . . panicked sometimes. I see expectations again. Sometimes I fear I'll try to find the empty place again." He glanced at Tallis then, as if he had just divulged the dirtiest secret of all.

"It's terribly interesting . . . ," Tallis mused aloud.

Kardus waited expectantly, and Tallis grimaced. He'd been forming an observation and didn't like to speak without thinking it through.

"What?" Kardus finally demanded. "Do you know how much I'm enjoying this? Real talk! Not my own speeches." He took the amphora and refilled their cups. He pushed Tallis's cup toward him. "Come on, talk."

Tallis grimaced. "I'm thinking as I speak, for which Callimachus would have fits, but what strikes me is this: The man in the boat brought you back to pain. Good, honest life pain."

Kardus got an uncertain but hopeful glint in his eye.

"The demons took away life, with its dilemmas and uncertainties. The man brought it back. He didn't fix everything—he just gave you a chance to have it square in your lap again."

Kardus sat back. When his eyes filmed with tears, Tallis busied himself with inspecting the vintner on the amphora.

"Good, honest life pain," Kardus murmured. "Yes, he gave it back. He gave me back what was mine, and mine alone. He gave me back responsibility." Then he said clearly, "But they never took anything I didn't surrender first."

This time Tallis sat back, bottle still in hand, remembering a certain Two Truths. "Why, of course. You can choose, and I suppose you can choose to give that right away."

"That's what I keep talking about, night after night. But they don't get it. Not this. Not what you and I are talking about. They see I have my old voice back, and that I don't break shackles anymore. I don't do bad things anymore; I don't frighten them now. I'm a curiosity. But it's hard to tell them he did much more than chase the demons away—it's what is in their place. It's what he gave me back. That's hard to put into my story."

"It's all they see, Kardus. It's okay for now."

"I suppose." Kardus placed his hands on his belly. "We all have a place we're not meant to give away. But they came, and I gave, and I was wrong. I got to that place of silence I wanted to go so badly, but soon it wasn't silent at all. She lied, they lied . . . it was the opposite of everything they promised, this . . . deafening prison, with no rest at all. I couldn't even kill myself, you know that? I can't tell you how many times

I tried. And then, like this . . . miracle . . . he came. And the sense of gratefulness I have . . ."

He shook his head. Then he looked at Tallis, and Tallis felt a thrill at the intensity in his strong remarkable gaze.

"He gave me back *people*. Life. Everything I tried to run away from. When he tells me to speak of God's mercy, *that's* what I'm talking about." Then his shoulders sagged. He found the charred twig and idled with it. "I'll need help, maybe, this time around. I don't want to ever return there; I don't want to ever go back."

Tallis delicately cleared his throat and pursed his lips. "Kardus—tell me what you did out there, with the man and the boy."

"You mean—just now?" He shrugged. "I told the demons to go. I said they had no right, that Jesus of Nazareth wouldn't put up with it, and neither would I and neither would the boy's father—not anymore."

"And they left."

"Of course. I told the father what they were, trespassers. I told him if he put up with it he was a lousy father. I said it was like having an intruder come in at night—I asked him if he would put up with *that*, having an intruder invade his home and ravage his wife and child and steal his things while he just sits by, and ho, that put some backbone in him. Then he knew what I was talking about."

Kardus grinned then, a deep glittering grin Tallis could almost call wicked.

"Then we made them leave."

"And you need help, Kardus?" Tallis spread his hands. "You have all the help you need. *Quandocumque impellunt, repelle.*"

Kardus thought it over for a moment. Then he smiled a wry little smile of agreement. He lifted his mug. *"Vero, amice. Quandocumque impellunt, repelle—solum Jesu a Nazareth. Solum Jesu."*

Push back, only with Jesus.

Tallis snorted and lifted his own mug. "Having been there, I can't argue with that. He's the one I'd want for an ally, with these particular foes."

How he managed to *do* it was another discussion entirely. And how he managed to cleanse the air of an entire region . . . why, that was an academy unto itself.

It seemed Kardus read his mind.

"Master Tallis, Tavi and I have grand plans, you know that? This area has long belonged to Dionysus, in ways you don't even know. You have to live here to understand it. He's done a great deal of damage. But Tavi and I will form our own academy, where people can come and learn of him, how he will wreck their lives if they let him. I want to do for them what Jesus has done for me. I want to tell them about the sacred place. How to protect it, so they won't ever have to go through what I went through. I want to give hope to people, for everyday living."

He pushed up his tunic sleeve to look at the bumpy scars on his arm. He ran his fingertips over them. "These can't be for nothing. It's all a waste if they're for nothing." He looked up. "Perhaps . . . you can help us form the academy." He sat up straight. "Think of it! *The* Academy— the Academy of Socrates, right here! What do you think?"

Tallis smiled a little. "Perhaps. I know Antenor has spoken of reviving it once more. And perhaps Polonus can help. He has a little experience running an academy."

"Yes . . . he does." Kardus cast a look about the room. "A school, right here at the inn—think of it: the very place my mother forbade learning. What irony. And this will be a *different* learning, *life* learning, like philosophy but so much more. Oh, we can have philosophy and mosaic classes and such things—Julia can come with her hard-luck cases— but I want to *help* people. Just look at this!"

His arm swept the room. "Can't you see it? Our very own school, a school of *life*? A place of healing? Think of it! The academy will live again!" He looked at Tallis eagerly. "You can take over teaching of Alexander! What do you think, Tallis?"

Tallis gazed on him. He thought on Callimachus and Aristarchus. Samir and Polonus. Jarek, who shackled his son. They tried the best they could for this boy, and that was something good. Then came someone to do for them what they could not, to take their good where they tried desperately to go, and that was something for which Greek had no word. He whom Kardus called Across the Sea was to Tallis Antenor's Great Good.

What did he think about a place of healing?

What did the father think, who at this very moment, guided his son home to his mother in what must be great joy?

"Kardus . . . I think it's marvelous."

To *Aristarchus*
At the estate of *Callimachus*
Athens

From *Tallis*
In *Palestine*

Greetings.
Your letter is next to me, on the desk.

Tallis looked long on the waters of the Galilee. It was hard to write past the ache in his heart. Aristarchus would not welcome any declarations of grief. If Cal hated trivialities, Aristarchus hated declarations.

I never imagined I'd be far away when he died. I'll keep my outpour brief, and say only this, that a color has gone from the sunset. It will never be the same to me.

Permit me to say too that I ache for your loss, as much as for my own.

How came I to his steps, so many years ago? Blind and broken, I came. He took me in, and I noticed the smell of jasmine, and I tasted food again. I believe in Great Good, Aristarchus; I met it first in Callimachus. I met it next in you. I met it here, on that which they have the temerity to call a sea. I watched Hell go forth, and watched as it prevailed not.

Kardus did not come broken to the steps of the one he calls Across the Sea; Across the Sea came to him. And this, dear Aristarchus, is Great Good.

Do a favor for me, since I will not return to Athens. Gather all my scrolls, all my work on the cultus of Dionysus, and go to the sea. Cast them on the waters for me. Like Lycurgus, Across the Sea drove Dionysus into the depths. When the pigs thundered down the slope, and when they drowned in the sea, I remember thinking Antiochus Epiphanes made the Jews sacrifice pigs to Dionysus. What an elegant sense of justice he has, this Jew, this Jesus of Nazareth. Maybe he did it on sudden fierce inspiration, in memory of the Maccabean who rose in revolt against Antiochus. Maybe, when the demons asked permission, he thought it an impeccable suggestion.

So, dear Aristarchus, cast the scrolls there for me, and this will be my tribute to Callimachus. He said I should not challenge the Maenads, but what moved them. Only then would real change occur. I have found it is so. I was not strong enough to challenge him on my own. It took you and Callimachus, a Parthian slave and his Two Truths, and the one Kardus calls Across the Sea.

I wish Cal could have met him. I saw him the other day, when he came to give a talk. It was the first time he'd been in this region since the day he came for Kardus a year ago. He had quite a welcome this time. Thousands gathered to hear him speak.

Thousands? Yes, because Kardus had done what he told him to do—he went home.

I won't tell you what happened when he came, because you wouldn't believe it. I'll simply say this: a few loaves, a few fish, and with this man, it's quite a feast.

I'll visit you someday, and I'll bring my wife. Yes, wife. You'll be pleased to know I have stayed my station—I've married a fellow servant. She is an innkeeper, and my, they are a tough lot. She scares me sometimes, as does Kardus's wife. They both remind me of you.

Aristarchus . . .

Kiss Cal's grave for me.

> *Your servant,*
> *Tallis*

Historical Notes

The material on Alexander the Great, his Maenad mother, Olympias, the notorious Antiochus IV, Epiphanes/Epimanes, and Dionysus was drawn from many history books such as, *Alexander the Great and His Time* by Agnes Savill; *Alexander the Great: Son of the Gods* by Alan Fildes and Joann Fletcher; *Women and Monarchy in Macedonia* by Elizabeth Donnelly Carney; *Alexander to Actium: The Historical Evolution of the Hellenistic Age* by Peter Green; *The Jewish People in the First Century*, Volume II, edited by S. Safrai and M. Stern; *Greek Legends and Stories* by M. V. Seton-Williams; and *Dionysus: Myth and Cult* by Walter Otto.

The law Tallis tried to revive, limiting the activities of the Bacchanalia, was passed in the Roman senate in 186 B.C.

Antiochus introduced the worship of Dionysus into the desecrated temple of Jerusalem in 167 B.C. "The altar was covered with abominable offerings, which the laws forbade. . . . On the monthly celebration of the king's birthday, they [the Jews] were taken by bitter necessity to taste the sacrifices, and when the Festival of Dionysus came, they were compelled to wear wreaths of ivy and march in the procession in his honor. At Ptolemy's suggestion a decree was issued to neighboring Greek towns, that they should adopt the same policy toward the Jews and make them taste the sacrifices, and that they should slay any who would not agree to adopt Greek customs" (2 Maccabees 6:5–9).

The miracle of the Gerasene demoniac is reported in the New Testament gospels of Matthew, Mark, and Luke. I drew heavily upon Mark's account and upon scholar Bargil Pixner's commentary on it.

I came across the name of Kardus in an excavation report of Kursi, published by the Department of Antiquities and Museums, Ministry of Education and Culture, Israel, 1983. I did not have access to this report when I wrote about Kardus in my first historical novel, *The Brother's Keeper*. I named him Jaren then, never dreaming of the possibility of an actual name. It was recorded in a tenth-century document by a fellow named Pseudo-Peter of Sebaste, as indicated in the Kursi report.

Many scholars believe Kardus was the first missionary, as the result of Jesus' injunction to him, "Go home to your people and report to them what great things the Lord has done for you, and how He had mercy on you" (Mark 5:19). As Bargil Pixner notes in his work, *With Jesus Through the Galilee, According to the Fifth Gospel*, pages 45–46, "Did the Christians of Hippos remember their first missionary by building the chapel which can still be seen at the site of his tomb-cave on the slope above Kursi?"

"Jesus himself was barred from coming into this region," Pixner observes, "and so he commissioned this grateful and devoted man to spread the Good News. A splendid sentence concludes this episode of violent conflict between the kingdom of God and that of Satan: *"So the man went away and began to tell in the Decapolis how much Jesus had done for him. And all the people were amazed"* (Mark 5:20).

—T.G.

Acknowledgments

To each of the following I owe one of my children, or at least a venti mocha:

Vicki Anderson, Albert Bell, Robin Day, Bart DenBoer, the indomitable Melissa Huisman from the Gary Byker Memorial Library, Todd Krygsheld, Candy Molette, and Paul Wright for various research matters; Anne-Marie Jacobson, Bob Jacobson, Chad Pierce, and Beth Steenwyk for reading the manuscript; my agent Kathy Helmers for believing in this project, and long ago, in me; my editor Andy McGuire for being the best kind of mean; my own personal copyeditor, on retainer, LB Norton, who exists to make me look good; Jen Abbas, Shelly Beach, Angela Blycker, Ann Byle, Lorilee Craker, and Julie Johnson, for watching my back; Evan, Grayson, and Riley (wait—you *are* my children) for your pure-hearted enthusiasm; and Jack, for your manic encouragement, your relentless belief in my capability, and for cheerfully pitching in whenever needed so I could write. Many husbands have done nobly, but you knock it out of the park.

More from Tracy Groot . . .

The Brother's Keeper

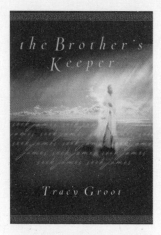

ISBN: 0-8024-3105-4

Thirty years after following a star to Bethlehem, one of the magi is back. This time he is sent not to an infant "king of the Jews" but to the king's brother, James.

James wants nothing more than to shut out the unsettling questions about his brother and have a normal life. But normalcy walked out the day his brother did. All the reports tell of strange healings and exorcisms. The family business is suffering and fanatical zealots descend on Nazareth to convince them to join the fight against Rome. And an eerie visitor with a strange accent tells James to "consider it all joy." But what James doesn't know is that someone has murder on his mind.